# The CAT'S MEOW

## VICTORIA ALEXANDER
### "One Magic Moment"

"Alexander's characters are distinctive. Her work is a refreshing addition to the world of historical romance!"

—*The Literary Times*

## NINA COOMBS
### "Heart's Desire"

*"Man's Best Friend* is an entertaining...tale of love in the human world seen through the eyes of a wise and wonderful dog."

—*Romantic Times*

## CORAL SMITH SAXE
### "Get Thee a Cat"

"Kudos to Coral Smith Saxe for giving us a reading experience that is pure ambrosia!"

—*Rendezvous,* for *Enchantment*

## COLLEEN SHANNON
### "Moonstruck"

"Colleen Shannon has infused her tale with all the drama, excitement and mystery of the classic and added her own magical style, turning this into a wondrous tale to be cherished."

—*Romantic Times,* for *The Gentle Beast*

Other *Love Spell* and *Leisure* anthologies:
**CELEBRATIONS**
**TRICK OR TREAT**
**INDULGENCE**
**LOVESCAPE**
**MIDSUMMER NIGHT'S MAGIC**
**LOVE'S LEGACY**
**ENCHANTED CROSSINGS**

# The CAT'S MEOW

## Victoria Alexander, Nina Coombs, Coral Smith Saxe & Colleen Shannon

LOVE SPELL BOOKS      NEW YORK CITY

LOVE SPELL®

October 1998

Published by

Dorchester Publishing Co., Inc.
276 Fifth Avenue
New York, NY 10001

ISBN 0-505-52279-9

# Moonstruck

# Colleen Shannon

*"I'll come to thee by moonlight, though hell should
bar the way."*
—*Alfred Noyes*, The Highwayman

# *Chapter One*

*Never stroke her fur backward.*

Peter Gabler's confident stride slowed as he approached the "Hub of the Center of the Universe."
He scowled. How like Bostonians to inflate their
own pretensions. He was a proud down-easter
himself, like his ships, and it went against his
grain to come calling, hat in hand, at this elite center of an elite town of an elite state. Still, he had
to go where the money was. Dreams were worth
a high price—even groveling.

But he didn't have to like it.

He paused across from the State House on the
lofty heights of Beacon Hill, tamping down his
brief insecurity, to survey the neat, brick-lined
sidewalks and ancient cobbled streets. No modern
electric lighting conveniences here, just gaslights,

which were remnants of a gentler time. A time when the best Brahmin families owned most of the expensive houses, a time when the Irish, the Italians and others of even lower status seldom ventured into this sacred domain of the wealthy, much less dared to purchase property.

Turning away from the sparkling gold dome and the proud columned portico of the State House, Peter continued his walk, consulting his pocket watch yet again. He was still ten minutes early, and he didn't want to appear too eager. He dawdled along the route he'd mapped out, grudgingly admitting to a curiosity about the rich. Given the high price they paid to live here, in social and monetary coin, he'd expected more than neat rows of townhouses, some with intricate ironwork, others flat-fronted and plain except for their fine shutters and tinted windowpanes. Doubtless even these edifices, which were spacious only by going upward instead of outward, cost more than his first ship. Still, he'd gladly trade this refined bastion for his plain clapboard house in Maine. Here, one could barely see the genteel flow of the Charles River. At home, spray crashed onto the rocky point below. There, gulls cried continually, as much a part of the landscape as the huge trees and clean air.

Still mourning his need to be here, he exited Mt. Vernon Street and made a left on Walnut. He walked half a block before he saw his destination. He froze in his tracks. This immense new house, with its vast lawn and ornate embellishments, shouted extravagance in an area where fantastic wealth was commonplace. Swallowing, intimidated despite himself, he pulled the advertisement from his pea coat pocket to recheck the address.

He glanced at the brass plate on the tall wrought iron gate surrounding the estate. This was it.

Peter pulled out his watch again. Two more minutes. He snapped it closed and stuck it back in his pocket. To prepare himself for the most important interview of his life, Peter reread the brief advertisement.

*To persons of good character, free feline to stable home. Chosen applicants will be given $10,000 to begin new business. Interview mandatory. Acceptance sole prerogative of current owner, but each applicant must agree to take exemplary care of the cat for so long as the animal lives.*

The article ended with the name and address of the owner, along with a number for one of those newfangled gadgets called a telephone, stating that applicants should set an appointment.

Peter had followed the instructions to the letter, but no matter how many times he read the enigmatic words, he could not understand why anyone, even a wealthy eccentric, would put such value upon the life of a cat. Cats were nasty, smelly, cranky animals who shed more hair than affection. He'd always detested them. They made him sneeze. Give him a large dog: a loyal, useful animal who came when called and could be trained to stay off of the furniture.

He folded the paper neatly and stuck it back in his pocket. Then, setting his captain's cap at a jaunty angle on his thick, wavy black hair, he shoved open the wrought iron swinging gate and walked toward the huge house.

As he drew closer, he could appreciate the talent

of the architect, if not the taste of the owner. While the white gingerbread trim curling at every eave and brimming from every roof peak was too frilly for his taste, he had to admire the deep red brick, the two octagonal turrets balancing the house and the widow's walk above. The view of the harbor must be glorious from there, he reflected.

He was approaching the steps that led to the wrap-around porch when a low growl made him freeze. Slowly, carefully, he turned his head—and came eye to eye with a tiger. The huge cat crouched on all four haunches, poised to spring, its fangs bared in a snarl. Out of the corner of his eye, Peter gauged the distance to the front door. If he jumped and ran like hell, he might make it. . . .

He tensed on the balls of his feet. The tiger did likewise, but the front door opened loudly and a tall, slim woman with red-gold hair hurried out, saying something in a vaguely Russian-sounding language to the great cat. The tiger's tail quit switching. It made a yowl of almost human disappointment. Finally it sprang up the three steps in one leap and shot through the door the woman held open.

Peter felt it brush his arm as it burst past him. He never would have made it to safety before the cat was upon him. Shoving his cap back, Peter wiped his sweaty brow on a clean kerchief, his hands trembling.

The woman soon came back out, saying contritely, "Forgive me, sir. Sheba has been declawed, but she does like to play. I keep her penned up when I know someone is coming, but she snuck out."

*Play?* Sticking his kerchief back in his pocket,

Peter retorted, "I do not think 'play' is what she had in mind." He bowed slightly. "Peter Gabler, at your service. I have an appointment with Mrs. Gisella Lowell."

The woman nodded. "I am Gisella. Won't you come in?" She stepped back.

He entered, wondering why she was answering her own door, and why she'd invited him to call her by her first name. He paused in the immense foyer, staring at the ornate woodwork of stairs that angled upward in perfect, dark squares for three stories above his head, leading to a balcony overlook on each floor. More ornately carved woodwork adorned the ceilings and baseboards, stained the same dark hue. In fact, the dark stain might have been overpowering if not for the house's relatively simple decor. No bric-a-brac in every nook and cranny, no lace antimacassars, or elaborate stained glass as had seemed so prevalent in the other houses in the neighborhood. Even now, in 1889.

An exquisite oriental rug was centered on the parquet flooring in the entry. Graceful arches led to adjacent rooms that held tasteful furniture in the Chippendale and Sheraton styles, rather than Empire or Rococo, as he might have expected from a woman who had married into money.

Mrs. Lowell swept a graceful hand toward the salon off the entry. "Won't you come in?"

Even as he followed, he stared, for this woman seemed both younger and more approachable than the eccentric widow he'd expected. Her lovely red-gold hair was pulled back by an emerald comb, and her eyes were a strange hazel that changed color with her surroundings. He wished he could peg her age. Her skin was almost totally smooth, and she had no gray hair. However, according to what he knew of her, she was the mother of a grown daughter—or at least had been before that young lady suddenly disappeared—so she had to be in her forties or fifties. She looked far younger.

As she walked into the salon, her graceful hips swayed under the simple flow of the tuniclike dress she wore. It was the strangest fabric he'd ever seen, a spring green watered silk so fine that as she moved under the modern electric lights, it shimmered with every shade of green between forest and chartreuse. Again, she surprised him. Her dress was no more subject to the strict mores of her time than was her taste in furnishings. No corsets or bustles for this fine figure of a woman. She wore what she pleased, the gossips be hanged.

For this, he had to admire her. By all accounts, she was an upstart, like himself. Down at the docks, with the exception of her own employees, she was not well-liked. The consensus seemed to be that she'd bewitched poor Alexander Lowell. She'd slowly taken over the refined Brahmin's life, wheedling him into tearing down the aging Federal-style mansion on this hilltop and building a modern new house. It was the scandal of Beacon Hill, a bastion of tradition. And each modern convenience they put into this behemoth—like the telephone, the electric lights, and even the mysterious elevator that supposedly led to a sealed tower she allowed no one else to visit—made this house as much an anomaly as its owner: an interloper.

For the moment, he squelched his natural curiosity. The interview that would decide his fate was about to begin.

Mrs. Lowell sat down in a Sheraton chair, waving him to the opposite one. "Now, Captain Gabler. I was impressed by your background."

He froze in the act of removing his cap. "You had me investigated, ma'am?"

She arched one well-shaped auburn eyebrow. "But of course. As you have, no doubt, asked about me."

Sitting, Peter cradled his cap on his knees and smiled wryly. Astute as well as beautiful. But then, from all accounts, the fisheries and the import-export shipping businesses she'd helped her husband run now thrived even more under her sole directorship. He nodded his shining dark head.

"Do you believe the rumors they whisper about me?"

He cleared his throat, wondering how to respond tactfully. The uglier rumors, Peter had dismissed with total scorn.

Mrs. Lowell still stared at him with those unblinking hazel eyes that suddenly reminded him of a cat's. In the mellow sunlight that streamed through the window, they looked golden.

He hedged, "Ah, I believe that you are a brave woman, thriving in a man's world, and that your policies of paid sick leave and vacation for your workers were bound to stir up controversy in this vastly competitive field."

She sniffed. "Your flattery does not impress me, sir. Do you believe I'm a witch?"

He quit twiddling with his hat and met her eyes. "No, ma'am, I do not. Nor do I believe that you poisoned your husband or had your daughter killed."

No matter what the rumors down at the docks, Gisella Lowell was no more a practitioner of witchcraft than he was. Eccentric? Obviously, and not only in her choice of dress, but he could scarcely condemn her for that when he was a bit odd himself. He'd heard all the tales about how she'd seduced poor Alexander Lowell when he was on a trip to Eastern Europe, married him, birthed him a daughter, took over his shipping business when he fell ill and then poisoned him to take everything else. As to the mysterious, abrupt disappearance of her only child, the lovely twenty-year-old Katarina, Peter was certain there was some sensible explanation. Belike the young heiress had run away with some fortune-hunter.

Besides, her history was none of his business and, frankly, little of his concern.

She digested his response for a moment, and then said abruptly, "Tell me, Captain Gabler, since we are being so frank—do you believe in witchcraft?"

Though he suddenly suspected she wouldn't like his answer, he had to be honest. He'd never stooped to lying in business, and he would not begin now, even if it cost him his last hope. "No, I do not."

Her lips curved slightly, whether in scorn or amusement, he could not tell.

"Do you like cats?"

His heart sank to his boots. He had hoped to avoid such a direct question. He shook his head firmly.

The smile deepened. "I thought not. That's why Sheba wanted to attack you. Animals sense things, you know. Unlike people, they trust their instincts. But I am impressed by your honesty. Now, tell me—what do you want the money for?"

This was easier. "To build a ship."

"But you've sailed many successful voyages, and should have little trouble raising funds from more traditional sources. From what I hear, you've been at sea all your life, and you made the Atlantic crossing in a record twelve days with your medium clipper. Is this not true?"

He nodded, bile rising to his throat, a bitter burning in the backs of his eyes. That last voyage around the Horn would have paid off his investors, and he would have finally, at the young age of thirty, been sole owner of one of the fastest ships on the waves. "Aye. But she went down around the Horn a year ago, taking all I owned with her. Ten of my men died."

"But your insurance—can you not use it to build a new ship?"

Huskily, he admitted, "My ex–business partner took care of those matters to leave me free to run the crew and ship. He told me he'd paid the premium, but . . ." He trailed off, unable to continue.

Her hazel eyes softened. "A pity. But why will no one finance your new venture?"

Nervously, he twiddled his cap between his fingers, wondering how to explain. Here was a woman who embraced everything new; he was an anachronism, a young man clinging to the romance of sail in an age of steam. There was no easy way to put it. He took a deep breath and said in a rush, "Most people want to build steamships. They say the era of the clipper is dead. Takes too large a crew, too much maintenance, too little cargo space."

"You don't agree?"

"No." He did not elaborate, but his conviction rang in the elegant room.

"I see. Well, if you are selected, the money

would be yours to do with as you please, though I do tend to agree that sailing ships are not as efficient as steamers. But that is neither here nor there. My only stipulation is that you must remain in Boston until November first. I have a lovely little townhome I can let you use, free of rent, for the next two months."

It was early September. The architect helping design the plans for the new ship lived in Boston, but Peter didn't expect the process to require two months. And as for living on Beacon Hill . . . He masked a shudder with difficulty and said cautiously, "You are selecting me, then?"

"The choice is not mine." Rising, the widow clapped her hands and called something in a language Peter didn't understand.

Heavy feet tromped down the stairs. Lighter ones came from every direction, and soon the salon was filled with cats. Cats of every description from a black panther to a cougar to the tiger to more traditional house cats of every hue and size.

The three great cats eyed him with predatory interest, but at Mrs. Lowell's hushed comment, they padded over to opposite corners of the room. They plopped down and watched, yawning, baring formidable fangs. The four house cats circled Peter's chair, yowling.

Peter sneezed.

Three of them sprang back, startled, but the fourth crouched directly in front of him, watching with that feline intensity that had always unsettled him. This cat was a small female, solid black, with huge gold eyes accented by the gold and diamond collar it wore.

For a timeless instant, Peter was transfixed by that gaze. The cat seemed to appraise him with an agenda of its own. What did she look for? A comfortable lap? A gentle touch? Someone who would feed her and water her, and take care of her? But no, even as he stared back into those luminous eyes, Peter couldn't shake the eerie sensation that the cat looked deeper.

Who he was. What he wanted. How he went about getting it. Things no cat should ever care about.

With one lithe spring, the cat jumped up on his lap.

Peter almost fell out of his chair. He crinkled his nose, trying to stop the urge to sneeze before it began, but strangely, now that the other cats had backed away, his nose didn't tickle. It was almost as if he weren't allergic to this particular feline. Or perhaps this shade of cat.

Ridiculous. Black fur was just as itchy. But the soft warmth on his lap began to seep into him, easing his discomfort. Compelled, he stroked the velvety fur.

Mrs. Lowell watched intently. When the cat began to purr at his touch, she sighed. A wistful sound, sadness and satisfaction mixed. "You have been selected."

Did he hear aright? His hands froze on the soft fur. It almost seemed as if the cat itself had more choice over who her new owner would be than the widow. Nonsense. Peter watched curiously, feeling as if he'd entered not simply an expensive world he'd never aspired to, but a fantastic domain where anything could, and would, happen.

He shifted his long legs. His hand moved, brushing the velvet fur backward. The cat stiffened on his lap, jumped down, walked over to a couch and sprang up. It circled around until it found the perfect spot, and then it lay down, curled in a ball, golden eyes fixated on him.

Meanwhile, Mrs. Lowell went to a tall cabinet against the wall and removed a slim red book. Moving silently, gracefully, like the cats around her, she brought the book to him.

*Her familiars?* came Peter's quick thought, but he squelched it and accepted the tome she held out. The expensive leather was lavishly gilded in a strange curlicue pattern, and a gilded cat's face, two emerald eyes winking at him, dominated the cover. The pages were also gilded.

"Open it. These rules must be followed religiously, or any bargain between us will be abrogated," the widow said solemnly, as if she offered her own personal copy of the Ten Commandments. Regulations he would break at his own peril.

Gingerly, he thumbed the book open to the title page. It read, *The Care and Feeding of the Modern Feline.*

He turned the next page and read five simple rules.

1. Never stroke her fur backward.
2. Let her sleep with you, eat with you, walk with you.
3. Talk to her and she'll talk back.
4. Give her independence and she will be loyal.
5. Love your cat, and she will love you.

Filled with a growing unease he could not account for, Peter turned the page, but the last ten heavy vellum pages in the book were blank. He closed it. Rule one he'd already broken, and the cat had made its displeasure immediately known.

Both pairs of golden eyes watched him steadily. The woman blinked no more often than the cat. Mrs. Lowell asked, "And can you abide faithfully by these rules?"

"I can't say I'm wild about sleeping with an animal, any animal—"

"These rules are not open to negotiation."

The gentle reprimand gave him little choice. He nodded. "As you will."

"And you will cherish her, as long as you both live?"

The similarity of the demand to a more sacred vow chilled him, but again, he reluctantly nodded. "Am I expected to take her to sea with me?"

"She loves the sea." Then, taking pity on his confusion, she stood and offered her hand. "You will grow to care for her in time. I promise. I sense something in you, something upstanding and wonderful."

He bowed over her hand. "Thank you for your trust in me."

"My banker will deposit the agreed-upon sum in your account." Mrs. Lowell turned her head to look at the cat still lying on the couch. She sat down next to it and spoke softly in her musical language. The cat crawled up her lap, setting its forepaws on her shoulder, and tucked its head under her neck, purring.

The woman's hypnotic hazel eyes filled with tears.

Moved for some reason he did not understand, Peter stepped away to give the leave-taking privacy. He walked around the beautifully appointed room, careful to skirt the lazing cats in each corner; he paused to admire the lovely mantel, glancing up at the picture above. He froze.

A tall, gorgeous young woman stood upon a grassy embankment in partial profile, blue black hair flowing down over her back past her hips, tossed in the breeze coming off the Charles River. In the painting, the harbor looked tiny, as if the ships spread at her feet were under her dominion. Her dress was emerald green, nipped in at a small waist, and there were frills of jet-flecked lace at her generous bosom. She held a wide emerald and black hat in one hand, the breeze catching the strings as if to snatch the proper covering away from a face and form that needed none. Her skin was ivory pale, finely textured, her black brows winging away from her huge golden eyes in reckless disregard for fashion or propriety.

He sensed the widow moving next to him, but still he stared up at the smiling young woman. The fierce strength and individuality in that face drew him more than its uncommon beauty, for the painter had captured the girl's vitality. He felt as if he could reach out and touch warm, living skin instead of cold canvas.

"My daughter is . . . was lovely, was she not?" came the widow's husky question.

"Was?" Still, he couldn't tear his eyes away from that wild face.

"She is . . . ill. Incognito. For a time." She cleared her husky voice. "Cat is ready for you to take her home." She thrust a piece of paper and a key into his limp fingers.

Finally, he tore his gaze away from the portrait. "Cat? Is that all you call her?" Surely a more exotic name was needed. Sable, or Dusky, or something.

"Cat is what she prefers."

He shrugged. "As you wish." He walked over to the cat and picked it up.

It spat at him.

Startled, he dropped it back onto the couch.

The widow shook her head. "Remember rule number four."

He wracked his brain. Oh, the one about independence. "She'd rather walk?"

"Always. On her own t—four feet."

He looked about. "Do you have a leash?'

"You will not need it. She will follow you."

Doubtfully, he watched over his shoulder as he walked toward the entrance. The cat traded last mournful looks between its former owner and its new one, but she padded after him, her whiskers trembling slightly.

At the front door, Peter paused. "But what do I feed her? The book says nothing of that."

"Whatever you eat will be fine."

Peter couldn't quell a scowl at that response. His parents had been conservative Swedes who immigrated to Maine, working dawn until dusk trapping lobsters to save enough money to buy their first boat. Those early years were a vague memory to Peter, but the lesson of reward for work had been a salutary one. "A penny saved is a penny earned," they had often said, quoting that great American patriot Ben Franklin.

Feed a cat human food? Nonsense.

But Peter merely tipped his cap to the widow and walked down the steps, pacing his strides to the cat's.

At the gate, he paused to look back.

The widow held on to a front porch post as if she needed support to stand. Even from here, Peter could see the tears in her eyes.

21

Touched despite himself, he snatched off his hat and turned it between his fingers. "Ma'am, ah, that is . . . visit us any time you please. And . . . I promise to take exemplary care of your cat."

She smiled and straightened, looking stronger. "Thank you, Captain Gabler. I can see we both made the right choice."

Peter smiled, his first genuine smile of the afternoon.

The widow blinked.

So did the cat.

Peter replaced his cap and held the wrought-iron front gate wide. The cat padded through, sending one last look over its shoulder at Mrs. Lowell. She waved.

Peter led the way up the street, feeling awkward, but his stride was as bold as ever. The cat followed obediently, its long tail swishing as it walked. Looking down at the sleek creature, he had to shake himself. He couldn't help feeling that the twitching tail was the cat's version of a lady's swinging hips.

An odd intuition he'd been denying grew stronger. Finally, he stopped, stuck one hand on his hip, pushed his cap back with a finger and stared down at the cat. "So, Cat. Did I choose you, or did you choose me?"

The cat looked back at him with slanted, mysterious eyes.

Amazingly, he heard a soft, musical voice, slightly accented, reply, "We chose each other."

Startled, Peter looked around to see if any of the passers-by had heard the voice. Several people looked at him curiously. Embarrassed at his foolishness, Peter walked on. The cat kept pace, but

Peter couldn't shake the feeling that he followed instead of led this fiendish feline.

Somehow, she would forever change his life.

For better?

Or worse?

# Chapter Two

*Let her eat with you, walk with you,*
*sleep with you.*

At the next corner, Peter pulled the scrap of paper from his pocket to look at the address again. Cat had trotted several paces ahead, and she stopped, looking back at him. She gave an impatient yowl and dashed around the corner. Panicked, Peter crushed the paper back in his pocket and hurried after. All he needed was to lose the cursed creature before he ever received the money. He rounded the corner, his heart pounding, but there the feline sat, calmly licking her paws to bathe her face.

Waiting. She looked at him as if to say, *My, for such a tall, strong man, you're slow*.

Impatiently, Peter shoved the fanciful thought away. No matter how unusually expressive this creature was, it was still a cat, small *c*, and not the capital kind, in any sense of the word. It would do as it was told. Peter drew even with the animal and gave it a stern look. "Bad cat! Stay close to me."

The cat ignored him, continuing to lick her paws.

Haughtily, Peter walked on, wishing he'd brought a map. He snapped his fingers at the cat, expecting it to follow, but when he turned his head, the cat was still ignoring him. Peter stopped, glaring at the animal.

She stopped licking, set both paws on the ground, neatly aligned, and glared back, whiskers flickering. And then, so fast that Peter blinked and missed it, the cat gathered itself on her haunches, leaped forward in a graceful arc, landed on all fours and streaked off in a black blur.

Again, Peter was forced to give chase, but this time he cursed a blue streak, not caring who heard him. He caught up with Cat at the next turn, following as the animal dashed through a wrought iron fence and up a pretty brick walkway lined with flowers. Peter checked the address on the small gate and froze. This was the house! How had the animal known?

Cat plopped down on the stoop of the tall, narrow townhouse, sighing heavily.

Strangely, Peter blushed, feeling inadequate. The rapid succession of emotions he'd felt in the past couple of hours had strained his patience beyond bearing. He was accustomed to giving orders, not taking them. Leading, not following. And choosing the company he kept in his rare leisure hours very carefully. These indignities could not continue. Time to show this animal who was captain here.

Shoving the gate open so hard that it slammed

against the fence, Peter followed the creature from hell for what he told himself was the last time. He'd lock the critter up while he did his business down at the docks. He hadn't promised the widow to take the cat with him everywhere, only on his next voyage; the thought appeased his conscience.

The key fit perfectly in the heavy brass lock on the glossy black door. As soon as he got the door open, the cat shot inside. More warily, Peter followed. The decor here was even more plain than in the mansion. Simple chairs and a sturdy wooden table centered the small dining room, which had a plain wrought iron light fixture above. Tasteful cream lace curtains hung in the bow window and in the opposite, equally plain parlor. Tall, narrow stairs led to the next landing, but rather than ascending, Peter explored the rest of the downstairs. The kitchen and pantry had all the modern conveniences. . . . He went still, gasping in shock.

The cat had jumped up on the counter, knocked over the milk bottle that had obviously just been delivered, and was in the process of helping itself to the milk pooling on the counter.

Peter reached out to swat the animal, remembered his promise and picked it up instead, roaring, "Enough! Bad cat!"

He opened the pantry door, thinking to confine the animal while he cleaned up the mess, but the cat spat at him and squirmed free, streaking up the steps to the next floor.

Sighing heavily, Peter cleaned up the spilled milk.

For several hours, cat and man were content in their own company. Peter arranged for his hotel to have his bags delivered, and when they arrived it was almost dark. Flipping on lights, Peter went upstairs to put his things away. The small townhouse had only two bedrooms. The first was tiny, with a narrow bed under a sloping ceiling. He would hit his head every time he got up. He closed that door and opened the second. This room was much larger, but it was already occupied.

Cat sat in the middle of the wide bed, eyes glowing green in the darkness.

Unnerved for a reason he could not define, Peter snapped on the overhead light. "Shoo! Scat! This is my room."

The long, graceful tail swished, but otherwise the animal didn't move.

Grinding his teeth together, Peter unpacked his few possessions and put them away in the large wardrobe against one wall. *Be patient,* he told himself. *It'll take some time for you to get used to her.* When he was done unpacking, Peter held the door wide, invitingly. "Hungry? Let's go eat."

The cat stayed put. With an almost human sounding sigh, she rested her head on her front paws and looked depressed.

Shrugging, Peter went downstairs, made himself a simple supper of cold ham and fruit from the groceries he'd had delivered and spread out his ship's plans on the dining room table. Tingling awareness made him lift his head. The swinging doors opened and the cat bolted through, her legs falling to the ground after obviously having pushed the doors open. She sat on her haunches to watch him hungrily.

Surprised, Peter put his glass of milk down on the table. He'd never thought cats intelligent enough to figure out how to open doors, but he was beginning to realize that, like her former owner, this cat was not ordinary. He went to the cupboard where he'd stowed the tins of cat food. He opened one with his pocket knife. He gagged at the scent. There was no way *he* would eat this stuff. Still, he scooped the food on a small plate, set it on the floor and went back to eating.

Ignoring the offering, the cat sat where she was, watching him. Her nose lifted slightly.

Peter tried to eat, but that unblinking stare unnerved him. He shoved his half-empty plate back and struggled with the impulse. *Oh, to hell with it.* He could show Cat who was boss later. The poor thing obviously missed its former home. Wouldn't hurt to spoil it a bit for one night.

Peter made a clicking sound with his tongue and set his plate on the floor. The cat bounded to the plate and crouched over it, eating the ham daintily. Peter expected her to sniff at and discard the orange sections, but to his surprise, Cat ate those too. A cat who liked fruit? Peter was still scratching his head when Cat's sudden tension alerted him.

Arching in that distinctive feline question mark that sounded an alarm, the cat peered beneath the squatty legs of a high cupboard against the wall. She hissed.

Peter bent beneath the table to look.

A large rat shuffled under the cupboard and poked out a sharp nose, whiskers flickering, eyes glowing red. Automatically, Peter stood and looked around for a broom but couldn't find one. Then he remembered. High time the cat was treated like one.

Pointing at the rat, Peter commanded, "Get him, Cat!"

The rat darted out, running for a small hole in a piece of baseboard.

Peter watched the cat, expecting it to expode in a flurry of movement and dash after the rat.

Indeed, the cat moved. . . . She spat and climbed the closest object—Peter's pant leg.

"Ow!" Needlelike claws stabbed Peter's leg to the thigh, and then his arm, and finally his shoulder as the cat clung there, still spitting down at the large rodent. Peter tried to pull Cat loose, but she scratched his hand. The rat bolted into the hole and disappeared.

Disgusted, Peter shoved open the swinging door and ceded the battle to the rat. Sitting down on the couch in the parlor, Peter tried to pull the cat away from his shoulder and rest her on the back of the sofa. He was about to use force, be hanged to gentleness, but as he touched the soft black body, he felt its trembling. Cursing inwardly, Peter awkwardly patted the haunches. Slowly, he felt the little animal relax. The cat jumped off Peter's shoulder to the back of the couch. In this position, they were almost eye to eye.

Peter scowled at the cat. "What kind of cat are you? Most cats love to hunt mice."

With a final shudder, Cat heaved a sigh and plopped down. That soft voice that was growing familiar said, "I despise the smelly, ugly things."

Peter started back, looking around to see where the voice had come from, but no one was there. He rubbed his forehead, thinking he'd really had a rough day. The strain of trying to raise the money to fulfill his lifelong dream was getting to him. Rising, he said wearily, "Maybe we'll both feel better after a good night's sleep. I have an important appointment tomorrow."

Trudging upstairs, Peter closed the bedroom door behind him. The cat would have to make do with the couch; be hanged if he'd awaken with cat hairs all over him.

The minute his head touched the pillow, he was asleep. In his dream, a familiar image grew. Boston spread out below in all its proper, prissy splendor while he stood above the city on a high hill. He was tired, for his meeting with the matriarch of the Coupland family had not gone well. She'd denied him the rest of the funding he needed to finish building his ship. He climbed up into the hills for solace. He stuck his hands in his pockets.

Suddenly, they were full of gold. Tens of thousands of dollars' worth of gold. Yet, oddly, the gold had no weight, as if once he won it, it would free him instead of pin him down.

Peter stared at the glittering bounty in his hands. Somehow, he knew he had to figure out the source of the wealth, and he also knew that his benefactor was not in the expected place. But where?

He looked around suspiciously. He was alone, but he heard laughter. Feminine, vivacious laughter so lovely that it drew him higher. At the top of the next hill, with Boston tiny in the distance, he saw a girl with long raven hair, and a black and green floppy hat in one hand as she twirled, laughing. Then she plopped down, green skirts and jet-flecked lacy frills flaring around her like leaves adorning an exotic flower. Slanted golden eyes lifted to his. Her smile faded. She waited quietly, as if she'd been expecting him.

Mesmerized by her beauty, Peter walked toward her, feeling a strange pull that he'd never known.

He was almost close enough to touch her when he whispered, "What is your name?"

She cocked her head on one side in a strangely familiar gesture. "When you want me, I will be there."

Peter was reaching out to touch her when she disappeared. . . .

Thrashing about in bed, Peter knocked into something. A piercing yowl made him start awake. He heard a slight thump and turned on the light.

He squinted into the darkness beyond the pool of light and saw familiar eyes glowing green in the gloom. "Cat?" he muttered sleepily. "How did you get in here?" Peter looked at the bedroom door. It was open. He was quite certain he'd closed it. And he'd apparently knocked the cat off the bed, so she must have been sleeping with him. How did she open the door?

Peter sat up and stuffed the pillows behind his head. The covers fell to his waist. He always slept in the nude. Chilled by the vivid dream, Peter needed comfort. Sighing in defeat, he patted the bed beside him. He had promised, after all, and since the animal didn't make him sneeze, it might as well sleep with him. He'd just have to change the sheets more often. "Come on up."

Cat didn't need asking twice. In one lithe leap, she landed beside him. However, she stayed on the very edge of the wide bed, her eyes running over his bare chest.

Peter reached out and picked up the cat. She stiffened, but when he set her near him and began to stroke her fur—in the right direction—she relaxed. "You're a queer one, Cat. You've been spoiled, I guess, but since I owe you a lot, I'll try to be lenient. There's something . . . compelling about you. Still, independence is very well, but you have to learn you don't own me—I own you."

The cat yawned. Her little head dipped as if she was too tired to pay attention to him. Snapping off the light, Peter set the cat on the pillow opposite his and settled down to sleep. For some odd reason, he felt comforted by the small presence. His sleep for the rest of the night was deep and dreamless.

The next morning, when Peter opened his eyes, a golden stare transfixed him. He'd seen those eyes before. Where? Tentatively, he reached out, but instead of touching the long black hair of his vision, he touched short, velvety fur. He jolted awake and bolted to a sitting position.

Dammit, what was wrong with him? Obsessed by a woman? He'd never been troubled by dreams or regrets for what might have been. He'd always been too busy trying to better himself and serve his investors and crew fairly. The life of a sea captain did not allow for close ties. Few women were suited to that life. While Peter had never been so profligate as to have a woman in every port, he'd certainly had his share. Throwing back the covers, still confused as to why he was so haunted by the lovely girl in the painting, Peter began to dress.

He stepped into his underdrawers and, with a supple wriggle of his hips, pulled them up.

The cat sat on the bed, watching him with very human eyes. She licked her lips.

A blush tinged Peter's cheekbones. Telling himself he was ridiculous, Peter nevertheless turned his back to finish dressing. When he was done attiring himself in the new suit he'd bought for this occasion, he turned to the cat and asked, "How do

I look? Would you give me twenty thousand dollars?"

The little black head bobbed. He laughed.

"I only hope Mrs. Coupland agrees." Turning smartly on his heel, Peter exited the room, unaware that Cat stiffened, her eyes widening in alarm.

As he went downstairs, Peter vowed to quit talking to this animal; he was beginning to imagine that she would talk back. Still, when Peter had collected his plans and gone to the front door, he said over his shoulder, "I'll be back in a few hours. Be good."

He closed and locked the front door, wincing at the pitiful yowl that followed. A black nose shoved aside the parlor curtains. Still yowling, Cat watched him leave.

Twenty minutes later, Peter entered the Coupland shipping office, his heart tapping at his ribs. While the money from the deal with the cat would certainly help, it was not enough to give him a majority holding in the new vessel and business. He'd heard that Tituba Coupland, the wealthiest woman in Boston and the current manager of the vast Coupland shipping enterprises, sometimes invested in other ventures, offering quite generous terms.

While he waited, Peter tried to avoid twitching in the stiff suit, but as time dragged on, he grew uncomfortable. Discreetly, he tried to check his pocket watch without the mustachioed, sideburned and natty male secretary noticing. Still, the man's lips thinned when Peter looked at the watch and slipped it back into his pocket. The woman had kept him waiting for over an hour.

Finally, the box on the secretary's desk buzzed

shrilly. When the secretary pressed the button, a cold voice said, "You may send in Captain Gabler now."

The secretary nodded at him. "Go in."

Peter had expected someone to exit the private sanctum, but when he went in, the office was empty save for a regal black-haired woman sitting behind a huge Louis XIV inlaid desk. The knowledge that this woman had kept him cooling his heels for an hour despite the fact that she had no other visitors ate at Peter, but he hid his annoyance behind a wooden smile and a deep bow. "Thank you for seeing me, madam."

A slender white hand with long fingers and curving, red-varnished talons waved him into a chair. Peter was surprised at how long her nails were. Few society women sported such a manicure, since it was almost universally considered slatternly, but with her deep red, lush mouth and voluptuous bosom, the nails looked somehow appropriate on Mrs. Coupland. The woman appraised him through inscrutable green eyes.

Determined to give away nothing, Peter looked about the office. A huge picture window boasted an impressive view of the harbor, but that was a sight Peter had seen many times. The plush Victorian sofa against one wall had a Sheraton table in front of it, and a Tiffany lamp rested beside a matching chair. Behind the couch was a painting of his hostess.

From the style of her dress, it had been painted years ago, but she looked no different today. She was beautiful, with perfectly balanced features and an hourglass shape, but there was something cold about her petulant mouth and challenging stare. In the portrait, she held a small black and brown puppy, while another gamboled at her feet, but either the artist had been indifferent, or she had been indifferent to the artist. The painting was flat, cold and lifeless, unlike the painting in Mrs. Lowell's house—of a girl he couldn't get out of his mind.

A bookcase next to the sofa and chairs held the obligatory classics, but the top shelf flaunted slimmer volumes with the look of frequent use. Peter squinted to read the titles. Why was such a wealthy, influential woman interested in Cotton Mather's *The Wonders of the Invisible World*, or the Egyptian *The Book of the Dead*, or even *The History of Magic*?

That long, sulky mouth moved into a smile. "You think my choice of reading material odd?"

Peter shrugged. "It is none of my concern, ma'am."

"A careful answer from a careful man. But you err, sir. If we are to be in business together, we should know much about one another." Mrs. Coupland stood, rounded her desk and offered him her well-shaped hand.

Peter shook it. A chill started at his palm and ran up his arm, but when she released him, the strange feeling went away.

"Now then. If I tell you something of myself, you must do the same for me. Agreed?"

"Agreed." Curiosity grew. Were all women of Boston so strong and direct? Or only its wealthy, eccentric widows? The woman was dressed in a maroon silk gown full of the furbelows and frills Peter despised, but they accented her awesome presence and hinted of the complexity of her character.

"I am named Tituba after a friend of one of my

ancestors. She was a great friend of the family, despite the unfortunate occurrences at Salem. That's why you see the books here. I have always been interested in my heritage. Understand a person's roots and you will understand how and when they will blossom, and what harvest you can reap from them." She nodded at him a cue to tell of his own background.

"I am the son of Swedish immigrants," Peter said reluctantly. "I was born by the sea, I live by the sea and I will die by the sea. There is nothing else for me."

"But I understand your last ship sank in the Cape Horn graybeards. And you were without insurance as well."

She used the sailing term for the treacherous waves in the "Roaring Forties," the southern point of the latitudes where the westerly winds made rounding the capes hazardous. But her critical comment made Peter's eyes narrow. "I will not be so again. I've fired my former business partner."

She nodded and went back to her chair, her hips swaying slightly. "Very well then. Do you have a design to show me?"

Heaving a slight sigh of relief, Peter spread his plans out on the desk and moved next to her. His nose quivered at her scent. The odd, musky perfume sent a tingle through his groin that he tried to ignore. However, over the next hour the feeling grew as she often brushed the side of a shapely breast against his arm as he pointed.

Still, Peter tried to maintain mental and physical distance as he explained the innovations that he and the designer had devised. ". . . she'll be almost three thousand tons, with a steel hull much stronger and lighter than wood, yet rigid enough for the width and length of a flat bottom that offers greater strength and stability. She'll not go down around the Cape this time. She'll ride any surge like a dolphin. And bark-rigged, with steel halyards, we can carry sails enough to make her faster than any sailing vessel afloat, yet they'll be large enough to require a smaller crew. And finally," Peter flipped a page and showed a drawing that would be a disgraceful waste of ink to every true-blooded clipper captain.

However, Peter had long ago learned that idealism and practicality had to share the same suit, if not the same hat. He pointed at the ugly screw. "She'll have an auxiliary steam-driven propeller, designed on a chain drive to be raised and lowered behind a trap door as needed so as not to cause drag. She'll not need any tugboats to pull her in and out of harbor, and even when she's becalmed, we'll be able to make headway."

"Hmmm, most impressive. But it's been my experience that designs that try to straddle two worlds end up conquering neither." She watched him quietly, obviously expecting a heated rebuttal. She shifted her body slightly closer.

Those green eyes were magnetic, drawing him into a verdant arbor where ivy clustered on cloistered walls. Come inside, learn my secrets, she seemed to say.

Peter's gaze dropped to that lush red mouth. His lips tingled and the ache in his groin made him grow hard. His head lowered toward that stunning, ageless face.

The exterior office door opened quietly. Assured footsteps approached in concert with deep, baying barks that sounded close by.

The secretary's voice protested, "Now see here,

madam, you can't just barge in like that—"

The inner office door opened and closed, cutting off the words.

Snapping back to a standing position, Peter looked at the intruder. Steady hazel eyes appraised him. Peter blushed. What was Gisella Lowell doing here? More to the point, why did he feel guilty?

After the one glance, Gisella ignored him. "You're really growing desperate, Titty. You cannot even wait for darkness anymore."

Titty? Peter blinked at the derogatory term tossed at the wealthiest woman in Boston. From her stiffening posture, Mrs. Coupland didn't appreciate the sobriquet.

Slender, shapely hands spread flat on Peter's plans, the curving nails bloodred in the sunlight. Her touch possessive, as if she already owned the impressive vessel—and its captain—Mrs. Coupland stood to her full, regal height. "You came to me, did you not? It is you who is desperate, and well you should be. Your little sessions in your tower haven't worked, have they? Nor will they— even after you've enlisted this handsome young man. I'm stronger. I always have been. I always shall be."

Peter's head jerked from side to side as he watched the women's expressions. His parents had never argued in front of him, and this was the first time he'd witnessed the full fury of two angry females. He finally understood the origins of the term catfight. But why did it seem they battled over him like cats scuffling over scraps? What did they want of him?

Gisella retorted, "Not for long. Soon enough, you shall face two of us—"

Mrs. Coupland tossed back her head in a husky laugh. Peter watched that long white throat work and was both fascinated and repelled as she said, still chuckling, "Your daughter will never return to you, but even if she does, I shall face you both, just as I did before. Now what do you want?"

Coughing slightly, Gisella drew a long, elegant envelope from her bag and placed it on the table. "I know you'll likely be busy on All Hallow's Eve, but I'm having a party to celebrate the return of my daughter, and I thought you might wish to be present."

The remnants of the smile faded. Green eyes narrowed to slits. "I shall be delighted to attend, you silly bitch."

Peter recoiled in shock at the unladylike conduct. Obviously, Tituba Coupland was a woman who followed her own rules. Even with her great beauty, it was difficult to see her as the social elite that she was reputed to be.

Mrs. Coupland turned to him with a contrite smile. "Excuse me, young man. But you've unfortunately been privy to a rivalry of long standing. Mrs. Lowell is not a graceful loser."

Coughing harder, Gisella turned toward the door. "Peter, I should like a chat with you when you have a moment. Good day to you both." The door closed and her quiet, dignified footsteps receded.

Uncomfortably, Peter cleared his throat. "Ah, well, if you've no further questions, madam, I shall go about—"

"But I do." Mrs. Coupland approached him, that luscious mouth quirked in a tempting smile. "Do you not want to kiss me?"

For some odd reason, Gisella's presence had

cleared Peter's head. The hypnotic stare, the curvaceous body, even the heady scent of this strange woman now left Peter cold. Pretending deafness, he sidestepped when she would have pinned him against the bookcase, rounded her and went to the desk to roll up his plans. "Ah, when you reach a decision about funding my venture, ma'am, you can reach me at—"

"I know where you live, Peter."

Slowly, he turned to face her. "You do?" How in the hell could she know that? He'd only moved in yesterday.

"And I know that you've adopted a small black cat that used to belong to that . . . witch. Tell me— do you like cats?"

Peter was growing a bit irritated at continually being quizzed on the subject, but he shook his head.

"Of course not. They never would have selected you otherwise. She bribed you, didn't she? To get you to take the creature. What name did she call the little animal?"

"Cat." Peter's voice was curt, for this woman was prying too closely into his private affairs for his liking.

That long white throat worked in delightful laughter again. "Cat? Oh, how lovely. Subtlety is not one of Gisella's failings." Her smile faded as those enigmatic green eyes fixed on something outside her huge picture window.

Peter turned to look but saw nothing.

"Excuse me, won't you?" She walked out a side door, shut it and disappeared.

Moments later, Peter heard excited, deep barks. Mrs. Coupland soon returned with a self-satisfied air. She nodded regally. "I do not need to contact you later. I know an honest man when I meet one. I shall be happy to fund half your venture. I will have my attorney draw up the documents."

All the strange feelings to which Peter had been subject since entering this room lifted away under the sheer awesome power of relief. "I cannot tell you how grateful I am, ma'am. I shall not disappoint you."

The barks outside had grown more threatening, interspersed with growls.

The lush mouth curved again. "No, you shan't. I shall see to it." She walked him to the door. "So, what do you think of Boston?"

Peter shrugged as they exited the red brick building. "It's very—" He drew off with a gasp.

Across the street, Cat cowered in a tree.

At the base, two huge Rottweilers stood on their powerful hindquarters, front paws clawing at the bark as they tried to climb the tree to get at the terrified feline. They snapped and growled, jumping, jaws baring huge fangs. One managed to claw its way to the first branch and lunge upward. He was only five feet away from Cat now.

The feline scampered higher, but the branch bent even under her slight weight. She had nowhere else to go.

Angry that Cat had followed him but fearful for her safety, Peter started to rush forward. He hesitated. The dogs were close to two hundred pounds apiece, and he didn't even have a broom. Vaguely he sensed Mrs. Coupland's watchfulness, but he was too busy frantically looking about for a weapon to wonder why. Seeing the little animal so threatened brought home to him how quickly Cat had become important to him. He was about to move forward and kick the dogs away, regardless of his own safety, when two police officers hurried up the street, obviously drawn by the commotion.

They took in the scene with one glance, relaxing a bit when they saw that the only entity in peril was a cat. They each pulled out a nightstick and stalked forward. "Here now, ye bloody beasties, who's let ye loose?" the older one demanded. When the dog at the foot of the tree snapped at him, he popped it on the snout with the stick.

To Peter's intense relief, the Rottweiler whimpered and backed away. The other officer looked about, spied Mrs. Coupland and called across the street, "Ye've been warned, ma'am. Keep these beasties penned up or they'll be put down. We'll have no more attacks on my beat."

Sighing, Mrs. Coupland clapped her hands.

Immediately, the second dog stopped growling. Turning his head, he looked at his owner. With a last yip of defiance, he clambered down from the tree and trotted over to Mrs. Coupland. The first dog followed.

They sat at her feet, tails wagging, as she patted each powerful head. "I'm sorry, officers. I don't know how they got out."

Peter glared at her. What a good liar she was, he reflected grimly. The officers apparently thought the same, for they scowled suspiciously until she opened her office door. She waved blithely back and took her hounds inside. The door closed quietly.

Chilled for a reason he didn't understand, yet profoundly relieved, Peter walked to the foot of the tree. He held out his arms. "Come along, Cat."

Whiskers quivering, Cat stayed put.

"Is this your animal, sir?" asked the older officer.

"Yes." Why wouldn't she come down?

"I'd not let her loose around here. Those dogs are dangerous. They've killed other dogs, cats, even attacked a child once."

"Why aren't they put down, then?"

Swinging his club back at his waist, the officer harrumped. "Some people got more money than sense, is all I ken. Good day to ye, sir." The two Irish officers walked off.

When they were alone, Cat looked about several more times, side to side. She stared down at him, her golden eyes huge and reproachful. She still quivered, obviously terrified.

Peter swallowed harshly. "Come on, Cat. Here, kitty, kitty, kitty." She ignored him, still peering about. Then, in a black streak, she darted down the tree, leaping past Peter's outstretched arms, and ran for home.

Feeling tired when he should have been invigorated, and depressed when he should have been glad, Peter followed, prey to new doubts. How could he ally himself with that woman? Mrs. Coupland had let those dogs out quite deliberately. The malicious act troubled him, especially given the easy way she'd lied about it. She must have seen Cat at the window.

Why did she hate Cat? And why did the woman despise Gisella Lowell? Peter's steps dragged. He was on the verge of achieving his heart's desire, but for some reason the elation did not come. Instead, guilt weighed him down. He felt as if he'd failed both Gisella Lowell and Cat.

Why that should bother him so, he didn't know. His head ached. He longed for simplicity: the

43

snap of canvas above his head, the sweep of a limitless blue horizon, salt spray in his face. But he resolutely ignored the harbor's siren call and set himself to the task at hand.

One, find and comfort Cat.

Two, talk to Mrs. Lowell and discover what in tarnation was going on.

Twenty minutes later, he found a louvered window half-open and an empty townhouse. His heart beating a panicked tattoo, Peter locked the townhouse and hurried toward Mrs. Lowell's. No matter how he told himself that his life would be simpler minus one cat, fear gnawed at him. He had to find the critter and tell her he was sorry. He should have beat those hounds off with his bare hands if he'd had to.

Let her be there, let her be there. . . . The mantra kept time with his clicking heels. He virtually ran, but the distance of a few blocks seemed to lengthen with each step.

# Chapter Three

*Talk to her and she'll talk back.*

Trying to stay calm, Peter tapped at Mrs. Lowell's front door. When a whole ten seconds passed, he pounded harder. Eons seemed to lag, but in less than a minute, Mrs. Lowell peeked out the door.

"What do you want, young man?" Her voice would have made an iceberg seem warm.

"I . . . that is . . . Cat. She ran off. She . . ." He swallowed, unable to continue under that hostile stare.

The door opened another crack. "Perhaps you were not the right person for her after all. You may leave if you wish, especially since you find her so distasteful to live with. I will still see that the money is deposited into your account. I do not doubt that Mrs. Coupland will fund your venture, so you don't need us any longer anyway."

*But I do*. The thought popped into his head, unbidden yet undeniable. Something about Cat drew him in an inexplicable way he could barely contemplate, much less understand. She was so much more to him, evoked so much within him. A friend he'd desperately needed and hadn't known it. However, he couldn't face the ramifications of his feelings at the moment, for one need overrode all else. "Please, ma'am. I must see Cat. To be sure she's all right."

Another eon passed. Mrs. Lowell turned partly away and said something in that strange tongue. A moment later, she opened the door.

Peter noted that she was pale, but icily composed. Without a word, she waved him into the salon. There, Peter almost dropped in his tracks with relief, for Cat was curled up on a sofa cushion.

Her pretty pink nose quivered as he drew near, but when he reached out to touch her, she slapped at him and hissed. He drew his hand away and sat down in the same chair he'd occupied an age earlier. Had it truly been only yesterday? He felt as if his entire world had turned topsy-turvy in the space of the past twenty-four hours. He watched the furry little creature intently, trying to understand how she'd become so important to him so quickly. Ignoring him, she licked her paws and cleaned her face. Her graceful movements, the gleam of midnight hair, the slanted golden eyes reminded him of someone—

Gasping, he spun in his chair and looked at the portrait above the fireplace. The smiling girl there was the same girl he'd seen in his dream. The same girl who'd beckoned him and then disappeared, leaving him aching with need. Peter turned back around and glanced at Cat.

Slowly, her raised paw lowered. Propping both her little feet neatly together, Cat stared inscrutably back. Daring him? Luring him? How? And where? Realizing it was important to understand what the feline communicated, Peter closed his eyes, dismissed the rational part of his brain and let instinct guide him.

Two faces appeared in his mind and slowly superimposed one on the other. Cat's whiskers disappeared. The nose lengthened to a regal tilt. Her soft hair began to fade away, becoming ivory skin over well-shaped cheekbones. Only the eyes, slanting, mysterious, remained the same. The same eyes that haunted his dreams; the same eyes looking down at him from the portrait.

Jumping to his feet so fast that he overturned the chair, Peter forced the image away. He was tired. Depressed even, subject to fanciful notions. And yet, when he looked back at Cat, she seemed almost . . . disappointed. Sighing heavily, she plopped down, curled her tail over her body and pretended to go to sleep.

Mrs. Lowell shook her head at his confusion. "Sometimes our imaginations speak truer than our minds. Tell me—why did you not fight the dogs?"

Peter froze in the act of lifting the chair to set it upright. "How did you know that?"

She ignored him. "Did you kiss that . . . woman?"

Slowly, Peter set all four chair legs on the carpet. "Forgive me, ma'am, but I do not see that my personal life is any of your concern."

"Oh, no? If you become involved with that . . .

woman, what do you think would happen to Cat?"

Peter clenched the chair back tightly. "I will not let anything happen to her." His quiet voice rang in the tall, airy room.

Mrs. Lowell walked up to him to stare deeply into his eyes. He let her look, hiding nothing, even though he felt stripped bare under the power of her gaze.

Some of her hostility faded. She moved back and fell more than sat down upon the couch next to Cat. Pulling a handkerchief from her pocket, she coughed into it. Cat sat up in obvious alarm and hurried over to rub repeatedly against the widow's arm, as if trying to comfort her.

As the widow coughed, blood dotted the fine embroidered linen. A new realization struck Peter like a blow between the eyes. Mrs. Lowell was ill. Perhaps even dying. No wonder she was so determined to see her pets settled in good homes. Yet, while that part of the mystery made abrupt sense, Peter still wondered why she and Mrs. Coupland were such bitter enemies, and what Cat had to do with their rivalry.

Sure as sunrise, Cat was involved. And Mrs. Lowell had chosen him to help in that battle, which was why he'd disappointed her by appearing susceptible to Mrs. Coupland's allure. When her coughing grew louder, shaking the slim shoulders, Peter went to the sideboard and poured a glass of water. He took it to the widow, knelt and held the glass to her lips, supporting her wobbly head so she could drink.

After she took a few sips, the coughing eased. Wheezing, she sat back. "I would have preferred that you not know yet," she said between breaths. "But . . . I have consumption. The doctors don't believe I'll survive the year." The effort she'd expended in the explanation seemed to exhaust her, for she sat back weakly.

Cat was frantic now, rubbing and turning, turning and rubbing. She kept looking up at Peter, yowling with piercing demand. *Do something*, that soft voice begged in his head. *Help her.*

Feeling helpless, he dabbed water on his own clean kerchief and wiped the sweat away from Mrs. Lowell's brow. "Ma'am, should I get your doctor?"

"There's nothing he can do." The widow caught his wrist, her grip surprising him with its strength. "Peter, promise me you won't accept money from Mrs. Coupland. Indebt yourself to her once and she will enslave you for life. Don't take my word for it—ask around." She released him and leaned back, heaving a deep, exhausted breath.

Awkwardly, Peter patted her hand. "I must admit, something about her bothers me. It seemed as if she released her dogs deliberately, to attack Cat."

"She did."

"But why?"

Her breath still ragged enough to make the lace at her bodice flutter, she replied obliquely, "When you are ready, you will understand."

Peter waited, but she didn't elaborate.

Finally, she looked away and said softly, "You would not believe me, anyway. But did you know that, according to ancient beliefs, a black cat brings good fortune and much gold upon the household where it resides?"

Stunned, Peter sank back down in the chair he'd turned upright. The previous night's dream of finding gold in his pockets came back to him with vivid clarity. Somehow his own good fortune was tied both to Cat and to the girl in the portrait.

At the look on his face, Mrs. Lowell smiled slightly. "I've said enough for now. All I ask is that you trust your instincts. A wise man is always guided by his heart."

Peter eased away, uncomfortable with that advice. He'd spent a lifetime learning to trust his head first and ignore his heart. A chill slithered up his spine, freezing him in place as she continued, with greater strength, "Tell me, how old do you think Mrs. Coupland is?"

He shrugged. "Forty-five or thereabouts."

"She's sixty-eight years old."

Startled, Peter dropped the kerchief he had moved to put back in his pocket. "You jest."

She shook her head. "I will leave it to your imagination to wonder how she achieves such a youthful appearance."

"And you, ma'am? How old are you?" The words were out of his mouth before he could stop them.

Cat stiffened. Peter looked at her. Her tail switched back and forth, and Peter had the strangest feeling that the tense feline understood and listened intently to the entire conversation. She looked up at him, her golden eyes seeming to chide him for asking such a bold question.

But Mrs. Lowell smiled. "You *are* beginning to understand. I am fifty-nine."

Peter contemplated that in silence. Jamming the kerchief back in his pocket, he rose, unable to withstand any more. He already had too many things to think about.

Mrs. Lowell stood with him, looking stronger. "Before you leave, I must know one thing—do you want Cat to go with you? Are you willing to fully abide by the terms of our agreement?"

Truth welled to his lips like water from a spring, all the purer because it had only recently been tapped. "Yes. I want her." I do? he asked himself.

Mrs. Lowell seemed to understand, for a smile stretched her lovely mouth. "And what if she's attacked again?"

"If she stays where she belongs, she won't be," Peter said, with a cautionary glance at Cat. The little nose lifted in the air as she stared back, unrepentant. Peter sighed and admitted, "I will do whatever is necessary to keep her safe."

Mrs. Lowell's penetrating hazel eyes probed past the facade of skin to bone, to mind, deep into his heart. Oddly, he stood very still and accepted the invasion, somehow knowing that she had both the right and the skill to plumb his deepest thoughts and hopes. Elation thrilled him when she gave a satisfied nod.

"If Cat wishes it, you may take her home now."

Holding his breath, Peter looked at Cat. She glanced between her former owner and her new one and hesitated. In one lithe leap, she jumped off the couch to rub against Peter's trouser leg, purring.

At sea, time was marked by bells, tides and maps. In port, it was marked by gaslights, milk deliveries—and the internal clock of Peter's new friend. Nightly, Cat went to sleep on the pillow next to his. When dawn painted the sky, she invariably awoke him by licking his face with a rough tongue. Peter would glance at his pocket watch; it always read six-thirty.

There were some advantages, it seemed, to owning a pet. Peter had always been a slow riser, and sometimes his first mate had to wake him twice. Not so with Cat around. Gently, but persistently, she would rub her soft body against him, purring, or lick his cheek until, yawning, he got up. It was a much more pleasant way to awaken. And sometimes in the night, on that blurred plateau between the dale of sleep and the mountain of awareness, he could almost feel the girl in the painting against him, kissing, embracing. But when he awoke there was only Cat. Like a woman, Cat was soft and warm. And always, when he reached out to kiss the girl in his dreams, she dissolved in his arms, back into a feline who could enrich his days and warm his nights but never share his heart or his body.

In the bright autumn sun, he'd tell himself that he was being ridiculous. So what if the girl in the painting had golden eyes? Or that her hair was the same color as Cat's? Or even that Cat's former owner was possibly a witch.

Cat was an unusual little animal, that was all.

She was extremely smart for a cat.

True, she was intuitive to his feelings, and would only eat people food. But many spoiled pets were that way. Strangely, she was fastidious even for a cat. She seldom spilled so much as a crumb, and even then she would quickly eradicate any trace. She was always immaculate.

Routine had always ruled Peter's life, and when the days and nights with Cat began to follow a pattern, he started to relax. To cherish the warm little body that liked to sit beside him while he worked on finalizing his plans. To stroke her, and pamper her. Even her habit of escaping the house to follow him wherever he went stopped bothering him. As October dawned brisk and bright, he began to accept that Cat was the best companion he'd ever had. In the peaceful moments of their quieter time he surprised himself wishing, wishing . . . well, it could not be.

Finally, he began to accept the soft voice as real. Somehow, this amazing animal communicated with him through his mind. With every day that passed, the soft voice grew more insistent, and more loquacious. He grew to expect its musical accompaniment to their walks and their meals. Often, he had to bite his tongue to keep from answering back.

Then, one day over breakfast, that musical, slightly accented voice said, "I have been to sea many times, you know. I used to travel with my father."

Peter no longer had the urge to look around for the source of the voice. No one shared the kitchen with him but Cat. And Cat sat in a chair at the table, her little head cocked to the side as if to gauge his reaction. Peter buttered his toast to keep from asking her where she'd traveled.

The voice continued, "But steam is such a nasty, smelly way to travel across the gift of the ocean God gave us. On a sailing ship, you feel like a giant bird, wings spread to the draft of wind and tide. Convenience, even efficiency, should never mean the death of something so beautiful as a tall ship."

Stunned, Peter dropped the toast. A flush warmed his high cheekbones. No one, not even his own crewmen, had ever expressed his own feelings so perfectly. Maybe he was crazy, maybe he was desperate, but whatever spirit that inhabited this neat little feline was kindred to his own. "What type of ship did you sail on?" He cleared his throat, unable to believe he was actually talking to an animal.

What might have been a smile curled that dainty little face. "A schooner, a medium clipper, even an old-style frigate."

Now that he'd done the unthinkable, Peter was flooded with questions and interest. "And where did you sail?"

"All over. Once I even traveled with him around the Horn. It was one of the most exhilarating experiences of my life."

"You weren't afraid?"

"No." The little shoulders almost shrugged. "I'm a strong believer in destiny. Those who don't dare, don't truly live."

Peter's world narrowed to two golden eyes. Longing made him tremble so that he had to clasp the table edge to steady himself. How he wished . . .

Cat set her paws on the table to look at him even more intently. "Peter, I—"

A loud knock made Peter start and return to himself. Sighing with mingled regret and relief, he rose to open the door. At the entryway Tituba Coupland, dressed in sable and diamonds, gave him a smile that shivered down his spine and tingled in his groin. My, she was a beautiful woman. That musky scent she wore was the headiest he'd ever smelled, though he'd never been fond of perfume. Odd.

"Good morning, Captain Gabler. I wanted to see you myself and give you the papers my attorney drew up. May I come in?"

Flushing, collecting himself, Peter opened the door. "Certainly, ma'am. But did you not get my note?"

"What note?" She blinked at him, her green eyes clear and fresh as spring. And equally inviting.

"Please be seated." Peter led her into the small salon and waved her into a chair.

Cat padded in and crouched in the doorway, her eyes slitting. She hissed slightly.

Mrs. Coupland's smile widened. "What a lovely little creature."

"You didn't think so upon my visit to your office." Peter kept a careful distance from her. He seemed to think more clearly when he couldn't smell her perfume.

Huge green eyes blinked at him in shock. That voluptuous mouth, red and luscious as ripe cherries, pouted. "Hades and Vulcan got out on their own. They're truly not vicious. They were just being playful." She held her elegant, red-tipped fingers out toward Cat. "Kitty, kitty, kitty. Come see me, little darling."

Cat's head lowered on her shoulders. She growled, her tail switching with displeasure.

Peter frowned. He didn't particularly care for the woman either, but he'd not have his pets being rude to guests. "Cat, behave!"

Cat relaxed slightly, but her eyes never left Mrs. Coupland.

"Never mind, Captain. I am more of a dog person anyway, to be honest. Tell me—might I have a cup of tea?"

Peter bolted to his feet. "Certainly. Excuse my manners." He hurried out.

When he returned with a laden tray ten minutes later, Cat and Mrs. Coupland sat exactly in the same place, their gazes locked.

Peter's discomfort grew, but he went through the ritual of pouring tea and ignored the creepy feeling that he was an unwilling spectator in a titanic battle of wills.

Mrs. Coupland sipped her tea and grimaced slightly. "I'm sorry to ask this, but I prefer milk with mine."

Setting down his own cup with a clatter, Peter jumped up. "I'm sorry. I seldom partake of tea. I'll be right back."

After he'd returned, poured a dollop of milk into Mrs. Coupland's cup and sat down, Cat curled about his legs, mewling frantically. When he moved to pick up his cup, she placed both paws on his knee and stared up at him, making an unearthly yowl.

Her cry was so loud that Peter set his cup down to clap his hands over his ears. "What's the matter with you, Cat?" Cat quieted and sat at his feet, her gaze glued to his cup.

Mrs. Coupland gave the cat a piercing glance, then sipped her tea, unconcerned. Peter relaxed. "Now, about my note—"

"I think I remember now," Mrs. Coupland interrupted. "Some nonsense about you no longer needing my funding."

"Yes, well, it is true." To his relief, Peter had finally heard from an old college friend who'd agreed to give him the rest of the money. And so Peter had gladly sent a polite thanks, but no thanks, to Mrs. Coupland's office. While he might distrust his instincts about such arcane things as spells and witches, he did rely on his instincts about people.

Tituba Coupland was not to be trusted.

With the elegant grace of an offended queen, Mrs. Coupland set down her cup. "I'm disappointed. I am truly impressed by your innovative vessel." She glanced at his cup and back into his eyes, her brows arched slightly, as if to say, *Do you refuse to drink with me as well*?

Clearing his throat in embarrassment, Peter picked up his cup. Immediately, Cat started yowling again. Glaring at his pet, Peter raised the cup to his lips.

Cat leaped into his lap and clawed the back of his hand.

Grunting in pain, Peter dropped the cup. Hot tea spilled on his lap. With an unearthly yowl, Peter leaped up. He brushed at the front of his pants with his napkin. Cat went flying but nimbly landed on her feet.

Even in his pain, from the corner of his eye, Peter saw Mrs. Coupland hide a smile. His dislike of her grew. When the stinging pain had faded enough for him to compose himself, Peter picked up the broken cup pieces and laid them carefully on the tray. Quietly he said, "If that is all, ma'am, I fear I have another engagement."

Spring green eyes blinked in shock at his dismissal. Slowly, they turned putrid, like vibrant foliage rotting to feed the things of darkness. . . .

Transfixed, Peter stared at the richest woman in Boston. A veil seemed to be torn from his eyes. Flawless skin took on wrinkles, sagging at the jowls. Lush black hair was streaked with gray. Pearly teeth grew long and yellow.

Unable to stop himself, Peter backed a step.

And then, in the blink of an eye, Mrs. Coupland smiled, lovely once again. She stood. "I will keep you no longer, then. Thank you for your time, Captain. I am certain we shall meet again." With a swirl of sable and a glint of diamonds, she was up and out his front door.

Though he listened intently, Peter could not hear her footsteps retreating. Sighing with relief, he collapsed into his chair. Shivering, Cat jumped up and curled on his lap. Absently, wondering what on earth he'd seen, or not seen, of the true nature of the woman who'd just left, Peter asked without thinking, "Why did you make me spill my cup?"

"She put a potion in your tea." Cat still shivered, so he stroked her fur—the right way.

"What kind of potion?"

"Most likely a love potion. To weaken you and make you desert me. . . . Do you understand now, Peter, why I don't want to be alone? She wants to kill me."

His throat tight, Peter patted her, holding her safe in the curve of his arm. And somehow, despite the fact that he was a reasonable man in a reasonable age, he had to fly in the face of all he'd clung to. He, too, shivered as he recalled the ghastly image that Mrs. Coupland had become in her anger at being dismissed. The ugly crone he'd seen was her true entity—body and soul. "She's a witch."

Cat turned her head to look up at him. A smile tinged the lovely, musical voice. "I thought you did not believe in witchcraft."

"I've never liked cats, either."

She propped her paws on his shoulder to look deep into his eyes. "Is this an admission that you . . . like me?"

Tenderly, he rubbed her favorite spot behind her ear. She nudged against his hand, purring. "Yes, little one. And crazy though I may be, I'm beginning to understand. Mrs. Lowell is a good witch, isn't she? The archenemy of Mrs. Coupland."

Cat nodded against his hand.

"Are you her familiar?"

She quit rubbing and jumped down to the floor. "It seems you are still not ready for the whole truth."

"Please, wait."

At the door, she stopped, her proud little back still turned away from him. "Yes?"

"Why did you not warn me of the potion while she was here?"

"She could hear me, and I'd rather she didn't know that I can talk to you." Cat glided up the stairs.

Sighing, Peter checked his pocket watch. He'd be late to his meeting with the ship's designer if he didn't leave now. "Cat, you'd best come with me in case she returns."

A quiet voice responded from the top of the stairs. "I'll go to my . . . former owner's house. I shall be fine. I'll see you back here this evening."

Peter hesitated, but finally, reluctantly, walked out.

Somehow, he knew he had let her down again.

But the final revelation that hovered just beyond his conscious mind was more than he could bear. For, in cherishing Cat, he had lost all hope of winning the girl in the portrait. He didn't know how the two were linked, but in his heart he feared he could never have both. . . .

That night, behind the filmy barriers of sleep, dreams again consumed him. This time, he peered through a gauzy curtain at a brilliant masquerade ball, spectator but not participant. Boston Brahmins danced in Mrs. Lowell's gleaming ballroom, gay in costumes of every color and guise.

A full moon squatted on the velvet tablecloth of the Halloween night sky. It looked as tasty to Peter as a huge, succulent orange. He wanted to slice it up, suck it dry, consume it to fortify himself. In some strange way, he understood that the moon must be his salvation.

If he could only accept its power . . .

Restless, Peter tapped his evening slippers in time to a Strauss waltz. He longed to dance, but the one partner he yearned for was not there. And where was Cat? He felt an urgency to find her, but somehow, he couldn't move.

Tituba Coupland glided toward him. She was dressed like a forest nymph, green leaves beaded with brilliants barely covering her lovely bosom. Green chiffon floated down from the form-fitting sheath of leaves, baring her long, supple legs. At her shoulders, a cape had been cleverly stitched to look like branches supporting a lush sweep of moss feathers that tossed behind her as she walked.

Ripping the gauze veil aside, she beckoned to him.

The scent she exuded filled his head like tendrils of smoky musk twining about him, drawing him to her. He took one hesitant step, aware on some deep level that the choice was his.

Abruptly, Cat was there. Peter took two more steps, staring at the lovely woman, so perfect under the brilliant lights—too perfect. Then he looked at Cat, the quiet, graceful, intelligent little feline who'd somehow wriggled into his heart. His steps slowed, stopped. Torn, he peered between the two creatures. Finally, in a movement that felt easy because it was so right, he held out his arms to Cat.

She jumped into them, preening under the bright light of the moon, still shining down over Peter's shoulder. Mrs. Coupland leaned toward him, showing her generous cleavage, and her scent became so overpowering that he could barely breathe. Instinctively fighting her power, Peter looked down at the soft warmth in his arms. Through the fog of arousal, wise, elongated gold eyes shone like a lighthouse in the gloom, leading Peter home.

The brilliant illumination seeped through his self-imposed blindfold. Truth beamed into his heart and mind. *Trust your instincts*, Mrs. Lowell had said.

Mrs. Coupland faded into the background like so much woodwork. "Katarina," Peter whispered.

Cat was the girl in the portrait.

Immediately, between one blink and the next, the cat in his arms transformed into long legs, silky black hair, a full bosom and a smile that did, indeed, welcome him home. Like Cat, the girl in the portrait had golden eyes that beamed at him in the darkness. Riches had always been his for the taking. All he had to do was reach for them.

She held out her hands to him. "See? I was always there. I will come to you, when you believe."

The music came to a stop, as if even Strauss wanted to witness something wonderful. Hungry to touch this woman his heart had recognized long before his eyes, Peter reached out. Their fingertips brushed.

Glass shattered, spraying them like broken dreams. Razor-sharp shards pelted Katarina, cutting the skin of her throat and arms. With a cry of pain, she backed away, slipping on the crushed glass.

Peter lurched forward to save her, but he was too late.

The hellhounds burst through the broken windowpanes, jowls agape, slavering at the scent of blood. One dog savagely caught Peter's arm, shaking it, dragging him away from his Katarina, his newly found heart's desire.

The other leapt for Kat's throat. Its teeth sank deep, tearing into the vulnerable white skin.

Kat went down, blood from her gashed neck spurting warmly over Peter.

Peter's own pain faded. He kicked, he pounded at the Rottweiler with his free hand, but he couldn't shake the cursed beast, for it outweighed him by close to thirty pounds. Peter was forced to watch as Kat's struggles faltered and then stopped.

Blackness swam before his anguished gaze. His arm was numb, and he realized that the hound's sharp teeth had cut his artery. Weak now, he tried to free himself, but his arm felt as if it were about to be severed from his body.

But he could still hear.

Hideous growling, smacking noises.

And an equally ugly sound.

Laughter.

Tituba Coupland's laughter . . .

Screaming, Peter awoke. His heart thudded against his ribs. He reached out in the darkness for Cat, but she wasn't there.

Panicked, Peter snapped on the light. He drew a deep breath of relief. Cat sat before the window, gazing mournfully out at the moon.

His heartbeat slowing, Peter lay back, mentally calculating. Indeed, the moon would be full on Halloween night, some two weeks hence.

Chilled, he pulled the covers over his shoulders,

telling himself that it was just a dream. He'd heard too many tales of witches of late. He was just unnerved. That was all.

But even as he stared out at the moon cavorting across the sky with a glittering banner of stars, Peter knew on a bone-deep level that his dream had been a warning.

Should he listen to reason?

Or, he sighed, should he listen to his heart?

# Chapter Four

*Give her independence, and she will be loyal.*

Fortune, it seemed for once, smiled on Captain Peter Gabler. The new vessel was coming along nicely. Financing was now complete. However, the imminent culmination of one dream made Peter's others all the more unsettling. How the proud little feline had become so important to him, Peter still did not know. But as Halloween grew nigh and the moon fatter with every night that passed, Peter was certain of one thing: If Cat wasn't there to share the fortune he'd make with his new vessel, his victory would be pyrrhic.

Wealth lurked in the gold of her eyes. Treasure beyond price, for these riches no one could touch—and no one but he could hoard. Her purrs soothed his pains; her company filled his loneliness; her conversation stimulated his mind. She was unique—and irreplaceable. If he lost her, the seven seas could not sweep him away to forgetfulness.

While acceptance of these facts grew in Peter's quiet moments, his fears loomed in equal proportion. He had to keep Cat safe. Tituba Coupland wanted her dead, but she'd have to kill Peter Gabler to get to Cat. Witch or not, Tituba was not the first and probably would not be the last powerful person Peter Gabler had fought, perhaps literally, tooth and nail.

Despite his best efforts not to betray his concerns, Cat seemed to read his thoughts. At first she tried to reassure him. "I shall be fine walking over to . . . Mrs. Lowell's house," she said three days before Halloween.

"Nevertheless, I shall walk with you." Peter held the door for Cat.

She stalked through it, haughty as only a cat can be. "I'm touched at your concern, but they won't dare try anything in broad daylight."

"You mean they wouldn't try to chase you up a tree?"

Cat's easy stride paused. Slitted golden eyes glared up at him. "That attempt failed, didn't it?"

*Not through any action on my part.* Peter still felt guilty about his momentary cowardice. When the time came again, as it might, he wouldn't hesitate. But he only replied, "No, but there's no sense in giving them easy opportunities."

Doggedly, despite her prickly independence, he tailed her to Mrs. Lowell's and watched her go safely through the door. Waving to the older woman, he walked down to his meeting with the attorneys near the State House.

Upon exiting some hours later, the glow he felt

at the transacted first payment to a famous Maine shipyard almost warmed him enough to chase the chills away. In the late afternoon light of a crisp October day, witches, familiars and evil spells seemed figments of his imagination. However, when he saw Tituba Coupland driving past in her elegant barouche, her two monstrous dogs sitting opposite, his pleasure was spoiled.

He stared at her, wondering how anyone could be so evil, yet so lovely.

She turned her head, saw him and said something to her driver. The carriage halted. She beckoned him with a black-gloved hand.

He walked down the hill toward her but stopped a goodly distance away. Too far away for her perfume to waft in his direction. He tipped his billed cap. "Good day, madam."

A perfect black eyebrow formed an inverted question mark on that exquisite ivory forehead. "Madam, is it? Really, Captain, I thought we were better acquainted than that."

Peter waited politely, neither demurring nor agreeing.

The black brow lowered and met its match. "I wonder if you might meet me for a late supper tomorrow night? At my home on Joy Street?"

A refusal trembled on Peter's lips. Both Rottweilers watched him with the intent hunger of born predators. Peter bit back the denial. Perhaps there was some way he could circumvent his bad dream, and he might learn it if he were to go to her lair.

His indecision must have been apparent, for her eyes narrowed and she said coldly, "It is not wise to make an enemy of me, my dearest captain." She scratched one of her hounds beneath its huge chin. It drooled on her lacy glove, but she didn't seem to mind.

Pulling his cap down to cover his disgust, Peter answered, "May I send word to you tomorrow morning?"

"I did not realize your . . . consequence was so . . . large. Do you have a pressing engagement?" Her avid gaze traveled to the front of his pants.

To his embarrassment, under her scrutiny Peter felt himself harden. He'd been in Boston too long, away from his lady friends in Maine. With an effort, he kept still, pretending this beautiful woman's obvious lust didn't affect him. "Well, actually, I have to find a costume for the masquerade ball at Mrs. Lowell's." He watched her closely.

"Ah, I see." That was an excuse that apparently satisfied her, for she nodded her shining dark head.

Peter wondered why she so obviously wanted him at the party, but she gave him no time for questions of his own.

"Very well then. I shall wait until noon to hear from you. You may go, driver." The barouche lurched forward.

Thoughtfully, Peter turned toward home. He stopped. Home? A temporary abode, certainly. But the presence of Cat made the strange, elegant townhouse home.

Indeed, as soon as he fetched her, they strolled home. The sunset painted the clouds, creating a burst of color and form that even that strange painter would envy. Now what was that fellow's name? Peter had seen the artist's work once in Europe, and he'd never forgotten those vivid strokes. Van Gogh, that was it. He'd always intended to return and purchase one of that man's paintings.

The work had struck him on a primal level, beyond thought, deep inside his secret heart.

Which is why Cat, and that strange girl in the picture, tugged at him so. Peter unlocked the townhouse door, but Cat dallied on the stoop, her head tilted back as she watched the impressionistic pantheon of light and dark playing out over the hill sloping down to the river. "I wish," she sighed. Her head drooped.

He sat down on the stoop and picked her up to cradle her close. Poignant longing shook him, but for what, he could not say. Save that, enjoyable as her company was, he wanted more. . . .

Again, Cat proved her uncanny ability to empathize with him. "This used to be my favorite time of year. Not too hot, not too cold, the world is most vivid when it's about to slumber for the winter."

Odd sentiments for a cat, but Peter had long since stopped wondering how a feline could be so wise to the ways of humans. "Used to be?"

"Last Halloween my life changed."

Peter's stroking hand froze in the velvety fur. "What happened?"

She jumped out of his lap. "You'll know soon enough." She nosed open the door and went inside.

Peter sensed her need for privacy, so he sat on the stoop until the sun went down in a last fiery blaze of glory. Then, sighing, he stood and went in. He looked for Cat in the kitchen. She wasn't there. He checked the living room. Nothing. He went upstairs to his room, but she wasn't there either. Finally, his heart pounding with fear, he checked the tiny water closet.

She leaped off the commode he'd been astonished to learn that she used. "Can I not have a moment to myself?"

Feeling like an intruder, he murmured an apology and closed the door.

That night, their dinner was eaten in silence. Something weighed on her, and not just fear of the dogs. She was tense, irritable, and grew more so with every day nearer to Halloween. He'd questioned her several times as to what was wrong, what sad association she had with this time of year, but she always turned away from him.

She picked at her food, hopped down off the chair and streaked off to a corner. Sighing, Peter quelled the urge to go after her. Instead, he decided to have a bath. The exterior doors were locked. She'd be safe enough by herself for all of an hour.

Humming, he lounged in the huge copper tub, scrubbing his hairy chest and muscular arms with pine-scented soap. A draft of cold air was his only warning. He looked up, his arms raised as he lathered his thick black hair.

The door creaked open the rest of the way. Peter hadn't bothered to turn on the lights in the hall, so at first he could see nothing in the darkness. He blinked, his arms sagging down, wishing he'd brought a weapon. He was about to stand and go find Cat when he saw her eyes glowing at him in the blackness.

He lounged against the tub. "Hello, little one. Have I given you independence enough?"

No answer. Just those uncanny eyes, glowing in the darkness. They stared at him with a longing that flustered him. He was torn between a need to cover himself with a towel and a peculiar urge to haul her into the tub with him, hoping, praying, she might become the woman of his dreams. His cheeks reddened. He'd definitely better bed a woman, and soon. Yet even as he castigated himself for being an idiot, the heavy curtain he'd dropped between reason and longing began to lift.

There, in the black of night, with an almost full moon beckoning outside, Peter Gabler let emotion dictate truth. His nostrils flared as the image he'd struggled against grew large in his mind. Her supple little shape elongated into an equally supple, graceful form, black fur became ivory skin, curving claws morphed into long-fingered, graceful hands.

Peter felt his body respond. Peering into Cat's ageless eyes, he knew he saw the intensity of an independent woman. Something drew him to her, something stronger than rationality. On some instinctive level, he recognized in Cat his spiritual, if not his physical, mate. With her stubborn independence, her love of the sea, her intelligence and her thirst for knowledge and beauty, she was all he'd ever wanted in a woman.

And she had the form of a cat.

He moaned with longing and despair, biting his knuckles to quiet the sound.

But his eyes had adjusted enough to the darkness for him to see Cat's back arch. She gave a low, keening growl that grew in intensity to a yowl of desperate longing.

It was the loneliest sound Peter had ever heard.

"Cat," he pleaded huskily, reaching out to her.

With a spin and a patter of paws, she was gone.

Hastily finishing his ablutions, Peter threw on his breeches and bolted after her. He called, searching, but she didn't answer. He finally found her hiding under the bed in the second bedroom.

He knelt and reached out for her. "Come to bed, Cat."

She batted at his hand. "Go away!"

He sat back on his heels. "What have I done?"

No answer, and than a small, cold voice whispered, "Nothing. It's hopeless. You'll never believe . . . and even if you do, you won't be able to find the spell in time. I . . . might as well learn to like mice."

The hairs raised on the back of Peter's neck. "What do you want of me?"

"Solitude." But the musical voice broke. Cat turned her back on him. The despair emanating from her in waves penetrated him, driving him to misery.

Helpless, he stood and left the room to seek his lonely bed. Hours passed, and still she didn't come. His arms crossed behind his head, Peter stared out at the moon. It was almost full. Cat's moodiness was linked to the phases of this orange harvest moon. Three more nights until Halloween. Peter had seldom celebrated the holiday, even as a child. He'd been too busy tending to the concerns of this world to consider the possibility that on this one night, when living souls reveled, enslaved souls could also rise.

And so, as an adult, he was learning a lesson that every child knew: Halloween was a night when magic made all things possible.

Believe . . .

As if the thought had conjured her, there she stood. Watching. Waiting.

"Cat," Peter whispered, sitting up in bed and holding out his arms.

Mewling like a hungry kitten, Cat jumped into his arms. "Promise me, Peter," she said softly. "No matter what, you'll keep me with you."

He stroked her velvety head. "I promise."

She suffered his touch for a moment, then moved to the edge of the bed, sat up and stared at the moon.

Glad she'd come back to him, where she belonged, he dozed off, watching the moon bathe her in healing light. And, sleepily, he knew that, whatever the outcome, this night he'd never believed in would transform him—and Cat—ever after.

The horizon stretched into forever, sparkling like a gay ballroom where waves frolicked with fluffy clouds. But the music was a joyful sound only nature could devise: roaring wind, pounding waves and exultant heartbeats thrumming in tune.

Peter's new ship bounded over every mighty crest like a Thoroughbred, gliding down the slough with barely a quiver. Raw power, all the more impressive in its sleek, bridled vigor, vibrated in the huge wheel beneath his hands. Peter pressed his stubbled jaw to the smooth cheek below his and clasped his hands next to the smaller, feminine hands. Gold wedding bands glowed on each left hand.

"Did you ever feel anything so wonderful?" he shouted over the roar of slapping waves and crackling canvas. The sleek clipper seemed to fly across the sea, her canvas drawn full by the brisk breeze.

"She's beautiful, Peter," his wife shouted back. "At this rate, we'll set a record around the Horn."

Peter dropped a possessive hand over his wife's distended abdomen. "And be home in plenty of time." Within, the baby kicked.

"Mother says I'm having a girl. Do you mind?"

"Mind? Give me a lovely, black-haired daughter, half as beautiful as yourself, and my joy will be complete."

"And if I want to teach her the arts?"

An old Calvinistic denial tugged at Peter; a stronger instinct pushed back. His habitual restlessness was gone. Oh, he still loved the sea, but he could be happy in port now for months on end. A missing part of his life—nay, a missing part of his soul—had been filled . . . on a night when the moon was full and magic ruled.

Sighing, Peter kissed her velvety cheek, remembering a furry little cheek he'd often caressed. "Teach her all you know, my love. Some gifts exceed all understanding, and they are priceless. I know that now."

A beautiful, mischievous face turned up to his. Katarina smiled at him, expression full of Cat's playful wisdom, elongated golden eyes glowing at him with an almost feline intensity. "So you believe, Peter of my heart?"

Peter clutched her tighter. "I believe."

Peter snapped awake. Dawn slipped through the window, tripping in on little cats' feet. Peter reached out, but the opposite pillow was cold. He sat up, his heart thrumming with the certainty his mind had denied for so long. "Cat," he called huskily.

No answer. Peter threw on his clothes and searched. The louvered window was open. Peter hurried over to Mrs. Lowell's and knocked briskly. She opened the door quickly, as if she'd been expecting him.

"Cat's here?"

She nodded.

"I have to see her."

She opened the door, watching him with the quiet expectancy of her former pet.

Peter rushed into the salon, his heart pounding. Three times now he'd dreamed of the girl in the portrait, each dream ripping away another veil between his conscious and subconscious minds. If magic was real, then so was shape-shifting. All the signs had been there from the beginning. He'd just been too stubborn—and too "sensible"—to heed them.

Yes, they were all there. Cat's tenderness toward Mrs. Lowell. Her speech. Her talk of going to sea with her father. Her knowledge of the location of the townhouse. Her understanding of human foibles and human needs.

And her fear of the dogs and Tituba Coupland. *Trust your instincts*. For the first, best time in his life, he did exactly that.

"Cat?" he called softly. At first he didn't see her. She wasn't in her customary place on the sofa, or under any of the chairs. Peter walked deeper into the room. Mrs. Lowell watched him intently, nibbling at her full lower lip.

He felt her tension, but he was too busy searching to answer the questions in her eyes. And then he saw his "pet." Lying beneath the tall secretary opposite the portrait, her chin propped on her front paws, watching him mournfully.

"What do you want, Peter?"

Ten feet away, Peter stopped. He knelt before her. "I want you, Cat of my heart. Or should I say—Katarina?"

Mrs. Lowell sagged onto the sofa, her hand at her bosom.

Kat's head lifted. Golden eyes fixed on Peter's

tender face, searching in her intense feline way.

No longer was her gaze inscrutable to Peter. He saw the flashes of joy, pain and hope in the golden mirror of her eyes. But she still didn't jump into his arms. She glanced at her portrait and then away, as if she couldn't bear to look at how she used to be.

"What if . . . what if . . . I'm always this way?"

"I shall love you anyway. But allow me to be your champion, Kat. I will fight Tituba and her hellhounds to the death, if need be." Peter held out his arms. "If we have one lifetime, or nine of them, we belong together."

Kat crept out into his arms, snuggling against his shoulder, purring. "I don't want you to be hurt."

Nestling her close, Peter stood. "How did it happen?"

Kat tilted her head back on Peter's shoulder. "She put a potion in my wine last Halloween night, just before Mother and I could combine our powers to nullify her latest incantation and destroy her. By the time Mother realized my wine was enchanted, it was too late. . . ." Her voice trailed off, and she hid her little face again.

Mrs. Lowell continued huskily, "My beautiful daughter changed into a cat before my terrified eyes. And Tituba walked away laughing, but promising that this Halloween, her hounds would make a meal of all that was left of Katarina."

Shivering, Peter clasped Kat so close that she squirmed in protest. He loosened his clasp. "Sorry." He walked over to the portrait. "So, are you a witch as well?"

"Yes. But apparently a very inept one."

Mrs. Lowell stood and came over to them. "We

still have some time to work on that before, well, while I'm still . . . available."

Kat buried her face in Peter's jacket. "I detest it when you talk that way, Mother."

"Death is a natural part of life, my child. Once you are yourself again, together we can defeat Tituba. It shall be my memorial, my legacy to you and your children."

Peter's throat clogged with emotion. "Is that why you advertised? To leave a legacy?"

"Of course. Kat will need help running my estate. Someone knowledgeable about ships and sailors. And my other respondants will hopefully be able to help as well. One quarter of my estate will give you and Kat a good start, but the true beauty of your time together will be making a new dynasty out of an old legacy."

This woman astounded Peter. No wonder she'd remained so lovely. Wisdom and kindness made the best fountain of youth in the world.

Kat lifted her head. "It's time, Mother."

Gracefully, Gisella nodded. She swept a hand toward the elevator. "Peter, since you want to help us fight Tituba, I need to show you something."

Peter's heart lurched against his ribs. The octagonal turrets had loomed large in his imagination since he'd first seen them, and he wasn't sure he was ready to learn their secrets. But he had no choice. Tenderly setting Kat down on the sofa, Peter removed his cap and tossed it on a table, figuratively readying himself for battle.

"I'm ready, ma'am."

Gisella's lips curved. "Your taste was excellent, as usual, Kat."

A rasping sound that might have been a laugh came from Kat. "I'm glad you approve, Mother.

You go ahead, Peter. I hardly slept last night." Kat yawned, showing sharp white teeth. "I'm going to take a nap."

And so Peter completed the shortest, most important journey of his life. A journey that had begun when he talked back to Kat, and had grown more hazardous now that he'd admitted she was his soul mate trapped in a feline body. With this foray into the arcane world of magic, the safety of rational skepticism would protect him no longer. When he exited this elevator, he would not be the man who had entered, and his life's happiness would depend on how skillfully he exercised the tutorial he learned here.

All these thoughts ran through Peter's head as he stepped off the small elevator into a new world. Beveled windowpanes sent rainbows flitting about the fantastic eight-sided room. Dried herbs and flowers of every type hung from the exposed wooden rafters, crisscrossing the vaulted tower. The shelves were crowded with books on potions, spells and talismans. In the center of the room stood an enormous octagonal walnut table with sphinx-head gilded legs supporting it on a triangular base. A gauzy lace cloth fell over the table edge to the plush red carpet lining the floor. An ornately carved wooden box sat in the center of the table.

The walls were lined with artifacts of cats throughout the ages: Egyptian tomb paintings, rubbings from Gothic cathedrals depicting demon cats, a Greek black-on-red pottery vase showing cats dancing with maidens. But it was a massive shield that drew Peter.

It hung on a wall opposite the windows, where the sun sparkled off its vermillion coat of arms and the gilded and silver-leaved raised design in the middle. The symbol depicted a lithe cat, standing on its back legs, an olive branch offered in one paw, a sword in the other. The metal worker had displayed such artistry in creating the bossed design that the cat seemed ready to walk off of the wall. Fascinated, Peter stepped closer, his hand reaching out.

Golden eyes glinted a warning, glowing in the feline face. Peter jumped back, his hand dropping to his side. "My God, it's alive!"

A musical laugh shivered down Peter's spine. Mrs. Lowell's soft hand touched his shoulder. "The eyes are topaz. You're merely seeing the sun's reflection."

Yes, well, Peter had seen enough strange things of late to make him back away, still facing the shield. He was taking no chances.

Mrs. Lowell smiled as she sat down at the table, waving a hand to indicate that he should sit opposite. "You really hate this magic rigmarole, as my husband would say, don't you?"

Peter shrugged. "I'll accept anything if it will give me Katarina as my bride."

"Don't you wonder why we selected you?"

Peter sat opposite her. "I think I know. According to the spell, Kat's champion probably had to be a man who hated cats, who didn't believe in witchcraft—"

Gisella took up the tale. "—willing to risk his life to save her. If the stroke of midnight passes and none of these requirements are met, Kat will remain a cat forever." Gisella shook her head. "Tituba tried to make the terms of Kat's transformation back as difficult as possible. She told us the terms to torment us, never believing we'd find anyone suitable."

Praying that he would be that man, Peter stared at the shield. "Is that coat of arms your family crest?"

She nodded. "The cat was sacred to ancient religions," she told him matter-of-factly. "All this evil familiar nonsense was propagated by primitive Christians whose best notion of justice was burning people at the stake. Did you know that the only women accused of witchcraft in the Salem witch trials who survived were the ones who confessed?"

Fascinated, Peter shook his head.

"Those of character enough not to lie were the ones who were executed."

"And Tituba's ancestor? How did she survive?"

"She didn't. Not in human form."

She opened the box.

Peter peered into the shadowy contents. He was disappointed when she pulled out a yellowed clump of brittle parchment papers; no ornate, gilded cover here. But she spread the plebian square before her, unfolding it nine times until it covered the huge tabletop. The significance of the number did not escape Peter.

Realizing the words were written in Latin, Peter squinted at the spidery writing and tiny pictures of animals and plants. "What is this piece of paper?"

"The accumulated knowledge of the women of my family, handed down from daughter to daughter." She spoke reverently.

Alarmed, Peter scooted his chair back, just in case. "You use it to cast spells?"

She gave him a chastising look, as if she lectured a child. "I use it to understand the mysteries of life, and to commune with nature. I occasionally cast spells, but only when forced to combat evil."

"Like Tituba Coupland?"

She nodded. "What I tell you must not leave this room, but my daughter has selected you as her soul mate, so you should know. Agreed?"

"Yes." Peter braced himself, expecting to be regaled with tales of flying broomsticks and bubbling cauldrons.

"My husband came to Hungary precisely to find a white witch among the descendants of the Magyars. He was the only person in Boston society to realize that Tituba's power stemmed from black magic. He tried to fight her by himself, and she almost killed him. When he found me, I agreed to wed him because he had given a huge sum to my people. But a marriage of convenience soon developed into love. At first, I was able to combat Tituba's spells. Her influence began to wane."

"Is black magic stronger?"

"More treacherous, more insidious. But not stronger. We were at a stalemate for many years. I was teaching Katarina my skills so she could ally her powers with mine and we could defeat Tituba for once and all, but I became ill. I should have realized what Tituba was doing last Halloween, but by the time I tried to stop Kat from drinking the potion, it was too late. And I fear, exactly as Tituba had planned, the last year of my life has been spent trying to save my daughter. Tituba has become so powerful now that, even together, I'm not certain Kat and I can defeat her. We only have one chance."

She folded the book back up, letting him wonder.

Fearing the answer even as he asked, Peter said, "And that is?"

"We must know which spell and potion she used to transform Kat. Kat and I can't get near her house without alerting those cursed dogs. We've already tried. But I'm assuming she's invited you there, since she's tried to seduce you?" At his nod, she took a deep, relieved breath and continued, "If, by the light of the full moon on Halloween, we say the spell backward and duplicate the potion in opposite proportions, Kat will become a woman again." She smiled as she saw the change in his expression. "I can see I have your attention now."

"Most acutely, ma'am. What can I do to help accomplish this?"

"You can go to Tituba's house. In her basement, she keeps her spellbooks."

"But how will I know which one to choose?"

"The transmutation spellbook is a huge black volume with a goat's head on the front and large brass hinges. It will probably be in Latin, but the illustrations should depict which spell is used to transform people into cats." She handed him the same red book she'd given him when he adopted Kat. "I took the liberty of fetching this. If while touching the other tome, you open this one to the blank pages and sprinkle this on the spellbook," she offered him a small vial of glittering powder, "the words will be duplicated in this book."

Gingerly, Peter accepted the slim volume. He stuck the book into his inner coat pocket and walked before the huge mirror on one wall. To his relief, the outline didn't show. "And if she catches me?"

Gisella's eyes darkened. "See that she doesn't." She pulled an ancient-looking carved wooden cross out of the box on the table. "Wear this. If the dogs attack you, touch them with it. If their power comes from hell, as I believe it does, the cross will burn them."

The reverent way she handled the cross told Peter how valuable it was. "Where did this come from?" He slipped the cross on its plain silver chain over his neck.

"It's been passed down through the women in my family for centuries. It is to be used only in extreme circumstances, against evil. It is rumored to be carved from a chunk of the true cross."

Peter gasped, cupping the small cross in his hand. Was it his imagination, or did it seem to pulse with a life and warmth of its own? "I shall take good care of it."

Spent, Gisella leaned back in her chair and coughed into her handkerchief. "I . . . know you will."

Alarmed, Peter went to help her up. "Come, ma'am, you must rest."

"I don't have time to rest. Only two days to Halloween. Do you have your costume for the party?"

"I intended to go today—"

"No need for that." She went to a small closet and beckoned him over. Peter went and looked inside. He stared at the full suit of armor, glinting in the gloom. He flushed, then went white. He was no knight in shining armor, though he admitted to being flattered that Gisella apparently felt otherwise.

He tried to keep his protest gentle. "Ah, I shall feel ridiculous in that."

Gisella coughed again, then put the handkerchief back in her pocket. "It's not your feelings I'm trying to spare, Peter," she said grimly. "On Halloween night, you shall need all the protection you can get."

# *Chapter Five*

*Love your cat, and she will love you.*

Later that night, Peter stared up at the most exclusive Federal-style home on the most exclusive street near the top of Beacon Hill. The harvest moon was almost full, and it smiled down on him with a benign gleam that he prayed heralded good fortune. Two more nights. The role this woman would play in Kat's destiny terrified Peter when he paused to think. So he decided not to think.

*Trust your instincts.* Gisella had been dead right—well, exactly correct, anyway. Instincts had brought him to Kat, and instinct would bring her to him in human form.

Pausing on the brick walkway, Peter looked up at the massive house. It was old and rather plain, save for the pediment and two fluted columns. In fact, the house looked quite respectable, far more respectable than Gisella's home. A facade as false as Tituba's charm, Peter reflected. The house loomed over him like the night's darkest shadows, a symbol of the power of black magic. With a potion and a spell, Tituba could transform him, too. What would she choose? A dog? A pig? Or perhaps a rat.

Shadows curled around his feet, lapping at his toes, but Peter closed his eyes and banished them with a luminous vision. Kat, in her true human form, smiling radiantly as they walked down the wedding aisle. He would endure anything, fight anyone, even a witch and her hellhounds, to make that dream a reality.

Drawing a deep, steadying breath, Peter stared steadily ahead, lifted the ram's head door knocker and banged it on the massive front door.

Earlier, he'd sent word that he'd meet Tituba for apperitifs but had to politely decline her dinner invitation. Gisella had made it plain that he was not to eat or drink anything at Tituba's house, and after Kat's fate, he knew he had to follow that edict at all costs. As he waited, Peter straightened his tie and patted down his dress black frock coat. Good; the jacket was loose enough to disguise the bulge of the book in the inside pocket.

The door opened slightly. A petite maid in a mobcap and frilly apron peeked outside. "Be ye Captain Gabler?" she whispered, still holding the door partly closed.

Peter heard dogs growling. Automatically, he reached for the cross hidden on a long chain beneath his jacket, but he forced himself to relax and doff his cap instead. "Yes. Mrs. Coupland is expecting me."

The maid said, "Get back, Hades! Move, Vulcan!"

The door opened wide enough for Peter to slip inside. His feet sank into the plushest carpeting he'd ever stepped on. He stared down at the design, fear gnawing his insides. Leaves, twigs and moss made a lovely medley of autumn hues, the carpet so cleverly sculpted that each leaf seemed to tremble, about to fall to the mossy forest floor.

Green velvet curtains shielded every window, and even the woodwork was dark brown. The decor offered the effect of an intimate forest grotto. Any moment now, Peter expected to see a nymph or a satyr canter into view. However, as Peter took another step and the door closed behind him, low-throated growls focused his attention on the most dangerous part of the ambience.

Both Rottweilers were planted beside the massive curving stairway, one at each carved newel post like a living gargoyle. Their bared teeth showed impressive fangs, but only until Mrs. Coupland walked through an arched doorway down the long vaulted hallway.

She clapped her hands. Immediately, the hounds' mouths snapped closed. They ducked their heads like repentent puppies as she chided them, "Hush, boys. Is that any way to welcome a guest?"

She sauntered toward him, all grace and beauty, her lush curves complemented by the tight red silk gown she wore. Black lace peeped at her low-cut bodice and drifted from her mutton sleeves. The gown's skirt was swept back to a slight bustle. Rubies glittered at her throat.

She was dressed to kill, Peter decided; probably quite literally. He masked his fear behind a wide smile that he knew showed his perfect teeth and the dimple in one cheek. "Good evening, Mrs. Coupland." He bowed over her hand.

"Tituba. And I may call you Peter?"

"Of course."

Tucking her hand through his arm, she led him into the drawing room down the hall. The forest decor was repeated there, right down to an ornate wooden mantel that was carved to resemble a tree populated with birds and nocturnal creatures. One bat was poised for flight; it looked so realistic that Peter barely avoided ducking his head.

She noted his interest. "I had the house redone a few years ago, and I wanted some unique touches that would set Coupland House apart from the hoi polloi." She sat down on a deep forest green davenport, patting the spot beside her.

Peter sat where she indicated. "You have succeeded, ma—uh, Tituba. Your home is as unique as its owner."

She touched the back of her upswept hair. "You flatter most prettily, young man. Tell me, have you found all the funding you need?"

Nodding, Peter said, "But if, after our first voyage, I still need a loan, I shall come to you first." He smiled, showing his dimple again. Subterfuge had never been one of Peter's strengths, but he'd never had so much at stake before. And he found that it was easier to lie to someone he detested.

Long-lashed green eyes searched his, but when he didn't blink, she leaned back. "Excellent. Now tell me—what costume have you selected for the ball?"

Peter shifted in his seat. "Uh, well, the only thing I could find at the last minute was, ah . . ."

She leaned forward, her bountiful cleavage on display. "Yes?"

That damnable perfume was going to his head again. What on earth did she put in it? Some sort of aphrodisiac, no doubt. Peter dragged his gaze up from her breasts in time to see the flicker of a satisfied smirk on her mouth. "Well, to be truthful, I'm embarrassed. . . . I shall come as a knight."

She clapped her hands. "But that's marvelous!"

Vulcan and Hades bounded into the room, ears pricked forward, sharp dark eyes alert.

Scowling, she waved them off. They slunk away, tails tucked between their legs.

But Peter wagered the moment he poked his nose outside this room, they'd be waiting. How on earth was he to get to the basement unseen? He dragged himself back to the conversation.

". . . you be a black knight or white knight?"

"Ah, just a knight, I guess. A most reluctant knight, I fear." That, at least, was true.

"All the best champions are. The bravest person in the world is the one who uses his might as wisely as his heart." She leaned toward him, her gown slipping off one shoulder. "And the bravest souls make the best champions. Would you be my champion, dear sir?"

Peter's gaze dropped to her breasts. In truth, she had a beautiful bosom a woman half her age might envy. Since she seemed to expect it, he reached out to touch one luscious breast. She leaned into his palm. When she pursed her mouth, reviling himself, he kissed her. Softly, sweetly, like a knight as gallant on the field of love as he would be on the field of valor. Her scent twined about his will, drawing him deeper into her spell. Peter kissed her harder, desire wrenching his gut. He might have been lost then had she not purred into his mouth.

Shock dashed over him like icy water. Kat made that sound when he touched her. If he had to risk his life to hear her make it standing within the circle of his arms in her true form, then so be it. Peter leaned back, panting slightly. "You take my breath away, Tituba. Might I have a drink of rum?"

She pouted up at him. "Rum? That's a commoner's drink."

Peter kept his smile in place. "Indeed. Or a sailor's choice. Straight, please." Rum was clear, so he could see if she put something in it.

Her hips swaying, she went over to a blank wall and pressed a hidden lever. A full bar swung outward. While she worked, her back to him, Peter stood and pretended to wander the room, touching the intricate figurines and strange art objects with apparent awe. In reality, he inched closer to the door. He peered out.

Just outside the threshold, Vulcan and Hades lifted their heads. Even from here, Peter could see a shadowy, curving staircase at the very end of the hall. Instinctively, he knew that must be the entrance to her lab. He ducked back inside and beamed at his hostess just as she turned with two crystal glasses. She offered him a clear amber liquid and kept a blood-red glass of wine for herself.

Peter quirked an eyebrow. "This is rum?"

"But of course. The best available. Aged ten years in Barbados."

Peter lifted the glass and swirled the liquid, inhaling. "It smells wonderful."

Her lovely arm lifted high, the liquid in her glass

sparkling under the brilliant lights. "To future business partners."

"To a new partner." Kat's lovely face swam in the liquid, giving him strength. He made as if to sip, taking in very little. Smiling, he nodded his appreciation.

She drank deeply, waving back at the sofa. He preceded her. When his back was turned, he spit the sip back into his glass. They fenced verbally for fifteen more minutes, Peter toying with his glass. He played out his little game as long as he could, but when her eyes narrowed on the unchanging level of the liquid in his glass, he stood and raised his arm. "To sailing ships. May they live as long as beautiful women."

Accepting her due, she stood and drank with him, watching until he took a swallow large enough to half-empty his glass. She smiled slightly and turned to refill her own glass. Immediately, Peter spit the rum into a potted plant beside the couch and poured out all but a dribble of liquid from his glass. Here came the tricky part. He had to guess what she'd given him. Either a sleeping potion or a love potion. Perhaps both.

When she sat down beside him again, Peter patted a yawn. "Excuse me. Too many late nights working." *And too many nightmares about you, you witch.*

Idly, she played with her huge ruby necklace. Waiting.

Sure now, Peter yawned wider the second time. Thank God he didn't have to make love to her. He moved to set his glass down on the table before the couch. The crystal missed the table edge and fell to the plush carpet. "Sh . . . sorry," Peter whispered. Then he fell sideways, his eyes closing.

Immediately, she stood and went to the door. "Quickly. Tell the footmen to get him below. I gave him enough to keep him out until tomorrow. And tell no one he was here, understood?"

The maid gave a weak assent. Then heavy footsteps approached. One pair of strong hands caught Peter's arms, the other his feet. Like a sack of grain, he was carried down the curving steps.

Peter could scarcely contain his excitement. They were taking him precisely where he wanted to be! Darkness increased behind his closed eyelids, and then a bright light flickered on. He felt himself tossed, none too gently, on a plush sofa. One of his legs dangled off the edge.

"Leave me," Tituba commanded. The heavy footsteps retreated.

Smaller, more tender hands lifted Peter's leg up onto the couch. He felt her staring down at him. He kept his breathing even. He sensed her leaning down, and then her hands, icy cold, touched his privates. He was so shocked that he had to shield his gasp with a groan and a drowsy settling of his limbs, as if he'd shifted in his sleep.

Tituba stared down at him for what felt like hours, but when she seemed reassured that he was still asleep, she whispered, "You are as well endowed as I thought, Captain. Pity I can't keep you." Her footsteps retreated. The light snapped off.

Peter wanted to sit up immediately, but he finally understood how treacherous she was. He lay very still. He didn't hear her come back, but suddenly the light came on again. He had not moved. This time, when the light went off, he hoped she was gone. He heard the door lock.

He opened his eyes to pitch darkness. He didn't

dare turn on the light, so he contented himself with a small box of matches he'd brought in his pocket. Their flickering light led him to a candelabra. He lit the three candles and began to search the room.

This spell chamber, or whatever a witch called her haven, was larger than Gisella's. It had the same herbs and tomes, but jars of disgusting things, some of which Peter recognized and some of which he didn't, lurked in every shadowy corner. Eye of newt and toe of frog, no doubt.

Search as he might, Peter couldn't find a black book as Gisella had described. Then he remembered Tituba's fondness for secret compartments. Peter noted a long blank wall that seemed to have no purpose. He tapped it and finally found a hidden spring. He jumped backward as a black cavity yawned wide.

The smell made him gag, but he held his breath and ducked into the cavity. Dead creatures hung from hooks. A cat, a fox, a rat, lizards, snakes and even the head of a deer. An ornate table supported by two carved demon's heads sat in the middle of the small room.

On it was a very sharp knife, a bowl and various vials, unmarked. Next to the bowl was the black book. Peter thumped the candles down, opening the book to thumb through it. When he found a cat's picture, he drew the red tome from his pocket and followed Gisella's instructions.

Nothing happened. Peter tried again, sprinkling the sparkling powder over the blank pages, lifting the candelabra high. Still, nothing.

Peter thumbed through the spell book again, but he saw no more pictures of cats. Dammit, what did he do now? He was almost out of powder. He tried one more time, but still saw nothing. Cursing to himself, Peter stuck the vial and the cat book back in his jacket. He brushed the residue of sparkling powder into his palm and tossed it into a waste basket in the corner, setting crumpled paper on top of it to hide it.

Putting back the black book exactly as he found it, Peter turned to leave. As he moved the candles, flickering light caught the tip of the knife. It glowed red. Peter stared at the residue in the bowl. He remembered something Gisella had mentioned about a witch's most potent spell.

"She mixes her blood with milk, catches the blood of the animal she wants to change her enemy into and tricks her foe into drinking both—"

That was Tituba's blood.

Automatically, listening to the instincts that had brought him this far, Peter took his clean kerchief from his pocket and cleaned out the bowl, folding the kerchief to protect the sample. He put it back in his pocket. He closed the hidden door behind him and began to look for a way out. The entrance door was made of iron, and it didn't budge when he shoved hard. Far above his head, he saw a rectangular crank-type frosted glass window. Peter tied several lengths of rope together and formed a loop. He tossed the loop over the crank handle and yanked. It seemed to hold.

Scanning the room, memorizing its layout, Peter blew out the candles and felt in the darkness to put the candelabra back where he'd found it. Then he began to climb, putting his feet flat against the heavy plaster wall. When he drew even with the window, he tried to shove it open, but his weight held the lever closed. Removing the cap he'd stuck in his pocket, supporting his weight with his legs and free arm, Peter used the cap to shield his hand. He slammed his fist with all his might against the glass.

It broke with a shattering sound. Peter held his breath, listening. He thought he heard a whuffling sound outside and heavy footsteps, but then the noise stopped. Breaking the rest of the glass, he hoisted his arms out of the narrow window. He barely fit. He wriggled, managing to brace his legs firmly enough to spider walk up the wall and force his bulky torso through.

The whuffling sound came back. Closer.

Freezing, Peter looked about. The moon had risen on the opposite side of the house, but it was bright enough for him to see an ornate walled garden. While he hung helpless, half-in, half-out of the window, another noise sounded. This one made Peter squirm frantically to free himself.

One growl. Then two. Low, throaty and hungry.

Heavy footsteps ran up, and Peter Gabler was eye to eye with the two ugliest, most dangerous dogs he'd ever come across.

Vulcan bared his fangs, salivating.

Hades tensed to spring, his ruff bristling on the back of his powerful neck, his jaws gaping to bite.

Two nights later, Nature herself seemed to beam, as if she, too, enjoyed this night when all souls reveled. The moon, a plump, succulent orange spread on a black velvet banquet table sprinkled with diamonds, looked close enough to pluck. The brisk winds whipping off the water up Beacon Hill had eased to a gentle caress. The temperature was mild. Lights glowed from all over, but they blazed brightest from the Lowell household.

A line of carriages wrapped around Walnut

Street like an exotic Oriental spice train, disgorging emperors, queens, Cleopatras, Caesars and exotic animals from across the globe. At the door stood Mrs. Lowell, dressed as a gypsy, as if she wished to flaunt her Magyar heritage. She kept glancing at the watch pinned to her sequinned costume and peering over the shoulders of her guests, as if looking for someone. Every time a knight arrived, she gasped, but drew a disappointed breath when she shook hands with him.

Almost all the guests had arrived when a black carriage drawn by six black horses careened around the corner, passing other carrriages dangerously close to the sidewalk. A footman held open the ebony door. Tituba Coupland minced down, her feet clad in green velvet slippers to complement her sumptuous gown of leaves, moss and chiffon. She exuded vitality and ancient but mystical life. Last in line, she offered her hand to Gisella as she scanned the room.

"Good evening. My, have you ever seen so many knights . . . errant?" She smiled, her red lips matching her red nails and the spark of red deep in her eyes.

Gisella glared at her rival, lowering her voice to a menacing whisper. "Where is he, Titty?"

The smile faded. "You know I detest that nickname. What, haven't seen your little champion?"

"Not since he came to your house. What have you done with him?"

Elegant shoulders shrugged. "I really haven't the faintest notion where he is." Tituba sashayed forward, her hips swaying in the revealing embroidered gown.

"Only you could make a tree look vulgar," Gisella said. She glanced down the street one more time in both directions, sighed and nodded at her butler to close the door.

Tituba arched an eyebrow at the crowded rooms and noisy guests. "Well, I must say you've learned a lot from me. Pity you haven't learned the most important lesson of all."

Gisella picked up Kat from a cushion near the door and cradled her close. "I was born knowing the most important things in life, Titty. Things you'll never understand."

Kat stared anxiously, her eyes huge, at the front door.

"Well, tonight will tell the tale, won't it?" Tituba patted a bored yawn. "I'm quite thirsty. Do you have any decent wine in this pomposity?"

Gisella nodded at the men serving punches and wines at a long banquet table in the salon. Tituba glided off, seeming to float in the gauzy dress.

As soon as she was out of earshot, Kat said, her voice agonized, "Mother, where could he be? Do you think she's killed him?"

"I don't know, dear one. But if he doesn't bring the book within the hour, we're lost."

Oblivious, the guests danced and drank and dined, whiling the minutes away to the witching hour. The ornate grandfather clock against one wall tolled the half-hour. Gisella hovered near the front door, neglecting her guests. Her slender fingers fidgeted with the full folds of her skirt.

Kat wrapped herself about Gisella's legs. Across the salon, Tituba mockingly toasted Kat's picture. Then, her arm still raised, she nodded at Kat and Gisella. She glanced at the clock and smiled. Fifteen minutes to midnight.

A soft knock sounded at the door. Gisella waved her butler away and answered the door herself,

Kat on her heels. Gisella sagged against the wall, propping herself up with one hand. "Thank God," she said simply. "Peter, where have you been?"

"No time to explain." Peter tried to bend to caress Kat, who'd propped her paws on his metal-plated knee, but he winced and had to straighten.

Closing the door and stepping out on the stoop with him, Gisella tipped his face plate back. Peter's face was scratched, healing scabs lining both cheekbones, and his nose was bandaged.

Kat mewled pathetically. "Peter, what happened?"

"I'll be all right. The dogs attacked me as I escaped from Tituba. Without the cross, I would have been dead. I managed to climb the garden wall, but then I passed out cold for hours in an alley a block away. A man found me and took me to the hospital. As soon as I could walk, I dressed in my armor and came here. Now, where is she?"

"Inside," Gisella answered. "But you're wounded—"

Peter shifted painfully. "It's just this damn armor. My shoulders and arms took the brunt of the attack. I'll be all right. No time to argue." Peter lowered his voice. "This is what we need to do." Peter handed Gisella a small sharp knife.

A few minutes later, a new knight wearing very old armor walked stiffly into the salon. His mail was dented in many places and was rusty in others, but those close enough to see the gleam of blue eyes beneath the faceplate froze in their tracks. Somehow the wounds on the knight's face only seemed to accent his purity of heart, and soul, and mind—and purpose.

*So Sir Galahad must have looked when he protected the grail,* Gisella thought, *or Lancelot when he saved Guinevere.* This knight errant walked to the loveliest woman in the room. If he paled slightly when he got a good look at her dress, no one remarked on it.

Peter almost gagged on his nausea when he recognized the dress. So many elements of his dreams had come true that he wasn't certain any longer of the dividing line between imagination and reality, or even if there were a line. Only clinging to the warm memory of his most recent dream of rounding the Horn with his wife gave his aching, weary body stamina enough to stay strong.

Holding Tituba's gaze, Peter stopped in front of her and bowed slightly, stifling a groan. "Happy Halloween, Tituba. Surprised to see me?"

Even standing still, her cloak whipped about behind her, as if she were caught in a windstorm. Her face was drawn and she apparently labored under strong emotion. "Not really. I knew you'd be back. You've made your loyalties quite plain. . . . My oleander doesn't like your notion of fertilizer, Captain." Tituba's walk was graceful as she clasped her hand on his chain-mail–clad arm and accepted his escort to the bar. "You were quite clever to fool me that way. Few can play dead before me and get away with it."

"I shall endeavor to get away with even more, tonight. May I get you another drink?" Peter asked. She nodded. He took her empty glass and gave it to a servant to refill with red wine.

Gisella said from directly behind them, "See, Titty? Faith can move mountains—or strike the heart of evil. All we have to do is believe."

Startled, Tituba whirled. When her back was turned, Peter quickly pulled a small vial from a concealed pouch and dumped something in her drink. He whirled the wine around and gave it back to the startled servant. Tituba would be suspicious if he gave her the glass. Peter turned back around, smiling beneath his visor.

When he was ready, Gisella let her gaze drop to the cross hanging outside Peter's armor.

Turning back to see what she stared at, Tituba absently accepted the wine from Gisella's servant. Hissing, she took a step back, her gaze glued to the small brown cross. Some of her wine splashed on the carpet.

Peter lifted his own glass high. "To belief in magic on this night when all things are possible." He stuck the cross back beneath his breastplate.

Immediately, Tituba relaxed. "To the power of magic." She sniffed her wine, then drank it deeply. The other two did likewise.

When all the glasses were empty, Gisella invited, "Would you care to see the new statues in the garden?"

Scarcely masking her glee, Tituba set down her glass with a thump on a passing steward's tray. "I should be delighted."

Clanking awkwardly in his armor, Peter followed the two women through the wide doors, down the veranda, to the lawn. He beckoned to Kat as he passed her. Looking frightened, she slunk down the steps after them.

Peter's heart pounded so hard that he was surprised it didn't echo in his armor. They all walked up a grassy knoll to an artful arrangement of statues and benches. The moon beamed down on them fondly, silvering Peter's armor and bathing Kat in its healing light.

A faint rustling sound came from the bushes a hundred feet away.

Kat jumped up on a bench, her whiskers dotted with milk. Peter hovered over her protectively, praying that good magic was stronger than bad. He wished a sword had come with this ridiculous armor, or that he'd had time to purchase a gun. Every second was a precious commodity now. Each tick of the clock moved them closer to victory, or to ruin. Peter took a deep breath and watched the bushes.

Gisella sat down on another bench, her fingers drifting to the capacious pocket in her full gypsy skirt.

Her beauty luminous in the moonlight, Tituba dabbled her fingers in the small fountain between two statues. "I'm pleased to see you're being reasonable about this, Gisella. This is so much better than calling my hounds through the window, as I originally intended. If you'll cease this foolish resistance, I might even stop before Kat's dead." Regretfully, she glanced at Peter. "And I should hate to see such a handsome young man killed for some foolish, hopeless notion of goodness." Tituba clapped her hands.

The rustling became a crashing sound. Two muscular canines burst through the bushes, their eyes glowing red in the night. The Rottweilers padded forward, growling, their ears laid back as they glared from Peter to Kat. Each had a cross-shaped brand on its forehead.

Peter picked up Kat. The dogs crept closer, their great paws almost soundless.

Tituba held up a staying hand. The dogs froze. As she turned to face Peter and Kat, her eyes, too, glowed red. "Concede all of Boston to me or die," she said coldly.

For a timeless moment, all was quiet in the garden. Even the moon ducked behind a cloud as if it couldn't bear to watch.

The hellhounds tensed on their haunches, preparing to spring.

Peter held Kat protectively, waiting for destiny to play its hand.

Tituba smiled at him, her true nature bared with her long, pointed teeth. For an instant, Peter swore he saw her voluptuous form stoop, her long black locks thin to gray wisps. But then the moon peeked out again, and she was an avatar of evil, more frightening in her false beauty than she was in her truest form.

In a flash, Gisella had the red book out. She laid it flat on the bench beside her and opened it to the blank pages in the back.

Tituba's laughter echoed like a banshee's as her hand fell. "Your little spells are useless against me, you bitch."

Both dogs leaped for Kat, their teeth snapping.

Peter lifted Kat up into the tree beside them. Without a moment of hesitation, he moved between Kat and the dogs. He held out his chain-mailed arm to shove one hound away, brandishing the cross before the face of the other.

In the house, the grandfather clock began to chime. One.

Gisella chanted softly in Latin, holding the blank pages wide. Slowly, the moon at its apex in the sky beaming brightly on the blank pages, silvery writing appeared.

Two. Vulcan had Peter by the arm, growling as he tugged, trying to move Peter aside so Hades could get at Kat. Peter resisted, but blood appeared as sharp fangs pierced the thin chain mail.

Three.

Her little face turned upward, Kat moved out on a branch to bathe her full form in the healing moonlight.

Four.

Vulcan shook his head, his powerful neck muscles flexing as he bit down harder. Peter's planted heels began to drag. Desperately, he held out the cross in his other hand to keep Hades at bay, but Tituba threw a rock at him, hitting his hand. He dropped the cross.

Tituba laughed, the sound echoing over the garden like an evil omen. Kat yowled in despair, for the moonlight hadn't begun to change her.

Five. Hades leapt up, snapping, his teeth almost reaching Kat's little feet.

Gisella chanted louder and faster, reading the writing, her finger moving rapidly from the bottom of the right-hand page toward the top.

Six. Hades jumped harder. A fang grazed Kat's foot. Blood dripped down into the frenzied hound's mouth. She moved a little higher, but any farther and she'd be out of the moonlight. Tituba's laugh was as frenzied now as the snarling of her hellhounds.

Seven. Peter kicked at Vulcan's legs, trying to bend to retrieve the cross, but the armor wouldn't flex. Vulcan released his grip as he fell, but he scrambled up quickly, his jaws gaping, his saliva glistening in the moonlight.

Eight. This time when Vulcan opened his jaws to bite, Peter rammed his fist into the dog's throat. Gagging, Vulcan moved back.

Nine. Tituba's smile faded. A strange look crossed her face. Gisella spoke so fast that her voice had become one long chant. Her finger was nearing the top of the left-hand page now.

Ten. Kat's eyes widened. The branch began to bend under her weight. Pearly toes formed where her paws had been. This time, when Hades snapped at her, she kicked his nose. He howled and jumped sideways. Peter rammed his hand even farther down Vulcan's throat, making it impossible for the hound to bite. Catching the dog's neck in the crook of his elbow with his other arm, he began to squeeze.

Eleven. Tituba's hands were at her own throat. She made an odd, choking sound and began to scream curses. Curses in Latin, curses in French, and finally, her voice changing with every word, "You stupid woman, what have you done to . . . meow!" Her tight green gown began to sag upon her. Tituba's arms shortened, became coated with white fur. Her long face grew small, rimmed with whiskers and sharp, feral teeth.

Twelve. Kat's tail disappeared. Instead of crouching on all fours, she sat on the branch now, her black fur smoothing into soft white skin. Her back straightened. Her paws turned into long, lovely fingers. Gisella stopped reading and slammed the book closed.

For an instant, silence ruled in the garden.

The branch snapped under Kat's weight. She tossed the broken collar away like a slave breaking her manacles. She landed lightly, on her feet, as graceful as the lovely woman she'd remained inside. When Hades recovered and lunged, she picked up the broken branch and whacked him over the nose with it. Howling, he backed off.

Meanwhile, Vulcan made a gagging sound as Peter strangled him. The red eyes began to dim.

Weakly, Gisella supported herself on the bench, as if casting the spell had taken her remaining strength. With a wisp of sadness in her wise hazel eyes, she watched Tituba's final transformation.

The green gown was piled on the lawn now, its sequins glittering in the moonlight. A small pink nose poked out of the heavy fabric. Big green eyes stared at Gisella, looking dazed.

"We mixed your blood with Kat's, Titty," Gisella said softly. "It was in your wine."

A piercing, despairing yowl rang through the garden. The white cat wriggled free of the fabric, claws bared as it leaped toward Gisella.

Hades had stiffened at the sound. He turned away from his much larger foe, his nostrils flaring as he scented the hated feline smell. Growling, he leaped for the cat. His teeth snapped down on her tail.

Howling in pain, the white cat clawed his eyes. His jaws relaxed.

Panting, Peter dropped a dazed Vulcan to the ground, cradling his bitten, bleeding arm. Vulcan's head shook as he coughed several times. He blinked, focusing on his brother chasing a white cat over the lawn. His eyes took on an ugly red gleam again. Baying loudly, he galloped after the other two animals.

Gasping for air, Peter ripped off his helmet and tossed it away. He looked around for Kat. He'd been too busy fighting Vulcan to see what had happened, but he had noted the white cat running off. He saw Gisella first, white as a sheet, barely able to sit on the bench. Peter hurried over to her. "Are you all right, ma'am?"

She nodded. "See . . . to . . . Kat." She handed him her long shawl.

Frantically, Peter searched the cleared space for Katarina. He didn't see her at first. Had it worked?

Had he helped save her, or was he too late?

Then, under the shade of the tree, an embarrassed, musical voice he'd heard many times said, "Don't look, Peter. I'm naked."

Joy rocketed through Peter's veins, blasting away his various aches and pains. A world of happiness beckoned now. "Kat?" Peter had to clear his throat before he could speak plainly. He held out the shawl, keeping his eyes averted.

He heard the rustle of the shawl, and then the girl in the painting, the same girl who'd haunted his waking and sleeping hours for the past two months, the only girl he'd ever wanted for more than a night, stepped out into the bountiful moonlight.

Long black hair covered her full, barely clothed bosom. The shawl shielded her hips, but her legs were bare. They were long and perfectly shaped. Her knees trembled.

But those eyes. Those elongated golden eyes gleamed at him even in the darkness with a tinge of phosphorescent green. Peter held his hands out to her, vaguely aware of dogs growling in the distance. A sharp yowl came, and then there was silence. Peter smiled, his eyes glistening with tears. "Katarina of my heart, I pledge the rest of my life to make you happy, and keep you safe. I believe."

Sobbing, Kat threw herself against his chest. Her long hands caressed his battered face, touched his bleeding arm. "Peter, I love you. Knight of my heart, come to me at last. Hold me and never let me go." Pulling his head down, she kissed him.

Pain tore through Peter's sore arms and chest, but he welcomed it. Pain was as much an affirmation of life as the elation sprouting goosebumps all over his body. And then, as he felt, thigh to thigh and heart to heart, the vibrant life and passion that was Katarina, even his pain faded. He kissed her deeply, his head swimming with her clean, fresh scent. He ran his hands over her velvety back and was delighted when she arched into his touch. A sound very like a purr escaped her lips.

Gisella smiled tiredly. "One settled. Three more to go." She wiped a tear away, watching the passionate embrace.

High above, the huge harvest moon smiled down on the garden and three other, very special cats. . . .

As for Peter Gabler, he'd come home. In trusting his heart and his instincts, he'd found the perfect companion for his mind and his soul. Katarina snuggled against him, purring louder.

On some dim level, Peter Gabler smiled.

He'd been wrong about this, too.

He could have Kat and Cat. . . . A friend and a love for all time.

# Get Thee A Cat

## Coral Smith Saxe

# Chapter One

"Please wait in here, miss," said the dark little man in the impeccable morning coat. "Madam will see you shortly."

"Thank you," Bess Fielding murmured as she stepped past the butler and entered the parlor. She stopped short just across the threshold, frozen in shock. She gave a little jump as the heavy pocket doors closed behind her.

"What are *you* doing here?" she demanded.

The tall, sandy-haired man who stood before the hearth on the other side of the room hooked one elbow on the mantel's edge and grinned at her. "A gentleman doesn't say."

Bess stepped toward him. "If there were a gentleman here, Ben Carruthers, I wouldn't be asking," she retorted.

"You mean there's a way to silence you?" His light brown eyes danced.

"Odd," she said coolly, lifting her chin, "that's what everyone always asks about you."

"Can't stop talking about me, eh?"

"I can. But they said they were desperate."

"I can imagine they were, the way you do go on and on about me."

Bess waved a gloved hand at the door. "You should be the one to go on. I have an appointment here." She smoothed her cashmere afternoon dress and took a seat, some distance from where Ben stood by the fire. She looked up. "What? Still here?"

He grinned again. "You're mad at me for not dancing with you at the Stoddards' ball last month, aren't you?"

Bess sighed. "You're too full of yourself, sir. I assure you, not every female you encounter is smitten by your meager charms. As a matter of fact, I am hoping that we two can become better strangers." Her eyes narrowed. "But why are you here? You can't possibly know Mrs. Lowell. She's terribly reclusive and, I'm told, quite exclusive as well, which would leave you out in any circumstance."

"I should tell you—"

The pocket doors whispered open. The butler stood at attention in the doorway. "Madam will see you now," he announced in sepulchral tones.

Ben and Bess looked from the butler to one another. A prickle of alarm climbed Bess's spine.

"Which of us—?" Bess and Ben spoke in unison, halted in the same way.

"Both." The butler turned. "This way, please."

"This can't be right," Ben muttered, starting after him.

"It certainly *isn't* right," Bess hissed, jumping up

**110**

and hurrying after them. "This is a private matter."

"As is mine."

They paused, staring at one another. Bess felt the prickle at her spine begin again.

"You wouldn't—" she gasped.

"You couldn't—I was here first!"

"My appointment was for one o'clock."

"As was mine!"

Bess picked up her skirts and hurried after the butler, who was disappearing down the long paneled hallway. "A gentleman would bow out now," she shot back over her shoulder.

Ben caught up to her. "You just said there weren't any gentlemen here. However, a lady would never insinuate herself into a man's business affairs."

"Business, my foot—"

"You may go in." They fell silent as the butler pushed wide another set of double doors. Bess aimed a narrow glance at Ben Carruthers and sailed into the parlor.

Bess had seen Gisella Lowell only once before, and that had been but a brief glimpse of the mysterious widow through the window of her carriage. The woman who greeted them now seemed both older and younger than all reports, and far more handsome than any had rumored. Her pale auburn hair, untouched by gray, glinted in the light of the fire in the hearth behind her and the cut of her elegant tea gown was a style Bess recognized as the latest in French fashion. By rumor and by all appearances, Gisella Lowell was a most unusual woman.

Bess decided she'd better speak now or the all-too-glib Mr. Carruthers was likely to have the first, middle and last words. Why in heaven the man hadn't gone into law, she'd never understand.

"Mrs. Lowell," she began.

"Gisella, please."

"Gisella, I'm afraid there's been some confusion about the times of our appointments. I had thought I was to meet with you at one o'clock, yet Mr. Carruthers believes his interview was at the same hour."

"You are both perfectly punctual and correct," the woman replied. "Won't you please sit down?"

"Forgive me, Mrs. Lowell—Gisella," said Ben, "but I don't understand."

"You both replied to my advertisement, yes?" She took a seat on the straight-backed Sheraton settee and motioned for them both to take two lyre-backed chairs nearby. "And both of you replying on the same day, within moments of one another . . . well, I thought, such unity of mind and spirit would never brook a separation. So, I set this interview for both of you."

Bess felt her heart sink. Sharing an interview with Ben Carruthers? If there was any unity of mind and spirit between them, it was in their mutual contempt. But what about the cat?

Ben beat her to the question. "I'd be very interested to hear more about the cat you're giving away," he said, flashing his most charming smile.

Gisella Lowell smiled. "As you already know, I have many cats. They are a—passion of mine, you might say."

"Was that really a panther we saw as we came through the front garden?" Bess asked.

"Panjit, yes. Quite a little mischief-maker. I hope he didn't bother you."

"Is—is that the cat—your ad—?" Ben's voice sounded strained, much to Bess's amusement.

"No, no." Gisella's laughter was soft, murmuring. "No, Panjit is too set in his ways. He'd never take to another master. Or mistress." She leaned forward and fixed them both with a keen stare. "Before you meet with Henri, I would like to hear more about yourselves. You two know one another, I presume?"

"Yes," said Bess, reluctantly. "Mr. Carruthers and I were children together."

"Ah, how lovely. How I wish I'd had a lifetime to know my Alexander." Her eyes grew misty for a moment. "Still, the time we had was as full of love as three lifetimes."

"I'm very sorry for your loss."

Bess looked at Ben. The expression in his golden brown eyes seemed sincere. *A first,* she added, skeptically.

"Bess," Gisella said, fixing warm hazel eyes on her. "Tell me more about your plans for the money attached to my offer."

Bess smiled. "I know that your advertisement said the money was to start a new business, but I hoped you might make an exception in this case. I have been for these past two years a sponsor and sometime aide at the Bennet Street Clinic for Women and Children. It's a small hospital, but it does so very much good for the people of that area, who otherwise could not afford to see a physician, or be provided with even the most basic medical care."

"Are you a physician?" Gisella asked.

"No, no!" Bess laughed. "No, I'm hardly the serious and studious sort. But my heart was so touched by the good work being done there by doctors and nurses who could be earning a far better living than the small stipend they claim at Bennet Street. I help out from time to time, with small bookkeeping matters or running errands, but my chief task has been to raise money to support the clinic's efforts."

"And you wish to use the money for this purpose?"

"Yes." Bess leaned forward, excitement filling her, as it always did when she talked about her work. "Their cause is so worthy, yet they are threatened with closure due to lack of adequate funds. I cannot hope to solicit the necessary amount from my connections, however generous they may be, and I have no money of my own until I marry. It is my hope that your generous offer will allow me to at last be of some substantial service to these good people."

Gisella nodded, slowly. "A most interesting and worthwhile use." Now her smile shone on Ben. "And you, Ben? What would your plans be?"

Bess thought he looked a bit dismayed, but he seemed to gather himself and rise to the occasion. She waited, wondering what Benjamin Carruthers of the Beacon Hill Carruthers might want with ten thousand dollars and a cat.

"Though I cannot claim such a noble cause as Miss Fielding's," he said, shooting a smile Bess's way, "I can say that my plans fit more into the line of your advertisement."

"Yes, you told me in our telephone conversation that you are with a shipping and manufacturing concern."

"Yes. The land out west is being settled up fast, especially with all the territories being admitted to the Union. Families and businesses need goods out there that they can't make or obtain for themselves. The river routes, as well as the new railroads, will be a tremendous boon to them. It's my plan to supply them with the goods they need." He paused, his eyes meeting Gisella's in a meaningful stare. "At a fair price," he said firmly.

Bess sensed that more was said in that exchange of looks than in Ben's words. What was he up to? Was he planning to start his own business? And why would he wish to leave Thomas Duke, when all Boston was abuzz with the fabulous success of Duke & Company's business ventures?

Gisella reached up and pulled a long velvet rope. A muffled bell rang somewhere below them.

"Henri will be here in a moment. Before he comes, I should like to commend you both on your forthrightness and your energy. Two such bright young people as yourselves may go a long way together in this world."

"But—" Bess started to protest.

"Excuse me, but I believe there's been a misunderstanding," Ben said quickly.

Gisella tilted her head questioningly. "Has there?"

Bess leaped in. "What Mr. Carruthers is trying to say is that he and I—that is, we are not—"

"Together," Ben said.

Gisella smiled. "Of course. I apologize for my implication. Though it's odd, you know. Mr. Lowell and I were so very *simpatico*, shall we say, that almost from the first, we, too, would finish one another's thoughts."

Before Bess could protest, the doors whisked open and a small gray cat, scarcely more than a kitten, trotted confidently into the room. It had a stocky build yet all the grace of a typical feline, and when it came to stand beside Gisella, Bess saw that its round, friendly face held a pair of uncommon copper-colored eyes.

"Henri," Gisella said softly, stroking the cat's long tail, "these are two new friends, Bess and Ben."

The cat looked from Bess's face to Ben's and back. Bess had the oddest feeling the animal was taking their measure. After a moment's consideration—or so Bess fancied—it walked toward the two of them. With a small *prrpf* of a mew, it sat down squarely between them.

"Excellent. He likes you," Gisella said.

Bess shot a glance at Ben. He looked decidedly uncomfortable and more than a bit bewildered. She took this as a cue for her to press for an advantage.

"Henri," she said softly, reaching out toward the cat's thick, velvety coat. "It's nice to meet you."

The cat arched affectionately under her hand, purred loudly, then turned and plopped itself down by Ben's chair. Bess could scarcely stifle her smile as the cat sat there, plainly waiting for him to make an overture.

Ben lifted a hesitant hand and patted the cat's head. Henri gave another resounding purr and snaked his way around Ben's legs.

"Oh, dear," said Gisella. "This does present a problem."

"What do you mean?" Ben asked.

"Henri is interested in both of you. Yet you are, as you say, not together." Gisella bit her lip gently. "Hmm. This calls for a special arrangement, I believe."

Bess felt her heart flutter, then sink. This wasn't what she had planned on, hoped for. Why, why had Ben Carruthers, of all people, come along to generally mess things about? What if the widow was only offering half the prize? It wasn't nearly enough to preserve the clinic. She turned an anxious face toward their hostess.

"Yes, I believe Henri is correct. I, too, am interested in both of you. Let me propose a plan. I shall set a time of trial for each of you—say, one week? That should give Henri time to get to know each of you and a decision may be reached. Moreover, it will bring us closer to All Hallows' Eve. What say you?"

Hope flooded into Bess's spirit. "It would be acceptable to me."

"And you, Ben?"

Bess clasped her hands tightly in her lap. Please say yes, she prayed. Please let me have this chance to prove I have something to give.

"All right."

She could breathe again. Henri gave a little mew and trotted over to her. With one graceful bound, it landed in her lap. Startled, she put her hands on it to steady its perch on the gathered front of her overskirt.

"Henri has chosen to be with Bess for the first week." Gisella smiled, her eyes dancing. "He is a true gentleman: ladies first!"

"So I see," Ben said dryly.

# Chapter Two

"I can't believe this," Bess muttered as the door closed behind them.

"You can't believe it!" Ben followed her down the steps of the Lowell house. "I'm not the one who turned calf's eyes on the woman! At any moment, I thought you were going to recite the death of Little Nell in there!"

"Heavens above," she cried, swishing through the gate that was being held open by her carriage driver. "Dickens, yet. Don't tell me the man can read."

"You're not going to win this," Ben said evenly as he watched her load the sturdy leather carrier into the carriage and take the seat beside it. "The cat will be mine. Cats love me!"

"For which the women of Boston are eternally grateful." She tucked in the skirts of her saffron yellow dress and gave him a saccharine smile. "Good day, Mr. Carruthers."

Ben stood glaring as the carriage pulled away and rolled down the brick-paved lane.

"There is no way you're going to get custody of that little orange-eyed furball," he growled. "And there isn't any way that I'm going to wait a whole week to take charge. This is war."

He squared his shoulders, clapped on his hat and set a course for the wharf area and the finest fish market in all of Boston.

Bess took the tray from the maid and closed the door quietly behind her. "All right," she said softly. "Little cat, here's your treat."

Her cousin, Helena Fielding, was curled on the carpet next to the brass bed, peering into the cat's carrying case. "He's so very quiet, Bess," she said, her slender arms hugging her knees. "Are you sure he's well?"

"I don't know," Bess said, shrugging. "I've never had a cat; have you?"

"I played with one the cook kept to keep the mice from the pantry when I was small, but once I was in school, Mama said I mustn't romp with creatures."

Bess set the tray on the bedside table and bent over the latch on the cage. "I suppose we shall have to learn together, eh?" she murmured to the wide-eyed young tom.

When the door was opened, she stood back, allowing the animal to emerge at will. She splashed cream from the little pitcher on the tray into a blue and white china bowl. Carefully, she placed the

119

bowl on the floor by the bed, then joined Helena on the carpet.

"He'll come out when he's ready," she said, arranging the deep sleeves of her kimono. "He needs to get used to his new surroundings."

"Oh, I'm sure he will. Now, tell me, why was Ben Carruthers at Gisella Lowell's? Did he say anything about my Carl?" Helena stretched out her arm to smile at the diamond ring that glinted on her left hand. Betrothal rings were all the fashion and Helena Fielding's fiancé, Carl Randolph, was nothing if not a young man who kept up with the times. "Can you believe it's only two weeks to the wedding?" She sighed.

"With all the commotion around here, you'd think it was only two days!" Bess gave her cousin a hug, her dark head near Helena's fair one. "I couldn't be happier for you, dear. I wish you all the joy in the world."

Helena's soft gray eyes shone. "And that's what I want for you! So, tell me, what about the estimable Mr. Carruthers of Duke & Company Shipping and Manufacturing International?"

Bess sniffed. "Estimable, indeed. The only thing that can be esteemed about Ben Carruthers is the width of his head."

Helena smiled but clucked her tongue. "How am I ever going to dance at your wedding if you keep rejecting men right and left for their littlest faults?"

"Littlest faults! Do you know what that fellow was doing at Mrs. Lowell's today? He was there to get the cat. My cat!"

"Oh, look, he's coming out!" Helena cried softly.

Bess looked to the cage. The fine gray head, with its charming full cheeks, emerged from the opening, wide eyes peering in all directions. Whiskers of considerable length twitched, as if they could sense the character of the room and its inhabitants like delicate divining rods. At last he stepped out, paws treading lightly on the thick counterpane of embroidered Japanese silk.

"He's adorable!" Helena cooed. "What a cunning little face! He looks as if he's smiling."

"That's what I first noticed about him, too," Bess said, keeping her voice low. She chuckled. "He looks like he fell in the cream pail and loved the washing up."

"But why on earth would Ben Carruthers want a cat?" Helena asked, smiling as the kitten began to pad about on the bed.

"I don't know. I can't believe he wants it as a pet. And he certainly can't need the money. His family is as rich as yours, and he's well employed at Duke's."

Helena put her hand on Bess's arm. "You know I would lend you the money you need for the clinic, if only you'd let me."

Bess patted her hand. "I know that. But you have a home to make with Carl, and your father has been all too kind to me since my parents died as it is. I want to be the one to earn this money." She took up the tasseled end of her kimono sash and dangled it. The cat batted at it with a soft paw. "I have to be worth something in this world other than a smile and a light remark."

Helena laughed. "Leave it to my Bess to find the most unorthodox method of earning her way!"

"I know," Bess said, her eyes dancing. "When I saw the ad in the newspaper, quite by chance, I was too intrigued not to want to learn more. And the idea of earning ten thousand dollars just for taking this handsome little fellow home with me—well, it was too good to resist."

"And the Bennet Street Clinic for Women and Children shall have the funds it needs and more!"

"Meowrr."

The two women looked at the cat and laughed.

"He agrees," Helena said.

"Either that, or his claws are trapped in the counterpane! Here, puss, let me help."

Bess gently extricated the cat's claws from the delicate threads. She put a hand under his soft belly and lifted him up. "Are you ready for a bit of milk?" she asked. "Actually, I think Moira put in cream. Will that be all right, your highness?"

She set him down by the dish of cream and stood back, watching as the cat nosed forward, testing the safety of the situation.

Helena shook her head. "What on earth would Ben Carruthers want with a cat?" she repeated.

It was the biggest fish in the market. Beside it, in the heavy wicker basket, lay a paper-wrapped package of fresh chicken livers, a lobster tail, a ball of rich butter and a sizable bundle of dried catmint, tied round with straw. In addition to the foodstuffs, there was a skein of bright red yarn, a small feather pillow and a small, stuffed ball covered in soft black rabbit's fur.

Ben smiled to himself as he hefted his purchases up onto the table in the kitchen. He'd given Mrs. Johanssen, his cook and housekeeper, the night off, saying he'd eat at the party tonight. And so he would. But not until he'd stocked his armory and made his first foray into enemy territory.

"No cat can resist me," he intoned, laying the great fish, neatly sliced into thick fillets, in the icebox in the pantry. The butter followed, along with the lobster tail. He selected two of the choicest of the chicken livers and stowed the rest with the sea-food.

Whistling, he took up a heavy knife and diced the chicken livers into bite-sized pieces, scooping them afterward into a bit of waxed paper. The cat-mint was given similar treatment, only when it was thoroughly chopped, he carried the bits to his bedroom and deposited them throughout the pockets of his evening coat and trousers. Still whistling tunefully, he looked at his dusty hands. Smiling, he chose a fresh pair of gloves from the bureau and thrust his hands into them. He rubbed his hands together, gave them a satisfied clap, then removed the gloves, taking care not to disturb the herbs he'd left within.

Bess Fielding was lost, he thought to himself as he prepared his bath for the evening. By this time tomorrow, that fuzzy, four-legged bankroll she'd hauled home would be his alone, utterly devoted to him. She'd never be able to charm her way into the cat's affection—not when he'd so cleverly stacked the deck.

Sometime later, bathed, dressed and refreshed, Ben placed the packet of chicken liver into his coat pocket, pulled on his specially scented gloves, clapped on his top hat and was off to the home of Lionel and Antonia Fielding, to the ball held in honor of their daughter Helena's upcoming nuptials.

Whistling as he went.

"I can't believe it's come to this," Ben said, giving Carl Randolph a playful punch on the arm. "Not yet thirty and no longer a bachelor."

123

Carl grinned and pretended to be wounded. "The wedding's not until Friday next, old boy," he said, rubbing his arm. "I'm still a bachelor tonight."

"It's the same thing. You're hooked, you're netted, you're gilled. Even if the parson hasn't said a word over the proceedings, you're already there, in matrimonial exile from the world of men." Ben shook his head in mocking disapproval.

Thomas Duke joined them. "Ah, but look what he gains," the big, dark-haired businessman said, nodding in the direction of the dance floor. Helena, a vision in cloud pink, was taking a turn with her father. "If Randolph here is exiled, I'd say he's been banished to Paradise."

Carl's eyes sparkled. "She is the loveliest in the room, isn't she?"

"I can see she is," Tom replied, amused.

"All *I* can see is her and that outrageous cousin of hers," Ben said, his expression belying the sweetness of the champagne punch in his cup. "I'll say one thing for you, Randolph, at least little Helena doesn't take after Miss Elizabeth Pile-on-the-Agony Fielding."

Tom grinned. "You seem to think a lot of Miss Elizabeth."

Ben glowered. "I knew her of old. She could teach a Philadelphia lawyer how to argue."

Carl leaned confidingly toward Duke. "He and Bess were childhood sweethearts."

"Watch yourself, young trout," said Ben, poking a finger at Carl's fine starched shirtfront. "Unless you want tales of your misspent infancy to reach your Helena's ears."

"You wouldn't!"

"Wouldn't I?"

The dance had finished and Bess had joined Lionel and Helena as they left the floor. Helena glanced at the three men and sent a dazzling smile at Carl. Carl blew her a kiss and she turned to bury her rosy blush in her cousin's shoulder. Lionel led them away to the dining room.

"So?" Carl demanded, spreading his arms. "Am I in matrimonial exile now?"

"Lord, yes," Ben replied. "If you could only see yourself. The hook is dangling out of the corner of your lip, just there—"

Laughing, Carl pushed his hand away. He wrinkled his nose. "Phew! No wonder you're a bachelor, Carruthers. You never launder your gloves. What sort of scent is your barber using these days—grass cuttings?"

Ben colored slightly. The damn catmint. That cat was already trouble. He gathered his wits to put a good face on his blunder.

"Exactly my plan, old married fellow. The ladies love me, but I never let 'em get too close to throw the noose around my neck."

Tom Duke waved a finger at him. "I'll see you tie that noose there yourself someday. And smile while you're doing it, too."

"I'll hang for murder before I hang for a husband."

"Oh ho, be careful what you wish for!"

Ben looked about the room, taking in the measure of the company assembled for this event. "I see Regis and Barnewall are here tonight. How goes it with the western shipping scheme? Will they come on board, do you think?"

Tom nodded. "Oh, yes, they'll see things my way. Barnewall's holding out for a better share, but when he sees that Timmons might beat us to the western territories, he'll scramble up the gang-plank like a good little seagoing rat."

Ben winced inwardly at Duke's words. Tom Duke was the fastest rising young entrepreneur in Boston—maybe on the whole Eastern seaboard—but he had a contempt for people and a habit of cutting around such niceties as fair trade and legalities that sometimes made Ben uncomfortable. Still, he was the star of the hour in Boston, and if he could only buy into a partnership, Ben could hope to pressure Tom into more ethical practices. All the more reason to get that money from Gisella Lowell. Which meant getting that cat away from Bess Fielding.

*Speak of the devil and up she pops.*

"Ah, the lovely bride-to-be and her charming cousin," Duke drawled. "How about it, Carruthers? With Miss Helena safely tucked in Randolph's pocket, I'd say Miss Elizabeth seems a perfect match for you."

"Sir, the only match I desire is one to light my cigar. Good evening, gentlemen." Ben bowed to the men, made a hasty bow to the approaching ladies and headed for the nearest exit.

Tom and Carl looked at one another in astonishment at their friend's sudden departure, then shrugged. The ladies were soon upon them and they devoted themselves to more lighthearted matters.

"Mr. Carruthers." The butler bowed his head crisply as Ben rounded the corner into the foyer.

"Just going to have a bit of a smoke in old Lionel's hideaway, Johnson," Ben explained, tossing a grin over his shoulder. "You know I've never been much of a dancer."

"Very good, sir."

At the top of the stairs, Ben cast a glance over the balustrade to see if the butler was still standing guard. He was, but his attention was on the front door. Ben took advantage of the moment to slip away from the direction of the study and down the hall toward the family's quarters.

"Where the devil does she sleep?" Ben muttered, going softly along the carpeted hallway. He approached one of the several doors along the hall, listened and tried the knob.

The time was now or never. Bess Fielding would be occupied at the ball, probably dancing—and arguing—with Tom Duke. He had only to search her room, find the cat and work a little magic.

He patted the packet of chicken livers, still in his pocket. He grinned to think what the very proper crowd in the ballroom below would think if they knew that one of the guests was traipsing about with chicken entrails in his trouser pocket. *Heavens! Disgraced for life!*

Ben sobered. He might make light of them, but he did, in fact, like and respect many of the set in attendance tonight. He'd been raised among them, even if his family was not one of the very first of the first in society. And he needed their goodwill if he was to begin his own company. Boston was a small town, still, when it came to business. His father's fame as a clever and successful entrepreneur was a towering mark to aim for, and expectations of Charles Carruthers's son were extraordinarily high. Not to mention those of Charles himself.

So—he had to find the cat.

"Rrrwr?"

He froze.

"Prrr—row."

Payday! Ben backed up and tried the door on the opposite side of the corridor. It opened easily, quietly, to his relief. And there, on the bed, eyes wide and tail twitching, was the object of his search.

# *Chapter Three*

"Hey, puss," he said softly, closing the door behind him. "I have a treat for you."

The animal stood, paws lifting up and down on the coverlet, as if waiting for him. He smiled and approached slowly, pulling off one glove. Hand outstretched, he bent toward the cat.

A rapturous sniff caused Ben's heart to surge. The plan would succeed! The cat would be so attached to him by this time next week that Gisella Lowell might as well just hand over the bank draft now.

"Fitzzz-ztt!"

It was off the bed with a graceful bound and up on the shelving above the mantel, which was constructed of many compartments full of porcelain figurines. It sat there quietly, that odd smiling look on it face, peering down at him. Was it mocking him? Ben tried to stay calm.

129

"Hey, what is it, eh? Are you trying to tell me you don't like a bit of the old catnip now and then, is that it?"

The cursed thing just stared at him with those big round eyes. He started over.

"How about this, then, Henri, old pal?" he said, reaching into his pocket for the waxed paper package. "Mm-mm, delicious chicken livers. Fresh from the butcher's, *n'est-ce pas?*"

He opened the package and held it aloft for the cat to inspect. It put out a questing paw. Ben pulled the food back.

"Uh-uh," he said. "You need to come down here and get it."

He looked around for a chair, but there were none to be seen. With a shrug of resignation, he folded his long legs and sat on the floor. He placed the open package before him.

"Come on," he called softly. "Here, puss, puss, puss."

It was astounding. One instant the cat was there on the mantel. In the next it was airborne, launching itself into a perfect arc that ended with the animal clinging with all four paws—and all claws—on the red silk flowered drapes at the window. Ben leaped to his feet, aiming to catch the creature before—

Too late. The fabric shredded, sending the cat sliding down for almost a yard before it leaped off and skidded to the top of the mantel once again. Several silk fans flew off the wall behind it. A fragile-looking porcelain clock in the shape of a pagoda teetered on the edge of one shelf. Ben leaped for it, catching it just before it could leave the edge.

The cat leaped again, this time to the tall carved

130

table holding the chinoiserie pitcher and basin. It might not have tipped over, but it was clearly unbalanced, prompting Ben to hurl himself toward it. The cat hit the floor with a thud and raced away as the basin and pitcher tipped and slid toward the edge of the table, then gave in to gravity and came thumping down, first to Ben's shoulder, then with a shatter to the floor.

It was war now. The cat had flung down the gauntlet and Ben Carruthers was no man to refuse a challenge. He clambered to his feet, searching the room for his opponent.

"There you are," he panted, noting the cat on the bed once more. "You won't get away this time. You're going to eat chicken livers and roll in catnip and you're by Jove going to enjoy it!"

Ben bent to retrieve one of the hatboxes that had toppled off a chest by the wall. A blue velvet bonnet had tumbled halfway out. He tossed the hat aside and took up the box. His collar had burst loose and was wavering to one side of his neck. The knees of his trousers were dusty, and his hair stood on end in places. He limped a little on one bruised knee. Shoulders squared, jaw set, he started once more to the bed.

"Rrrwr?"

"That's for damned sure, *rrrwr*," he muttered.

He kept the box low until he stood within inches of the cat. Then, with a swiftness born of desperation, he raised it and clapped it down over the animal.

"RRRRowww!"

The cat's tail was caught under the edge of the box. Ben lifted it, slightly, just to free the tail, but the imp shoved under the opening with the skill of an otter and scrambled toward the end of the bed, claws digging in for dear life.

Ben clapped the hatbox down again. "Got it!" he cried, triumphant.

"Got what?"

At the sound of the voice behind him, Ben whirled. Under his hand, the cat scrabbled and thumped at the imprisoning hatbox.

"I repeat," Bess asked, hands on her hips, "got what?"

The man's gall was unparalleled. Unmitigated. Unbelievable!

Bess stood in the doorway and took in the scene before her. Her carefully decorated Japanese-style room looked like the aftermath of a bad nor'easter: water puddled on the floor, hats and hatboxes rolled into corners, fans scattered everywhere, drapes hanging in tatters, china smashed to bits. And here was Ben Carruthers, collar askew, his evening clothes in wild disarray, holding a box over the cat she had only yesterday sworn to care for and protect.

He gave her a sickly grin.

"This is low, even for you," she began. "Trying to harm an innocent animal just because you couldn't get your way—"

"It's not like that!" he protested. "I don't want to harm the confounded thing! I was trying to—"

"Kidnap it!" She gasped. "Of course! You were going to take the cat and let me think it had been stolen or lost and I'd have to tell Gisella Lowell that I couldn't take care of it!"

"No, no. That's not it at all."

Bess was having none of his excuses. "And look what you used as a lure—chicken livers!" She swooped down on the offending pile of red bits. "Let it out," she commanded.

"But you don't—"

She marched over and pulled his hand off the box. Cooing softly, she lifted it up. "Come on, little one," she coaxed. "It's all right, no one's going to hurt you now."

The cat stepped out, mewing piteously. It gave Bess a stricken look and went to rub against the front of her gown.

"That cat is insane!" Ben pointed around the room. "Look what it did!"

"And no wonder, with a grown man trying to abduct it, chasing it all around. It's a wonder the poor thing didn't die of heart failure!"

Bess bent to scoop up the cat. It shot away from her, bounding to the carpet, and was out the door in a flash of gray.

"Oh, heavens, now look what you've done!" she cried.

"What I've done?"

"Oh, for pity's sake, just do something worthwhile for a change. Help me get it back!"

Bess lifted her skirts and dashed off in pursuit. She heard Ben's footsteps pounding after her. A flick of its thick gray tail, and the cat rounded the staircase.

"He's going to the kitchen," Bess cried. "We can corner him there."

They raced down the narrow, spiraling back stairs. A scream issued forth from the kitchen before they even reached it. They clattered into the room, where the staff was preparing the dessert course. The pastry chef stood stone-still, a flattened soufflé sagging in his hands.

"Did you see a cat?" Bess asked, breathless.

"A cat, miss?" The butler exchanged glances with the chef.

"*Mais non*, mademoiselle," the chef said with a terse smile. "I would *never* have a cat in *my* kitchen." He looked pointedly at his failed masterpiece.

"Oh no," Bess wailed, spying the open back door. "It must have gotten out! Hurry, hurry!" she said, pulling at Ben's sleeve. "He might go out into the street! Or Uncle Lionel's dogs might get him!"

The night outside was cool, with a brisk little wind rising and falling. The small garden at the back of the house was quiet, filled only with the whisperings of dry leaves on the breeze. Bess stood in the center of the garden, turning this way and that.

"Which way?" she asked. "Which way would he have gone?"

Ben squinted. "Up there," he said in a hollow, resigned tone.

She looked where he pointed. High in the branches of a nearby chestnut tree, two red-gold eyes flickered. The cat gripped the slender branch, causing the last leaves to shake over their heads. It gave another of its pitiful mews.

"The poor thing! It's stuck up there, terrified." Bess started for the tree, calling in a soothing voice, "It's all right, little cat, I'm coming!" She gave a jump up to the lowest branch and swung there, her skirts belling around her.

"Bess, this is ridiculous, it's only a cat—"

"What kind of a monster are you? What kind of a man are you?" she huffed, inching, hand by hand, toward the trunk of the chestnut.

"But you don't need to—"

He was insufferable! Here she was, risking life

134

and limb for a poor creature that he had scared so badly that it had taken refuge in a terrifying perch, and he was telling her that she was being ridiculous?

Suddenly, she felt his hands encircle her ankles. She struggled, but her grip on the branch was loosening.

"Let go of me!" she yelled, trying to kick outward.

"Bess, will you just listen—oww!"

She felt an instant's gratitude that her blow had connected, but in the next instant she lost her hold on the branch. Down she slid, into Ben Carruthers's arms. The sudden weight toppled them both to the ground.

They lay there in silence for a brief moment. Then she raised up and began pummeling him with her fists.

"What were you doing? Are you mad? You want to kidnap my cat and now you want to kill me?"

He warded off her blows with ease. In a quick motion, he gripped both her wrists in one hand and held her still. His face was tight with anger.

"I-was-not-trying-to-kidnap-the-damned-cat!" he said through clenched teeth.

"No, of course not! You were just petting it with a hatbox!"

"I was trying to keep it from tearing up the entire house."

"If you hadn't terrorized it, it wouldn't have torn up anything! And now, thanks to you, it's up a tree and can't get down! And you nearly killed me trying to stop me from rescuing it! What kind of a man are you?"

She stared down at him, waiting for an explanation. He said nothing, just lay there, regarding her with the oddest expression on his face.

Odd, indeed, she thought suddenly, out of no-where. *I never noticed what long lashes a man can have. Or how firm their chests can be. And the curve of his jaw . . .*

Great auk! She was sitting on the man! Skirts rucked up, décolletage displayed, legs bared and thinking about his eyes—and more!

She scrambled off of him, tumbling over into the leaves and grass. "Get up," she whispered urgently. "Get up before you disgrace us both."

He groaned but easily pulled himself up into a sitting position. "Are you ready to hear what I have to say?" he asked, brushing leaves from his hair.

"I'd rather hear my horse talk. I want my cat out of that tree!"

"Very well, then." He jumped nimbly to his feet, extending his hand. "Here, I'll give you a boost."

She allowed him to help her up but snatched her hand away as soon as she was standing. "You'll do nothing of the sort," she said, brushing at her skirts and yanking at her bustle. "If you were any sort of a man, you'd go up that tree yourself, this instant."

"Not I. I've had enough damage done to my person on behalf of that cat, thank you. If you will excuse me, Miss Fielding?"

He turned and headed back toward the house. She gaped at his rudeness, then rushed after him, limping on the one shoe she retained.

"You're not getting off so easily," she said, hurrying alongside him. "You started this, now you finish it."

"Madam, I intend to."

She was speechless as they climbed the back steps and entered the kitchen. She couldn't let him get away with this. She was about to grab his arm, but he raised his hand.

"Please, let me have a moment."

She stood back and crossed her arms. He was up to something.

He crossed to the table, where the scraps from the evening's sumptuous meal lay heaped in a basin, ready to be discarded. He picked up an orange rind, set it aside, then lifted an object out of the debris, holding it with thumb and forefinger. Bess and all the assembled kitchen staff stared.

It was a fish head.

*"Incroyable,"* the pastry chef murmured.

With a bland glance at Bess, Ben stalked out of the house once more and crossed the garden. At the base of the tree he dropped the fish head, then stepped back to peer up into the branches.

"You can have that if you want it," he called up. "Stay or come down, it doesn't matter to me."

He turned to Bess. "Good night, Miss Fielding. Please make my excuses to your aunt and uncle." With a crisp salute, he limped manfully to the back gate, passed through it and was gone.

When Bess looked back to the tree, the cat was on the ground, nibbling daintily at the fish head.

It had been a dangerous moment, Ben thought as he undressed for bed. There she'd been, angry enough to spit in his eye, blaming him for everything that blasted animal had done, telling him how much she hated him. And all he'd been able to think of was how magnificent she looked.

All right, all right, he thought. Maybe it hadn't been the only thing on his mind. But it had caught him off guard. Before she had slipped out of the tree and into his arms he had been thinking only of proving his point to her, that the cat would come down of its own accord.

But when he'd held her, when they had tumbled to the ground together, all his ambitions had suddenly changed. He'd wanted her to stop hitting him, true, but he hadn't wanted her to get up or move away.

The scent of her had been like the autumn breeze itself, with just the faintest hint of the last sweet rose on the vine. Her dark hair had come undone and one curl had wound itself around the slender stem of her throat, just below where her jeweled earbobs had winked in the dim light.

Lost in reverie, he brushed off his evening jacket. Bits of leaves and grass floated to the rug. From the state of his clothes, someone might have judged him to have been doing something altogether different than what he had done this night. It was a good thing he hadn't had to go back through the house. Tom and Carl would have split their sides with merriment over his dishabille.

But when she had been there, leaning over him, he'd had the surest, clearest impulse to stop her angry torrent of words with a kiss. And to drink his fill of the warmth of her body covering his. He had wanted, in that moment, to be doing exactly what his friends would have suspected he'd done.

His gloves fell from the breast pocket of his jacket. He shook them out, his mouth curling in disgust. Catmint. What a joke that had been on him. The blinking cat could stay in that tree for the rest of its unnatural life, for all he cared. As it was, he'd have to pay for the damages to Bess's room, and how was he to do that without explaining to her uncle what a perfect ass he'd made of himself? For that matter, how was he to explain what he was doing in Lionel's niece's bedroom in the first place?

The cat. The cat was trouble.

He finished undressing and shrugged into his dressing gown. After a short whiskey for a nightcap, he yawned and turned out the lamp. Crossing to the window, he lifted the sash, permitting the chill breeze to slip in over the sill.

Tomorrow he'd have to make a new plan. Another night like this one and he'd be ready for an asylum.

As was his habit, he was asleep within moments of stretching out. His breathing was slow and regular when the small form made the silent leap from branch to windowsill, from windowsill to floor.

The cat padded about the room, sniffing here and there in delicate interest, then got down to business. It was an easy matter to hop to the nightstand, then step lightly onto the puffy feather pillows the man had pulled around his head. Once, twice, thrice, the cat circled his sleeping form, tail sweeping up and over his body, so still beneath the coverlet. At the end of the third revolution it settled down at the man's feet and watched, its orangish-gold eyes glowing in the bit of moonlight slipping in over the bed.

The man's breathing quickened ever so slightly. His arms first clutched at the pillows around him, then began stroking, kneading. Deep murmurs of pleasure were uttered from deep in his chest, causing the bed to tremble.

The cat's whiskers curled in satisfaction. Silent as the moonlight itself, it left the room the same way it had entered and returned home by way of the woman's bedroom window.

# *Chapter Four*

Clouds surrounded her. No, make that *a* cloud, one big cloud that enveloped her and bore her up and rolled her about in great, wondrous swimming motions.

It's heaven, Bess thought. *I'm in heaven.* Or, at least in the heavens, she amended, hearing a glorious rumble of thunder that vibrated through her being.

Every place the cloud touched sang with sensation. It settled over her, pressing her down into a cloud bank. Deliciously soft, yet somehow solid and so very warm . . .

"Sweet Bess," a deep voice murmured, seeming almost inside her head. "Sweet, sweet . . ."

"I know that voice," she murmured drowsily. "I know you."

"Bess."

Her interest in the cloud's identity was short-lived. Such amazing, startling, wonderful things were happening in her body, she simply had to answer their demands. She writhed in pleasure, arching and stretching, lifting and twining and always, always, the sweet weight over her and the tender voice urging her on, cherishing her with murmuring sounds, enticing her to let go, to join in, to . . .

Bess woke with a start, gasping, as the last tremors of pleasure ebbed from her body. She cast back the bedclothes, allowing the breeze from the open window to cool her heated form.

What had just happened? Surely she'd been dreaming, but it had been so intense, so real! Even now, she sensed that her entire body had been caught up in the vividness of it, that it had believed that she had actually been . . . been what?

Making love. She'd never had relations with any man, but her friend, Dr. Irene Warren, had patiently and forthrightly answered Bess's questions as far as the physical and anatomical aspects of the union of man and woman were concerned. But Irene hadn't told her how marvelous it could feel, how devastating and yet pleasing. . . .

"Oh my lord!" Bess sat straight up. "Save me for a fool."

The voice. It had registered at last.

The voice of the wonderful, loving, arousing cloud had belonged to none other than Ben Carruthers.

"Mmrrow?"

Bess jumped at the sound, then gave a shaky laugh. "Ah, so you decided to come in after all, did you?" she asked, snapping her fingers lightly to beckon it.

The gray cat padded up from its place at the foot

of her bed and gave her arm an affectionate bump with its head. She smiled and lay back, rubbing the velvety fur and feeling the purring begin deep in the cat's throat.

"It was just a dream, Henri," she said softly. "Thank goodness."

"Rrrow."

Ben sat in his small dining room, sipping pensively from the strong coffee Mrs. Johanssen had brewed at his request. He'd felt he needed something like a slap in the face this morning, and his housekeeper's disintegrate-the-spoon version of coffee was the next best thing.

What a night! He'd slept, but he'd woken this morning with the distinct sensation that he'd been running races from midnight 'til dawn.

And those dreams. Even now, well into his second cup of his housekeeper's black brew, his thoughts drifted off, his breathing becoming quick and shallow. Dreams of the headiest delights. Dreams of long caresses, deep kisses, exquisite embraces. Dreams of a woman's body that in every way fitted his to perfection. Dreams of explosive pleasures.

Dreams of Bess Fielding.

He groaned and set down his cup. Bess Fielding! The most argumentative, unreasonable, contentious female in all the world? It was unthinkable.

And yet he had thought it. More than that—he'd dreamed it, felt it, wakened with what he would have sworn was the taste of her on his lips. And he would have known it was her, even if he hadn't touched that lustrous dark hair or seen those wide blue eyes closing with ecstasy before him. He had murmured her name a hundred times last night.

"No," he muttered. "Not Mrs. Carruthers's lad Benjamin." He wasn't going to give into a ridiculous fantasy, a—a—quirk of indigestion or a trick of the mind. That was all those dreams had been. They meant nothing and he would pay them no mind.

And yet . . .

He seized a piece of toast and munched it. He would put the whole night out of his thoughts, right now, forever.

He finished his toast, drank the last of his coffee and rose from the table. He'd lose himself in work. But first he'd pay his debt to Lionel, his father's old friend, for the mess he'd made last night. That was the best way to put an end to this nonsense.

As he strode out into the crisp October air, he saw a feather come whirling past on the wind. Feathers floating, feathery touches, feathery kisses . . .

"Gad!" he exclaimed, slamming his hat on his head. He decided it was better to walk the distance to the Fielding house. The chill, refreshing breeze would snap some sense into his addled brain.

"There you are, mademoiselle," Bess said, patting the child on the head. "Your dolly's as good as new." She handed over the much-loved toy and the little girl scampered out the door of the Bennet Street Clinic.

Dr. Irene Warren chuckled as she washed her hands in the basin Bess had filled for her. "You have the skill of a surgeon when it comes to doll repair. Have you ever considered going into medicine for humans?"

"Oh, no." Bess laughed. "I simply couldn't stay serious long enough to learn all that. Dolls and whirligigs and jacks-in-the-box are much better suited to my temperament."

Dr. Warren dried her hands on a clean towel and sighed. "I suppose you're right. You certainly don't lack for intelligence or good sense, but your wit would probably get you thrown out of every medical classroom in the nation." She put her hands on her hips and looked around the neat, clean little room that served as the primary examining room of the clinic. "Besides, I don't know what we'd do without you to cheer people up and charm open the purse strings of our most necessary benefactors."

Bess reached for her hat. "And I couldn't be happier doing anything but that."

"Oh?" Irene took her own hat and coat off the rack near the door. "And what if a gallant knight comes riding up and sweeps you off your feet?"

Bess grinned as she buttoned up her coat against the brisk October air outside. "I should beat him about the head and shoulders with my umbrella until he put me down!" she cried. She pulled her own silver-headed umbrella from the stand and brandished it before her.

"Ah, but what if he were handsome and wise and rich?" Irene countered, her eyes twinkling. "What if he went down on his knee before you and promised his undying love?"

"Is he a man?"

"Yes."

"I'd rather be courted by a snail."

Irene laughed and waved Bess ahead of her out the door. "If you keep up your crusade against these poor fellows, a snail may be all you'll get."

"Most of the men I know have more hair than good sense," Bess said, as she waited for Irene to lock the clinic doors. "A snail doesn't change his shell with each new sunrise."

"Are we talking about one man in particular?" Irene's blue eyes regarded her friend shrewdly. "Perhaps a certain young man who'll be in the wedding party with you soon? Ben Carruthers, for instance?"

Bess sniffed. "Please. I'm ashamed that I can even remember his name."

Irene tucked her arm through Bess's and they started down the steps. "You cared for him once upon a time, didn't you?"

"Once upon a time I believed that little fairies brought the dewdrops each morning," Bess replied airily. "I've a bit more under my hat of late."

Irene shook her head. "All right, all right. I give up."

Bess hugged her friend's arm. "Why are you so hot to have me married off? I don't see you panting for a husband."

"I am a doctor," Irene said, her expression growing serious. "A female doctor. It's hard enough to be taken seriously and do my job without having to worry about the obligations of a home and a family." Her eyes were fond as they regarded Bess. "But you say you have no such ambition. And yet I can't think of anyone I know who is wiser and more comfortable with children, warmer of heart or as capable of making any place she enters into a haven."

Bess felt herself blushing. "Pshaw. I'm comfortable with children simply because we speak the same language. And as for havens, I can't imagine that the addition of two trouser legs and a beard will improve any spot more than say, a vase of flowers and a warm hearthfire."

"I give up!" Irene laughed. "You are too much for me. I—"

"What?" Bess asked as the doctor fell suddenly silent. "What is it?"

She looked where Irene was staring. A man in a heavy dark coat and battered hat slouched against the wall of the building at the corner ahead.

"Is it someone you know?" she asked, lowering her voice.

Irene shook her head. "No. But I've seen him before. Last week. In the alley behind the clinic. I thought he might need medical help, but he never came near and he turned and went off before I could speak."

"Perhaps he lives hereabouts."

"Let us hope so. All the same, I'd rather cross here, if you don't mind."

Bess nodded, and they steered across the avenue in midstreet, picking up their skirts to avoid the piles of refuse and damp fallen leaves. They cut around a slow-moving lumber wagon and gained the opposite sidewalk. Bess cast a look across to the other corner. The man had vanished.

"I don't like this," she said. "You're not the least afraid of the biggest, meanest man who lumbers into our clinic. I've seen you wrestle women twice your size, wild on illicit drugs or drink, and win out like a veritable John L. Sullivan. Why does this fellow frighten you?"

"I don't know. It's just an instinct, a hunch. Silly of me, a woman of science, I know, but I *am* a woman and I don't pretend to cast off the gifts of my sex just to serve in a male-led world. That fellow seems malevolent, somehow."

Bess looked where the man had stood and shivered. If Irene was worried, it was a matter to take seriously, to be sure. Nothing must happen to the clinic or to Irene, who did so much good for so many, with so little recompense.

*Little cat*, she thought as they approached the trolley line. *You must stay with me.*

Cap in hand, Ben waited in the west parlor of the Fielding mansion on Commonwealth Avenue. A quarter of an hour had passed since the last time the butler had come to tell him that Lionel would see him shortly. He had inquired whether Miss Elizabeth Fielding was at home and was told that she was not. He was both relieved and vexed. In part, he never wanted to cross paths with Bess Fielding again in this lifetime. Last night's humiliation, coupled with his night of disturbingly . . . warm . . . dreams had been enough to unsettle him for quite some time. Yet, if she were here, perhaps she could add a word or two about the cause behind his cat-chasing debacle of the past evening and lend at least a dram of credence to what was, of course, a quite incredible tale.

Then, too, if she were here, he might look again at her and see if those lips he'd gazed upon last night in the garden, those shoulders he'd touched in his dreams . . .

"By Jove!" He bounded up from his chair. "This has to stop."

With determined strides, he crossed to the parlor doors, flung them open and proceeded to hunt for Lionel Fielding himself. After all, he'd been in this house many an afternoon as a boy, when he and Helena and Bess had played pirates, Indians, big game hunters and circus performers in nearly every nook and cranny of Richard Henry Hobson's extravagant architecture.

147

The study, he decided, was the place to begin. Lionel used to while away odd moments there, he recalled, especially on those occasions when Antonia was on a rampage of cleaning, decorating or entertaining. He searched out the good oak doors at the end of the second floor hall and found them open a crack. Voices inside caused him to pause there.

". . . so you think the lady's smitten, eh?"

"Smitten? According to my Helena she's headless!"

Ben scowled. It was Carl and Lionel, discussing the idiocy of love.

"And does Carruthers return my niece's feelings?"

Ben straightened at the sound of his own name. What was this?

"All I know is what Helena's told me," Carl said. The sound of a long draw on a stout cigar ensued. Ben shifted impatiently. "She says Bess is half mad for Ben, writes all manner of poems to his eyes and his noble brow, droops about the place with his name in her sighs."

Ben sank against the wall. What was he hearing? Bess in love with him? It was impossible! Wasn't it?

"Of course, she wouldn't dare tell him," he heard Lionel say. "The way that man goes on against love and marriage, you'd think they were all the plagues of Pandora's box rolled into one. She'd never hear the end of it, poor girl."

"And after the way they've warred against each other all these years, I always thought she abhorred him," Carl replied. "She's been as stern with him as he with her."

"I believe I've seen her acting somewhat differ-

148

ently these days, here about the house. But are you sure it's real? She's not just playing some game?"

"To what purpose? You know Bess. She always shudders at the very idea of marrying one of us 'fool males,' as she calls us." More puffing. "No, this has to be the real thing. Nobody knows her like Helena, and Helena swears it's love."

"Well, for heaven's sake, don't let Carruthers hear of it. He'll never let her live it down!"

"I don't know. Let me think about it. I think he ought to know. But I'll ask Helena what she thinks. Will she be back from shopping soon? I can't imagine that she and her mother can be still—"

The words faded in Ben's ears. He felt as if he'd been pasted to the wall. Bess? In love? Bess in love with him?

"It's impossible," he breathed. This had to be a prank.

But Lionel himself had said he'd seen her! And Lionel Fielding, good man though he was, lacked both the imagination and the lightness of spirits to join in any such high jinks. No, it had to be true!

He stumbled away from the door, thankful for the thick runner that muffled his steps. In a daze, he descended the stairs and let himself out the front door, ignoring the butler who pursued him in an effort to return his hat and coat.

Upstairs, a small gray cat slipped out through the crack in the library door. It looked back over its shoulder, to where the two men now sat talking and smoking as if they had never a notion of the cat's presence in the room, snaking around their ankles even as the smoke from their cigars wreathed their heads. If anyone had been present to witness, they would have seen the cat's whiskers curve upward, and they would have sworn they'd seen it smile.

# Chapter Five

"Oh, lord," Bess murmured as she saw the hatless, coatless figure approaching her on Commonwealth. Ben Carruthers. The man was like a bad penny.

As he drew closer, he reached up to raise his hat, found none and gave her a lopsided smile. He bowed.

"Miss Fielding," he said. "It's a lovely afternoon, is it not?"

Bess pushed her hands further into her muff and grimaced. "Perhaps for Greenland bears," she said tersely, shivering against the wind.

He grinned. "Greenland bears! That's good!"

"No, it's not," she responded. "But it will have to do. Good day to you, Mr. Carruthers."

"And a great good day to you, Miss Elizabeth." He bowed again as she brushed past him. "I hope we have the pleasure of meeting again soon."

Bess shook her head as she pushed open the gate and followed the walk to her uncle's front steps. She mounted the steps slowly, then turned to look at the lone figure that still stood in the street, gazing after her. Ben Carruthers was fast losing what little wit he'd had to begin with, she thought. Yet there was something in his eyes . . .

The butler held open the door for her, a coat and hat in his arms. Bemused, she added hers to the lot and went upstairs.

Helena and her mother were returning from yet another shopping expedition. Bess heard them coming up the steps from the back entrance, packages rustling in their arms.

She was happy for her cousin, but she wasn't in the mood to hear any more animated discussions of the cut of a trousseau gown or bonnet. She ducked into the morning room and waited for them to pass.

Helena and Antonia carried their goods past the morning room door, but to Bess's annoyance, they paused just beyond it, taking off their hats and coats at one of the hall tables. She sank into a chair to wait out the delay.

"Now, tell me more of what you heard last night from those gentlemen friends of Carl's," she heard Antonia say. "Can they really have meant that Mr. Carruthers is enamored of our own Elizabeth?"

Bess sat up straight. What on earth were they talking about?

"That's what they said," Helena said confidingly. "Mr. Carruthers is so very much in love with her that he can scarcely do his work!"

"Are you going to tell her?"

Bess shot out of the chair and ran on tiptoe to the door, straining to listen.

"Oh, no!" Helena whispered. "I told them to tell Mr. Carruthers to forget her, for she is so against marriage and him that she would only fill him as full of barbs as a pincushion!"

Bess felt her cheeks flame. Was she really that harsh?

"Ah, yes, I suppose you're right." Antonia mused. "But doesn't Ben deserve better than that? After all, he's from one of our best families, a respectable businessman in his own right, and well thought of, or so I hear from Lionel."

"I think he deserves much better than the way she treats him, especially now we know he adores her. But Bess is so firm in her position, I swear Adonis himself could go down on one knee before her and she'd tell him his crown was on crooked!"

The pair in the hallway dissolved into giggles at this, but Bess grimaced. This is what I get for eavesdropping, she thought.

"Well, I hope my niece comes to her senses before long. A fellow like Ben Carruthers doesn't offer up his heart lightly and that makes the gift all the dearer. And I would love to see her happily settled. Now, what of the peach silk you saw at Slater's? I say a morning gown; what do you think?"

Bess listened as they proceeded down the hall, chatting about dresses and trimmings. Her cheeks still stung with the heat of her embarrassment and excitement.

Ben in love with her? Was it possible?

And was she so forbidding, so distant, so crotchety that he wouldn't dare speak of it to her?

She paced about the morning room, picking up objects and idly examining them. Never had she felt such a jumble of emotions, all at once. Happy, yes. Excited, yes. Confused and fearful, yes. Add a bit of embarrassment to the mix, along with a dash of outrage—after all, if she was supposed to be so smart, why hadn't she seen that Ben was in love with her?—and you had the recipe for as fine a state of absolute giddiness as you could wish.

In love. Someone loved her! Ben loved her!

And she had treated him like a fly at a picnic, swatting him away and flapping words of scorn at him. And all the while he had been hiding his most tender feelings.

She went to the window and swept aside the drapes. The wind had risen and more leaves swirled on the air and danced about the small garden. Only last night she had stood in that garden in the moonlight with Ben. She felt herself coloring again. Actually, she had done more than simply stand with him, hadn't she?

"Poor man." She sighed, leaning her flushed cheek against the cool pane. She had flailed at him, pounded on him, railed against him. And, manfully, he'd concealed his passion and restrained himself from any outbursts or declarations. All because he knew she would only mock him.

"This can't go on," she murmured, spinning about. "He's held his devotion in check for too long already!"

"Bess? Elizabeth? Is that you in there?" Helena's voice sounded in the hall outside the library.

"Yes, I'm here." Bess could hear the note of high excitement in her voice as she answered her cousin.

"If you're coming with us to the Appletons' party tonight, you'd better begin getting ready, hadn't you?" Helen stopped inside the door and tilted her head, regarding Bess. "Is something the matter? You look as if you've been running races or something."

"I'm fine!" Bess exclaimed, skimming over the carpet to hug her. "Perfect! And a party is just what I need tonight!"

She whirled past Helena and hurried to her room, where the next few hours were taken up in feverish preparation and many impromptu bursts of song. And no one noticed when a small gray cat stepped lightly out from under the hall table and trotted down to the kitchen for a bite to eat from the generous cook's helper.

The door was locked, but that was no problem for him. Working in the shadows as he did, lock-picking was just part of his trade. A noisy dog, now that was a problem. But no animals would be found in this place, he was sure.

The lock snicked open in response to his tools and he slid inside the darkened building. He paused, waiting to see if anyone might be hiding inside, and allowed his eyes to adjust to the dim light. A stub of a candle, the scratch of a matchstick and a small circle of light bloomed around him.

He found the tiny office with no trouble—his accomplice had been thorough in her description of the place. Once inside, he set down his light and went to work on the rolltop desk that flanked one wall. In short order, he'd found what he required.

He pocketed his findings and carried the light back out to the main room. Lifting a desk clock and weighing it idly in his hand, he began to grin to himself. Now the fun part began.

\* \* \*

Bess felt as if she were a Roman candle, all fizzy light and sound inside. Helena and Antonia had been abominably slow in getting ready for the ball tonight, she thought. What if he had arrived early? What if he had come, seen she was not there and left? Or worse—what if he had come and then left with some other partner?

She edged around the dance floor, endeavoring to peer over heads and around potted palms. Was love always like this? she wondered. Did it always turn people into giddy tops, spinning in circles with but one object in mind?

*Ben is in love with me.* For the past few hours, that one phrase had echoed round and round in her head and still she scarcely dared to believe it. What was more astonishing, perhaps, was that she liked the idea. She, who had always held that marriage was slavery for the woman and that men were nothing more than mustaches. She, who had sworn never to marry until the good Lord made men with more sense than He provided for sheep. She—even she—was ready to accept and welcome with open arms a man's love.

She tapped her fan against her gloved palm, wishing she had some way to climb up into the gallery and peer down upon the throng in the Appletons' ballroom. Then she could gaze upon Ben without him even seeing her, and she could drink her fill of him, uninterrupted.

But, alas, the orchestra had filled the gallery to capacity. There was no way she could steal up there and gaze down, wedged between a bass viol and the grand-sized harp.

And then she saw him.

His sandy brown hair gleamed in the light of the candles and the soft glow from the gasoliers. Resplendid in formal evening coat and immaculate white shirtfront, sporting a red rose bud in his lapel, he, too, seemed to be scanning the crowd for someone. She hardly dared hope she was the one he sought.

The crowd was packed tightly around the edges of the reception hall, which had been converted into a ballroom by the removal of the deep carpets and heavy brocaded furniture. Bess wished she could simply elbow a straight path through the chattering throng of partygoers. It was maddening to lose sight of him in the crush of feather headdresses and dark-coated shoulders.

"Miss Fielding."

She whirled at the sound of a deep voice at her side. Relief and pleasure flooded through her. It was Ben.

"You look very lovely tonight," he said.

Shyness overcame her. For once, she was at a loss for words.

"Th-thank you," she stammered. "Lovely evening, too, isn't it?" *Great auk, she sounded like a parrot!*

"Is it?" he asked smoothly. "I would have sworn it was preparing to rain."

"Not in here." *That was it. She'd lost her wits. What an idiotic thing to say.*

To her astonishment, he laughed. "Let us hope not. I was hoping perhaps you'd dance with me, but if you're afraid of a cloudburst in the middle of a schottische—?"

"No, no. I'd love to dance."

He led her to the floor as the music began. It wasn't a schottische, it was a waltz. She felt herself coloring as his arm came about her waist and they stepped out to the music.

"I'm glad you're here tonight."

"I am, too," she replied. *Lord, did love make blockheads of everyone it touched? What an insipid remark.*

"How is our feline friend? Not up a tree, I hope."

"No. No, he's safe at home. He seems to be quite content."

"I feel certain he must be, with such a charming roommate."

She felt uneasy. Ben Carruthers wasn't cut out for flattery, and though she couldn't detect any signs of insincerity in his voice or on his face, she felt as though they were suddenly playing a game. Had Helena and Aunt Antonia been wrong about his feelings for her?

Still, when she allowed her heart to get a word in, she knew she felt wonderful in his arms, gazing up into his cleanly-shaped features. The small lines about his eyes spoke of the laughter she knew he so enjoyed and the smiles that used to warm her like sunshine.

"You will be pleased to know that your trick with the fish head worked to woo him from the tree," she said, remembering her social training at last.

"Ah, would that every pretty puss were so easily wooed and won."

She gave him a hard look. "What do you mean by that?"

"I don't know. Only that most men have to make idiots of themselves many times over in order to win the hand of the lady of their choice."

She pursed her lips as they dipped and turned with the flow of the dancers around them. "If you would win a lady with a dead fish, you can only hope to catch a dumb creature."

"You'd never be won that way, eh?"

"With a fish head? No, sir. Nor do I live in a tree."

His eyes began to snap. "I don't deny it. The birds themselves would have to find quieter quarters to do their mocking."

She stiffened in his arms. He was at it again. "I only mock what goes past begging for it," she said evenly.

"Beggars seem to be ever at your door, from the generosity of your tongue. You must be close to bankruptcy with all you give them."

"No, sir, I have only one mocking charity and that's the Ben Carruthers Benevolent Fund. And a great boon it is to society, too. I save them a world of effort."

He was silent for a long moment.

"My goodness," he said at last, softly. "Such a beautiful gown. But you should insist that your dressmaker give you back your money."

She didn't want to, but she had to ask. "And why is that?"

"She forgot to put in space for a heart."

Bess stopped still and pulled away from him. "That was—that's—"

"That's right," he said, making a stiff bow. "I do apologize, Miss Fielding. I won't trouble you with my rudeness anymore."

He led her, speechless, from the floor, bowed once again and vanished into the crowd.

She felt tears sting her eyes. What a horrid man! What a horrid mess.

Why, why couldn't she have kept silent, just once? Old habits die hard, she'd always been told. Sparring and exchanging jibes with Ben Carruthers was almost automatic with her.

But he'd been abusive, too. Only a statue could fail to take offense at his words.

She sagged and started toward the door to the library. She just wanted to get away. She'd been so happy, so overjoyed to see him. She'd almost believed the things she'd heard Helena and Antonia saying in the hall that afternoon.

"Miss Elizabeth Fielding?"

Bess turned to the white-coated serving man. "Yes?" she said, hastily wiping her eyes.

He offered up a silver tray that held a folded piece of paper. Frowning, Bess took it as the man backed a few discreet steps away. She bit her lip as she read the contents.

"Will there be a reply?" the servant asked.

"No," Bess said, glancing wildly about the room for a moment. "No, but if you would, please find my cousin, Miss Helena Fielding, and tell her that I've been called away. Tell her not to worry."

"Very good, miss." The man gestured to another fellow, who waited near one of the doors. "Miss Fielding is leaving," was all that he said.

In a twinkling, Bess found herself wrapped in her warm, hooded cloak and seated in one of the Appleton carriages, on her way. The Appletons were one of the old families of Massachusetts, like the Fieldings and the Carruthers, and hospitality was a fine art in those circles. It was a blessing on this night, for she couldn't have been less in control of her own forces.

The driver pulled up before the clinic and Bess was out of the carriage before he could even descend and help her out.

"I don't know how long I'll be—" she said to the driver.

"I'm to stay with you, miss."

159

She could see his eyes stray to the shabby buildings, the refuse on the walkways. A small crowd had gathered around the steps up to the clinic door and many of the people were decidedly not of the social strata to be found on Beacon Hill that evening.

"Thank you," she said simply and pushed her way through the crowd of onlookers. She took the steps two at a time, despite her gown, and burst through the doors, breathless.

"I'm so sorry I had to call you away from your party," Irene said, coming forward, her hair down in a thick braid over her shoulder. "But I just couldn't—you wouldn't believe—"

Bess put her hand out to her friend, even as her own horrified gaze took in the sight around her.

# Chapter Six

Cases of supplies and medicines had been up-ended and overturned, papers strewn about like the leaves out on the Common. Obscenities were scrawled on the walls—the walls that she and Irene had themselves scrubbed and whitewashed to make the place clean and bright. Ink was seeping into the floor in one corner, while iodine dripped down the face of the smashed mantel clock. Chairs were broken, light fixtures wrenched from the walls, clean bandages unfurled and draped over the messes on the floor.

"What happened?" she whispered. "What . . . how . . . ?"

*"Who* is the question I want answered," Irene said. Irene, who was cool and calm in the face of the worst sights, sufferings and pains, choked on her words, and Bess saw tears sparkle in her eyes. "And then I want to know why."

"A madman, surely," Bess murmured, still stunned by the rack and ruin around her.

"Not so mad as to leave yer safe untouched." A stout policeman entered the room from the doorway of the little office. "Was there anythin' in it, Mrs. Warner?"

Irene nodded. "Not a great deal, Lieutenant Castleberry. Most of my patients can't pay much. I keep only a little cash—perhaps fifty dollars—for the out-of-pocket needs of the clinic."

"Well, yer out of pocket for it now, I'd say," the man said, making a note on his pad. "The inside o' that safe is the cleanest thing in this place, to be sure."

"Oh, dear." Irene sat down and covered her mouth with her hands.

Bess squatted beside her, her satin skirts ballooning around her. "Irene, it's fifty dollars. I can replace that easily."

Irene shook her head. "No. I just remembered. I had the money for the rent in an envelope, ready to carry to the leasing agent tomorrow."

Bess felt her heart sink. "In the safe?"

Irene's eyes lifted to hers, wide with anguish. "Yes," she whispered.

"Oh, dear."

"Yes. It would be one thing if it were only the petty cash, but the cash, the rent, and all the repairs and replacements—Bess, whatever are we to do?"

Bess chewed on her lip for a moment. Then it came to her. It couldn't be more providential.

"I'll have the money before the end of the month, and then some. Do you think you can persuade the leasing agent to give us a week's extension, given the circumstances?"

"I can try. But how can you possibly raise so much money in so short a time?" Irene took Bess's hand in hers. "You've already gone begging for us to your friends so many times and they've been so generous. How can you ask for more?"

"Never mind how," Bess said, starting to grin. "You wouldn't believe me if I told you. You work on the leasing agent and I'll manage the rest."

"If you don't mind, Miss Warning," Lieutenant Castleberry interjected, "my men'll be needin' a list of medicines that was taken. Some of 'em may show up on the streets, as you may know."

Irene looked stricken. "Bess, this is dreadful," she murmured.

Bess gave her a quick hug. "Don't worry. And don't punish yourself. You had no way of knowing someone would do this."

"You're right. We have to think of the people who need this facility, don't we?"

"And who need your fine skill and caring heart."

"Miss Doctor Warman?"

The two women smiled at one another. "Go, do, before he mangles your name beyond all recognition and you forget who he's talking to," Bess whispered. "And then get some rest. Put a closed-for-repairs sign on the door and sleep in late tomorrow, please. I'll meet you here at nine o'clock."

"Nine o'clock?"

"Don't look so shocked," Bess said with a grin. "People have been known to sleep as late as nine-thirty!"

Bess settled herself back into the Appletons' carriage and gave the driver directions to her home. She was in no mood to return to a party, not after this. And not after her dreadful encounter with

Ben on the dance floor. No, she needed to be home, in her own room.

The room that was still under repairs since Ben's recent escapades. The man was nothing but trouble. And he wanted Henri!

Well, he was not going to get him. She would think of a way to ensure that the little gray cat didn't fall into the hands of that two-faced weather vane, Ben Carruthers. Or perish in the attempt!

Henri the little gray cat was sitting comfortably on the settee next to Gisella Lowell. He gave a desultory lick to one of his paws and looked up at the Mistress.

"*Oui*," she said, tapping her chin with one tapered fingertip. "This does seem to be *très compliqué!*"

The cat raised its back and stretched. Gisella stroked it idly, her bright gaze falling on the pleasant fire that danced in the hearth.

"Mmrr," it murmured.

"Yes, quite so, *mon* Henri. They do indeed seem to be most uncommonly stubborn. And yet such passion, such feeling! How can we make them know it?"

Henri hopped off the settee and stalked to the bookcase. Sidling up to the lowest shelf, he rubbed against a set of well-worn books, bound in ancient but carefully kept leather. He tilted his head toward Gisella.

"A spell, you think?" she asked, rising. "Hmmm. They did prove susceptible to the dreaming charm you cast over them."

"Rrrmr."

She chose one of the gilt-edged volumes and carried it back to the settee. Slowly, she turned the pages, tracing the narrow columns of writing with one finger. "Let's see . . . charms for sleep, invisibility, shape-changing—what of shape-changing? You could—*comment?*"

The cat repeated its soft mew.

"Ah, that's what I thought you were saying. So, you don't believe it would be a good idea for you to change into human form and challenge our Mr. Carruthers for Miss Fielding's hand? I agree. Mr. Carruthers is not the sort to feel proprietary over any lady until she has spoken her own devotion, and Miss Fielding is not easily moved by male charm, magic or no."

Gisella shook her head. *"Non, mon Henri le plus fidèle,* we must come up with something that brings them together rather than tests them by estrangement. Here—I have it!"

The cat bounded over and sat on her lap to look where she pointed. He put a soft paw over one short passage.

"Yes," Gisella said. "That was the very one I chose. Do you think you can work such a charm on these two warring lovers?"

For his answer, he bumped his head against her arm. She laughed softly and rubbed behind his ears.

"Henri, my dear young friend, I believe this is more fun than a night on the Champs-Elysees. If only my Alexander were here to share it."

Loud purring floated up from the cat, who was writhing against her hand. It laid a paw on her arm and bumped her chin.

*"Merci,* Henri," she said, her gaze soft and distant. "I love you, too."

\*     \*     \*

Ben folded the newspaper and scowled. The Bennet Street Clinic had been burglarized and ransacked, the report said. Losses were estimated in the thousands of dollars.

He was furious with Bess, but not angry enough to take delight in this news. Just because she was a harridan with a heart of brick and a tongue like a penknife didn't mean that the clinic wasn't a worthy establishment.

She must be stricken, he thought. That was a great deal of money—

"Oh, no," he exclaimed, jumping up. Money! She needed money more than ever now. And how was she to obtain it?

The cat.

He smacked his fist against his palm. Damn! Could matters get any worse? First he had made an utter fool of himself in her room, chasing after the silly feline. Then he'd imagined he was in love with her, besotted just because of something he overheard. He knew men, how they'd say almost anything over cigars and good whiskey. That was likely all it was. And last of all he'd allowed himself a moment of sympathy for the chit just because of a burglary in a notoriously bad neighborhood.

*Three times a fool, that was Ben Carruthers.*

Well, no more. The cat was to come to him shortly and he was going to take full advantage of it. Let Bess Fielding go find the money she needed among all her rich friends and relations. That befitted a woman. But he was a man who had to make his way in the world. He couldn't expect charity from anyone, nor did he want it. He'd earn his ten thousand by showing the little gray minx the best time in its short little furry life!

Buoyed by his anger and renewed resolve, he

dressed and went off to work. The offices of Duke
& Company were as bustling as ever and he was
soon lost in the usual round of meetings, visits to
warehouses, reviewing manifests and setting up
orders for goods of every kind. Statehood for the
Dakota Territories, Washington and Montana
meant yet another boom in Duke's affairs as people's confidence in their futures rose. It was while
he was sorting through mail orders from the west
that he saw the slouching fellow emerge from Tom
Duke's office.

Bundled in an overcoat and a hat, even in the
cozy warmth of the coal-heated building, he
looked nothing like your run-of-the-mill Duke &
Company customer. Nor was he an employee; Ben
made it a point to know everyone in the company,
from janitors to partners.

His curiosity roused, he slipped out of his office
and followed the man, at a distance, down the
stairs. At the ground floor, just before the front
doors of the Duke Building, the man suddenly
turned and confronted Ben.

"Why're you after me?" came a rusty voice from
deep within the overcoat's upturned collar.

Ben raised his hands. "Just wondering who you
might be," he said, smiling affably. "I make it a
point to know everyone I work with."

The man looked him up and down contemptu-
ously. "I don't work with no one."

"Sorry. My mistake."

"That's true enough." The dark fellow turned
and sent a spray of tobacco juice arcing toward a
corner. With one last sour glance in Ben's direction, he sauntered out.

Ben climbed the stairs and found Tom Duke in
the hall near his office. "Who was that old rascal

that was just here?" he asked, grinning. "Looked like he could use a bath in mineral spirits."

Tom shook his head. "No idea who you mean."

Ben stared quizzically. "Wasn't there a scruffy, dark fellow in your office just a few moments ago?"

Tom raised his shoulders. "Nobody here but us robber barons," he said with a smile. "Say, did you get an order from those Norwegians out in Seattle?"

Ben let the matter slip past. Either Tom was telling the truth or he was telling Ben in subtle terms that it was none of his business. It wasn't up to Ben to figure it out, at least not when business was booming.

The days passed quickly and the little gray cat with the enigmatically smiling face finally moved into his bachelor quarters. Ben found he liked the companionable little fellow who accompanied him about his rooms, padded around the edge of the tub when he bathed and who seemed to always know and quietly understand his moods.

"Not bad, just the two of us, eh, Henri, old fella?" Ben asked, rubbing his knuckles on the cat's soft head. "Two males on their own in the world, beholden to no one, ready for adventure at a moment's notice."

"Frrrp."

Two days passed without incident, but on the third day, when Ben returned home from work, he found the front door unlocked and the cat missing. He sped from room to room, searching under beds and in cupboards, but Henri was nowhere to be found.

It was on his third pass through the parlor that he found the handkerchief. Of frothy Irish lace, the tiny square of lawn at the center bore the white embroidered initials E.A.F. Elizabeth Abigail Fielding.

He was out the door in a flash, on his way to Beacon Hill to confront the thief. So bent was he on his revenge that he failed to notice one of the Fielding carriages as it passed him, moving at a respectable clip, toward his own part of town.

When Henri had shown up on her windowsill, Bess had been delighted to see him.

"So, you came back, eh?" she asked, scooping him into her arms for a cuddle. "I can't blame you. I'm only surprised it took you so long."

"Frrp."

"Hungry?" she asked. "Why don't we find a little something for you in the kitchen?"

A bowl of cream seemed to please the visitor, though the pastry chef and the cook both frowned their extreme displeasure at the sight of any live animal's presence in the well-scrubbed kitchens of the Fielding household. Bess assured them she'd take all the blame.

"He came blocks and blocks by himself, just to get here," she told them, stroking the luxurious gray pelt. "I'm sure Mr. Carruthers has been treating him just abomin—Oh, no!" she shrieked.

The pastry chef, who had been checking the cake pans in the oven, jumped at her scream, allowing the heavy metal door to slam shut. The room went silent.

Slowly, with a look of exquisite pain on his face, he opened the oven door and peered in. The cook groaned as he lifted out what would have been a light and airy yellow sponge cake, save for the large crater in its golden center.

"Oh, no—oh, I do beg your pardon, Luc," Bess pleaded, "but you don't know what he's done! The miserable cad! He won't get away with it!"

She swept the cat into her arms and stormed upstairs. The cook looked at the chef, who gazed with deep sorrow at his fallen masterpiece.

"A bit touched in the head, is what I hear," she told him comfortingly.

Almost immediately, Bess was at the Regale Hotel, carrying Henri up the stairs to Ben's apartment. The cat was tucked inside a hatbox—she had apologized profusely before setting him in there—and she was gaining indignation with every step.

"What a mean, low trick," she muttered. Dropping the cat at her uncle's house just so that he could arrive, all innocence, and claim that she took Henri on purpose just to make it look like he, Ben, wasn't fit to care for the animal. He'd been underhanded before, and this was no different.

She knocked on the door of Number Ten and waited, tapping her toe with impatience. When no answer came, she rapped again, harder.

"Fitzz," came the sound from the hatbox.

The door swung open.

"Ben Carruthers?" Bess called, stepping across the threshold. "I know you're in there, hiding like the coward I know you are!"

There was no answer.

"You're not going to get away with it," she called, stepping into his parlor. "I have the cat with me and he's going to stay with you until Gisella Lowell says I can take him home with me for good."

Her voice fell silent against the simple striped wallpaper and the good pieces of dark furniture that stood about the room. Where was he? Ben was tricky, but was he so idiotic as to hide from her when she knew what he was up to and confronted him with it? No, that was not his style. He'd come and try to talk his way out of it.

"I'm going to leave the cat right here," she called out. "Your little trick didn't work."

Something pricked at her. His door had been unlocked. It was an hour at which most businessmen would be home before their hearths. Had something happened to him?

A piteous little cry came from within the hatbox.

"Oh, I'm sorry, little one," she said, setting the box down on top of a nearby table. "You must be suffocating—"

The cat shoved the lid of the box open and made a wild dash out of the room. Bess hiked up her skirts and raced after it.

"Henri! Henri, come back. You mustn't just run off. I don't know this place."

She located him in the kitchen, standing on the counter, tail twitching. She relaxed.

"Still hungry?" she asked, approaching him. "I'm sure Mr. Carruthers has been stuffing you with lobster and fresh crabmeat, if I know his ill-begotten ways."

She went to the pantry door and searched for the icebox. Sure enough, there was cream, fish, butter, lobster, crab and even a dozen fresh oysters waiting for the cat's pleasure.

"I'm surprised he didn't lay in a supply of mice," Bess commented, taking some of the crabmeat. "Just wait, it'll occur to that scheming brain of his." She shut the pantry door and saw that the cat was gone. "Oh, not again," she moaned.

Setting the crab on the sideboard, she went in search of the wandering Henri.

171

# *Chapter Seven*

Ben Carruthers's apartment was an intriguing place. As she went from room to room in her search, she discovered some very revealing bits of information regarding her childhood friend and latter-day nemesis. For one thing, it was obvious that he did read and read a great deal, if his library was any indication. Floor-to-ceiling bookcases lined the walls, and comfortable chairs and a well-worn leather sofa clustered around the fireplace.

In the bath, she noted with amusement that he failed to hang up his towels on the rack provided and that the whole place smelled appealingly spicy. "Bay rum," she murmured, recalling how her late father had doted on that scent.

But still no cat.

In his bedroom, she found books piled on the bedside table, a plate of leftover cheese and biscuits and a veritable mountain of pillows heaped at the head of the large mahogany bedstead. She hesitated to step inside such an intimate place in a bachelor's apartment, but a soft mewing and scratching from the deep wardrobe propelled her forward.

"So, you got yourself trapped," she called softly, pulling at the heavy brass handle. It refused to yield. She looked below the latch and saw the keyhole. She heaved a sigh of exasperation.

"All right, wee one," she called to the cat. "You've managed to get yourself locked in, I see. A moment, and I'll find the key."

She turned, surveying the room. Where would Ben keep the key to his armoire? Why would anyone need to keep his clothing locked up in his own home, anyway? she wondered.

It didn't matter. She couldn't leave Henri locked inside. Who knew when Ben might come rolling in? It could be hours from now or it could be moments.

"Saints preserve me," she cried softly, realizing her peril.

Frantically, she began to pull open drawers, tossing aside papers and packets, cigars and matches, whatever came to hand that wasn't a key. She hunted through the bedroom, with no result. She raced through the other rooms, upending boxes and rifling through cupboards. Still no key of any sort.

The kitchen and pantry were her last hopes. Flour dusted her hands, cornmeal spilled across the front of her dress, tea and coffee scented the air around her. Her anxiety built to a fever pitch as she rooted through the potato bin and then shoved pitchers and coffee cups aside in the china cupboard, leaving brown fingerprints on their pristine surfaces.

The sound of male voices in the hall outside the front door nearly stopped her heart. In a panic, she thought to hide in the pantry, but it was too close to suppertime. He or his housekeeper would be there in a moment.

Fleet as the wind, she raced for the back of the apartment. It would at least take him time to get back there, allowing her at least a moment to discover a hiding place. If Ben Carruthers were to find her tearing up his apartment in search of a key to his personal wardrobe in order to let out the cat he would claim she had kidnapped in the first place—well, by its very complicated nature, it was unthinkable.

She heard footsteps in the hall. Her only choice was the bedroom. Under the bed? She couldn't possibly get all her skirts under there. And the cat was still in the armoire.

Panicked, she yanked on the brass handles and miraculously, the heavy mirrored doors swung open. She shoved aside suits and shirts and climbed inside, just as the footsteps sounded outside the bedroom door.

"I'll be with you in a moment, Carl," she heard Ben call nearby. "I just want to shed my jacket."

Quickly, fervently, she prayed that the armoire had a trap door in its floor that would open now and swallow her up.

Ben shrugged out of his coat and tossed it on the bed. His fingers went up to loosen his tie but halted when his eyes fell on his nightstand.

"What the—"

The drawer of the nightstand stood open and his

books had been flung to the floor. He turned slowly, surveying the room. While it hadn't exactly been ransacked, lampshades were slightly askew, the bedcovers were rumpled—something Mrs. Johanssen wouldn't have permitted—and the portraits on the mantel had been shuffled.

He retraced his steps through the hall, checking each room as he went. Things were definitely amiss.

Carl waited for him in the front hall. "Has the cat returned?" he asked cheerfully.

Ben shook his head, then shrugged. He proceeded to the kitchen, Carl at his heels.

"Something wrong, old fellow?"

Ben nodded slowly as he crossed to the pantry and went inside. He took in the condition of the shelves and bins and nodded again.

"What is it?" Carl asked.

"Either the estimable Mrs. Johanssen has given up her Methodist ways and has taken to the jug with a vengeance," Ben replied, "or I've had a visitor."

"The cat?"

"Something like a cat. But I'm sure they're gone now." Ben turned and put a hand on his friend's shoulder. "Why don't you go ahead to the club and I'll meet you there. I'm sorry I was such a wild man at the Fieldings', but I was sorely pressed."

"Think no more of it. Just hie yourself down in time for supper. I hear that Throckmorton's back from the Continent and has a tale or two to relate that is decidedly not for mixed company."

"Uh-huh," Ben said distractedly, guiding his friend to the door. "I'll see you later."

He shut the front door behind Carl and started out on another quick review of the rooms. The foyer yielded nothing. The dining room was minimally disturbed. The parlor was decidedly ruffled and featured a lady's hatbox set prominently on one of the tables. The library desk and tables were awry, but he was grateful the shelves had not been routed.

That left his bedroom. And he was fairly certain what—and who—he would find there.

He slowed as he approached the door and went in quietly, taking care to step onto the soft area rug that centered the room. He paused, listening and looking about him.

Then he saw it: the merest scrap of rose taffeta peeking out from the very bottom edge of the wardrobe door. A wicked grin spread over his features.

"I think I'll have a bath before I go out, Carl," he called out into the hall. "Make yourself at home. There's brandy in the library and some good smokes."

His image in the armoire mirror quivered, as if something moved inside. He could only imagine Bess's dismay that any moment now he might open the door and stand before her, naked as a newborn. She was quaking in there, he hoped.

Perching on the edge of the bed, he undid his boots and let them fall, loudly, to the floor. He snapped off his collar and cast it onto the polished floor near the wardrobe. Gleefully, he snapped his suspenders and bounced on the bed, making the springs squeak.

She was determined to stay in there, was she? He thumped his feet on the floor as he crossed to the doorway.

"What's that you say, Carl?" he called out to the

empty hall. "Sorry, can't come out now, old fellow. No trousers and so on."

He whirled and ran silently to the armoire. With a grand gesture, he yanked it open.

The scream she produced was gratifyingly shrill. He wanted to laugh at the sight of her, crammed into that little space, hands over her eyes, quivering like a willow in a high wind.

"You can uncover your eyes, Miss Fielding," he drawled. "I am not undressed, despite your worst fears. Or is it your deepest desires?"

She lowered her hands and then launched herself at him. "You blackguard!" she shrieked. "You unmitigated, overbearing, underhanded—"

He ducked under her swinging fists and backed off. "I?" he exclaimed. "Who the deuce broke into my home, stole my cat, then had the nerve to return, ransack the place and hide in my clothes cupboard?"

She advanced on him. "Stole your cat? Stole your cat? Who was it brought him to my house and left him, trying to make it look as though I had sunk so low as to kidnap him?"

"This is complete bosh! I left the cat here, in the safety of my own digs, where he is, I may say, more than content to remain!"

She swung at him again. He dodged to the side.

"You tried to make me think you were naked!"

"Serves you right for hanging about in a gentleman's bedroom."

"You're no gentleman!"

"You're no lady!"

"Cat thief!"

"Burglar!"

She leaped, hitting him square in the chest with her full weight. He toppled like a tree, landing on his back on the carpet, his head making a resounding thump. He lay there for a long moment, stunned, the world tipping and the sound of his own blood thundering in his ears.

"Oh goodness! Ben! Ben? Oh, dearest Ben, are you all right?"

She was on her knees next to him, peering into his face. Her hand caressed his cheek. He was only mildly surprised at the tenderness of her words and voice. It was . . . nice . . . he decided dreamily.

"Oh, no. You've hurt your head. Let me get you a cold compress! No, some scented water. A drink! Oh, all this time at the clinic and I can't think what to do when someone bumps his head—"

He grasped her hand, pulled her down to him and kissed her, long and thoroughly. When he released her, she was staring at him, wide-eyed but not outraged, he noted.

"Why—why did you do that?"

He sat up with a groan. "How else was I going to stop your sweet, chattering mouth?"

"Oh." Her fingers ran over the fresh-blushing lips he'd just tasted. The gesture made the world swim again. She grabbed for his shoulder. "Here, let me help you."

He leaned blissfully upon her, one arm snugly about her waist as he got to his feet. He couldn't recall what they had been fighting about, but it didn't matter now, did it? His lovely Bess was here, holding him, and he was holding her and maybe there could be more of those kisses. . . .

"You look very ill," she said, her astonishingly blue eyes searching his with a narrow glance.

"Oh, no. I'm fine." He smiled and leaned his forehead against hers. "I'm fine."

"Your wits are addled and it's my fault." She let

him go and he plopped onto the edge of the bed. "Oh, Ben, can you ever forgive me?"

"I'll try," he said, gesturing magnanimously.

"It's the cat. And the money. I got carried away and thought the worst of you." She knelt down next to him. "I don't know how I can make it up to you."

"Oh, I think I can think of something," he murmured, reaching for her.

"No," she said, rising just out of his reach. "I must make amends."

He tilted forward, trying to take her into his arms, caught himself just before he fell to the floor. She paced about the room.

"I should go to Mrs. Lowell and tell her—"

"Mr. Carruthers? I'm here to leave your laundry, sir."

Bess froze, shock registered in her every feature. Ben shook his head to clear it.

"Quick," he whispered. "It's my housekeeper. Into the wardrobe."

"The laundry?" she asked, waving her hands about.

"You're right. Lord, what to do—uh, duck down on the other side of the bed. I'll keep her at bay."

She darted around the bed and disappeared out of sight just as the firm footsteps of Mrs. Johanssen came to a halt at the bedroom door.

"Mr. Carruthers," she said, "I thought you was not home. I yust brought you your laundry. Shall I put it away for you?"

"Uh, no. No. I—uh, I was just changing and I'm in a hurry to meet some fellows at my club. Perhaps you could put it in the guest room?"

"Ja, I can do that. Then I have to be off, unless there's someting else you'll be needin' this night."

"No, Mrs. Johanssen. Thank you, but I'm fine."

She peered at him. "You look kinda puny, if you don't mind my sayin'. A cup of tea won't take but a moment, sir."

"No, I'm fine. I just need some peace and quiet, that's all."

"Very well. I'll be here first thing in the mornin', same as always."

"Good night, Mrs. J."

Ben heaved a sigh of relief as he at last heard the front door close behind his worthy house-keeper. He turned to see the cat, Henri, seated on the bed, looking at him with that enigmatic smile.

"You can come out now, Miss Fielding," Ben said, giving the cat a suspicious stare. "Our mutual friend is here on my bed."

"I didn't kidnap him," Bess said, rising and brushing off her skirts.

"And I didn't leave him at your uncle's house so that it would look like you kidnapped him."

They eyed one another cautiously. They turned as one to look at the cat, who was now blissfully engaged in washing its face.

"It couldn't," Ben said.

"No, it certainly couldn't."

"Well. That's that. Matter settled."

"Yes, I suppose so."

He stood, looking at her. He decided he liked her a bit disheveled. She looked deliciously soft and vulnerable, two words he'd never associated with Bess Fielding before. He was reminded of the dreams he'd had of holding her, in this very bed.

"Oh," she said, jumping and coloring. "I must go. It's getting late and I don't know if I should—certainly I can't—I mean, you and I shouldn't—"

He stepped closer. "Shouldn't we?"

Her eyes went wide. "No, I think not. Don't you?" she asked in a small voice.

"No."

# *Chapter Eight*

He took another step closer to her. He could just catch a hint of the creamy vanilla scent of her now. It curled around his senses like a trail of smoke.

"But, I—oh, my!"

She gave a small squeak as his arms came about her, snugging her close in his embrace. He found he liked the tight curve of her waist, bracketed by her very proper corset. The feel of it reminded him of what softness was hidden beneath. It promised secrets that might only be revealed to a man in the stillness and the lamplit privacy of the night, secrets he alone would unveil.

"I don't think we should be doing this," she said, her voice husky.

"You said you would make it up to me. I like to pay my debts promptly, don't you?" He leaned forward and placed a mere breath of a kiss on the bare spot just above her collar.

Her reply was a quickly indrawn breath. Encouraged, he slid his hands over her back, pressing her against him and taking sweet, small tastes of her neck, her jaw, her cheek, her lips. His boldness was rewarded with a soft moan, deep within her and a sense that she was melting in his arms, warming him as she flowed against him.

"Bess," he whispered. "How could I know those argumentative lips of yours would taste so sweet?"

He didn't wait for a response, only raised his hand, tilted her head back and kissed her, parting her lips, tasting of her, nibbling at her. All the world was in that kiss, he felt. All his world, all his hopes and dreams. He wanted to somehow make the touch of his lips speak more than the torrents of words they'd exchanged over the years. He wanted to pour his soul into her with just this one kiss.

When he lifted his head at last, he was almost dizzy. She clung to him and they swayed together for a moment. Slowly, she lifted her arms and pushed herself back.

"We shouldn't do this," she said.

"No?"

"We're too sensible to fall into such an easy trap."

"Are we?" He gazed at her. He didn't feel in the least bit trapped. He felt oddly liberated, as if he'd been waiting all his life, breath held, just to kiss Elizabeth Pile-on-the-Agony Fielding. But perhaps it was just a dream, again. A nice moment that meant nothing in the grand scheme of things.

"I must go," she murmured. "I shouldn't be here."

"I suppose not," he said reluctantly. "How did you get in, anyway?"

"Your front door was open."

"The devil it was. I recall locking it before I rushed out to your uncle's house."

She shrugged. "All the same, it was open, and Henri and I just came in. I assumed that because it was open, you were at home."

"Curious."

He cast a glance at the windows. It was already nearly dark. "I'd better get you home."

"Oh my goodness." She stopped, stock-still in the middle of the room. "What if someone sees me coming out of your house, alone, at this hour?"

"I'll stand guard and you can go when I signal."

"But I have no carriage! I let the driver go when I went in, though I can't think why. How could I be so stupid?"

"Hmm." He stood back, surveying her from head to toe. "It'll be a stretch, but I think I have a solution."

Not long after, Mr. Ben Carruthers was seen leaving his apartment, jaunty in his evening clothes. Another young man walked with him, in street clothes, a bowler hat clapped low on his head. Mr. Carruthers and his companion climbed into his carriage and rode away without exciting a word of comment from anyone.

Except Helena, when she encountered her cousin stealing up the back stairs, dressed in a man's suit and carrying her own clothes under her arm.

"Please don't ask," Bess told her wearily. "Let's

just say it's close to Halloween. Right now, all I want are a hot bath and a bed."

Bess awoke with the chill of the approaching winter spreading its fingers under her partly open window. She ran to shut it, then raced back to bed and huddled under the covers.

The cold was sobering and she was glad of it. She'd made an utter fool of herself yesterday and she had to face that. Not only had she been wrong about Ben trying to trick her with Henri, but she'd hidden in his wardrobe and then succumbed to his kisses. Such idiocy!

No matter how many dreams she had about Ben Carruthers—and last night had borne a whole new crop of them—she wasn't in love with him. She wasn't in love with anyone.

No matter how lovely it had felt to be held in his arms and hear his voice so close to her ear, she wasn't going to go all moony over some man. And certainly not Ben Tyrant-to-Women Carruthers.

And no matter how much her traitorous body urged her to devise ways to make him kiss her again, she wasn't going to get herself compromised into a love affair or into marriage. She was too sensible to fall for that.

She bounced out of bed and began to prepare for the day. Irene needed her. She had work to do at the clinic.

Besides, in less than three days, she would be the owner of mischievous little Henri and the delighted benefactress of the renaissance of the Bennet Street Clinic. No man was worth sacrificing that.

She hurried to the clinic before any more treacherously sensual thoughts or foolish love notions could overtake her. When she arrived, she saw that while the clinic was very nearly restored to cleanliness, something was troubling Irene. Over a break for tea, Bess urged her to talk. She didn't like what she heard.

"Are you sure?" Bess asked.

"As sure as I'm sitting here." The expression in Irene's eyes reflected the grim set of her mouth. "Thomas Duke is the owner of this building. And he wants us out."

Bess sank into a chair. "But—why? We meet the rent, we maintain the rooms, we provide a beneficial service in this neighborhood. Why should he wish to be rid of us?"

Irene began sorting through the papers that were still in disarray after the break-in. "I imagine he wants to use the building for more profitable purposes. And besides . . ." She ducked her head, avoiding Bess's eyes. "We are no longer in a position to meet the rent and I have no idea how long it will be before we can begin to provide any sort of service here again."

Bess put out her hand. "You mean it's all gone? All of it?"

Irene shrugged. "What there was of it. It will cost three times what we have just to replace the medicines and instruments. Most of them were donated, you recall. Then there are the repairs, the furniture to be replaced, and that doesn't even begin to cover an honorarium for a qualified nurse or a less-than-qualified orderly, let alone an assisting physician."

"How could this happen?" Bess sank her chin onto her fist. "We couldn't be more completely ruined if this had been planned."

Irene was silent. Bess felt a small shiver of apprehension. "Irene? Is there more?"

The doctor sighed. "I can't."

"Can't what?"

"I can't be sure. It's best to say nothing."

"Not to me it's not. I say something even when there's nothing to say, and you definitely are not saying something." Bess threw up her hands. "Now, see, I've lost all sense. Tell me," she urged, taking Irene's elbow. "You know you can tell me."

"It's what you said. About it being planned."

Bess gulped. "You believe it was planned? By whom—oh, my lord."

"I know he's Ben's employer and his friend. But it's all too perfect. No other suites or offices in this building were broken into, nothing harmed. Only ours. I haven't talked to any of the other tenants, but I'm willing to wager that we're the only ones who were unwilling to move."

"But Tom Duke doesn't need to stoop to this sort of low trickery. He's already richer than Croesus and a gentleman besides."

Irene looked at her, a plea in her gray eyes. "See? It's likely I'm wrong. You know him better than I. That's why I didn't want to say anything."

Bess rose. "I've never known you to be wrong about something this important." She began pulling on her coat.

"Where are you going?"

"To the offices of Duke & Company."

"You can't mean to confront him?" Irene took her arm. "I shan't allow it, Bess. I can manage."

Bess faced her, her eyes dark with purpose. "You're a doctor, my dear. Be one; it's what you do so wonderfully well. But when it comes to dealing with the rich and mighty of Boston—let me take the lead."

\* \* \*

The gray cat had waited for exactly the right moment, then darted out of the carriage under the swirling hem of the woman's skirt. An ash can by the steps afforded him a convenient hiding place until she had gone up the steps and into the building.

With his tail at a jaunty angle, he had trotted off. Around the corner, down the alleyway, and then he was there. The woman's smell was strong in the piles of board and paper and plaster that were mounded at the back-door stoop.

This was the place she went to when she came home with the very odd scents on her clothes and shoes. This was the place she was worried about, the place she wanted him for.

The woman needed him. And she needed the man.

The man would have to wait. For now, the cat would find a way to lessen his lady's worries. It might take a while, but the opportunity would come and he and Mistress Gisella would work their magic together. He was in the right place.

"Bess? Here?" Ben bolted up out of his desk chair.

Carl grinned at Ben. "Awfully eager, aren't you?"

Ben sat down hastily. "No, no. I was just surprised, is all. Why would she be here to see me?"

"Did I say she was here to see you?"

Ben glared. "Watch yourself, boy. I don't josh well this time of day."

"Mr. Carruthers?"

She was there to see him. He shot a cold glance at Carl, who simply widened his Cheshire cat grin.

"If you will excuse me, Miss Fielding," Carl said, backing out of the office, "I have work to finish before I embark on my wedding trip."

"Of course," she murmured.

Ben rose. "Forgive me, Miss Fielding," he muttered, coming around his desk. "I was caught unawares. Won't you have a seat?"

"Thank you," she said, taking the chair he drew up.

He perched on the edge of the desk, enjoying the look of her. Her cheeks were rosy from the brisk air outside, her lovely dark hair tucked up under an emerald green hat. But her expression was grave, a look he wasn't accustomed to seeing in warmhearted, witty Bess Fielding's blue eyes.

"What is it?" he asked, his tone softening.

"I've heard something . . . a rumor."

"A rumor? What about? It's not like you to listen to gossip, at least not if memory serves." He smiled. "As I recall, you always said that any stories you thought up on your own were better than the work of a dozen tattletales."

The corners of her mouth raised slightly. "That's because you were always tattling, Benjie Carruthers."

"It was my only defense," he protested, laughing. "You tormented me past all endurance and my mother told me it wasn't nice to hit little girls, even when they pasted your trousers to a chair seat."

Her smile broadened. "You were a sight, trying to wriggle off both the chair and your trousers, in order to get free."

"And your mother made you write notes of apology to me, my mother, my tailor and the upholsterer."

She joined his laughter then, and he was struck again by her beauty. "Now you look like the Bess

I remember," he said softly. "No hat, no jewel, no gown becomes you so much as your smile."

She colored instantly and looked away. "I was going to say something much the same to you," she murmured.

"Why don't you?"

She shook her head. "I don't have the words. Is that not rare?"

He chuckled. "I would say so, if it didn't mean risking a sound beating over the head with your umbrella."

She looked at him at last. "Have I been so truly awful?"

"No. No more than I."

"Lord, then I must have been intolerable. But now . . ."

"Yes? Now?"

"I can't tell you."

"Then perhaps you'll let me tell you, sweet Bess." He paused, gathered his courage and took the plunge. "I have one or two words to say to you. First of all, that I'm sorry I've been such a tyrant to you these past years. I think perhaps it was my way of avoiding a dangerous truth. I don't know any other way to tell you this, so I'll just say it straight out—I love you."

Her lips formed a perfect *O*. She looked away again.

"I know. It's ridiculous, of course."

"No," she cried softly. "No more ridiculous than what I was going to say to you."

"And what was that?"

"I told you, I don't have the right words. I can't tell you all that I'm feeling, how much I'm feeling. It's as if my heart were many times larger than it was but a week ago, I have so much—" She broke off.

"So much hate? Derision? Revulsion?"

"Very well—love! There, are you satisfied?"

He was laughing as he knelt down before her. "Only you and I could court in such a contentious fashion! Bess, sweetness, you love me!"

"Yes."

Her answer was both joyous and tearful. He reached up to catch a tear as it spilled over the heavy fringe of her lashes.

"Don't cry, sweet," he whispered. "We love each other. Isn't that a good thing?"

To his astonishment, she threw her arms around him and kissed him, hard, on the mouth. His arms came up and pulled her close, his whole being suddenly overtaken with the power of her response, the wonder of these wild new feelings.

"Yes," she whispered fiercely against his neck. "Yes, it's the most wonderful thing in the world."

"Then why are you crying?"

She lifted her tearstained face. "Because I can't love you."

"Uh-huh," he said slowly. "And why is that?"

"Because you work here."

"And you'd prefer I were unemployed?"

She whacked him on the shoulder. "No. See? You don't understand me at all."

He took her hands in his, partly to comfort her, partly to protect himself from another attack. "Take me with you," he said, struggling for patience. "You love me, but you can't love me because I work here and I don't understand you, is that right?"

"No! Yes. Listen." She cast a glance at the door. "May we speak in confidence?"

"Sweet, if we haven't been speaking in confidence thus far, I can only tremble at the idea of what you might want to say to me next—wait! Wait, before you assault me again, I'll go shut the door."

When the door was closed, she sighed and shook her head. "I know you must think it the height of impropriety, but I must be sure that no one else is listening."

"I'm all attention." He drew up his desk chair before her. "Tell me."

# Chapter Nine

"It's about the Bennet Street Clinic. You know that I work there and that I care deeply about it."

"I do."

"It is being closed down. Not by authorities, and not for lack of use. It is being closed because Thomas Duke wants it closed."

"Bess, that's silly. Why would Tom Duke want to close a charity hospital?"

"It is in his building. And he wants us out."

"Is that what he said?"

"No. At least not directly. Not as a true man, an honest man would."

Ben straightened. "What do you mean?" he asked slowly. "And mind what you say about my employer."

Her hands twisted together in her lap. "I don't know any other way to put it. But a week ago, the clinic was broken into. The other businesses in the building were also broken into, but little was taken and none were vandalized. Only the clinic. We lost every cent we had in the safe, and the whole suite of rooms was torn apart in the most vicious and destructive manner."

"What could this possibly have to do with Tom Duke?"

"Irene—Dr. Warren, who runs the clinic—has confided in me that Thomas Duke approached her this past summer and asked her to cut short her lease on the clinic. She refused, knowing as she does that it is a haven for that area of the city's poor. He asked again, and again she refused. She thought him a gentleman, but soon she began receiving threatening notes, which she has only just recently shared with me. She believes the other tenants have already given in to Mr. Duke's pressures. She is the last obstacle to his getting what he wants."

"But she has no proof that all these events happened on his orders?"

"No. But there can be no other explanation. The man is a villain."

"You don't know that."

"It's all the proof I require!"

Ben got up and paced about. He ran his hands over his hair, lost in thought.

His own suspicions leaped to the fore. Duke's business practices had often made him uneasy. But vandalism? Threatening women? Burglary? It seemed preposterous.

"Will you confront him?"

He halted, shocked. "I?"

"Yes, of course. You know he won't listen to the pleas of two women, nor would any judge or magistrate in the city. I need your help to stop this outrage." Her blue eyes no longer sparkled with tears. They snapped with fire.

"I cannot."

"You will not."

"He is my employer. Soon to be my partner, I hope. I cannot accuse him, especially not just on your word."

She stiffened and went pale. The light in her eyes went from blazing to freezing in an instant. She stood, gathering her coat about her.

"Very well, then. I am sorry to have bothered you, Mr. Carruthers. Good d—"

"Bess, no, don't go!" He caught her arm as she turned toward the door. "We can work this out somehow."

"I don't think so." Icicles hung from her words. "I had thought you a gentleman, but I see I was wrong."

"Bess—"

"I had thought you loved me, but I see I was wrong." Now her voice filled with tears.

He pulled her to him, made her face him. "I do love you and I won't let you deny that you love me. But do you really believe that Tom is behind these events?"

"As I live and breathe, yes."

"Then I'm your man. I'll speak to him."

Her eyes searched his face. "Truly?" she asked, her voice still choked.

"Truly."

This time it was he who did the kissing. And when they parted, he was more than converted to her cause.

Bill Sanderson was sleeping when the cursed animal went mad. His heavy overcoat bundled around him, a pint of rotgut, half empty, curled in his fist, he was minding his own business, snoring away on the old mattress in the alley. Next thing he knew, all the demons of hell itself were unleashed upon him in the form of one small gray cat.

For no reason he could think of, it had launched itself upon him, spitting, yowling, scratching, frightening him so quickly out of his stupor that he almost wet himself. The thing seemed to be everywhere at once—on his head, around his legs, ripping at his chest, nipping at his knees and ears in the same instant.

His bottle fell and smashed, drenching them both as he rolled over and over, wrestling with the creature. Then, as suddenly as it had begun, the cat quit, bounced a yard away down the alley and sat, tail twitching, watching him with eerie reddish eyes. He staggered to his feet, intent on wringing its miserable neck.

"Fzzzt."

Starting toward it, he toppled to the bricks, then sat up, shaking his head and blinking. The reason was evident: his bootlaces had been fastened together. He squinted blearily at the animal. The wretch was grinning at him!

"Think you're s' clever," Sanderson growled, ripping the laces apart. "I'll make mincemeat of your carcass!" He struggled to his feet and lunged toward the cat. It sat there, stone still, right up until the instant he knew he had it in his grasp. But when he clapped his hands around its neck, he found he held only air.

"RRRrrrwr."

He lumbered about in a circle. The cat was nowhere. Then it was there again, behind him.

Sporting that mocking smile. His rage was boundless.

"I'll skin you alive!" he roared, advancing on it once more.

The alcohol was still in his blood, so his going wasn't smooth, but on he came, his quarry dancing before him with a twitch of the tail and switch of the whiskers. Bill lunged, missed, gathered his forces, lunged again, missed.

On down the alley they went, the ragged man and the sleek little cat, him roaring and the cat only smiling. It was only a matter of time before they reached the street at the end of the alley, where the spectacle had gathered quite a crowd.

Sanderson had just caught the beast and was raising it over his head in triumph when a madwoman attacked him from behind.

"You're mad." Tom Duke puffed at his cigar and stared mildly at Ben.

"If I am, then so are Randolph, Dr. Irene Warren, Beckett of New York and the Boston Mercantile Bank."

"There's no way you can prove anything," Tom said, rising from his desk chair and going to the window. "Besides, you were in on it."

"I? Odd, I don't recall committing burglary and vandalism."

"Nor do I. That was all Sanderson's doing, and he was handsomely rewarded for his efforts. But you were in on the deals that brought me to this desperate state. You were the one who speculated with me, cut corners on the legalities and willingly signed off on all those shipments that somehow, tragically, never made it all the way out to those dangerous frontier territories. And you were the one who resold those same shipments to another poor fool, doubling our money."

"There was never any—"

"No, I was very careful. You're not as smart as you imagine. Or, at least, not until now. But you're right. I need that building. I've had to cover some deep losses as well as bribe some officials to keep silent about certain things." He turned, his broad shoulders silhouetted against the window. "Do you think I could do the same with you?"

Ben fell silent. All he'd worked for, all his hopes, were destroyed. Bess had been right in her suspicions about Duke, and it hadn't taken Ben long to uncover not only Duke's treachery at the clinic but a great many other things as well. Last night, after hours, he had returned to the office and searched through file after file in Duke's private safe, compiling evidence that was irrefutable. Somehow, he hadn't been surprised when Henri the cat had trotted into the office and explored with him.

Yet now it looked as if he might indeed be dragged under with Duke.

"I don't know," Ben said, crossing his arms and perching on a corner of the desk. He hoped he looked more confident than he felt. "I think we can come to an understanding, don't you?"

Duke's eyes gleamed. "Perhaps you're cleverer than I thought, Carruthers."

"Let's say that you cut me in for a partnership, eh? Full partnership, with full say in all Duke and Company dealings. How does that sound, for starters?"

"It might be arranged. If you agree to forget what you've found out."

"It might be arranged." Ben reached into Tom's humidor and drew out a cigar. "And why don't you take off for a bit of a hiatus, old fellow? See the country, take the Grand Tour, maybe?"

"And leave you here to run things?"

"Just in your absence, of course."

Duke's expression darkened. "Trying to squeeze me out won't work," he said. "I built this firm and I can take it down, and you with it."

"But I don't think you will. You've burnt too many bridges. I looked into your affairs in the South, as well. You don't have many friends left, Tom. Boston was your last refuge."

"I won't let you do this."

"Oh, but you will." Carl Randolph stood in the doorway.

Tom Duke's fury was coming to the fore. "You pale, green boy," he growled. "Go home, Randolph, and have your mummy help you dry behind the ears."

Ben drew out another cigar and handed it to Carl. "Duke here doesn't seem happy about our new partnership," he said, shooting a cool glance at their boss. "Perhaps what you have to say might cheer him along."

"This is trash," Duke said.

"Well, what you did to the Bennet Street Clinic certainly fits that description. And just in case you're feeling a wee bit unsettled, let me clear your conscience. Your man Sanderson gave you up." Carl clipped off the end of the cigar and held it as Ben applied a match. "Sang like a canary, that fellow." He turned to Ben with a wondering smile. "Had cat scratches all over him. Said a blue-eyed brunette assaulted him from behind and laid his head open with an umbrella. Can you beat that?"

"You'll never do this! No one will believe an old

rummy like Sanderson. And even so, there's no proof!"

"True," said Ben, holding out his cigar and admiring the drift of gray smoke from its glowing end. "But once all the other matters come to light, I think you'll be blamed for the Great Fire of '72 and the fall of Pompeii, don't you agree, Carl?"

"Indubitably."

"Get out," Duke snarled. "Get out. You've made your point. I'll have the papers to you in the morning, *partners.*"

Ben and Carl started for the door. "Oh," Ben said, turning about. "Just in case you might wish to skip town before those papers are signed, I took the liberty of having them drawn up and signed already. Carl here slipped them in with a pile of invoices. You've already signed."

Carl grinned. "I knew you'd never suspect anyone still wet behind the ears. My old nurse always said I'd go far with this face."

Tom Duke's only reply was a strangled oath.

"Ah, one more thing." Ben flung a companionable arm across Carl's shoulders. "This fellow's getting married in the morning. Hope you can make it to the wedding. Wouldn't do to start rumors flying in this old town, would it? It might hamper your future."

With that, the two men left the building of Duke & Company and headed for the Bennet Street Clinic, where a celebration was already underway.

Bess looked with longing at Ben's tall form capering around the front hall of the clinic, Irene struggling to keep up with his impromptu polka. Miracles had happened, all in the space of a few days. Tomorrow, after the wedding, they would go to Gisella Lowell's, and that would be the end of their connection. She was in love, but she knew there was no real reason behind it.

"Ten thousand dollars for your thoughts," a voice said next to her ear.

She turned, smiling shyly. "Aren't you being a bit premature, Mr. Carruthers? I thought the decision was up to Mrs. Lowell."

"Actually, I think it's up to Henri," Ben said, nodding to where that fellow was lapping up spilled ice cream. "But I want to tell you this now, before we go to Gisella's. I'm bowing out. You can have Henri and the cash."

"But why?"

"Well, I'm fairly sure that our charges against Tom Duke will hold. Add to that his signing over the firm to Carl and me, in large part, and I just don't need the money anymore. And much as I've grown fond of old Henri, I think he'll be happier with you. I'll probably be gadding about the country on business for quite some time."

She swallowed hard against the lump in her throat. So this *was* good-bye.

"That's very kind of you. I know the money will be put to good use here."

"Carl and I are already planning investments in the name of the clinic. That way there'll always be an income here. And, of course, the building is yours for as long as you wish to stay."

"That would be up to Irene, of course," Bess murmured.

"Bess, I—"

"Yes?" Her breath caught, waiting.

"I—I should be going. I have to get Randolph to the church on time tomorrow."

She smiled. "Yes. What a happy day for him and Helena."

"So it will be." He bowed. "Good-bye, Bess."

"Good-bye."

She watched as he and Carl bade good night to the few merrymakers left on the premises as the two men sauntered through the doors of the clinic. That was that, she thought.

She'd known it was too good to be true. She'd lost her wits, her good sense. It had been the passion of the moment, the excitement of the competition over the cat that had prompted them to think and act and even begin to believe that what they felt was love. Now that things were settled, there was no spark left. It was over.

She straightened up and began clearing away the party debris. "Heigh-ho," she sighed softly. "Many a good hanging has prevented a bad marriage. Perhaps it's just as well."

But later that night, in her bed in the chill darkness of her room, hot tears fell, and in the morning it took several cold compresses to soothe the headache that had sprung from her heartache.

# Chapter Ten

"There. You look stunning."

"Do I? Truly?" Helena's face was grave, despite the high color in her cheeks.

"Have you ever known me to lie?" Bess raised a hand. "Don't answer that," she said laughing. "But I promise you, you're a vision. And that gown is only a prop for my little cousin's natural loveliness."

Helena nervously touched the orange blossoms that held her delicate Venetian lace-trimmed veil. "I hope these stay on at least through the ceremony. Is it time? Papa's not here yet. He should be here, shouldn't he? Oh, Bess, what if he has Carl with him when he comes?"

Bess went to the door, her own heavy silk gown rustling with each step. She peeked out. "He's coming even now. And no bridegroom with him to chance ill-luck with a glimpse of his bride before the ceremony. Though I suspect that if Reverend Talcott doesn't pronounce you man and wife with all due haste, Carl is likely to astonish us all."

"Bess!" Helena's cheeks went scarlet.

There was no time to reply. Lionel stood in the doorway, resplendent in his deep gray morning coat.

"It's now or never, daughter," he said gruffly. "And if it's to be never, it won't matter to me, but your mother will have the most extravagant fainting spell ever seen on Beacon Hill."

"It's now, Papa," Helena said. "I'm quite sure."

"Then let's be off. Your young man is champing at the bit."

Helena held him still for a moment. "Let him wait," she said softly. "This is my last walk as my papa's daughter. In a few moments I'll be Carl's wife for the rest of my life. And though that thought makes me very happy, let's take our time, all the same."

Bess felt her own throat close as the two linked arms and proceeded to the flower-scented chapel. She almost wished . . .

"No," she whispered. This was Helena's day. She wouldn't let herself think about her own abandoned hopes.

She ran to catch up Helena's yards-long satin train and settle it before the open chapel doors. With a last loving hug, she took her place and began the procession down the long aisle to the altar.

Ahead of her, Carl and Ben waited, their faces more sober than she'd ever seen. She wanted to giggle. How frightened men became at the thought of marriage, even when it was clear that most of the advantages were on their side! Still, she knew that Carl and Helena were utterly right for one another.

How handsome Ben looked, she thought as she passed the halfway mark, the bouquet of orange blossoms and calla lilies fragrant in her arms. His light brown hair shone in the candlelight, and his unusually serious demeanor did have a certain charm about it. He looked solid, strong, and—

She turned her gaze quickly away and fixed it on the stained-glass window high above the altar. She must keep her mind off Ben or she'd not make it through the day.

At last, she reached the front and took her place before the minister. The strains of Mendelssohn's processional sounded, her cue to turn and face Helena and Lionel as they came down the aisle. Helena's radiant smile beamed out, even through the delicate mist of her veil. Bess couldn't help smiling in return. It wasn't exactly proper for a bride to look anything other than shy and demure on her wedding day, but Helena had never been one to hide her feelings. She was in love and glad simply to behold her groom, waiting to take her hand and keep it. Tender joy seemed utterly appropriate.

The ceremony began with the usual words of admonition and prayer and proceeded to the vows. Bess listened with only marginal attention as the minister pronounced that the state of matrimony was not to be entered into lightly and that if anyone present knew of any impediment to the joining of these two persons, they should speak now or forever hold their peace.

Bess smiled at him, then at Helena. No such announcements would be made at this wed—

"I do," Helena said softly.

Bess started and stared at her. What on earth? she thought. Could she possibly have heard what she thought she heard?

Then Carl spoke, removing all doubts about her hearing. "I do, too."

The minister frowned at them over his spectacles. A murmur of alarm and shock rippled back through the rows of assembled guests.

Reverend Talcott cleared his throat. "Miss Fielding, what have you to say?"

"I will not be married, sir, unless my cousin Elizabeth is married first."

"Helena!"

Bess felt as if the world were tilting on its axis. She lifted her bouquet to refresh herself. She loathed women who fainted at the slightest hint of emotion. Yet the scent of orange blossoms seemed only to make her giddier. From somewhere deep within her, hope began to bloom. She struggled to stuff it back in its place. Had the world gone mad? she wondered.

Reverend Talcott held up his hand. "A moment, please. Miss Helena, this is a most unorthodox, shall we say, objection. Are you quite sure you understood the question?"

Helena nodded, her veil shimmering. "I will not be married until my cousin is likewise married."

Bess tried again. "But you can't—"

"And I will not be married," Carl said, interrupting her with a raise of his hand, "until my friend Benjamin Carruthers is married."

"Now, see here," Ben cried, coming to life. "I—"

"Can you deny that you love Elizabeth?" Carl demanded.

"I can and do!"

"Oh-ho," said Carl, reaching into his pocket and pulling out a finely wrought gold ring. "Then why was this ring delivered to your office just two days ago?"

Ben made a grab for it. Carl held it away, peering closely inside its golden circle. " 'Sweet Bess—For Always. Love, Ben,' " he read aloud. "Now do you deny it?"

Helena broke in before Ben could reply. "And I have here a locket of my cousin's, in the shape of a heart, and inside it a lock of sandy brown hair and a scrap of paper containing the monogram B.E.C. in her own handwriting." She dangled the necklace before her.

Bess felt her whole face suffused in heat. "You told me you hadn't seen it," she said lamely.

The minister cleared his throat once more. "This is a most unusual circumstance. Is there—" He lowered his voice. "Is there any reason that these two must be married at once?" he asked, looking meaningfully at Ben.

"NO," Ben and Bess said at once.

"Yes!" Helena turned to Bess, then to Ben. "You must be married at once before each of you talks yourself out of it. You would not believe how these two can argue, Reverend."

"But where their love is concerned, they can't debate," Carl put in. "No amount of argument can change the love Helena and I have seen between these two."

"So they must be married now," Helena said firmly. "Otherwise," she said, turning large eyes on Ben, "Carl and I won't be married and you will be responsible for our deepest unhappiness."

Bess looked at Ben. He looked stunned for a moment, then, slowly, he began to grin.

"We've been hoodwinked," he said softly.

"By our own hands," she replied, the corners of her mouth twitching.

"Shall we?" he asked.

"All right," she said with mock sternness. "But only for the sake of Helena and Carl."

"Of course. And for the sake of that cat."

Bess looked where he pointed. Gisella Lowell sat on the far end of the front pew. On her lap, a soft white satin bow about his neck, Henri sat smiling.

"It seems you can't keep it safely at home where it belongs. You obviously need help." Ben moved to take her hands. "So, will you marry me, sweet Bess?"

"I will, my love," she answered, tears starring her vision. "After all, you already bought the ring and I hate waste, don't you?"

She went into his arms, laughing.

The two married couples exited the church in a storm of cheers and rose petals. As they made their way to the flower-trimmed carriages that waited on the street outside, Ben caught sight of a stocky fellow flanked by two uniformed police officers. The three stepped up to Tom Duke as he came down the steps of the chapel.

"Ben?" Bess asked, taking his arm. "What's happening?"

"Call it a wedding present," he said, watching as the officers placed his former employer in handcuffs.

Duke glared at Ben and Carl as he was led away. Ben tucked Bess's arm more tightly in his as he called out to the retreating figure, "Duke! You look glum, old fellow! 'Get thee a wife,' " he said, quoting Shakespeare.

Bess stooped and swept Henri up in her arms. "No, get thee a cat, sir," she called. "Get thee a cat!"

And with laughter and joy and the ringing of the church bells, they climbed into the carriages and trotted away to start the rest of their lives.

# One Magic
# Momemt

# Victoria
# Alexander

*This story is for Cathy Griffin, who went above and beyond to lend a hand, and for Bob Griffin, who was smart enough to know a gem when he saw one!*

# Chapter One

*Laura.*

The name flashed through his mind, then vanished as quickly as it had appeared. It was a mistake he hadn't made in years and, no doubt, could be blamed on the sights and smells of the seasons changing around him. Autumn always brought back memories. And regrets. Neither of which could be altered.

Still, his error was not surprising. The young woman hurrying in his direction, head bent against the crisp October breeze, was the image of her mother at the same age. Bridget Templeton O'Neill drew nearer, and he corrected himself. No. Laura Templeton's coloring was not quite as intense as her daughter's, her hair not as dark, her eyes not as blue. No doubt the differences could be attributed to the heritage of the Irishman for whom Laura had abandoned her own legacy. A small twinge of remembered pain shot through him. He shook his head to clear the memories, both bitter and sweet. That he had loved his closest friend's sister and she had loved another was part of a past long since laid to rest.

"Good day, Miss Templeton." He nodded. "Bridget."

Bridget jerked her head up. Blue eyes in a delicate face widened and flashed with unease, as if she'd been caught at something unsavory. "Colonel Gordon." She smiled in a tentative manner. "How nice to see you again."

Colonel Josiah Gordon raised a brow. In spite of her words, Bridget did not seem at all pleased to see him. Was the girl up to something untoward? Nonsense. In this she was as different from her mother as night was to day. Bridget did not have a defiant or disobedient bone in her body. She did not flout the rules of proper behavior dictated by society or the more stringent regulations laid down by her aunt and guardian. Yet eighteen-year-old women did not typically appear in public without so much as a servant, even in the middle of the day. Josiah glanced up and down the street. "Surely you are not out and about unaccompanied?"

"Well, Colonel." She bit her bottom lip, obviously groping for a plausible explanation. "you see I . . . it's simply that . . . what I mean to say . . ."

If this had been any other young woman, he would have been amused by her obvious discomfort. But from the moment he had met her—as a frightened twelve-year-old coping with the death of her parents and a new life in the home of an uncle she had never known—and had realized, had things been different, she would have been his own daughter; he had privately thought of her as such.

"I suspect you have simply lost your companions. Either they have fallen behind or you have." He stifled a chuckle at the relief washing over her face. "Am I correct?"

"Exactly." Her smile, genuine now, returned. "That's what must have happened."

"Then might I accompany you home?" He held out his arm. At least with him by her side she would not have to endure the speculative looks of passersby wondering why a fashionably dressed young woman was alone on the streets of Beacon Hill.

"Yes. Thank you." She looped her arm through his and they started off.

He slanted her a quick glance. Her brows knit together in a serious manner, as if she were considering an issue of great concern. What was bothering the child? Even though his position as trustee of her Uncle Albert's estate certainly permitted him the liberty of asking, he suspected it would be wiser to wait and see if she would confide in him on her own.

"And how is your family, Bridget? It has been several weeks since I last spoke to your aunt. She is well, I trust?"

"Quite well, thank you," Bridget said politely, her tone as even as if she were commenting on the weather.

Of course the girl was far too well mannered to ever reveal her true feelings about Claudia, although he had no doubts on that score. Josiah's own mood darkened at the thought of the woman who'd married his lifelong friend. While she had apparently made his life comfortable, and provided him with two ready-made sons from a previous marriage, Josiah had never liked her, nor she him. Now, with her finances firmly in Josiah's hands, Claudia was forced to treat him with courtesy. However since Albert's death, his widow had made no secret of her opinion of her late husband's niece, at least among friends and relations. Regardless of Bridget's legitimate claim to the family name, Claudia never failed to express disdain for the girl's heritage: She was the daughter of an ungrateful rebel and a working man; a fireman, no less, and poor Irish to boot.

Still, Josiah could not fault the woman's public treatment of her niece. Claudia had followed Albert's wishes to the letter, launching Bridget into society with all the ceremony befitting a Templeton. She had made certain Bridget met all the right people and was seen in all the right places. Albert had provided for a respectable dowry and Claudia had no qualms about mentioning that fact to any suitable young man who happened along in an obvious attempt to rid herself of the child once and for all. To Claudia's frustration, Bridget's shy demeanor and quiet nature had discouraged all potential suitors thus far.

Still, recently, hadn't Josiah detected a slight change in the girl?

"And Stephen?"

A deep blush swept up Bridget's face. "Stephen is wonder—" Her gaze dropped to the street before her. "—fine."

Josiah studied her thoughtfully. Surely she did not have feelings for Stephen Templeton? Certainly the young man was appealing, with his dark, handsome looks and his charming manner. But Stephen Templeton was in every way his mother's son: interested in little more than money and appearances. No, Stephen was not the man for Bridget. Still, the look on her face was cause enough for at least a moment of concern and a private vow for further observation.

"And is Paul fine as well?"

"Oh, yes," she said quickly, her reticence at once replaced by animation. "Paul is, well, Paul."

"How is he finding Boston these days? I have scarcely seen him since his return from Europe."

"To be honest, I'm not entirely sure he likes Boston anymore."

"Smart man, Paul Templeton." Josiah chuckled. "Mark my words, he'll do well in life."

"I think so, too." Enthusiasm rang in her voice. "Paul is very progressive. He says we are living in the most wonderful time on earth and every day mankind is making unbelievable strides forward. Why, he is always reading about adventurous explorations to uncharted places in the world or amazing new discoveries and inventions. You should hear him speak of the potential of electricity or the possibilities of steam power or—" She stopped and turned toward him, pinning the colonel with a surprisingly firm gaze. "—did you know even as we speak there are men very close to developing a horseless carriage? In Germany, I think."

"Is that so?" He couldn't quite hide the amusement in his voice.

"Indeed. And Paul also says there are even those tinkering with," she leaned toward him in a confidential manner, "flying machines."

"Remarkable." The corners of his lips quirked upward.

"Isn't it?" She considered the colonel for a moment. "You knew all this, didn't you?"

"You've found me out." He laughed. "I must confess, in spite of living in Boston, a city that I firmly feel pays far too much homage to the past and far too little attention to the future, I am aware of the immense progress being made in all manner of endeavors. Paul and I share an interest in new inventions and findings. As did your uncle."

"I know." Sorrow flashed in her eyes. "I dearly miss him."

"As do I." Josiah took her arm once again and they walked on. "You did brighten his life, you know."

"Did I?" Bridget said softly.

"Indeed you did." Memories washed through him. "Albert never forgave himself for not standing up to his father when your mother married against his wishes."

Odd how those days were still so vivid in his mind. Laura Templeton had committed the unpardonable sin, at least in the eyes of her father and society, of falling in love with the wrong man. Thomas O'Neill, a big, laughing Irishman, had stolen the heart of the Boston heiress. Her father had cut off all contact with her, going so far as to forbid any Templeton to so much as say her name. Not until the senior Templeton had died had Albert tried to find her.

It was the account of O'Neill's death in the newspapers that had ultimately led Albert to his beloved sister. But the reunion came too late. Laura Templeton O'Neill's heart had died with her husband. When Albert found Laura, she was gravely ill. He'd moved her from the small South Boston house she'd shared with her husband to the Templeton's Beacon Hill mansion and hired the finest doctors. They'd shaken their heads and said there was nothing they could do.

Josiah was out of the country when it happened, and had heard the sad tale from Albert the very day he returned. Both men had sat in the Templeton library that night, awash in fine brandy and the past, speaking of what was and what might have been if Laura had loved Josiah instead of Thomas O'Neill. Still, they admitted O'Neill had been a good man, and from all accounts, Laura had been happy with the life she'd chosen. It was all either of them had really wanted. They had agreed that night that Albert should have had the courage to follow his heart as Laura had followed hers, and ignore his father's dictates forbidding contact with his sister. And they'd acknowledged it was no illness that had claimed Laura. She simply could not bear life after the death of the man she loved. Josiah had wished then that he, too, could have known such a love.

Bridget was all that was left of the woman they'd loved. The girl was quiet and scared, but in appearance the very image of her more independent mother. The men had sworn that night to take care of Laura's daughter as if she were their own. A vow Josiah had renewed upon Albert's death.

Bridget's eyes glistened with unshed tears.

"I am sorry, my dear." He squeezed her arm. "That was thoughtless of me. It would distress Albert to see you still mourning his passing. He would want you to go on with your life."

"I am." Bridget sniffed and raised her chin in a vaguely defiant manner he'd first noticed after Albert's death. Today it seemed more pronounced, more determined. More like Laura. He raised a brow in surprise. Did Bridget in fact inherit more from her mother than he'd suspected? Was strength of purpose coming with age? A parental pride stirred within him. "Colonel?"

"Yes, my dear?"

"I was wondering . . ." She drew a deep breath. "You have done a great deal of traveling."

Josiah smiled with pleasure, images of a world exotic and wonderful flickering through his mind. Journeys to places others only dreamed of had filled his life, and the books he now wrote about his travels and adventures gave that life purpose. "I have seen much of the world."

"Tell me, are people truly different from place to place?"

"Certainly there are different languages. Customs vary and—"

"No, no, I don't mean that." Bridget shook her head. "I mean people themselves. How they think and see . . . well, life itself. In terms of morals and standards, things like fair play and honesty and virtues, as it were. Take the Swiss or, oh, I don't know . . . Hungarians perhaps. Yes, Hungarians, for example, just for the purposes of discussion."

"Hungarians?" He laughed. "Interesting choice. But only for purposes of discussion, you say?"

"Yes, of course," she said quickly. "I quite suspect the possibility of running into a genuine Hungarian here on the streets of Boston is practically nonexistent."

"No doubt." He could only think of one. One fascinating Hungarian. He had always wished to know that particular Hungarian better and regretted the opportunity had never arisen. Now, of course, she was the talk of Boston, with her strange offer of cats and fortunes. Could that have anything to do with Bridget's curious question?

Absurd. He pushed the outlandish thought aside. Bridget might well wish for a pet, but she had no real need for money. Albert had made certain of that. Still . . . For the second time today he vowed to keep a closer eye on the girl.

"So then, Colonel"—she favored him with her brightest smile—"tell me all that you know about the virtues prized by Hungarians."

"Poor child," Gisella Lowell murmured to herself, and idly stroked the head of the animal purring in her lap.

In one corner of the fashionably appointed parlor, a cat batted at a tassel dangling from fringed hangings. Another lay before the tall window, lazily attempting to capture a shaft of autumn sunlight drifting through the slightly uneven panes of glass. Various other cats groomed themselves or simply napped in the spots each had claimed as its own. A few studied her with calm intensity, as though they expected little but hated to miss any possibility of excitement. What appeared to be a thick, orange-colored fur throw lay in a heap at her feet. Gisella fixed her unseeing gaze on a point across the room, her thoughts on the interview just concluded.

The girl, what was her name? Ah, yes. Bridget. Bridget Templeton O'Neill. The name alone spoke volumes about the young woman. Obviously, the use of *Templeton* was the doing of her aunt. It was just the sort of thing Claudia Templeton would insist upon. The woman was so deeply embedded in appearances it was rather surprising she allowed the child to use her father's name at all.

Gisella dimly remembered the lingering gossip

about Laura Templeton's scandalous elopement with a poor Irishman, a fireman if memory served. Even though it had happened a few years before her own arrival in the city, Boston's elite had a long, unforgiving memory, especially when it came to a defection of one of their own. Any number of society matrons were still clucking over the scandals of a century ago. And Claudia Templeton was one of the worst.

Gisella drew her brows together thoughtfully. Bridget had claimed she wanted Gisella's offer of ten thousand dollars for the man she planned to marry. If indeed she was betrothed, certainly Gisella would have heard. It was impossible to separate business from society in this town. Even an outsider like herself couldn't help but know the tiniest details about the lives of the upper crust. It was no secret that Albert Templeton had left strict instructions as to the fate of his niece. And it appeared that Claudia was indeed acquiescing to her late husband's desire to introduce Bridget to society and make certain the girl found a suitable husband. Everyone knew of Claudia's concerted effort to marry Bridget off. Regardless of her aunt's feelings about the girl, an engagement, especially a good match, would have been trumpeted in the papers, and more than likely on the streets as well. Claudia would never have passed up the opportunity to crow about a successful pairing she'd had a hand in.

If the child considered herself engaged, Gisella had no doubt it was without Claudia's approval or knowledge. Indeed, while Bridget had sat in this very room, the perfect image of a proper Boston young lady of good breeding, her hands had nervously toyed with the gloves in her lap. Gisella prided herself on her intuition. It obviously took a great deal of courage for the girl to come to her. Like her cats, she had an unerring instinct when it came to people. Who was trustworthy and who was not. Bridget Templeton O'Neill was no liar, yet Gisella knew the story the girl had told was not complete. And knew as well that the girl needed help.

Gisella smiled. Bridget had come to the right place. "Sebestyen."

There was no response.

Gisella rolled her gaze heavenward. "Very well, then." She sighed. "Smudge."

The pile of fur at her feet shifted and uncurled. Slowly, as if every movement required an inordinate effort, the heap of mottled orange rearranged itself. Gisella tried not to laugh. Sebestyen, or rather Smudge, as he preferred to be called for reasons known only to himself, got to his feet in an unhurried manner. His back arched upward in a long, leisurely stretch that extended every inch of his feline form to its impressive limit. Between his thick coat and a substantial amount of excess weight there were indeed a great number of inches to extend.

*Fat cat.*

Smudge swiveled his head toward her, his green eyes glittering with reproach.

"Do not look at me like that." Gisella laughed. "You are fat, you know. You do not partake of nearly enough exercise and I suspect you have had one mouse too many."

Smudge sat on the Persian carpet before her and raised his chin to meet her gaze, resembling, as always, nothing so much as a monarch whose girth equates his status in the world.

"But, my darling, you are magnificent." And indeed, Smudge *was* one of her favorites. He was of a standard height but round, very round. His coloring was an intriguing shade of orange save for the exception of a blotch of black smeared just above his nose—as if the creature had investigated a coal bin and bore the mark of his curiosity ever after. His full coat did nothing to diminish the impression of obesity and, in fact, added to the overall effect.

Smudge appeared satisfied by her declaration and turned his attention to a vigorous washing of his right front paw.

Gisella studied him for a long moment. His personality was as unique as his appearance. Sebestyen was his true name, "revered" in the language of her homeland. A distinguished name befitting a cat of his breeding and regal nature. But when he'd been barely more than a kitten, Gisella had once laughingly called him Smudge. Much to her chagrin, he'd refused to answer to Sebestyen ever since. She suspected his refusal had a great deal more to do with his desire to annoy her and assert his obvious belief that he was the master and she the pet, rather than any preference for the name itself.

"I shall miss you, Smudge."

Smudge halted his ablutions and cast her a lordly glance.

"There is a young lady who may well be precisely what I am looking for."

Smudge stared unblinking.

"She is charming, very pretty and quite nice."

Suspicion colored the cat's eyes.

"Now, now. Do not be difficult. You knew this moment would come." Regret coursed through her. She was exceedingly fond of Smudge. "Miss O'Neill will provide you with an excellent home and you, in turn, will provide her salvation. Unless I am mistaken, and I am never mistaken"—her voice softened—"she has a good heart. She deserves better than what she has been given—or even that for which she wishes—though she does not realize it yet. It shall be up to you to make certain the path she chooses is true."

Smudge appeared to consider her words, then favored her with a slight smile of consent.

"Excellent." Gisella reached forward and scratched him under his chin. Smudge leaned into her hand, his eyelids nearly closed, and sighed in feline ecstasy. "I have much left to do in this world and I should very much appreciate the successful completion of this task. Do not fail me, Smudge."

The cat purred in contentment and perhaps, agreement.

"And do not fail her."

# *Chapter Two*

*India. Mexico. Brazil.*

Paul Templeton stared at the globe spinning beneath his fingertips.

*China. Madagascar. Persia.*

Exotic names flashed in and out of sight, mesmerizing him, catching his imagination.

*Japan. Russia. Egypt.*

There was so much more to the world than Boston.

"Damnation." He smacked his hand on the globe and glared at the now-still sepia-colored sphere. The real places represented by the tiny black print were as far out of his reach as the moon or the stars.

*Why?* The question he'd avoided for months shot through his mind like an accusation. Why, indeed? There was nothing to keep him here. He had graduated from Harvard and gone on to pursue two years of study at Oxford before finally returning home like the dutiful son he somehow managed to be. Even so, his stepfather had left him no actual business to manage, just a large number of profitable investments now in the capable hands of Colonel Gordon and his bankers and attorneys.

Paul couldn't prevent the smile that curved his lips whenever he thought of his stepfather's method of controlling his wife even after his death. Perhaps his private amusement was due to his mother's continued complaints about her late husband's influence over her finances from the grave. Although she had nothing, in fact, to complain about. The funds available to run the household, to provide clothing not merely serviceable but in the height of fashion, and allow for entertaining as well, had not been at all diminished. In addition, Paul was certain she retained assets from both her first marriage to his father and from her own family as well. Still, it was a constant annoyance to his mother that her finances were not at her unfettered disposal. It bothered his brother as well.

Stephen considered himself an expert investor, and indeed it was the only topic of study Paul had ever seen him actively pursue. Stephen was convinced he could manage money with an aptitude that would transform the Templeton fortune into a wealth comparable to that of the Astors or Vanderbilts. When he chose, he spent his days in a well-appointed office in the business district, allegedly trying to do just that with his mother's private funds. Paul often wondered why his brother hadn't managed it thus far.

Publicly, Claudia disdained the idea of putting

herself in the same category as New Yorkers, proclaiming Boston had higher standards that had nothing to do with mere wealth, but her eyes gleamed at the prospect of building their fortune. Albert had obviously known what he was doing when he had kept his legacy out of her hands and those of her sons'. Still, both Stephen and Paul would receive control of sizable trust funds in another four years. Stephen would be thirty then, and Paul, twenty-six.

Paul sighed and absently spun the globe. At least his brother knew precisely where his interests lay. In spite of his academic training, Paul had failed to narrow his attention to a single topic. History and architecture captivated his mind while art and literature tugged at his soul. Science intrigued, mechanics and engineering beckoned, exploration called to a restless nature long held in check. The future stretched before him, offering limitless possibilities. He raised his gaze to the books filling every inch of the shelves lining the walls of the library, stretching in an endless march around the room. He knew each and every volume by heart. Why didn't he know his own heart as well?

He and his stepfather had shared the love of this room and of the books that could take them to all the places on the globe. While Stephen was his mother's favorite, Paul had been Albert's son in every way but blood. Perhaps it was because he'd been younger when his mother married. Perhaps it was a result of Stephen always being closer than Paul in spirit and temperment to his mother. Or perhaps it was simply affection and yes, love, that had developed naturally between a kind man wishing to be a good parent and a boy needing a father.

Lord, he missed him. What would Albert advise him to do now? He ran his fingers impatiently through his hair. Paul knew his mother would be appalled by the very thought of him pursuing any activity outside of those approved for sons of prestigious families: banking and business, primarily. She would no doubt swoon dead away if he even brought up the suggestion of his leaving Boston permanently. Still, he knew, as he knew little else in his life, that the future expected of him here would surely cost him his soul.

Perhaps he should discuss his dilemma with Colonel Gordon. The man had been a hero in the War Between the States, promoted to colonel at an unusually young age. He'd spent the next twenty years traveling the world on and off, experiencing all the things that now so fired Paul's imagination. Surely the colonel would understand. Perhaps he'd even encourage him to cast off the expectations of his mother and pursue his own life. After all, there was little for him here. The good people of Boston would barely note his absence. No one would miss his presence, and there was no one he would leave behind.

*Except Bridget.*

An odd sensation settled in the pit of his stomach. Odd but all too familiar. The same sensation had gripped him upon his return from England, barely a month ago, when he had seen her again and realized she wasn't the child he had left behind. Far from it.

Features he'd never particularly noted before now captured his attention and left his head swimming and his mouth dry. Her hair was dark as the night and unruly curls drifted down the back of her long neck, escaping from the severity of the all-too-proper style she now wore. Time and again he wondered what it would feel like against his flesh or entwined in his fingers. Her skin seemed to glow, as if lit from within. More than once he had to stop himself from reaching out to make certain it was as soft as it appeared to be. The young woman who'd greeted him on his return bore only a vague resemblance to the girl who'd bidden him farewell, a girl who'd been a mere shadow of the woman to come. A woman he had never expected to meet outside of his dreams, who now caught his heart unawares.

He was not prepared for a figure that narrowed and swelled in all the right places. Unprepared for the subtle fresh scent of spring that accompanied her when she entered a room and lingered when she left. Unprepared for thick lashes that swept her cheek and shaded eyes so blue they put nature itself to shame.

Were the unmarried men of Boston complete and utter fools? Her face and dowry, coupled with his mother's eagerness to see her wed, should have procured her a suitable husband long before now. Oh certainly, she was retiring and reserved with those she didn't know, but it seemed to him that many men preferred a quiet nature in a wife. Whatever the reason, he was grateful that her charms had so far been overlooked, although how any healthy, living, breathing male could do so escaped him.

And what of *her* feelings? Did her breath come faster in his presence? Her pulse race with his smile? Her heart flutter when he stepped near?

Probably not. He blew out a long breath. Bridget cared for him, no doubt, but her affection seemed that of a sister for a brother or a friend for a friend.

Indeed, while he suspected she'd had friends at school, he knew of no one in Boston, with the exception of himself and possibly Colonel Gordon, with whom she ever dropped her reserved, quiet manner. Even though they had both been sent away to school, through letters and those rare holidays when they were home, Bridget had always confided her deepest secrets to him, and he had shared his confidences with her. Always, until now, when fear kept him still. Despite his long absence, she had resumed their easy camaraderie as if they'd never been apart.

Perhaps if he told her of his feelings . . .

No. He would never risk what they already shared.

Still, wasn't there a chance that she could love him as he loved her? She was a woman now, with a woman's emotions. It hadn't taken him long to realize that he was in love. Wasn't it possible that, with time, she could share his feelings? Surely his desire to leave Boston could wait. Bridget was well worth any delay, any sacrifice. He would have to be patient and bide his time. And quell the overwhelming impulse to take her in his arms whenever she smiled at him or her laughter rang out to echo in his heart.

He pulled in a deep, steadying breath. It would not be an easy task. The mere thought of her fired his blood. His behavior was exactly like that of any other lovestruck twit he and his friends had made sport of during his school years. He shook his head with unexpected sympathy.

Now he, too, had joined their ranks.

The Templeton mansion loomed ahead and Bridget's step slowed. It would not do to run into

Aunt Claudia, with her disapproving stare and inevitable questions. *Where have you been? What are you up to? Why were you unaccompanied? What were you thinking?* Followed by the inescapable lecture. *You are a well-bred young lady and I expect you to behave as such. We shall never find you a husband if you continue to refuse to curb your behavior.*

"Is something amiss, my dear?" Colonel Gordon's tone was mild and as steadying as an anchor in rough seas.

Without thinking, Bridget lifted her chin a notch. No one, except Aunt Claudia, had ever accused her of improper behavior. But from the moment she'd first stepped inside the Templeton home, nothing she did could please her aunt. Although, this once, Aunt Claudia's ire might well be deserved. If she even suspected the purpose of Bridget's sojourn today . . .

"No, of course not." Bridget pushed aside her apprehension and favored him with her brightest smile. "Would you care to come in for a moment? Perhaps for a cup of tea?" Aunt Claudia couldn't possibly upbraid her with Colonel Gordon present. Or at least Bridget hoped not.

"Thank you, Bridget. I'd like that." They climbed up the wide front steps. "Perhaps I can take this opportunity to have a long chat with Paul. I've been meaning to—"

The front door flew open with a frantic swish and an urgent Irish brogue.

"Thank the dear Lord you're here at last, Bridget O'Neill. It arrived just a minute or two ago and I didn't know how in the name of all that's holy I'd keep it out of the sight of the mistress. She won't like it at all, I tell you, whatever it is, and I can't say as how I want to be . . ." Emma Malone's gaze slid from Bridget to Colonel Gordon and her eyes widened. "What I mean to say is . . . Miss O'Neill, I . . ." The maid stammered, her Irish accent growing more pronounced with her obvious dismay at having been caught being less than formal with a member of the family.

"It's all right, Emma." Bridget laid a hand on the girl's arm and slanted a quick glance at Colonel Gordon. He appeared amused rather than annoyed at the display of familiarity. Emma wasn't much older than Bridget, and the two had become as friendly as their respective positions would allow, but no closer, much to Bridget's dismay. The Irish inflection in the girl's speech never failed to remind Bridget of the happier times of her childhood. But Emma needed her job to help support a large, and from what Bridget could gather, loving family, and the maid was always conscious of Aunt Claudia's ever-present threat of discharge.

Bridget stepped past her into the foyer and pulled off her hat and gloves. "Whatever is the matter?"

Emma cast another glance at Colonel Gordon and drew a deep breath. "A delivery came for you. Just a moment ago." Emma turned and picked up a large basket covered with a loosely woven, celery-colored cloth. A large forest green bow decorated the handle.

Colonel Gordon raised a brow. "What have we here?"

"I have no idea." Bridget handed Emma her cloak and accepted the hamper in exchange, noting that it was far heavier than it appeared. "It must be a mistake. I'm not expecting anything." She walked into the parlor, set the basket on the floor and sank to her knees before it. "Who on earth could be sending me a gift?"

"Well, open it, girl"—Colonel Gordon's lips quirked upward in amusement—"and we'll find out."

"It's like Christmas." Emma's eyes sparkled with anticipation.

"Very well." Bridget laughed, excited in spite of herself. She pulled off the cloth and peeked into the wicker container. At first, she saw nothing but a mound of orange fur. "What on earth?"

The fur shifted in a slow, fluid motion and two green eyes stared up at her. Bridget gasped. "A cat! Oh, look, it's a cat!" She reached into the basket and carefully picked up the unresisting animal, placing him gently on the carpet. "Oh, isn't he lovely?"

The cat stretched in an unhurried manner and glanced around the room, as if assessing the suitability of his surroundings. He emitted what sounded like a sigh of resignation. Perhaps the parlor was not quite up to his standards. Bridget stifled a laugh. Somehow she suspected he was not the sort of cat who tolerated humor at his own expense. He settled back on his haunches and stared straight into her eyes.

"Oh my." Bridget breathed the words. "He's magnificent."

Emma snorted. "He's fat is what he is."

"Not at all," Bridget said firmly.

"He is rather overlarge, my dear." Colonel Gordon's tone was wry.

"He's . . . well . . ." Bridget studied him for a moment. "Grand. That's what he is: he's grand." She stretched out her hand.

The feline glanced at her fingers then fixed his gaze on hers and stretched his neck forward to rest his chin on her hand. Delighted, she scratched him gently. His eyes closed in contentment.

Colonel Gordon chuckled. "It appears you have made a conquest, Bridget."

"As has he," she said softly.

"It won't do you a bit of good." Emma shook her head. "Your aunt will never let you keep him. You know how she is about anything or anyone that might be a bit of trouble." Emma sniffed. "Not that her highness would be doing any of the work herself now."

"I see no problem with Bridget's keeping the creature," Colonel Gordon said in a casual manner. "I shall speak to Claudia—"

"No." Even to her own ears, Bridget's voice was surprisingly firm. "I shall deal with my aunt myself. I do thank you but"—her gaze met his—"this is my home as well as hers. Beyond that, I shall very likely be married soon and I cannot continue to allow my au—others—to control every aspect of my life." She scrambled to her feet. "It's past time I stood my ground."

"As you wish." Was that approval in the Colonel's eye?

"Oh, Lord, I nearly forgot." Emma pulled a small packet from the oversize pocket on her apron. "This came with the basket." She handed Bridget a brown paper parcel, tied with twine.

Bridget turned the package over in her hand. Her heart beat faster. In the excitement of receiving the cat, she'd nearly forgotten exactly what his presence meant. Her hand trembled with anticipation. Impatiently, she slid off the string and tore away the paper.

"It's only a book." Emma shrugged with the disgust brought on by so impractical a gift.

Bridget barely heard her. She stared at the slim red volume in her hand. Emerald cat's eyes gleamed at her from the leather cover, the feline face centered in an ornate design of curls and flourishes, all gilded and twinkling in the afternoon light. Gold edged the pages in a perfect frame. Gently she opened the book to the title page.

*"The Care and Feeding of the Modern Feline,"* she read, more to herself than to her companions. She turned the page. An admonishment in bold letters caught her eye:

*There is no better judge of human nature than a feline. Their instincts are infallible when it comes to character. Never disregard the reaction of your cat to the people around him. If your cat takes a dislike to a person, beware! The person in question is not worth liking.*

Bridget glanced at the cat, who wore an expression that could only be described as smug. Again, she struggled to hide a smile and quickly returned her attention to the book, flipping through the pages. Toward the middle of the volume, she found a piece of expensive vellum, covered with an elegant yet firm penmanship, tucked in the spine.

*My Dear Miss O'Neill,*
  *By now you must realize I have indeed selected you as a beneficiary of my grant. I know it was my financial offer that compelled you to find the courage to approach me . . .*

How on earth did Mrs. Lowell know how difficult it was for Bridget to call on her?

*. . . yet the money is not as significant as the creature I now entrust to your keeping. I am confident you will understand that as well. You would not receive this bequest were I to think otherwise.*

*Sebestyen is an unusual feline. Judging by his appearance, I believe he is descended from some of the revered cats of ancient times, possibly in Asia. Judging by his temperament, there is no doubt he is of noble blood and fully knows his worth. You shall suit each other well. It is my wish that each of you learn from the other.*

Bridget glanced once more at the cat now diligently washing an upraised paw. He was wonderful, of course, but what could she possibly learn from him? The creature threw her a quick, condescending smile and returned his attention to grooming.

*Trust in yourself, my dear. Follow your heart for the truth you will find only there.*

> *Your servant,*
> *Gisella Lowell*

Follow your heart? What did she mean?

*I nearly forgot. While his true name is Sebestyen, he prefers to be called Smudge.*

"Smudge." The name had a satisfying feel on her tongue. Not nearly as majestic as Sebestyen, but, given the streak of black above his nose, quite fitting. Besides, Sebestyen was the title of a creature suited for worship and adoration. Smudge was the name of a pet to be loved.

"Smudge?" Emma and the colonel exchanged glances.

"That's his name." Bridget pulled the note from the book. A narrow piece of paper fluttered to the floor.

"I'll get that." Colonel Gordon bent to retrieve the paper. He glanced at it and a frown creased his forehead. Without another word he handed it to Bridget.

It was a bank check for ten thousand dollars. Her gaze met the colonel's worried eyes. "Bridget, I think perhaps—"

"Colonel." She squared her shoulders. "I meant what I said earlier. Please don't be offended, but I need to run my life and make my own decisions. This is my business, and mine alone. I would prefer not to discuss it and I would appreciate it if you would respect my wishes."

Their gazes locked and held. He considered her silently. She wasn't foolish enough to think Mrs. Lowell's advertisement hadn't caught the notice of many a Boston resident, and the colonel was more astute than most. He no doubt had already put together the arrival of Smudge and the small fortune she held in her hand and surmised exactly what Bridget had done.

"Very well." He nodded. "But we will speak of this later."

"Thank you," she said with a rush of relief.

Male voices sounded in the hall: Paul's and Stephen's. Her pulse raced. In many ways, Stephen was a great deal like his mother. It might well be wise to delay introduction of the cat to the rest of the family.

"Emma, would you take Smudge into the kitchen? For a bowl of cream, perhaps?"

Emma cast the cat an uneasy look. Smudge returned it with disdain. "I don't think he's going to let me be picking him up, now."

"He appears to be a fairly intelligent animal," the colonel said. "He may simply follow you."

"Do try it, Emma."

"If you say so." Emma heaved a long-suffering sigh, grabbed the basket and started toward the door leading to the back hallway. She glanced at the cat. "Come along with you."

Smudge got to his feet as if he had all the time in the world and, indeed, the world would well wait until he was ready. With a superior sway of his hips he padded after Emma. She stopped and opened the door. Chin raised, the animal stepped delicately over the threshold. Emma grinned. "Seems we've got another highness in the house."

The door swung shut behind her just as Paul and Stephen strode through the open pocket doors from the foyer on the opposite side of the parlor.

"Colonel Gordon." Genuine pleasure shone on Paul's face and he stepped toward the colonel with his hand outstretched. "I was just thinking I needed to pay a call on you."

"Good to see you, too, my boy." Colonel Gordon shook Paul's hand with the obvious affection of an uncle for a favorite nephew. Indeed, even though there was no true bond of blood between them, the colonel's long friendship with Uncle Albert had put him in the position of a warmly received relation.

"Colonel." Stephen smiled politely. Bridget bit back a frown. She would never understand why Stephen did not share the affection she and Paul felt for her uncle's best friend.

"Stephen." The colonel nodded briefly and turned his attention back to the younger of the brothers. "Forgive me, Paul. It seems that in spite of my best intentions, life, in the form of a minor calamity here or an unexpected crisis there, seems to interrupt at the most inconvenient times. I've been meaning to sit down and have a long talk with you. And today I was fortunate enough to run into Bridget, who kindly invited me to tea." He favored her with an affectionate smile. "I'm extremely curious as to your thoughts on your studies, now that you've put the hallowed halls of England behind you and come home."

Paul shook his head wryly. "I'm not certain my thoughts are at all worth relating, although I do seem to have a great many of them."

"Excellent," the colonel said with a grin. "I rarely believe in the importance of quantity, except when it comes to thoughts and ideas and hopes and dreams. You can never have enough, and who knows, in my own case at any rate, when one might actually prove worthwhile."

Gordon laughed and Paul joined him. For the barest moment, there was a startling resemblance between the two that had nothing to do with appearance. Colonel Gordon's coloring was much darker than Paul's, his tanned skin a testament to long years of trekking through exotic places like Africa and India and the South Seas. His once black hair was now streaked with gray, although his mustache remained untouched by the marks of age. Why, the colonel was in his fifties, after all, positively ancient, and Paul was only a few years older than Bridget herself.

Physically, although both men were tall and shared a build that hinted at athletic prowess, they couldn't have been more dissimilar. Paul's hair was a warm, sandy color somewhere between blond and brown. His hazel eyes sparkled with intelligence behind gold-rimmed glasses.

No, the resemblance between the two was more a similarity of spirit than body, an enthusiasm for life and all of its secrets that surrounded Paul and the colonel, creating an almost palpable bond. Regret shot through Bridget at the realization that this was one connection she would never be allowed to share. Oh, she, too, was excited by the thoughts of great explorations and discoveries, but such endeavors were not open to women. It would be different if she were a man, but even in this thoroughly modern age of wonders, women were expected to marry and raise families and keep homes and leave the world and all its newfound glories in the hands of men like Colonel Gordon. And perhaps Paul, as well.

"Bridget?" Paul stared at her with a quizzical half-smile on his lips. "Did you hear me?"

"What?" Bridget shook her head to clear the distant sound of far-flung adventure from her mind.

"I said, Colonel Gordon and I have a great deal we should like to discuss. We will be in the library. Would you ask Emma to bring us tea?" Paul's eyes narrowed. "Bridget?"

"Of course," she murmured. Odd, how thoughts of exploits and exploration seemed to grab at her mind with increasing frequency these days. Paul's influence, no doubt.

"Are you certain you're quite all right, my dear?" Colonel Gordon's tone was even, but she read far too much speculation and an overabundance of questions in his eyes.

"Yes." She met his gaze straight-on. "I'm fine." *And I know what I'm doing.*

"Very well." The colonel turned to Stephen, who leaned against the Italian tiled mantel, arms crossed over his chest. "Good to see you again, Stephen. Give my regards to your mother."

"Of course. I assume you shall see her yourself at the Harvest Ball next week." Stephen's tone held not even the merest note of interest, as though he really didn't care if he saw the colonel again, soon or not, and was simply being courteous.

"That's right. Next week is Halloween. I had nearly forgotten." A grin of delight broke across the colonel's face, and Bridget recalled that he had been considered something of a rake in his younger days. "I wouldn't miss it for the world. Why, unless I was abroad, I've not missed a Harvest Ball yet." He glanced at Bridget. "You will reserve a dance for me, won't you, my dear?"

Bridget laughed and dropped an exaggerated curtsy. "Why, I'd be honored, kind sir."

"Save one for me as well, Bridget." An odd, intense light flickered in Paul's eye.

"And for me," Stephen said.

"You shall, no doubt, be the belle of the ball. I must say, I am quite looking forward to it." Colonel Gordon nodded at Paul and they headed toward the hall. "Now then, my boy, Bridget tells me you've been reading up on the efforts to produce . . ."

Their voices trailed away behind them.

"Bridget," Stephen said softly.

"Yes?" Her heart thumped in her chest.

"Could you remain here for a moment? I wish to speak with you."

"Of course, Stephen." She shut the doors and

turned toward him. She held her breath. "About what?"

His manner was at once insolent and charming. Lord, he was handsome. He shrugged. "Oh, we could discuss any manner of things."

"Could we?" She struggled to keep her voice even.

"Indeed we could." In two long strides he was at her side. "But I should like to begin with this."

He pulled her into his arms and bent to claim her lips with his.

# Chapter Three

"Albert's extensive accumulation of books has never failed to amaze me."

Josiah glanced around the library, with its dark wood aglow from years of polishing and a warmth that came as much from the memories of times shared as from the welcoming fire burning in the hearth. He could almost feel his friend's presence and wouldn't have been at all surprised to turn and see Albert offering him his best brandy or a fine cigar.

"The library is impressive for a private collection. You can find almost anything in here." Paul gestured at the far wall. "On this shelf, prominently displayed, are the complete works of one Josiah Gordon. Fine reading. Informative and enjoyable."

"To everyone except the critics."

Paul drew his brows together. "I thought your books were rather well-received."

Josiah snorted. "It all depends on how one defines *received*. If you were to judge by comments made exclusively by reviewers—is Albert's brandy still in the same place?"

"The cabinet to the right of the window. Bottom shelf."

"Thank God. I thought we might actually be forced to drink tea. Vile, weak-willed stuff. No real reason for it." Josiah stepped to the cabinet and pulled open the door. "It's good to know some things can be counted on not to change."

"I think Stephen can be thanked for that," Paul said mildly. "My brother does enjoy his comforts."

Josiah bit back a sharp reply. In terms of temperament and outlook, Paul was as different from his brother—and his mother, too, for that matter—as if he had been born into another family altogether. Oh, certainly Claudia's sons shared some physical characteristics. Both were handsome men, taller than average, with a definite similarity in the shape of their mouths and set of their eyes. But Stephen's eyes seemed more often than not lit with a calculating gleam, whereas the spark in Paul's was that of curiosity and a desire for knowledge. Their interests, too, were worlds apart. For two years, Paul had studied abroad, while his brother had spent twelve months on an extravagant Grand Tour. Josiah and Albert had often discussed these very differences and whether they were the result of heritage or home, or something as yet unexplained.

Josiah selected a decanter and held it up to the light, studying it with a critical eye. "This will do nicely. I don't suppose you can find a cigar. . . ."

Paul laughed and shook his head.

"I didn't think so." Josiah sighed in resignation. "As I was saying, if one was to pay too much attention to my critics, you would believe my writing to be—how was it put once? Ah, yes, 'the self-indulgent stylings of a man who refuses to discard the adventurous nature of boyhood.'"

He poured a glass and raised it in Paul's direction.

"It's rather early in the day. Mother won't approve."

Josiah lifted a brow. "And . . ."

"And as your host"—Paul grinned—"how can I possibly refuse?"

"How, indeed?" Josiah filled a second snifter and passed it to him. "It would be most inhospitable."

"Rude, in fact." Paul swirled the brandy in his glass and shrugged. "Besides, I have long thought it my purpose in life to annoy my mother. Or at least my lot."

"Claudia has always been easily annoyed. She has the soul of a critic." Josiah sipped the brandy, closed his eyes and savored the rich, heavy warmth of the liquor, precisely what was called for on a crisp autumn day. "I've suspected through the years that it's that adventurous, boyish nature of mine that she has always detested."

"Mother has never been particularly fond of passion in any form." Paul pulled a long sip. "I would wager she finds such extremes of emotion inconvenient. And she dislikes being inconvenienced."

"So the future does not bode well for Bridget's cat."

"What cat?"

"Bridget is the proud owner of a large, orange creature, allegedly feline, or rather, he may well be her owner."

"How very strange. It's not like Bridget to do anything she knows Mother will disapprove of. Still, if she had the courage to risk Mother's anger in the first place," he raised his glass in a toast, "the cat's future may be secure after all."

"And is Bridget's secure as well?"

"Who can say? Perhaps." Paul stared at a point on the bookshelf or maybe beyond, to the world outside the Templeton walls. He was silent for a long moment.

Josiah waited and sipped his brandy. Patience was one of the most important lessons to be learned on this earth. Patience and the need to appreciate, enjoy and even savor the good things in life. Like a fine liquor. Or a friendship that lasted beyond death and carried with it the responsibility to assist those left behind.

"I want to see some of what you've seen," Paul said abruptly. "Do the things you've done."

"Do you, now?" Josiah should have seen it coming. In spite of his heritage by blood, Paul was very much like Albert. And Albert would have joined Josiah in his travels if it had not been for his father and later his wife. Still, Paul's declaration at this time caught him unawares. "Claudia won't be especially happy to hear that."

Paul continued as if he hadn't heard. "I want to build great buildings or create great art or explore new worlds. Make my mark on the world. Frankly, I'm not entirely sure exactly what I do want to do; I only know that I want to do something. Something interesting and exciting. Something that does not depend on my family's name or influence or wealth. And I cannot do it here. I'm leaving Boston." The younger man's gaze snapped to his. "And I want Bridget to come with me."

"I see," Josiah said evenly. At once, the tiny details he'd noted but filed somewhere in the back of his mind for further study clicked into place. He should have realized the truth sooner, but he'd seen the boy so seldom since his return home. He drew another swallow of brandy and considered Paul carefully. "And what does Bridget want?"

Paul blew a long, heartfelt breath. "I wish I knew."

"You haven't spoken to her? Told her how you feel?" Good Lord, surely Paul wasn't as stupid as he himself had been in his youth? "Why in heaven's name not?"

Paul stared at him as if he'd taken leave of his senses.

"I assume by your manner that you care for her?"

"Very much, sir."

"Then tell her!"

"But what if she doesn't feel the same?"

"What if she does?"

"I . . ." Paul smiled weakly, "I don't know."

Josiah groaned. "Why on earth the fates decree the throes of love should be visited upon those too young to know how to handle it is perhaps the greatest mystery of life." He stepped to one of two leather wing chairs positioned to take full advantage of both the light from the window and the heat of the fire and lowered himself into it, gesturing to the other. "Sit down, Paul. If we are to continue this discussion—and there's no doubt in my mind that we need to do just that—we should at least be comfortable."

Paul sank into the other chair. "I feel like an idiot."

"And indeed you are, at least when it comes to this." Josiah leaned toward him. "All men are. It's the one area where women are probably superior to men. They're not at all like us, you know. I suspect it has something to do with evolution."

"Excuse me?" Paul stared in obvious confusion. "I don't understand. In fact, sir, if possible, I feel even more stupid than I did a minute ago."

"Get used to it. Love makes even the brightest of us question our own intelligence." He studied Paul closely. "You are in love, aren't you, boy? That's what you mean when you say you *care for her*, isn't it? This is *Bridget* we're talking about now, and if I thought—"

"Colonel!" Paul bolted upright in his chair. "I assure you my intentions are strictly honorable. I do care—love her."

"It does tend to stick in your throat, though."

"A bit," Paul said, a defensive note in his voice. "But then, I've never said it aloud before. And frankly, I'm finding the whole thing damned unpleasant." He pulled a deep swallow of the brandy and shook his head. "Bridget has been my closest friend for much of my life. I've always thought of her as simply my cousin, my family. But I'm away for a mere two years and return to find my dear friend transformed into . . . well, a rather astounding creature. A woman."

"Damned inconsiderate of her," Josiah murmured.

"It is indeed." Paul leapt to his feet and paced the room. "I can't even talk to her anymore. Bridget and I used to talk a great deal, you know."

He stalked to the liquor cabinet and refilled his glass. "I could tell her anything."

"And you can't now?"

"I can barely say hello." Paul glared, as if Josiah was somehow to blame. "My tongue gets tangled in my teeth. I stammer, I stutter. I can't seem to form a sentence. I told you—I feel like an idiot around her."

"She has grown into a lovely young woman."

"She's beautiful, but I've never especially had a problem with beautiful women before." His brows drew together, as if he was seeking the answer to an unsolvable puzzle. "That's not it. I don't know. She's good—"

"She's always been well-mannered."

"I don't mean her behavior. I mean her spirit. Her heart. She has a good heart. She doesn't think ill of anyone, even my mother and, God knows, she has reason enough to hate her. She sees the best in people and she's extremely trusting. Defenseless, in fact."

"She may not be quite as vulnerable as you think," Josiah said under his breath. Hadn't he noticed a growing strength of purpose in Bridget? That defiant little lift of her chin? The firm tone she'd taken in regard to her cat?

"I would give anything to keep her safe." A fervent light shone in Paul's eye. "I will allow no one to hurt her."

And her insistence that the check was her business and hers alone.

"Paul," Josiah said slowly, "in spite of your feelings, you have spent time with Bridget since your return, haven't you?"

"Not nearly as much as I'd like. Much of her time seems taken up these days with Mother's neverending crusade to marry her off. The effort seems to require a great number of dressmaker appointments and who knows what else." Paul sighed and plopped back into his chair. "I've even managed to make sense when I'm with her, although I have no idea how. She hasn't seemed to notice my, er, malady. Bridget treats me exactly as she always has."

"You've noted nothing unusual, then?"

"No." Paul shook his head. "Why do you ask?"

Josiah chose his words with care. "Do you know of any reason why she might need money? A great deal of money?"

"Money? No, of course not." Paul studied him carefully. "What is going on, Colonel?"

Josiah swirled his brandy in his glass and considered the situation. Bridget was as dear to him as if she were his own daughter. And if he'd had a son, he could wish for none better than Paul. He wouldn't hesitate to give his blessing to a match between the two, and he was certain Albert would have agreed.

But Bridget was up to something. Well-bred young ladies who never strayed beyond the bounds of proper behavior, who never gave their elders cause for concern, who, indeed, were quiet and reserved, did not typically seek cats who arrived complete with small fortunes. Josiah had heard all about Mrs. Howell's strange advertisement and had even considered responding to it himself. Not for the money—he had funds enough for his needs—but for the opportunity to get to know the intriguing widow. Besides, it would make an excellent story.

His reasons made perfect sense. What were Bridget's? By agreeing not to discuss the matter she probably assumed he had acknowledged it was her business and hers alone. Josiah thought nothing of the sort. In spite of the fact that he saw more and more of her mother's strength and independence in the girl, he shared Paul's views: Bridget was far too innocent and inexperienced to be allowed free rein to do as she pleased. He had no doubt the money was for a specific purpose, but while Bridget was reserved, she did not have a secretive nature; for her to keep secrets now worried him a great deal.

"Sir?" Concern colored Paul's face.

Paul loved her, and whether she loved him as well scarcely mattered. He was, and always had been, her friend. And right now Josiah did not doubt that Bridget needed, at the very least, a friend.

Josiah drew a deep breath. "Do you recall hearing anything at all about an advertisement placed by a Beacon Hill widow that offered a cat and ten thousand dollars?"

"It sounds vaguely familiar."

"I believe Bridget answered the ad."

Paul scoffed. "Bridget would never—"

"Indeed, she would. The cat is here in this house and," he paused for dramatic emphasis, "I have seen the check."

"But, why—"

"I think, Paul, that is precisely what you need to determine." Josiah drained the last of the liquor in his glass.

"I don't mind saying, I'm worried about her. I believe she's coming into her own, realizing she may have to make a few ripples on the still waters of her life in order to get what she wants. Discovering it's not always best to follow each and every rule. It's an attitude that's at once admirable and dangerous."

"I have noticed a certain determination about her since my return," Paul said thoughtfully.

"She's becoming her mother's child. High time, too. Still, I have a bad feeling in the pit of my stomach about all this." He held his empty glass out to Paul. Without a word the younger man rose and stepped to the cabinet, returning with the decanter. "Find out what she's up to, Paul. And while you're at it, tell her how you feel about her. Take it from a man who knows: Love is not easy to find on this earth."

"No?" Paul snorted in disbelief and filled Josiah's glass. "Coming from you, Colonel, that's a hard comment to accept. Your reputation precedes you."

"Do not confuse love with lover, my boy. They are different animals entirely. I have known any number of the latter, but only three real loves." He paused, and his mind drifted back a lifetime to three women, three sets of circumstances, three moments of magic. His voice was soft. "In that I suppose I have been luckier than most. Or more unfortunate. I know what is possible and precisely what I have missed.

"I'll tell you this, Paul: I lost two of those loves through circumstances I could do nothing about—war and death. But the third might have been different if I hadn't waited so long to tell her. If I hadn't been too damn scared of all the risks that go along with love. Don't let your mind rule your heart, boy. And don't let the woman you love get away."

Paul placed the brandy on a nearby table and turned to meet Josiah's gaze. His jaw was set and determined, and there was an air of newfound purpose in his stance. "I won't, sir."

"See that you don't. And do be nice to her cat, Paul." Josiah rolled his eyes toward the heavens. "Women tend to like men who are nice to their cats."

"Bridget," Stephen's lips whispered against the side of her neck, "how I've missed having you in my arms."

"Stephen." She sighed with the thrill of his touch.

He feathered kisses along the line of her jaw and her knees weakened. Stephen was the first man she'd ever kissed. The only man she'd ever kissed. She'd had no idea the sensations that swept through her when he held her like this would be quite so exquisite. Her body seemed to lean into his of its own accord. Oh, how she loved him. How she had always loved him. From the moment she'd first seen him when she was barely twelve years old, he, already a man of nineteen, had owned her heart. And now, miracle of miracles, he loved her back.

He held her tighter, crushing his lips to her. She melted against him, and the book she still held tumbled to the floor.

"Oh, dear." She gasped and pulled away.

"What is it, Bridget?" He smiled down at her and her heart fluttered. Dear Lord, he was a handsome man.

"I . . . I have something for you." He released her and she drew a steadying breath. She bent and picked up the slim volume, her hands still trembling with the power of his embrace.

"A book?" He raised a brow. "That's very

thoughtful, but are you sure you haven't confused me with my brother? Paul is the one who always seems to have his nose stuck in a book. Whereas I," he took her free hand and kissed her palm, and excitement shivered through her, "have other things to keep me occupied."

She swallowed hard and withdrew her hand from his grasp. Now was not the time to explore the odd and wondrous effect he had on her. She struggled for control and stepped away. "This isn't the surprise." The book fell open to the page with the letter and the check. She held the check out to him. "This is for you."

A frown creased his forehead. He accepted the narrow slip of paper and stared at it for what seemed like forever. She closed the book and hugged it to her. Finally, his gaze rose to meet hers. His voice was cool. "How did you come by this, Bridget?"

For a moment panic stabbed her. Why hadn't she realized he would wonder about a sum as large as this? She pushed away her unease and squared her shoulders. After all, she had done nothing wrong. "It scarcely matters, Stephen. It is my concern, and I would prefer to leave it at that. Suffice it to say, it was not obtained illegally or through illicit means." Oh, certainly she had led Mrs. Lowell to believe she was engaged, but hadn't Stephen said he wished to spend the rest of his days with her? They were betrothed in every way except for a public announcement. "Regardless, it's yours."

"Mine?" His eyes narrowed. "Forgive me, my dear, but I don't understand."

"I realize this is rather unexpected. . . ." She paused to gather her thoughts into a coherent explanation. "It's for you to build your fortune. You said if we were to defy your mother and marry, she would cut you off without anything, and you won't get Uncle Albert's inheritance until you're thirty." The words tumbled out faster and faster, as if of their own accord. "You are always talking about how a clever man with a shrewd sense of investment and an eye toward progress, who possessed the skills to manage money, could build great wealth out of virtually nothing. Ten thousand dollars is scarcely nothing. Why, to many people, it's a fortune. I know it's not nearly enough for you to have the kind of life you envision, but I did think—"

"You procured this for me?" A pleased smile lifted the corners of his lips. "I don't know what to say."

Relief rushed through her and she nodded.

"Thank you, Bridget. I shall see what can be done with it."

"And then we can be together."

"Of course," he murmured, staring at the check in his hand.

"I love you, Stephen."

He glanced up and smiled, reached out and pulled her back into his arms. "Ah, Bridget, you are a wonder." He brushed her lips with his. "Is it any surprise that you have captured my heart?"

"Stephen, I—"

His kiss quieted her words and swept away all rational thought. Dimly, in the back of her mind, she noted a slight touch near her ankles and an odd, vaguely familiar cry.

Stephen jerked up his head. "Damnation, what was that?"

The sound came again. Unmistakable now, it

was the insistent meow of a cat demanding attention. Bridget glanced down. Smudge rubbed against the hem of her skirt and emitted yet another determined cry.

Stephen stepped back and glared. "Where did that—that *thing* come from?"

"He's mine," Bridget said quickly, and stooped to gather Smudge into her arms. The cat must have sensed this was not the moment to protest and allowed her to hold him without resistance. "His name is Smudge."

"Smudge?" Stephen studied the animal with obvious disgust. "It's huge. Fat, actually. And what an ugly color."

Smudge stiffened in her arms. He might not have understood Stephen's exact words, but he undoubtedly grasped the man's tone. She gripped him a bit more firmly, hoping to covey without words both safety and security. "I think he's lovely."

"Lovely? That's hardly the word I'd use. Where did you find it, anyway? On the streets? For heaven's sake, Bridget, whatever possessed you to bring such an animal into the house?" He grimaced. "Regardless, you must get rid of him at once. Mother will never permit you to keep a thing like that in her home."

"It's my home, too," Bridget said for the second time today. "And I have every intention of keeping him."

Stephen's eyes widened with surprise at the unyielding note in her voice. "What on earth has gotten into you, Bridget?"

"Nothing at all. I simply wish to have a pet. This pet." She met his gaze directly. "And I will not give him up."

Stephen shook his head. "I doubt Mother will give you a choice. And I can't say I blame her. Cats are scavengers. Filthy, disgusting beasts."

Smudge turned his head toward Stephen, opened his mouth to show sharp, pointed teeth and hissed. A thoroughly wicked sound.

Stephen paled slightly and stepped back. "He doesn't like me."

"I can't say I blame him," Bridget said sharply. "You obviously don't like him either."

Stephen's mouth dropped open and he stared. At once she regretted the curtness of her tone.

"I am sorry. I didn't mean to snap. I simply—"

"You've never spoken like that before." He studied her carefully. "It doesn't suit you."

"I did apologize. I don't know what else to say," she said under her breath.

"Very well." He glanced at the check in his hand and back to her. His expression softened. "I suppose the cat is your concern, too?"

"Yes, he is."

"As you wish. I'll leave it to you, then, to break the news of his existence to Mother." He shrugged slightly in an inconsequential manner and waved the check at her. "I would stay, but—"

"No, go right ahead," she said quickly. "I have a final fitting for my Harvest Ball gown. The seamstress will be here any minute."

"I will take care of this matter at once." He strode to the door, grasped the brass pull and slid open the wooden panel. Abruptly he stopped and turned toward her. "Thank you, Bridget, for having faith in me. For doing this for me."

"For us." Her smile belied the firm note in her voice.

He considered her for a long moment, as if he

had questions he wasn't entirely certain he wanted answered. Finally he nodded slowly. "For us."

He stepped into the foyer and closed the door behind him. Bridget stared at the walnut-paneled pocket door and absently scratched behind Smudge's ear, paying little attention to his contented purr, vibrating against her fingers.

How could she possibly expect Stephen to understand that she was not quite the same girl she had been when he left? It wasn't simply that she'd matured physically, but that she'd grown inside herself as well. He'd obviously seen her change of attitude and demeanor today and probably hadn't noticed before now because she had been too delighted with his attention to make her feelings known.

Ever since she'd returned from school last spring—to be thrust upon Boston society like so much excess punch at a poorly attended ball—her dissatisfaction had grown. Not with her lot in life so much as with herself. How could she tell Stephen that by the time he'd returned from Europe she'd admitted to herself how tired she was of her weak-willed nature. Tired of always doing what others thought was right and never uttering so much as a protest. Tired of having her entire life under the control of everyone except herself.

She wasn't entirely certain when these feelings had begun but suspected they'd always lingered somewhere in the dim shadows of her mind. Perhaps it was Uncle Albert's death two years ago that had first beckoned them into the light; and the realization that without her uncle's presence, with Paul off to study in England and Stephen still seeing her as nothing more than a child, she was very much alone and could count on no one but herself.

Perhaps it was the way she had changed through the years away at school, gradually finding her own voice among the other girls. Eventually discovering with equal parts surprise and pleasure that her thoughts and desires were as important as anyone else's, her suggestions and ideas often more astute and intelligent than she had ever suspected.

Or perhaps it had all stemmed from Stephen's recent declaration of love and the certain knowledge that if she loved him, she and she alone would have to take matters in hand. Bridget rather liked standing up for herself, rather enjoyed doing what she thought was best even if she knew the consequences might be unpleasant. It was at the same time terrifying and exhilarating. Oh certainly, Stephen seemed a bit disconcerted today but Colonel Gordon had appeared rather proud.

She pulled her brows together and heaved a wistful sigh. Shouldn't it be the other way around? Smudge glanced up at her as if he knew full well her thoughts, and she smiled.

"What do you think, Smudge? Shouldn't a man in love with a woman be somewhat pleased when she shows she has a modicum of spirit and a mind of her own and is not merely an insubstantial bit of fluff to be patted on the head and paid no attention to beyond a compliment on her dress or her management of a household?"

Smudge stared in obvious agreement with her rambling, and she laughed. "What a clever cat you are, agreeing with me so quickly—and without saying a word. It's quite impressive, you know."

She started toward the door leading to the back

corridor, but then turned on her heel and walked briskly toward the main hall, stopping before the closed doors. Gently she set Smudge on his feet upon the floor and nodded down at him.

"This is my home and now it's yours as well. I see no reason why either of us should have to hide our presence."

Smudge meowed his approval.

"That's exactly how I feel." Bridget pulled open the door and marched to the wide main stairs, refusing to so much as glance around to see if anyone observed them. She sensed, more than heard, Smudge directly on her heels and knew without turning that he walked with a certain arrogance that would serve her well. Perhaps she could learn from the cat, just as Mrs. Lowell had suggested. Bridget wondered what, if anything, he could learn from her.

Then her smile faded; Stephen didn't seem to like Smudge at all, and the feeling appeared mutual. All at once, the instruction from the book flashed into her head.

*There is no better judge of human nature than a feline.*

# Chapter Four

"For goodness' sake, Paul, do watch where you're going." Claudia snapped shut the door behind her and glared at her younger son. "You very nearly knocked me over."

"Sorry, Mother." Paul stifled a sigh of resignation. It seemed he was always apologizing to her for one thing or another. It was easier to beg her pardon and get the matter over and done with than argue. That would simply prolong a discussion whose sole purpose was to make certain he knew his place. Besides, he would not be living here much longer. "I was looking for Bridget. I—"

"She's in the sitting room. We've been meeting with the dressmaker." Claudia nodded at the door she'd just closed and pursed her lips. "I don't know what's gotten into that girl. She has been simply impossible to deal with."

"Really?" Paul said as though he didn't care. Still, given Colonel Gordon's revelations, even his mother's observations could prove worthy of interest. "In what way?"

"To begin with, since the moment she returned from school last spring, I have made certain she's met each and every eligible bachelor from the very best families in Boston and she has done absolutely nothing to encourage any of them. Not one has managed so much as a discreet inquiry, let alone a genuine proposal." Claudia's brows furrowed. "Bridget has become quite attractive in her own way. Why, many men seem to actually prefer that rather vulgar vivid coloring she has, with her black hair and bright eyes and lips that look suspiciously like they have been rouged—"

Paul groaned. "Mother, please."

Claudia ignored him. "It's the Irish blood in her. I'm sure of it. No Templeton ever looked like that."

"I thought Bridget was the image of her mother."

"There is a distinct resemblance, although Laura was more appropriately pale, as befitting someone with her legacy. Bridget looks like the kind of personage who would abandon all measure of propriety to dance under a full moon with gypsies or other disgusting creatures."

"Mother!" Paul choked back a laugh. "I've never heard you quite so . . . well . . . descriptive before."

"It's entirely appropriate, I assure you. The girl has tendencies that are just now beginning to reveal themselves." Her eyes narrowed in anger. "I made the mistake of allowing her to speak to the dressmaker without me regarding her dress for the Harvest Ball. I never thought she would choose anything other than white or a pleasant pastel. Now, I find she has selected something entirely inappropriate for a young unmarried woman. And at great expense, I might add.

"Furthermore, she insists this dress is what she will wear." Claudia clasped her hands before her and drew herself up ramrod straight. "I will not put up with this much longer, Paul. I have no idea what that school taught her, but she has not been the same since she returned home. Regardless of my dear Albert's wishes, the girl will not be allowed to do as she likes so long as she lives under my roof."

"I believe it is her roof as well, isn't it, Mother?"

"Only until she is married," Claudia snapped. "And as of this very moment, I vow to redouble my efforts to see her wed and out of this house." Claudia nodded sharply and swept away down the hall.

"As will I, Mother, as will I," Paul said under his breath. He pushed open the door to the sitting room and peeked inside.

His breath caught in his throat. His heart thudded in his chest.

Bridget stood, her profile to him, on a footstool in the center of the room, studying her image in a large standing mirror. Light from the floor-to-ceiling bay window bathed her with an unearthly luminance. The dress that so horrified his mother shimmered in the light. No wonder Claudia hated it. The fabric was a blue, intense and primal: the color of the sky at midnight. Or the sea just before sunrise.

Or Bridget's eyes.

Her hair, dark and shining, tumbled loose halfway down her back. Large silk flowers, as white as the alabaster swell of breast that the fashionably cut gown revealed, perched low upon her shoulders and caught the fabric of its short sleeves. Similar blossoms gathered in a large bouquet at the base of her spine to form a bustle, while others tumbled down the skirt of the gown in joyous abandon.

His mother was right: It was not a typical gown for a young lady, nor was it a dress suitable for most of the proper ladies of Boston. It was a costume, adornment in truth, fit only for a goddess of the sea. Or an angel of the night. Or Bridget. Only Bridget.

She turned her head toward him. "Oh, Paul, I didn't hear you come in." Excitement snapped in her eyes. "Tell me the truth now, what do you think? Aunt Claudia doesn't like it at all."

He struggled to force out the words. "I can see her point."

Disappointment washed across Bridget's face. "You don't like it, then?"

"Oh, no. I like it." Paul swallowed hard. "I like it quite a bit."

"Are you certain? Your mother thinks it's too . . ." She cast a critical eye at her reflection in the mirror. "Well, too daring, I suppose. The color is rather unusual, but I am so tired of boring whites and pale creams and sickly yellows." She crossed her arms over her chest and sighed. "Recently, it seems my entire life is made up of boring whites and pale creams and sickly yellows."

He moved toward her and held out his hands. "This is scarcely boring, pale or sickly."

"Thank you." She laughed and gripped his hands to steady herself. "I believe I've been abandoned by both Mrs. Howard—she's the dressmaker, you know—and your mother. They had a rather heated conversation about the gown." She stepped carefully off the stool to the floor.

"I understand your comments on the subject were rather heated as well." Her hands were warm and soft and he couldn't bring himself to let her go.

She winced. "I was somewhat outspoken. I'm afraid Aunt Claudia was a bit shocked." She raised her chin. "Nonetheless, I would do it again, and I suspect I will continue to do it in the future."

"You've always spoken your mind with me." Reluctantly, he released her.

"That's different, Paul. You've never judged me. Or my parents. I've always felt free to talk to you. About anything." She cast him an affectionate smile and his stomach twisted. "You've always been my dear, dear friend."

And couldn't friendship very well lead to love? Perhaps this was the moment he'd been waiting for. He drew a deep breath. "Bridget, I have something I wish to discuss with you."

"And I have something to tell you as well." Her eyes sparkled. "I'm not entirely certain where to begin." She twisted her hands together in a nervous manner. Would she tell him about the money? Was that what this was about? At long last she raised her gaze to his, a tentative smile on her lips. "I'm going to be married."

He sucked in a sharp breath. His heart dropped. His stomach churned. "Married?"

"I know it's a surprise. I really don't quite believe it my—"

"To whom?" His voice rang out with an curt edge.

Her eyes widened. "Paul, I—"

"To whom?" He clenched his jaw.

She stared at him with a puzzled look in her eye. He fought to remain calm, but a myriad of conflicting emotions battled within him. She straightened her shoulders and met his gaze directly. "Stephen."

Shock stole his breath. He stared in disbelief. "Stephen? My brother?"

"Yes," she said slowly.

"How did this happen?" He ran his fingers through his hair. "When did it happen?"

"I've loved Stephen since I first came to live here. Of course, I was sent away to school almost at once and rarely saw him. When I came home for good this past spring, I endured your mother's efforts to find me a husband. But when Stephen came back from Europe—"

"Barely a month before my return," he said under his breath.

"—he realized I was no longer a child." Wonder sounded in her voice. "He loves me as much as I love him."

"He's declared himself, then?"

"Oh, yes."

"But he hasn't said anything to Mother?" *Or anyone else?*

"Not yet." Unease flickered in her dark eyes. "But he will. Now."

"What do you mean, 'now'?"

She stared at him intently, as if trying to determine whether she should reveal her secrets. Her assessment left him vaguely chilled: She had never before hesitated to talk to him. She shook her head, turned away and paced the room. "I don't know—"

"Damnation, Bridget, it's me. Paul. You've never had trouble talking to me before." Impatience colored his words. "Stop this nonsense and talk to me now."

"Very well." She turned and faced him. "You know how your mother feels about me. She would never allow Stephen and me to marry. In fact, I think she's been looking for a suitable wife for him with much the same enthusiasm she has searched for a husband for me." She hesitated for a moment. "If we went against her wishes, Stephen is certain she'd cut him off without a cent and he—or rather we—would be poor. He doesn't get Uncle Albert's legacy until—"

"He's thirty," Paul said. "Wise man, my stepfather."

Bridget didn't seem to notice the implied criticism of his brother in Paul's words. "However, I know Stephen can make his own fortune—"

Paul snorted.

"—if given a significant amount of money to invest, and—"

"And you got the money from Mrs. Lowell," he said slowly. At once, everything became clear. Colonel Gordon was right to be concerned.

"Why, yes." She pulled her brows together. "How did you know?"

"Colonel Gordon."

"I should have suspected as much," she murmured.

"What did Stephen say?"

"Naturally he was pleased. He said he would invest the money at once." Her smile was bright, but there was something in her manner. . . . No. He was simply seeing what he wanted to see.

"Aren't you going to say something?"

"Are you quite certain, Bridget? Of your feelings and his?"

"I am." She nodded a bit more vehemently than was necessary. For a fleeting moment he wondered if she was trying to convince him or herself. "I know you and Stephen haven't always gotten along, but I hope you can be happy for me. For us."

He forced a smile to his lips. "I am happy for you. Of course. For you both."

She released a relieved breath. "Good. I thought for a moment . . ." She shook her head. An awkward silence stretched between them. Odd he thought. There had never been awkwardness or discomfort between them before this moment. There was so much he wanted to say. So much he'd never say now. "Well."

"Yes?"

She glanced down at her gown. "I should change. . . ."

"And I have a number of things I need to attend to." Abruptly, what he needed most was escape. He strode across the sitting room and jerked open the door.

"Paul," Bridget said quietly.

He stopped but didn't turn. He wasn't entirely certain he could bear to look at her right now. "Yes?"

"I wish . . . what I mean to say is . . . You are my dearest friend and . . ."

"And I'll always be your friend, Bridget."

He stepped over the threshold, closing the door firmly behind him. He leaned against it and stared with unseeing eyes down the wide corridor.

How could he have been so blind? There was no doubt that Bridget loved Stephen. Now that Paul thought about it, he should have seen it years ago. She'd always gazed at his brother as if he were the moon and stars. Of course, Stephen had always treated her like a child. Exactly what she had been until now.

Was it possible that he and his brother were more alike than he'd ever dreamed? Could the same thing have happened to Stephen that had happened to him? Could Stephen have traveled the capitals of Europe and returned to Boston to find in Bridget all he'd ever wanted in a woman?

Perhaps he was wrong about his brother. Perhaps he was interested in more in life than wealth. And perhaps he and he alone could make Bridget happy.

And wasn't that all Paul really wanted?

Bridget stared at the closed sitting room door. Never in her life had she shared so much as an uncomfortable moment with Paul. They had always known exactly what to say to one another. There were, in fact, moments between them when each seemed to know the very thoughts of the other. There was no one in this world closer to her.

Then why was it so difficult to tell him of her feelings for Stephen? Oh, certainly, the two brothers were as different as night from day. They shared nothing physically except a certain vague resemblance and in their natures were as unlike as complete strangers.

She'd expected to share the news about her marriage with a certain element of joy. Paul had said he was happy for her, yet somehow she wasn't quite as happy herself to be telling him.

She sensed a certain distance, a reluctance, perhaps, to accept her news. But was there reluctance on the part of Paul alone?

Nonsense. She'd known Stephen most of her life

and loved him from the very start. Of course, with the exception of the last two months he'd seen and treated her as a child. Perhaps they did not know each other as one adult knows another, but surely that would come in time. They did, indeed, have time; the rest of their lives.

Stephen was the man she'd always wanted. Always loved. Now she would have him. And they would be happy together.

Marriage to Stephen did not mean she could not remain friends with Paul. Did it? Would becoming his sister-in-law change forever their relationship?

The very idea chilled her heart and left her with a cold fear that nothing would ever be the same again.

# Chapter Five

"Paul." Bridget stepped into the foyer from the front parlor, a tentative smile on her face. "If you have a moment, I—"

"Not now, Bridget." Paul nodded curtly and continued toward the library. "I have some correspondence I must take care of."

"But we haven't spoken in several days, and I thought, that is, I hoped—"

Paul closed whatever was left of his heart to the pleading note in her voice. "Perhaps later."

He pushed open the door to the library but couldn't resist a quick glance in her direction. She stood silhouetted by the light, a figure of dejection and confusion. No wonder. He was supposed to be her friend, but he couldn't bear to be anywhere near her. Perhaps in time, but not today. He heaved a heavy sigh and stepped into the library.

The room that had become his safe haven. His sanctuary.

This was where he'd spent most of his time in the days since she'd broken her news, pouring over books and magazines, brochures and pamphlets. This was where he'd decided there was truly nothing to keep him in Boston now. He needn't waste another minute in vacillating between this interest and that. And this was where he'd finally reached a decision, late in the night and with the help of numerous glasses of brandy, a few good cigars and the words of Colonel Gordon. Gordon had even had the wisdom not to pursue further discussion of Bridget once Paul had told him about Stephen, although Paul knew from the expression on the older man's face that he would not let it rest completely.

Paul planned to leave Boston the day after the Harvest Ball. It was probably foolish to wait until then, even though a few days more or less would make little difference in the broader scheme of the rest of his life. It would simply be easier to tell Bridget of his decision at a relatively public event and easier for them both to say good-bye. At the ball there would be no possibility of over-emotional scenes. No likelihood of changing his mind. No chance of saying things that, once said, could never be taken back.

It was best to avoid any private conversations with Bridget right now. Paul wasn't actually avoiding his brother—they simply hadn't seen each other—but he would make it a point before he left to offer the groom his best wishes.

He hadn't lied to Bridget: He did have letters to write. Colonel Gordon had offered to provide him with letters of recommendation and introduction and promised to deliver them within the next day. Paul already had a lengthy list of names and organizations to which to send those.

He turned toward the far wall of the library and his stepfather's massive walnut desk. The well-polished piece of furniture dominated the end of the room, much as a royal presence reigned over a gathering of peasants. He took a step and pulled up short.

"Well, I was wondering when we would meet." He grinned. "I rather thought we might miss each other."

A large, no, a *huge* cat of an unusual orange color sat majestically in the exact center of the desktop, surveying him with an imperious gaze. Aside from his rather impressive girth, and the black streak above his nose that added a light-hearted touch, Paul imagined the creature had the regal nature of one of the carved cats found in the tombs of the pharaohs.

"Smudge, I presume?"

The cat seemed to nod slightly, and Paul bit back a laugh. This was no ordinary feline. Paul perched on the edge of the desk.

"I'm sorry we won't get to know each other. You seem like a decent sort, but I'm not going to be around much longer."

Smudge stared at him with an almost human intensity.

"You needn't look at me like that. It's not my idea to leave." He crossed his arms over his chest. "No, that's not quite accurate. It is entirely my idea to leave. I just hadn't thought I'd be leaving alone."

Where had he gone wrong? What would have happened if he'd arrived home before his brother?

Or if he'd declared himself to Bridget as soon as he'd realized his feelings? Or even later, after she'd told him about Stephen? Would she change her mind? See that she'd chosen the wrong brother?

But had she? He had to admit he didn't know. Stephen had never truly loved anything that money couldn't buy. But perhaps his brother, too, had changed through the years. Maybe Stephen could give Bridget the love she needed and the life she deserved. Paul could only hope so.

"At least she'll have you, won't she, Smudge?" He reached forward and scratched the animal under its chin. Smudge purred with contentment. Paul chuckled and stood. "Well, I do have a great deal of work to attend to and you appear to be sitting smack dab in the middle of it. If you would be so kind as to remove yourself . . ." He gestured with a dramatic flourish and a slight bow.

Smudge got to his feet and sauntered to the edge of the desk, pausing just long enough to survey his options, then leapt lightly from the desk to a well-used green velvet easy chair. He settled into the deep depression worn by years of well-cushioned bottoms shifting to find just the right position for comfort, curled into a perfect circle and gazed up expectantly. Paul wouldn't have been at all surprised to hear him say, "Don't mind me. I'll be quite fine right here. Do go on with whatever it is you're doing."

Of course, the cat said nothing of the sort. Paul grinned and shook the fanciful notion from his head. He circled the desk and sank into Albert's chair. Like all the other furniture in the room it was well worn and just as well loved. Paul would always be grateful that his mother had never cared

enough for this room to replace or rearrange anything within it.

He reached for the haphazard stack of notes and
papers he'd left here this morning, having intended to return to it as soon as he could. He
pulled the pages closer and sifted through the pile,
trying to decide what to deal with now and what
could wait until later. His hand stilled. A page of
his mother's personal stationery lay underneath
the uppermost sheet.

"How did this get here?" He picked up the expensive embossed ivory sheet, glanced at it idly
and set it to one side. He reached for another paper and stopped, the import of the words he'd
barely skimmed slamming into him with a shock-
ing force. Paul snatched up his mother's letter and
read it through. And read it once more.

His stomach churned. Anger surged through
him, then abruptly changed to a full understanding of exactly what his discovery meant.

"Dear Lord, this will break her heart." He raised
his head to meet Smudge's fixed gaze, his manner
slightly accusatory. Paul clenched his jaw. "You're
right, of course.

"I did promise to protect her."


"I hear congratulations are in order." Paul
strode into the fashionable office where his
brother played at having a legitimate job. If he was
using anyone else's money for his "investments,"
he would have been let go long ago. Paul leaned
over Stephen's desk and extended his hand.

"Congratulations?" Stephen stood and shook
Paul's hand, a puzzled expression on his face.
"Thank you, but I'm afraid I don't know what
you're talking about."

"Come now, Stephen." Paul released his hand and settled in the chair facing the desk. "You expect me to believe you've forgotten something quite so momentous?"

"Momentous?" His brow furrowed in confusion.

"I'd call marriage momentous."

"Oh, yes, of course." Stephen's expression cleared. "I simply had no idea you knew."

Paul shrugged. "You know how Mother is when she's gotten what she wants. She can barely contain herself."

"I thought she agreed with me to keep it to herself until the formal announcement."

"Even from family?"

"Perhaps not," Stephen murmured.

"Tell me about her."

"Well . . ." Stephen seemed to search for just the right words. "Louisa is a lovely girl. Very well mannered. She'll make an excellent wife."

"Certainly one must consider such things in a wife, but I gather she has other attributes as well." Paul leaned forward in a confidential manner. "Say, her father?"

"Jonathan Caldwell." Stephen chuckled slyly. "One of the richest men in Boston, in the country perhaps. His interests are far-flung and very profitable: railroads, coal, that sort of thing." A satisfied smile spread across Stephen's face. "I'll be working for him after the wedding and someday . . ."

"Someday it will all be yours." Paul's voice was cool. "So I gather your foray into the world of independent investment will soon be at an end?"

"Thank God." Stephen glanced around the well—appointed office with disgust. "I've discovered there's a great deal of difference between studying investments and turning a significant profit."

"Mother should be pleased that you're giving this up."

"She's ecstatic." Stephen snorted. "I have managed to lose a bit more of her money than I made."

"I understand Bridget also gave you funds to invest," Paul said casually.

"Yes. Well . . ." Stephen shifted uncomfortably. Immediately Paul knew that Bridget's money was gone. "It's a pity, but Bridget will be well provided for."

"Oh?"

"I'll see to that myself."

Paul studied him for a long moment. "She thinks you're going to marry her."

"She's mistaken." Stephen's voice was cool. "I never specifically mentioned marriage."

"What did you mention?" Paul's tone hardened. "Specifically."

Stephen's gaze met his. "I said we would be together, and I fully intend to honor that pledge."

"But not with marriage."

"Don't be ridiculous," Stephen scoffed. "Bridget is not the kind of woman one marries. Why, her background alone is simply—"

"Bridget is more a Templeton than we are." Paul forced a calm note to his voice.

"By blood, perhaps. But blood tainted by her father's common influence. No, I couldn't possibly marry Bridget." Stephen smiled. "But I do want her, and she will be mine nonetheless."

"She expects to be your wife."

"But she will settle for being my mistress." Stephen leaned back in his chair, a smug expression on his face. "She loves me, you know."

"She won't when she discovers you've betrayed her."

"Betrayed is a rather harsh word. She may see it that way in the beginning, but she'll come around. You see, I suspect Bridget has loved me since she was a child. Her feelings will not change simply because her expectations do." He considered his brother silently. "Why all the questions, Paul?"

"Bridget has always been my friend. I care for her." His jaw tightened. "I don't want to see her hurt."

"I don't plan to hurt her. Once she understands my reasoning I'm certain . . ." A speculative gleam appeared in Stephen's eye and he chuckled. "I can't believe I've been this stupid. *You're* in love with her, aren't you?"

"My feelings for Bridget are not—"

"Put it out of your mind right now, dear brother." Stephen stood, planted his hands flat on the desktop and stared down at Paul. "Bridget is, has been and always will be mine. Marriage is a minor detail."

Paul rose to his feet. His gaze locked with his brother's. "She won't consider it a minor detail."

"Bridget has always done exactly what she was told. And she'll do exactly what I want her to do now."

Paul shook his head slowly. "I wouldn't care to place a wager on it."

"No?" He raised a sarcastic brow. "You think you know her so well?"

"I know her better than you do."

"Do you, now? I doubt that. For example"—a slow, nasty smile spread across Stephen's face—"I doubt you know what it feels like to take her in your arms or touch the soft satin perfection of her skin. You don't know what it's like to press your mouth to hers—"

"Stop it, Stephen," Paul growled.

"—warm, supple and inviting, offering just a taste of the passion waiting—"

"Stephen!" A warning rang in his tone.

"—waiting to be unleashed and trained and tamed"—Stephen's voice grew intense—"by me, dear brother, only by me."

"Not if I can help it." Paul clenched and unclenched his fists.

"But you can't. Her mother threw away her heritage for the man she loved, and her daughter will just as gladly sacrifice her honor." He shook his head. "Laura Templeton didn't think twice about selling herself under the guise of love, and neither will Bridget. Calling it love somehow makes it permissible to be a slut."

Perhaps it was the ugliness of the word itself or the self-satisfied smirk on Stephen's face or the slight fear that Bridget did, indeed, love Stephen enough to take what he offered, but something inside Paul snapped. A red haze of fury fogged his vision. Anger clenched his fists once again, and he swung his right with unsuspected power, propelled by the need to protect the woman he loved and to defeat the brother he detested, cutting upward to connect with the underside of Stephen's chin.

The sickening thunk of flesh and bone colliding echoed in the small room. Stephen's head jerked on his neck like a broken doll. He stumbled backwards, hit the wall and slid to the floor.

Paul stepped closer and stared down at him, absently massaging his throbbing knuckles. At that moment, he could have easily killed his only brother.

"You've improved with age. I haven't the inclination to respond in kind right now, although I would enjoy it." Stephen rubbed his jaw and glared. "I hope you gained some measure of satisfaction from that, but it doesn't change anything."

"I'm going to tell Bridget everything," Paul said calmly.

"You do that, Paul, for all the difference it will make. She probably won't believe you, and even if she does, she'll hate you for telling her." Stephen struggled to his feet. "Just remember: It's often the messenger who bears the blame for the message."

# Chapter Six

Bridget paced the length of the library under the watchful eye of Smudge. The cat lay on the edge of an upper bookshelf, his full tail waving to and fro in a lazy rhythm. Briefly, she wondered how he managed to keep his significant bulk balanced, but she had far more serious concerns crowding her mind.

Every few minutes she glanced at the cabinet clock on the mantel. "Where is he, Smudge? Why isn't he back yet?"

Smudge's tail swished across the books in a silent reply.

Bridget had barely seen Paul since she'd told him of her feelings for Stephen. He was obviously avoiding her, and doing a fine job of it. Each and every time she made an effort to speak to him, he brushed her off, as if she was of no more importance than a persistent insect. He'd done it again just a few hours earlier and she'd had quite enough.

Why didn't he want to see her, speak to her? What horrendous crime had she committed to merit such treatment?

His evasion weighed on her more and more every day, dominating her thoughts, lingering always in the back of her mind. Even during those rare moments she and Stephen stole to be alone together, she couldn't stop wondering what had gotten into Paul.

Stephen's behavior, too, had been disturbingly different in recent days. His kisses were more demanding, his embraces more intimate. There was a subtle but definite insistence in the way he took her in his arms or whispered in her ear or brushed her hand with his lips. She found it all rather unnerving and a bit frightening.

Something had changed. Whether within Stephen or herself, she had no idea. The thrill of his touch was wearing oddly thin. She tried to tell herself that it was no doubt natural: eventually excitement gave way to comfort. After all, she had loved him for as long as she could remember.

Perhaps it was nothing more than her preoccupation with Paul's behavior that affected her time with Stephen; the moment she and Paul resolved whatever now stood between them, her unease with Stephen would vanish.

Still, there was the matter of the money. Every time she asked Stephen about it, he expressed a fair amount of confidence, then skillfully directed her attention elsewhere. It was only later that she would realize he hadn't answered her at all. That, too, was wearing thin.

She wrapped her arms around herself and

stared at the fire in the grate. The flames danced as frantically as the questions in her head. Questions that seemed to have no answers. Or none that made sense, at any rate.

She'd waited her entire life for Stephen to realize she'd grown up and to want her as she'd always wanted him. She loved him with her whole heart and soul.

She'd shared all her secrets, hopes and dreams with Paul for most of her life. He knew her better than anyone in the world. Paul was her dearest friend.

She shook her head. Why was she so much more concerned with one brother than the other? Why was the one she worried about most not the lover but the friend? An odd thought flashed through her mind.

*If you could choose only one, which would it be?*

"What are you doing in here?" Paul's voice sounded from the doorway.

She pulled her gaze away from the fire and looked at him for a moment. He was the one person in the world to whom she'd always spoken her mind. She refused to behave differently now.

"I was waiting for you." She nodded at the desk. "Your correspondence was still where you left it, so I knew this was where you'd come first. I didn't want to miss you. Again."

He stepped toward the desk. "Why?"

"I think we need to talk."

"Do we?" He ran his fingers through his hair, and she stifled the impulse to reach out and smoothe it back into place. "And what do you think we need to discuss?"

"What do we need to discuss?" She stared at him in disbelief. "I'd very much like to know what I've done to make you go out of your way to avoid me."

He looked at her with surprise. "You haven't done anything."

She heaved a frustrated sigh. "Then what in the name of all that's holy is wrong?"

"There's nothing—"

At once anger surged through her. "That is a lie, Paul, and you well know it. You have never lied to me before and I don't understand—"

"You can't marry him." Paul's words were clipped, his tone level.

"What?"

"Stephen. You can't marry him."

"Of course I can marry him." Her words carried the force of a conviction she wasn't yet prepared to doubt aloud. "Once he makes his fortune with the money I gave him we can be married."

"No."

"Why not?"

Paul hesitated, as if he was choosing his words carefully. "He's not right for you."

"Don't be silly. I know you two have never gotten along, but of course he's right for me. He's always been right for me."

"How do you know? He's been away for a full year. You've spent most of your life at school. You and Stephen have only really been together for the two short months he's been home."

A desperate intensity underlaid his words. "You don't know anything about him. About who he is and what he wants. He's simply been a handsome, distant figure that dominated a young girl's dreams of romance."

"That's not fair." But was it true?

"Isn't it?"

"I love him," she said staunchly.

"Do you?" His gaze pinned hers. "How can you love someone you barely know?"

"I know him." Her protest sounded weak even to her own ears. "I've known him all my life."

"And you've loved him since you were a child, but have you ever talked to him?" He moved closer to her. "Tell me, Bridget, about his likes and dislikes. His dreams, his desires, his values."

"That's not important," she said faintly.

"No?" His gaze searched her face. "Tell me this, then. Before now, has he ever shown the slightest interest in you as something other than a cousin?"

"Well, I—"

"Did he ever write to you?"

"I wrote to him."

"And did he respond? Did he write you long letters pouring out his innermost thoughts and feelings?"

"No!" She caught her breath. *But you did.*

She stared up at him. The moment between them stretched on endlessly. His hazel eyes seemed to darken behind his glasses. Her heart thudded in her chest and an odd ache swept through her.

"Bridget." Her name was scarcely more than a husky whisper on his lips. "I—"

"Paul, where on earth have you been?" Aunt Claudia swept into the room. Paul swiveled away from Bridget toward his mother. Bridget crossed her arms and stared at the fire, at once grateful for the interruption and strangely disappointed.

"What is it, Mother?" he asked, his voice strained.

"The ball is tomorrow night and I must discuss a matter of some importance with you." Claudia glanced at Bridget and pointedly raised a brow. "Alone."

"I'll be going." Bridget started toward the door, struggling against a confusing need to glance once more at Paul and the fear of what she might see in his eyes. What on earth was happening to her?

"Not quite yet." Claudia's imperious tone rang in the room and Bridget pulled up short. Her aunt raised her hand and pointed a long finger toward Smudge, still lounging on an upper shelf. "*What* is that?"

Dear Lord, she'd forgotten all about the cat. In the few days she'd had him, Bridget, assisted by a house full of servants who owed their livelihood but not their affection to her aunt, had kept Smudge's presence discreet. Apparently, Stephen too had kept his word.

"It's a cat, Mother."

"Obviously, it's a cat." Claudia glared. "What is it doing in my house?"

"He lives here." Bridget drew a deep breath. "He's mine."

"Get rid of him." Claudia's command left no room for argument. She turned toward her son. "Now, as I was about to say—"

"No." Bridget fought to hide the quaver in her voice.

Claudia swiveled to face her. "What did you say?"

"I said no." Bridget lifted her chin. "He is mine and I refuse to get rid of him."

A hot flush swept up Claudia's face. "This is my home and I will not allow—"

"This is my home, too. For as long as I want it to be. Precisely as Uncle Albert wished." Bridget met Claudia's angry gaze. "I'm no longer a child to be bullied and threatened." A calm brought by newly found courage washed through her. "You've spent a great deal of time and effort to marry me off these past months. You should know, Aunt Claudia, that I have no intention of allowing you to select a husband for me, just as I have no intention of allowing you to choose what dress I wish to wear or whether or not I will keep a cat or anything else, for that matter."

Claudia sputtered, "How dare you speak to me this way? I took you in. I gave you a home."

"Uncle Albert took me in. Long before it was yours, this was his home. And my mother's."

"Your mother? I have done everything in my power to make certain you would not turn out exactly like her. Apparently I've failed." Claudia fairly spat the words. "Let me tell you about your mother. She turned her back on her family and her class all for an ignorant, no-account Irishman. She was nothing more than an ungrateful wanton tart. And so, I suspect, are you."

"Mother!" Paul's eyes widened with shock. "How can you say such a thing?"

"I can say it because it's true." A nasty gleam of triumph flickered in Claudia's eye.

"I would suspect you of all people would recognize a tart when you saw one." Bridget's tone was cool. "After all, you did marry Uncle Albert for his wealth and position."

Paul choked.

Claudia gasped.

"Or perhaps"—Bridget paused—"*tart* is not a strong enough word."

Claudia sucked in her breath, then lunged toward Bridget, drawing back her hand and letting it fly.

Paul caught her arm, her palm inches from Bridget's face. "That's enough, Mother."

For a moment, the three stood frozen. Then Claudia shook off her son's grasp.

"For once you're right, Paul. That is quite enough." She straightened her bodice, collected her dignity and cast Bridget a venomous glare. "For the moment." She turned and stalked from the room.

Bridget stared after her.

"Are you all right?" Concern sounded in his voice.

"I think so." Bridget shook her head. "I can't believe I said that."

"Mother had it coming." Paul took her hands. "You're shaking."

She gazed down at her hands in his and uttered a weak laugh. "Courage takes rather more out of you than I'd thought."

"You stood up to her." He grinned. "I'm impressed and really rather proud."

"I'm somewhat proud myself." She stared at their clasped hands. He had wonderful hands. Large and warm and gentle. Why hadn't she noticed before? "You see, recently I've realized that I can't let other people run my life and make all of my decisions. The only person I can truly depend on is myself."

"You can depend on me."

She raised her gaze to his. Her heart stilled at the look in his eye. "Can I?"

"Always."

His gaze locked with hers. The world seemed to slow and stop and fade. He bent his head nearer to her and without thinking she leaned toward him until his lips brushed hers. She gasped but didn't move. Couldn't move. The pressure of his lips increased and he gathered her closer to him until she could feel his heart beat against hers, and still she couldn't pull away. Her breath mingled with his and warmth spread from his touch to suffuse her body and her soul. A wonder she had never dared dream of flooded through her, leaving her with a nameless ache that yearned for the release of tears or laughter or both.

Slowly, Paul drew back and released her, leaving her with a vague sense of loss.

"I shouldn't have done that. I apologize." There was a note of dismissal in his voice. He turned to the desk and rifled through the papers awaiting him. "It was probably nothing more than the emotion of the moment." He looked back at her. "After all, you love my brother."

"I do." How could she have forgotten? She nodded vigorously. "Yes, of course I do." Abruptly, she needed to leave. No—escape. She edged toward the door, Smudge at her feet. She hadn't even noticed his approach. Bridget bent down and scooped him into her arms. "I . . . I really should go." She turned and flew out the door, barely hearing his soft words behind her.

"As should I."

# *Chapter Seven*

He was a fool and worse. A coward.

Paul stared at the dancers circling the floor like so many brightly colored birds migrating to distant shores. All moving in the same direction, in time to the music, in step with each other. He barely saw them.

Somewhere in the crowded gathering of Harvest Ball guests, Bridget was more than likely in Stephen's arms. His mother was no doubt in a quiet corner planning her oldest son's wedding with the mother of his future bride. And Colonel Gordon was probably flirting with beautiful women, expounding on some point of interest with his contemporaries, or having a quiet cigar in a well-hidden corner.

He hadn't told Bridget about Stephen after all. He simply couldn't. Let someone else break the news to her, and break her heart as well. She'd had the courage to stand up to his mother, but Paul couldn't find the strength within himself to face her. She would find out soon enough. And Colonel Gordon would always be there for her. The man loved her like a daughter, and he wouldn't let her down. Not like Paul.

The music ended. Couples left the floor, to be replaced or to regroup and return. The orchestra started a new arrangement, the strains of a melody mingling with excited chatter and idle laughter. Paul heard none of it.

His cowardice, he realized, wasn't limited to his failure to tell Bridget the truth. It was her possible response that scared the hell out of him. Oh, certainly, he could have handled tears or despair if he'd had to. He'd even toyed with the hope that she'd turn to him, but dismissed the idea. He couldn't spend the rest of his life knowing that she loved his brother and he would always be second in her heart.

No, what truly terrified him was the thought that his brother was right. That regardless of what Stephen did, regardless of his callous plans, she would still love him. She would sacrifice not just her honor but her soul to be with him. The possibility chilled him to the bone and was the most compelling reason why he couldn't reveal Stephen's nature.

His gaze skimmed the crowd, seeking a midnight blue dress with white blossoms scattered amid its folds. At first he'd decided not to come tonight at all. He had bags to pack and preparations to make. But when the others had gone without him, he'd realized his original plan was best: He owed Bridget a private farewell. Whatever else there was between them, whatever else there might have been, he was still her friend and she deserved more from him than a good-bye in front of his mother and brother. Once he found her, he'd tell her of his decision, promise to write and wish her well. She'd protest of course, but Bridget, of all people, would understand.

It would all be very civilized and cordial, simply the parting of two dear friends. He'd resist the temptation to take her in his arms and press his lips to hers and tell her how he'd miss her.

And just how much he loved her.

Bridget slipped away from the too-warm, too-crowded ballroom and stepped out onto the terrace. The glow of a full, orange moon coupled with the flickering of well-placed gas lamps to throw the terrace into pools of golden light surrounded by deep shadows. A slight trace of perfume and the faint tang of cigar smoke floated on the breeze, evidence of others who had found sanctuary here before her. The sharp scent of autumn promised the winter to come, and the night was cool and crisp, calling for a cape or at least a shawl. But the fresh air soothed her overheated flesh and calmed her bewildered spirit.

Not since her father's death, followed far too quickly by her mother's, had Bridget been so confused.

Paul had kissed her. And Lord help her, she had kissed him back. A kiss she couldn't get out of her mind. A kiss nothing like that of the man she loved.

Stephen's kisses were hard and exciting and dangerous and weakened her knees. Or at least they had at first. Even before Paul had kissed her, she had noticed a change in Stephen's embrace.

*Or was the change perhaps in her?*

Paul's kiss was gentle, with passion restrained and promises unsaid but there nonetheless. And his kiss, too, weakened her knees.

Stephen's kiss made her blood race.

Paul's captured her soul.

She leaned against a stone planter and sighed. "What am I going to do?"

"What do you want to do?" Colonel Gordon's voice drifted from the shadows.

She stepped around the planter, guided by the smell of cigar smoke. Colonel Gordon lounged on a marble garden seat partially hidden in the shadows and patted the spot beside him. Without a word, Bridget joined him.

"I've always found a good cigar helps when I have a decision to make." He chuckled. "But I doubt if that's exactly what you're looking for."

"No." She smiled. "But thank you."

"Then perhaps you just need to talk."

She stared at her gloved hands folded in her lap. He was right: she did need to talk, but she wasn't quite sure what to say, or how to voice the conflicting emotions churning inside her. The colonel puffed on his cigar, waiting for her to begin. That was one of the nicest things about him. He had a great deal of patience.

"Colonel," she said finally, "how do you know if you're really, truly in love?"

He blew a long breath. "Are you sure you wouldn't rather have a cigar?" She shook her head. "I didn't think so. Pity. That's a difficult question, Bridget. I wouldn't doubt even Adam and Eve struggled with it.

"Love, real love, is a tricky animal. I've always suspected God created it just to keep men and women in a constant state of confusion. To keep us on our toes."

She heaved a heartfelt sigh. "Life would certainly be simpler without it."

"But not nearly as wonderful." He studied the burning tip of his cigar, glowing cherry red in the dark. "Did you know I was once in love with your mother?"

Bridget widened her eyes in surprise. "I had no idea."

"She was a wonderful woman. Full of fire and spirit. But by the time I declared myself to her she had already fallen in love with your father." He stared into the night, as if the events of another age hovered just beyond the shadows. "I don't recall the exact details of how they met, but I remember distinctly when she told me how she knew she loved him. Something about his gaze catching hers, and the rest of the world vanishing and leaving only them. One magic moment, she called it.

"She was right about that, too. I didn't realize it until later, but there's always that one special instant, the merest second frozen in time, when you know what you feel is right and true and—"

"Magic," Bridget said under her breath.

"Magic," he said simply, as if that one word left nothing more to explain. "There you have it, Bridget, advice from your own mother. And far better than anything I could give you." He glanced at her. "Does it help?"

"I think so. It's rather nice to receive advice from my mother."

"Sometimes the best advice comes where we least expect it."

"Does it?" she said absently.

"Indeed." He pulled a long puff on his cigar and blew the smoke out into the night.

"Colonel Gordon?" A familiar figure stepped into view.

"Good evening, Paul." Colonel Gordon pulled himself to his feet and grasped Paul's hand.

Paul laughed. "I thought you'd be out here. I could smell that cigar from the next county."

The colonel grinned. "One of the great pleasures in life, my boy. I didn't think we'd see you here tonight. Are you packed, then?"

Paul nodded. "I am, sir. I—"

"Packed?" At once Bridget stood and stepped forward. "Where are you going?"

"Bridget?" Paul appeared distinctly uncomfortable. "I didn't see you."

Colonel Gordon raised a brow. "I gather you haven't told her?"

"Not yet." Paul's voice was even.

"Tell me what?" Apprehension fluttered in her stomach. "Where are you going?"

"Well, I, for one, am returning to the party." The colonel glanced from Paul to Bridget and back again. "Good luck, son."

"Good luck?" Her voice rose. "Why is he wishing you good luck? What do you need luck for?"

"I'm leaving Boston." Idly, he snapped a branch from the holly bush growing in the planter beside her, as if his announcement carried no more significance than his action.

Her heart stilled. "What do you mean? Why would you leave Boston?"

"You of all people should know the answer to that." He studied the twig in his hand, turning it this way and that. "I've decided, since I can't narrow my interest down to any one area, to take up a profession where I sample everything that catches my eye. And indulge my desire for travel and adventure and all that goes with it. I'm going to write."

"Like Colonel Gordon?"

"Not exactly. I don't want to write books. I want to write for newspapers and magazines." His gaze met hers. "I'm going to be a journalist."

"That's wonderful. But don't they have journalists right here in Boston?"

"Rather a lot, actually." He shrugged. "But they're in short supply in the West."

"The West?" Visions of half-naked savages and gun-toting bank robbers flashed through her mind. "How far west did you plan on going?"

Paul grinned ruefully. "I don't know."

She stared at him, shock stealing her voice. A tight, aching band seemed to wrap around her chest, her heart. It was hard to breathe, hard to think.

"Aren't you going to say anything?"

What could she say? *Don't go! Don't leave me!* She didn't have the right. To him, she was nothing more than a friend. She forced a steady note to her voice. "It should be quite an adventure. You've always wanted adventure."

He stared at her as if there were something more he wanted to say but couldn't find the words. Finally he shrugged and flicked the twig into the bushes bordering the terrace. "I didn't want to tell you with the rest of the family. I'll tell them tomorrow before I leave."

"Tomorrow?" Her throat burned and she could barely choke out the word. "You're leaving tomorrow?"

"I think it's best." His voice was quiet.

*Is it?* "I shall miss you."

"I'll write, of course."

"Of course." There was so much more to say, but words failed her. She and Paul sounded like two strangers, polite and proper. She forced a light-hearted note to her words. "What will I do without you?"

"You're much stronger than you ever thought you were. Than I ever thought you were. You've grown up and you've turned out"—he smiled—"very well. You'll be fine. You . . . and Stephen."

"Stephen," she echoed.

"Good-bye, Bridget. I—" Once again he looked as if there was something else he wished to say. Instead he nodded sharply. "Good-bye." Quickly he turned, strode to the edge of the terrace and onto a garden path leading into the dark and out of her life. In an instant he was gone.

How could she let him go? But how could she keep him here? Keep him safe. Keep him beside her. She had no real hold on him. They were friends, dear friends, but no more than that. There was nothing between her and Paul. Nothing at all.

Just a kiss.

Just a moment.

Just . . . magic.

"Dear Lord, is it possible?" Could it be true? But she was going to marry Stephen. It was what she'd always wanted. What she still wanted. Wasn't it?

"Meow."

Bridget jumped in surprise, then squinted in the direction of the cat's cry. Two eyes glowed green in the shadows cast by the well-groomed hedge. She stepped closer. "Smudge? What on earth are you doing here?"

The cat sat gazing up at her with an expression

that seemed to ask where else he would be.

"I suppose it doesn't matter." She heaved a weary sigh. "Come along, then. I'll put you in the carriage until it's time to return home and—"

Without warning, Smudge jumped to his feet, stared into her eyes for a mere instant, then turned and bolted into the bushes with an uncanny speed she'd never imagined possible.

"Smudge!" Her call echoed after him. The very last thing she needed right now was to lose Smudge, on top of losing Paul. She took a step forward, her gaze scanning the tight growth of the bushes for any break that might allow her to slip through. She bent to look closer. There on the ground lay a familiar red leather book. With a shaky hand, she picked it up and turned it over.

A gilded feline face, centered in an ornate design of curls and flourishes, glittered up at her.

"*The Care and Feeding of the Modern Feline,*" she whispered.

She stepped into a pool of moonlight. Her hands trembled, the book fell open of its own accord to a point about ten pages from the end. Pages that were blank when last she looked now were covered with the elegant penmanship and script of a well-practiced hand.

*A Spell to Bring Forth a True Love.*

She gasped. Surely this was some sort of prank? Or at the very least sheer nonsense.

*But what if it wasn't?*

And certainly she didn't believe in things like spells.

*But didn't she believe in magic?*

The words seemed to leap out at her.

*When the hours grow short, the dark's*
*    shadows near through*
*'Neath the full of the moon, this will call him*
*    to you.*
*Once, again, and once more, in the moon's*
*    golden light*
*'Tis these words that will fetch him on*
*    Halloween night:*

*By the stars, by the heavens*
*By all ancient and new*
*Bring the one straight to me*
*With a love that is true.*

*With a love that is true.* Was it possible? Could this chant, this spell, answer her questions? Could it really show her true love? Surely not. But was it any more farfetched than Smudge or his book being here in the first place?

A shiver ran up her spine. Fear battled with excitement. Why not say the words? She had nothing to lose and perhaps a great deal to gain.

Bridget drew a deep breath.

"By the stars, by the heavens, by all ancient and new, bring the one straight to me with a love that is true."

She stilled and listened. Nothing. She skimmed the text again. Of course. Once, again and once more would be three times.

"By the stars, by the heavens, by all ancient and new"—her voice grew stronger—"bring the one straight to me with a love that is true."

The sound of the French doors opening caught her attention, and she swiveled to see a tall figure silhouetted in the light from the ballroom.

"Paul!" Her heart leapt. The book fell from her hands and she started forward.

"Paul?" Stephen sauntered out of the shadows. "Wrong Templeton, my dear."

Disappointment slashed through her like a sword. At once she knew what she should have known all along.

There was never a time when she hadn't believed she loved Stephen. But was there ever a single instant in which she knew with blinding clarity that this, indeed, was love? One magic moment?

No. Never. Not with Stephen.

Her breath caught. How could she have been such a fool as to confuse childish infatuation for love? The kind of love her mother had found with her father, that didn't depend on finances or money. The kind that lasted forever.

The kind a girl recognized when a man's kiss was like a promise unsaid and captured her soul.

"Paul said he wasn't coming tonight." Stephen stepped closer and smiled down at her. He was as handsome and dashing as ever, but it no longer mattered.

"He came after all." *And now he's gone.* "I thought he'd returned."

"So my brother was here?" Stephen said slowly. She nodded.

"And did he tell you . . ."

"Yes." She bit back a sob.

"Bridget"—he took her hands—"it won't be so bad. We can still be together."

"We can?" She stared at him in confusion.

"Of course. Louisa has an almost vulgar dowry, and once she and I are married, I'll have access to all her funds as well—"

"Married?" What was he talking about?

"I can provide you with a home of your own and see you as often as possible." He pulled her closer. "I know it isn't quite the future you envisioned, but it's better this way."

"Is it?" Her words were cautious.

"Indeed it is. You know Mother would never accept you as my wife. She'd make your life a living hell. But Louisa Caldwell is exactly the type of daughter-in-law she's always wished for and—"

"You're going to marry Lousia Caldwell?" Shock coursed through her. "Yet you still want to be with me?"

"Bridget, I care deeply for you. Nothing will ever change that." He drew her hand to his mouth and brushed the back of her gloves with his lips. "I want you in my life always. And with the Caldwell money—"

She pulled her hands from his, stifling the impulse to wipe her hands on her skirt, and took a step back. "And what happened to my money? Where is the ten thousand dollars I gave you?"

He shrugged in the carefree manner she'd always thought so charming. "Investments are exceedingly speculative. I'm afraid the money is gone." He stopped and narrowed his eyes. "I thought Paul told you all about this."

"Paul knew? He knew you'd lost my money and were planning to marry someone else and make me your"—she could barely choke out the word—"mistress?"

"Well, yes, you see—"

"He didn't say a word."

"Oh. I thought certainly . . ." Stephen paused. "He probably assumed you would be upset and couldn't bring himself to tell you. You see, my dear, Paul's in love with you."

"Paul's in love with me?" The words caught in her throat.

Stephen smirked. "I do hope you let him down gently. Although I would suggest, given our arrangement, that it would be best if you limited your contact with the rest of the family and . . ."

She barely heard Stephen. Paul loved her! She laughed with the sheer joy of it.

"Bridget?" Stephen frowned. "What is so funny?"

"You are, Stephen." She cast him a pitying glance. "You are such a fool, and I am no better for not having seen it before now."

"A fool." Astonishment washed across his face and his mouth dropped open.

"Oh, do close your mouth. You look like your mother." She snorted with disdain. "Did you honestly believe I'd agree to spend my life hidden away somewhere waiting until you had a free moment to favor me with your presence after you lost the fortune I gave you so that we could be married?"

"But you love me," he said with conviction.

"No, Stephen." She shook her head. "A twelve-year-old girl fell in love with a fascinating prince from a fairy tale and through the years failed to notice the prince was not a prince at all, but something of a frog. And failed to realize as well what can sustain the dreams of a naive child simply will not serve for a woman."

"You never used to speak this way to me, Bridget. I don't understand what's come over you." He glared. "You've changed. And not for the better."

"Indeed I have, Stephen," she said firmly, "and past time, too."

"You'll regret this." Stephen drew himself up in a haughty manner. "I shall not take you back."

"No, Stephen. It's I who will not take you back." She mustered her sweetest smile. "And I rather suspect it's you who will regret it."

He stared at her, stunned into silence. Then abruptly turned on his heel and stalked off.

Bridget released a long breath she hadn't realized she'd held. She had been right when she'd said courage took a lot out of you. Stephen's betrayal should have crushed her. Instead she felt nothing but a fair amount of relief and a vague sense of sadness. Poor Stephen. He really was a fool. And he didn't know her at all. Not the way Paul did.

Paul! He loved her. And she hadn't a doubt she loved him.

But was he her true love?

She glanced around the terrace and spotted Smudge's book lying near a planter. She fetched it quickly and stepped back into the moonlight. Now all she had to do was repeat the spell for the third and last time; surely Paul would appear.

But what if he didn't? What if her true love was someone else altogether? What if, Lord help her, it really was Stephen, after all? Bridget raised her chin. If that was the case, she would live her life without love and go to her grave old and alone. One way or another she would know.

She opened the book, glanced at the words and snapped it shut. Her voice rang without hesitation. "By the stars, by the heavens, by all ancient and new, bring the one straight to me with a love that is true."

The world around her seemed to skitter to a stop. She waited, her senses strained for something, anything. A symbol. A sign. A clap of thunder. A bolt of lightning. Nothing.

Except a quiet purr.

Bridget jerked her gaze to the path leading to garden. In the darkness, green eyes gleamed. A figure emerged from the night, Smudge carried in his arms.

"Paul," she whispered. Her heart thudded in her chest. She clapped her hand over her mouth. The book tumbled to the ground.

"I found your cat." Paul's voice was hesitant, as if he wasn't sure of his reception. "I don't know how he got there, but I opened the door of my carriage and there he was." Paul glanced down at the creature in his arms and chuckled. "The tyrannical little beast refused to let me get in, so I thought I'd better bring him back to you before anything happened to him."

"Thank you." She took Smudge, gave him a quick, grateful hug and set him on the ground."

"Well, I should be going—"

"No." Her voice was firm.

"Bridget," a weary note sounded in his voice, "I really think—"

"I spoke to Stephen." She studied him intently. "He told me everything."

"About Louisa and your money?"

"Oh, certainly about that." She waved a dismissive hand. "He also told me," she took a step toward him, "That you're in love with me."

Paul ran his fingers through his hair. "He told you that, did he?"

"He did." She stepped closer. "Why didn't you tell me?"

"How could I?" he asked sharply. "You love my brother. You told me yourself, you've always been in love with him. Telling you how I feel would only embarrass us both and make no difference whatsoever."

"No?" She moved nearer. Only a scant few inches separated them. "Perhaps you should make certain of that."

"Bridget." He stared down at her, puzzled. "I don't—"

"Tell me, Paul." She looked up at him, her gaze locked with his. Something in his eyes flickered. Hope? "Tell me."

"Very well." His tone was strained, as if he feared to say the words aloud. "I love you, Bridget."

"And I love you." She reached up and smoothed his hair back into place.

He caught her hand. "I thought you loved Stephen."

"I thought I did, too." She hesitated, groping for the right words. "I thought what I felt for Stephen the very first time I saw him was love. And that feeling never changed. But I did. I grew up. Even before I knew about Louisa and his plans for me, even before I suspected he wasn't quite what I'd imagined him to be, I had doubts. I confused the hero worship of a child for the love of a woman. I was a fool," she said simply. "And I was wrong."

"Are you certain you're not wrong now?" Tension underlaid his words.

"I'm certain I don't want to live my days without you. I'm certain what I feel for you is real and true and so much stronger than I ever dreamed possible that it's exciting and terrifying at the same time. And I have never been more certain of anything"—her voice broke—"than I am of this."

He stared into her eyes, as if searching for the

truth and afraid to believe it. Long moments passed by. Unease trickled through her.

"Paul? Aren't you going to say anything?"

"No." He pulled her into his arms and lowered his head to hers. "Only this." His lips pressed against hers, warm and firm and exciting. She slid up her hands to caress the back of his neck. At once his restraint broke. His kiss deepened, intense and demanding, and she met him with her own needs and desires. And love. Always love.

He drew back and gazed down at her. "You will marry me, won't you?"

She laughed. "Unless you have an heiress your mother would prefer."

"My mother has nothing to say about it." He paused, his gaze searching her face. "Besides, we'll scarcely ever see her once we leave Boston."

"We?"

"I'd always planned on going and taking you with me." He brushed his lips across her forehead. "Will you come with me? Marry me and explore the world by my side?"

"Explore the world." Wonder colored her words. She'd never even dared to hope for such a thing. She stared up at him. "And will we have wonderful adventures together?"

He grinned. "I promise."

"And do you also promise that our lives will never be dull and ordinary like—"

"—boring whites and pale creams and sickly yellows." He laughed. "No. We will always live a life of midnight blues and vivid reds and purples the color of the sky at sunset."

"And do you further promise to love me always and forever?"

"Always." He pulled her hand to his lips and

kissed the center of her palm, folding her fingers around the spot still tingling from his touch. "And forever."

"When did you know?" She hesitated, then plunged ahead. "Did you have . . . well, a magic moment with me?"

"They are all magic with you, my love."

"No. I mean one single instant when you knew you loved me." She held her breath.

"Absolutely." He nodded solemnly, but his eyes twinkled. "It was the moment I arrived at the docks and saw you standing there, slightly behind my mother and Stephen, to welcome me home. I think I would have known you anywhere, yet at that second it was as if I was seeing you for the first time. And not merely with my eyes, but with my heart and soul."

"Oh, my." She sighed the words. "I thought perhaps it was when you kissed me. It seems that, for many people, especially those who have known each other as long as we have, magic moments always come hand-in-hand with a first kiss."

"That was confirmation, if I needed such a thing." He raised a brow. "You certainly seem to know a great deal about magic moments."

"Girls in schools far from home tend to chat late into the night," she said primly. "Especially about men and magic."

"Now it's your turn. Was there a single moment when you knew?"

"I should have known when we were children and you told your mother you were the one who had broken her favorite vase. Or when Uncle Albert died and you found me crying and didn't tell me to dry my tears and stop such nonsense. Or when Smudge liked you at once. Cats have an unerring instinct about people, you know. But I'm apparently quite ordinary when it comes to these things . . . When you kissed me"—she gazed up at him—"it was magic."

"Magic." He bent to kiss her once more.

The indignant cry of a cat stopped him. She glanced around the terrace. Smudge lay on the edge of the planter, his bulk balanced precariously, his long, full tail swinging back and forth like a pendulum. He eyed them with the satisfied air of a job well done.

Paul laughed. "Always trust the instincts of a cat."

"And your heart," she said softly, and turned her face toward her own true love.

His lips met hers and joy surged through her soul and she marveled at the magic of this moment.

And all the moments to come.

# Heart's Desire

## Nina Coombs

# Chapter One

Hector shifted restlessly on Mistress's warm lap. He was comfortable enough there, and he liked being stroked, but he'd rather be outside running around with the other cats. Why did Mistress want to give him away, anyway? He hadn't been that mischievous and—

*You have done no wrong.* Mistress's voice echoed in his head. He knew her lips hadn't moved. She spoke to him often in this way. The first time it had scared him, but now he was used to it. *You have a task to perform,* she went on. *And if you do it properly, I will take you up to my special room and I will give you your heart's desire.*

Well, that made things different. He didn't know what his heart's desire *was* exactly—he'd have to think about it—but he did want to see the inside of that mysterious tower room. Though all the cats talked about it, only the most favored ever got to go up there. And when they came back, they wouldn't breathe a word about it. Even his very own mother wouldn't tell him what it was like up there.

*Patience*, Mistress said. *First you must finish your task. Then you will understand all.*

She smoothed the fur on his back in the exact way he liked, and he settled down to enjoy some good stroking.

But, too soon, the door opened and the butler announced another visitor. "Mistress Amity Phelps."

From his place on Mistress's lap, Hector looked the newcomer over carefully. Brown hair pulled back in a severe bun, brown eyes, a dress of brown stuff, too. A plain young woman, all brown, quite thin, and not beautiful like Mistress. But there was something about her—something that pulled at him right away. What could it be?

"Sit down," Mistress said.

Mistress Phelps sat, her back stiff, her hands clasped in her lap.

Hector listened closely as Mistress asked the usual questions.

"With the money, what business would you intend to operate?"

"I want to buy my former home," Mistress Phelps said. She had a strong low voice, pleasing to his ears. "My father owned several merchant ships. Unfortunately they went down in a storm, and we lost everything, including the house. My father died shortly afterwards, and two months ago my mother passed on."

She told the sad story without any change in her voice or expression, but Hector could *feel* her sadness. Deep inside him was an awful feeling of loss—*her* loss. He'd never felt anything so terrible before.

"And if you buy this home?" Mistress asked. "What would you do with it, what business would you operate?"

Amity Phelps shifted uncomfortably, but her voice was still strong. "Oh, I would open a boardinghouse for seafaring men. And to help me I'd hire back our old retainers, George and Martha." For the first time the woman smiled. Hector liked her smile—there was a kindness to it. "They're getting on in years," she said, "but they're two of the best people on earth."

"They are not already employed," Mistress asked, "this George and Martha?"

Mistress Phelps sighed. "I'm afraid they've had a bit of trouble finding work—because of their age, you see. The truth is, they'd still be with me, but I can barely feed myself these days. That's why I want to open the boardinghouse. To take care of us all."

Mistress nodded. Her hands kept moving upon Hector's back, but they didn't feel as soothing as they had. If only there was something he could do to erase the sadness, the loneliness, from this young woman's eyes, from her heart.

*Patience.*

"And you have kept cats before?" Mistress asked.

Amity Phelps gulped. "No, ma'am. My father disapproved of having animals about the house. But," she hurried on, "I would be very good to a cat." She lifted her hands in a gesture of resignation. "I don't expect to marry, you see. My young man went down with one of my father's ships. And there is no one else."

315

"There are dogs," Mistress said, "if one is lonely."

Hector stiffened. Was she trying to talk this young woman out of taking him? Amity Phelps was the only one of all the people Mistress had interviewed in this long day that he'd cared a bit about. If he had to leave home, he'd rather leave with her.

"I'm a very independent person," she said. "I think a cat would make a better companion for me than a dog. A cat and I could each go our own ways—and yet we'd have each other."

Mistress nodded again. She lifted a jeweled hand and picked up a book covered in red leather. It had been laying on the table beside her through all the interviews, but this was the first time she'd picked it up.

"This is the manual," Mistress said. *"The Care and Feeding of the Modern Feline.* You must agree to follow it precisely."

Amity Phelps got to her feet. "I'll have to read it first, ma'am. To see if I can do what it says."

"As you wish." Mistress handed it over. "It is a short book. Sit again and read it now. Then we shall continue."

Amity took the book and resumed her seat. Hector watched her face. What was in that book anyhow? And why was it important?

*Patience,* Mistress counseled. *In good time you shall see all.*

Amity read carefully. She had little more than the clothes on her back these days, but she would not lie to acquire the ten thousand dollars, though it seemed an almost unimaginable sum. If she couldn't—or wouldn't—do as the manual instructed, then she would just say so. And that would be that.

What a strange book. The cat picture on the cover, with the gilded cat's face and emerald eyes, might be expected. But to have such a book bound in expensive leather, and with gilded edges . . . that seemed odd. And the rules inside . . . At least once an hour she was to find the cat and speak lovingly to it. Stroke it then, too. But let it come and go as it pleased. Except for Halloween night, when she was not to let it out of her sight. She didn't particularly care to have the creature share her bed, as the book said she must, but if it was to be in the house it would undoubtedly sleep anywhere it pleased. And it would be nice to have company. She'd been lonely for so long.

She felt herself growing a little flushed. These rules—they made her think of loving someone else—not a cat, but a man. That, of course, was out of the question. She was a spinster, and it was foolish even to think about men—at her age.

"There is no proper age for love." The beautiful woman with the red-gold hair smiled at her from the thronelike chair, her eyes sad.

A shiver prickled down Amity's spine. "How did you—"

"Know what you were thinking?"

"Yes." Perhaps it had been a mistake to come here. That strange ad in the paper, and now—

"Most people think of loving when they read the manual."

That was probably true, but it still didn't explain—

"So, you have finished?"

Amity nodded. "Yes. But these blank pages in the back, ma'am—what are they for?"

"Not to concern yourself with." The woman leaned closer and scrutinized her face. "So, you are willing? You can take care of the cat? You can do as the manual says?"

"Yes, I can do it. And I will." Amity looked at the young tabby resting in the woman's lap. "Is that the cat?"

The woman smiled. "Yes. Hector. He is named Hector."

Amity tried to smile. "A hero's name. But I don't know if he'll want to come with me." Now that she was really thinking about doing this strange thing, it seemed even more weird. "What if he runs away?"

The woman shook her head. "This he will not do. I promise you."

Hector stretched and rubbed his head against Mistress's arm. He liked this young woman, this Amity Phelps, but he still wasn't sure he wanted to leave home. He had the whole big estate to roam around on here. And he would miss the others.

*This is the new mistress,* Mistress said. *This is the one.*

*But I want to stay here, where I belong.*

*Remember my words,* Mistress said. *Succeed in your task and you shall go up to the tower room— and be given your heart's desire. Fail and . . . But you must not fail.* She got to her feet, still holding him against her warm bosom. He wanted to dig in his claws and stay there, but he knew better. No cat ever touched Mistress with claws.

"I am satisfied," Mistress said to Amity Phelps.

Amity struggled to her feet. "You mean—"

"Hector will go home with you. He is your cat."

Amity looked a little stunned. "Oh. That is—thank you."

"The money will be in your hands this afternoon," Mistress went on. "I trust you will use it well."

Amity Phelps still looked stunned. No wonder. From the looks of her, she hadn't eaten much for some time. And now she was going to have ten thousand dollars. "I will. I will," she repeated. "And thank you."

Mistress handed him over then, and nodded at the book in its red leather cover. "Thanks are not needed," she said. "Only do what is required by the book and all will be well."

And then she was gone, leaving him alone in this strange young woman's arms.

# Chapter Two

Two weeks later Captain Adam Strong hefted his sea bag over his shoulder and looked back at his ship. He sighed heavily. He was a man of the sea, not used to the land and landlubber ways. And he hated to leave her—his ship—even for a few days.

But it was going to take some time to repair the damage done by that last storm. He shut out the image of raging waves and pounding rocks. He'd survived that storm and he'd survive others. The sea was his life. He knew no other.

But while they were repairing the *Beautiful Lady*, he had things to do landside. The first of which was to find a place to live, a temporary place, of course, till the *Lady* was ready to go again.

Leaving the shipyard behind, he strolled along Boston's main street, thronging with Boston citizens, all of them seemingly occupied with important business. At least they were all hurrying along and looking very busy—the men in their frock coats and top hats and the ladies with those odd things called bustles on the behinds of their gowns. Imagine *wanting* to wear such ridiculous things.

He sighed again. Anyway, they were all too high-faluting for him. He was a plain man, a working man, and all these richly dressed folk made him uncomfortable. So did the city itself. Too many buildings, too many people. He'd go mad if he had to stay long in this bedlam. Maybe he could find a place more isolated, away from the crowds and the din. A place near the sea.

He turned toward the newspaper office. That'd be the place to look.

An hour later, Adam made his way through sea oats and sand along a windy deserted beach. This was better. The city had been left behind. Here he could smell the sea, and look at it, even if he couldn't sail on it.

The huge house ahead sat alone on a rise of land, giving it a commanding view of the water. It had obviously been there for some time, battered by successive storms. Its widow's walk had a definite list to one side and a railing that looked as if it might fall at any moment. A shabby place, but with a certain dignity. A huge sign in front said SEAFARERS BOARDINGHOUSE. REASONABLE RATES. So this was it. He'd found the place from the ad.

He turned up the winding walk. In spite of its general rundown appearance, the house had a homey air about it. Flowers waved bravely in a flower bed under a porch railing that was missing several spindles. Bright curtains hung at each window, windows that sparkled in the sunlight. It looked like someone was trying to spruce the place up.

He went up the worn steps and knocked on the door. He wasn't a man used to creature comforts, so he'd have made the decision to stay even without the flowers and clean windows. After all, the place *was* by the sea. And that was what he needed.

The door opened and a woman smiled at him. She was a small woman, not young and not old, thin as a rail and dressed all in nondescript brown with her brown hair pulled tightly back in a bun. But her smile was decent, and the half-grown tabby perched on her shoulder purred contentedly.

"Hello," she said. "Won't you come in?"

"I'm looking for a room." He stepped inside. "My ship's been laid up for repairs, and I need a place to stay."

"Of course." She shut the door behind him. "You're in luck, sir. We just this morning opened our doors. And you're our first boarder, so you get your pick of rooms." She looked him over carefully. "I think you'd like the captain's room."

"The captain's?"

She smiled—a smile that lit up her plain face. "Yes, it's the best room in the house. Faces the ocean, you see."

"I'll take it."

"Or I can show you the oth—" She stopped, as though his words had just sunk in. "You don't want to see it first?"

He shrugged. "Why should I? I'm used to living in a very small space. Anything with a bed will do."

Her face fell. "Oh."

Now why did he feel as if he'd done something wrong? Hurt her feelings in some obscure way? "But let's go look at it anyway. I'm sure it'll be fine, and I can put my sea bag down and freshen up."

Her expression lightened. "Yes, yes. Of course." She made a little gesture with her hands. "You'll have to excuse me, Captain. I'm new at the boardinghouse business, and I've never dealt much with people. So I'm a trifle nervous."

"You're doing fine," he said. He looked around the foyer—its worn wooden floor gleamed with wax. "But how do you mean to manage this great place? I mean, for a woman alone this is a huge task."

She gave him a funny look. "Oh, I'm not alone. George and Martha are helping me. As I said, we just opened our doors. We've only had the house a week and there's a lot to do yet. But we wanted to get started."

Adam nodded. Why was he standing here making idle conversation with a woman he cared nothing about? There was little time in his life for women; just a casual evening now and then in some port or other. Women he barely *talked* to. Women whose names he didn't remember—if he'd ever known them.

As though she could read his mind, this one said, "My name is Amity Phelps. And you are?"

"Captain Adam Strong. My ship, the *Beautiful Lady*, is in for repairs."

"What a lovely name for a ship," Mistress Phelps said. She turned toward the staircase. "If you'll just come this way . . ."

He followed her up the staircase. Not even a hint of bustle on the back of her drab gown. Obviously she cared little for fashion. How did she carry that cat on her shoulder like that? She seemed almost unaware that it was there, never reaching up to steady it. The cat looked back over her shoulder at him, its eyes a deep dark green, reminding him of ocean depths—unfriendly ocean depths. But why did it stare at him so intently, almost as if it was trying to learn something from him? Or perhaps warning him?

Foolishness, he told himself. The woman was a spinster. She kept a cat. Many spinsters kept cats. So what?

"Here it is." She threw open a door as though he were about to meet royalty.

He stepped inside. It was a big room, vast in comparison to his cabin, and nicely put together with manlike furnishings. No frilly curtains or fancy bedcovers, no gilding or curlicues; just plain, solid furniture—mahogany, he guessed. And a magnificent view of the sea—she'd been right about that—with two comfortable chairs placed where that view could be appreciated.

"This room will do very well," he said, giving her a little smile. After all, she was going to be his landlady. And she was obviously working hard to make a go of this place.

"Good. Dinner is served at six." She drew herself up and tried to look stern. As far as he was concerned, the look was a failure. "Please be prompt," she said.

He chuckled. "Of course. I think you'll find seafaring men are always prompt for meals. We generally have huge appetites."

"Oh," she said again, that disappointed look settling over her face. Then she went back out the door, the cat still riding her shoulder. A strange woman. But a comfortable room. He put his sea bag on the stand. He was going to be all right here.

"Well," Amity said, back in her own room, "I wish I'd done better, but he did take a room." She reached up to lift Hector off her shoulder and looked into his eyes. "Do you know how much comfort you've been to me these last days?" she asked. "I love having you for my cat."

Hector purred. He liked Amity, too, but he wasn't so sure about that stranger in the captain's room. He was good enough to look at—human folk noticed that kind of thing, Mistress said—but there was no way to tell if what he spoke was truth. Mistress could probably tell, but Hector wasn't old enough yet. He hadn't had enough experience.

He switched his tail in annoyance. You'd think Mistress would give him some idea what this task *was* that she expected him to do, instead of just sending him off like this. How was he supposed to know what to do?

*Patience. You will be told.*

So, she could even talk to him here. Well, then, he wouldn't worry about things. He settled down in Amity's lap. It was about time for some good stroking and some loving talk.

"He's a strange man," Amity mused, absently stroking Hector's shoulders. "Our first boarder. But very handsome. Don't you think he's handsome?"

Hector purred. Amity could say anything she wanted as long as she kept petting him.

"He has such broad shoulders," she went on. "And his eyes are so dark. And that black, black hair. I like the way it curls around his collar. I like it that he's clean-shaven, too. No sidewhiskers on him, or beard, like a lot of men wear."

Those weren't the things Hector had noticed. Of course, he wasn't a human female. What he'd noticed first was the jut of the captain's jaw. This was a hard man, a determined man. A man used to giving orders and having them obeyed.

"I wonder if he has a wife," Amity said.

Hector stopped purring. Oh-oh. It looked like Amity was heading for trouble. He didn't know much about people yet, but he did know that human females could get in a lot of trouble if they started thinking certain thoughts about the wrong kind of man. Surely Amity couldn't be falling in love with this sea captain. Surely *that* wasn't what Mistress wanted.

*Patience.*

*But I need to know so I can—*, he thought.

*All will be revealed in good time.*

He switched his tail again. Good time, indeed. He'd been here two weeks already. How was he supposed to finish his task when he didn't even know what it was?

"A sea captain," Amity whispered in a voice that gave him chills of coming disaster. "I've always admired sea captains. Isn't it wonderful that he came here?"

# Chapter Three

Three days later Adam slumped in a chair by the big window, groaning in exasperation. Even a perfect view of the sea didn't help. He had just returned from the shipyard and the news was not good. The damage to *Beautiful Lady* had been even worse than that for which he'd prepared. Repairs were going to take some weeks, probably into the winter. And that meant he wasn't going to get out to sea again soon.

Being landside just didn't feel right. He had his land legs now, of course, but he missed the sea. He'd missed it the moment he had stepped off the deck and headed into Boston—missed the excitement, the adventure. Some men found cities exciting, but not him. He wanted to get back out on the water where he belonged. But he couldn't do that without the *Lady*, so he'd just have to—

A scratching noise made him raise his head.

Mice in the house? That could be, but this noise was at the door. He smiled to himself. As far as he knew, mice didn't scratch for admittance. Must be the landlady, though that was a peculiar way to announce herself. He rose and went to the door.

There was no landlady. The tabby cat stood there instead. "What do you—" Adam began. But the cat strolled by him and went to peer out the window, acting for all the world as if it owned the place. "What are you doing in here?" Adam asked. "Go on now, get out." He waved a hand at the door. But the tabby paid him little heed, going to a chair instead and rubbing against it.

Well, the animal wasn't likely to hurt anything, not while he was right there. Leaving the door open, Adam sank into his chair again.

Three days in this house and he didn't know the cat's name. Martha and George he'd met. Mistress Phelps had made a good choice there. Both of them obviously adored her and had only good things to say of her. Her retainers were getting on in years, though, and it was unlikely George was ever going to get that widow's walk repaired, though he spoke of doing it as soon as he "got a good day." Mistress Phelps would be lucky if the old man managed to repair things at ground level, let alone up on the roof.

Adam frowned. It didn't look as if this boardinghouse was going to become a going concern. So far no other boarders had shown up. But Mistress Phelps didn't seem dismayed by that fact. Maybe she wasn't as needy as she'd looked. He wouldn't know. He had little experience with women of her kind. He thought of his mother. A soft warmth and a gentle voice. A smiling face and a few stories. That was all he had to remind him he'd ever had a mother.

He couldn't envision Mistress Phelps as a mother, though he supposed she'd give it a good effort. Of course, she was a spinster, and not likely to be entering the state of motherhood. The cat would probably be her only companion. Of course she'd have the company of whatever boarders she managed to bring in. And Martha and George, of course.

He moved restlessly in the chair. Enough about Mistress Phelps and her boardinghouse. It was only August. What was he going to do through the long months until the *Lady* was ready to set sail again? How was he going to—

The tabby leapt up, landing directly in his lap. "What do you think you're doing up here?" He reached out to push it off, but then hesitated. "Well, since you've come this far, maybe I'll just see if you're a he or a she."

He lifted the cat, turning him over easily. "Ah, a he. Now, if I just knew your name, I could tell you to get out of here." He released it, but the cat didn't jump down. Instead, he settled down in Adam's lap like he owned that, too, and started to purr.

Well, there was no harm in it laying there. If he tried to move him, the cat would probably unsheath its claws. And these were new nankeen trousers.

The cat looked really comfortable. So relaxed. He'd like to feel that way, not a care in the world. For a little while, at least.

The cat's fur looked really soft. Before he knew what he was doing, Adam reached out to touch it. But one touch wasn't enough, and soon he was stroking the cat's back. There was something soothing about the process, and he kept doing it. So the *Lady* wouldn't be ready for some time. At least he was comfortable here, well cared for. He'd take a little rest from his captain's duties. He'd have to.

The tabby purred contentedly and, feeling more relaxed himself, Adam rested his head against the chairback. No wonder spinster ladies favored cats. They were wonderfully comforting creatures.

Hector licked a paw. He didn't understand why Mistress had sent him in here. Told him to visit the captain's room and climb up in his lap. Mistress was always so mysterious about things. But the command had been quite definite and, as always, he'd obeyed. No one ever thought of disobeying Mistress.

It wasn't too bad here either. The captain had seemed rather tense earlier, but now he was more relaxed. And he was good at stroking. Almost as good as Amity. Hector closed his eyes. This was a good life. If he just knew what he was supposed to—

"There you are!"

Adam jerked awake, his senses instantly alert. The cat was still curled up on his lap, still purring. And Mistress Phelps stood in his open doorway, her mouth agape, her face flushed.

"I'm so sorry," she said, her face flushing even more. "I didn't realize you were resting. I was looking for Hector, you see."

Adam got to his feet, holding the cat to his chest. "He found my room and scratched on the door. When I opened it, he came waltzing in like he owned the place." He glanced at the door. "I left it open so he could get out. But he seemed perfectly happy here."

Mistress Phelps swiped at some hair that had come loose from its moorings and curled around her face. "I'm so sorry. Hector shouldn't bother you. It's just that he's new at this business, too. He doesn't know enough to leave guests alone."

He deposited the cat in her outstretched arms. "I'm sorry," she repeated, as though the cat had committed mutiny or something. "I'll try to keep him from bothering you."

"He's no—"

But she was already gone, scurrying out the door as if he was going to bombard her with cannon balls. He turned back to the chair. Women were certainly curious creatures. Lucky he didn't have to worry about one of his own.

Amity held Hector close to her chest. It was his favorite resting place. Well, he liked it in her lap, too, or riding on her shoulder. Truth was, he liked being with her.

"What were you doing in *his* room?" she asked, putting a peculiar inflection on the word. "You know I'm supposed to stroke you every hour and speak to you lovingly. How can I do that if I can't find you? Or if I have to go looking through all the guest rooms?"

He wished he could talk to Amity as he did to Mistress. He'd like to tell Amity that he loved her, too. Of course, cats weren't supposed to actually *love* people. Cats were too standoffish for that. Or at least, that was what people thought. But he knew better. Cat love was just a different kind of love, more independent, than dog love. More satisfying than people love, too, from what he'd been able to observe of that. People seemed to have a lot of trouble loving each other. They couldn't seem to understand that loving didn't mean having your own way all the time, or telling someone else how to live.

Amity reached her room and went in, closing the door behind her. She dropped into her rocker, settling Hector on her lap. "I don't know what it is about you," she said, "but I can really talk to you." She scratched the favorite place behind his ears. "It's not just because the manual says I'm supposed to, either. I don't talk to you because it says so, and I don't pet you because it says so. Not anymore."

She sighed. "I love you, you know. I always will. But I wish . . . I really wish . . ."

Hector stopped purring. She was thinking about the captain! He could feel it. She was thinking about him with yearning. And it wasn't going to do the least bit of good.

The captain was a man of the sea. He was already fidgeting because his ship was in port. By the time it was fixed he'd be more than ready to leave. He would never settle down and stay in one place.

Hector was beginning to see that Amity needed someone, some *person,* to love. But he was afraid the captain wasn't the right sort. And Amity shouldn't be hurt. She was too good for that. He snuggled against her, trying to give her comfort.

He didn't see why good people like Amity had to feel so bad. Loneliness was an awful thing. And although he was the best cat around, he couldn't give her the kind of love she needed.

*Patience,* Mistress said.

# Chapter Four

Several days later the morning dawned bright and warm. Toward midmorning, Adam leapt from the chair where he'd been staring at the ocean and muttered an oath. He couldn't sit still a minute longer. He had to do something. Maybe a walk on the beach would help ease his restlessness.

Much as he wanted to, he didn't dare go back to the shipyard. Just yesterday, the owner had told him, his brows drawn together in a fierce frown, that every time Adam came to visit the yard, he put repairs on the *Lady* back another day. He supposed the man was right. He wouldn't like to work with someone peering over his shoulder all the time. But the *Lady* was his life.

Of course, landlubbers had no idea what it was like to be on the sea—the freedom, the thrill, the sense of mastering something wild and dangerous. And since they didn't know what it was like, they couldn't begin to imagine how much he missed it. Or how important it was for him to get back to it.

He grabbed his cap and jacket. At least on the beach he could smell the ocean. He could be near it. And walking would give him some activity.

He set off, away from the direction of town. The beach was empty—a long expanse of sand, broken by dunes where sea grasses grew and boulders were piled high. There were no more houses this far from the city, thank goodness. He didn't need people, didn't want people. He just wanted the sight and sound and smell of the sea.

The sun lay heavy on his shoulders, its heat baking through his clothes. Good thing he'd brought his cap to keep it off his face. But he should have left his jacket in the house. He slid out of it and slung it over his shoulder, loosening his collar with his other hand.

The sand pulled at his boots, but he marched on. A little heat wouldn't hurt him. He'd been inactive too long already. Working up a good sweat would be healthy. He certainly didn't want to turn into a fat landlubber like those he'd seen in town.

Around midmorning, he rounded a huge pile of rocks. What the . . . ? In front of a mound of driftwood, about a hundred yards down the beach, Hector sat at the edge of the water, his tail swishing from side to side as he stared intently into the waves. What was the cat doing out here? And all alone. His mistress would be worried.

Then, out of the depths, a female form rose. For the briefest moment Adam thought he was seeing the Sea herself, taking human form, and his heart jumped up in his throat at the sight. But the water sluiced off the form and revealed Amity Phelps.

She was soaking wet—hair, gown and all—and she stood there for a moment, wiping water out of her eyes. Then she calmly lifted her sodden skirts and started out of the water toward the cat.

Adam looked toward the sea. There was nothing she could have fallen off of or out of. No pier, no overturned rowboat. She must have gone out there deliberately—and wearing all those clothes.

Was the woman mad? It was a wonder she hadn't drowned.

He strode toward her, coming up to her just before she reached the cat. She stopped, her bare feet still in the water, and stared at him.

"Captain Strong!" She looked around rather wildly. "I—ah—what are you doing out here?"

"I'm taking a walk," he said. "But I think the question is more applicable to you. What are *you* doing out here?"

Red stained her cheeks and she looked down at her bare feet. "I—ah—I was just so hot. There was no one around, you see. And I just—" She straightened her shoulders defiantly and looked him in the eye. "So I decided to go for a swim."

"A swim," he repeated. "A swim with all your clothes on."

She bent and picked up the cat, holding him against her wet bosom. "Well, yes. I didn't think— That is—It was so hot and—"

"Thank goodness you didn't try it wearing one of those ridiculous bustle things. But you should have taken off your dress."

"Taken off—" Her eyes grew round with surprise. "Oh, I couldn't—"

"Of course you could." Why was he playing this game with her? She was obviously not the sort of woman who would walk naked into the sea—or anyplace else. "Men do it all the time."

She gave him an odd glance. "But I am not a man, Captain. I am a woman, a spinster woman." She sighed deeply. "And I have to be careful."

"You should be careful you don't drown." Now why had his voice gotten so sharp? This woman was only his landlady, nothing special to him. "Don't you know that all those clothes can pull you down? You could even be swept out to sea. Undertows can do that."

She met his gaze again, at her own level. "Yes, Captain, I know. But I also know where the currents are. I swam here often as a child." She gave him a timid smile. "Though I admit not wearing so many petticoats."

She kept the cat between them, like some kind of guardian. But in spite of that he could see how the gown clung to her figure, not a bad figure either. She seemed to have filled out some since he'd first seen her. Or perhaps it was because she was soaking wet and he could see better.

"My apologies for doubting your abilities," he said. "Was your swim as refreshing as you hoped?"

"Oh, yes," she said, glancing down at the cat. "It was quite cooling. You look very warm, sir. Why don't you try it?"

"I only swim naked," he replied, watching her downcast face. The flush he expected came, but she also gave a little chuckle.

"Then I had better go back to the house and leave the beach to you." She didn't raise her face to look at him.

The cat looked at him, though, intently, as if it was trying to tell him something.

"Don't go," Adam said. "I don't want to cut your fun short."

"But I don't want to keep you from a swim," she countered.

He reached for the top button on his shirt. "I'll make you a bargain. I'll just take off my shirt and my boots. Maybe you can shed a petticoat or two. And then we could have a swim together." Her head came up, her eyes bright. "You could show me where the dangerous places are. Don't you think that would be a good idea? You wouldn't want to lose a good boarder."

She stared at him, absolute incredulity on her face. Oh, oh, he'd done it now. For a moment he thought he'd offended her so badly she was going to throw him out of her house.

And then she laughed, a lilting, tinkling laugh he'd never heard from her before. "It's a deal," she said, putting the cat back on the sand. "If you turn your back while you take off your shirt, I'll shed a couple of petticoats at the same time."

"Good."

Hector backed away from the water that threatened to wet his paws. He didn't like the stuff and he hadn't wanted Amity to go into it in the first place. Why would anyone want to get in water on purpose? Humans! He would never understand them. Such strange creatures.

The two of them ran laughing into the water. Hector sighed and curled up in the shade of a rock. There was trouble coming—he could feel it in his bones. He was pretty much convinced now that the captain was a good sort. But that still didn't make him right for Amity. Amity needed someone who would always be there. Not a man who loved the sea more than anything else.

And for some reason Mistress wouldn't say what

to do about it. All he ever got for his pleas for help was that irritating *patience*. One more time of that and he was going to start screeching. Well, it looked as if he'd just have to wait. Wait and see what happened.

An hour later Amity opened her bedroom window wide to the sun and hot wind and stepped out of her wet gown. The women who stared back at her from her mirror seemed a stranger. Who was this creature with wildly curling hair and bright, shining eyes? This creature who had sported in the sea so brazenly? And when the captain had come, had stayed, actually *stayed* to go back into the water with him?

A flush rose to her cheeks and she turned away, stepping out of the rest of her wet things and picking up a towel from the stand. The sun had dried some of the dampness on her way back to the house, the sun and the unfamiliar heat that struck her body whenever she thought of what she'd done. Mama would have been shocked at such carryings-on, and Papa—she shuddered to think what Papa would have done. Probably confined her to her room and gone out with a horsewhip to look for the captain!

But Mama and Papa were gone. She was taking care of herself now. And she'd had a wonderful time at the beach. There was no denying that.

Hector jumped up on the window seat and switched his tail, looking at her with those green eyes of his. Looking at her accusingly. "Yes, I know," she said. "I've been neglecting you. Just let me get some clothes on and I'll be right with you."

She finished drying off and slipped into some clean things, then took her hairbrush and went to sit in the window seat. Hector climbed into her lap and settled down with a great sigh.

Chuckling, she stroked his soft back. "You're a great comfort to me," she told him, "especially when I do something foolish like I did today." She shook her head. "I still can't believe I did *that*. Me, a spinster woman. Thank goodness no one saw us. I'd never be able to get any more boarders if people knew I'd been swimming with the captain."

Hector rolled over on his back and presented his stomach for some stroking. "You're a spoiled cat," she said. "But I love you anyway. Now just lie still. I have to take care of my hair before it gets completely wild."

She brushed at it carefully, trying to get it to straighten out. But the sea air and the water had made it curl around her face, and for all her brushing and coiling and pinning, wisps still insisted on coming out of the chignon. Finally she dropped the brush on the seat. "Well, it'll just have to stay that way. The captain has seen it all wet and wild and—"

Oh, dear! She put a hand to her flushed cheeks. How was she going to face the captain now? It had been hard enough before, when she kept thinking how attractive a man he was, and what a shame it was for the sea to claim such a man for its own, especially when there were women on land who could give him all kinds of love. She'd promised herself to stay away from him, and then—

But she had tried. She really had. It wasn't her fault he had come to the beach when she did, or that he wanted to swim, too. Of course, she could have left him and come back to the house. She should have. Because now she knew what he looked like without his shirt, with the dark hair wet and curling on his chest, and moving down toward his belly, his strong bare feet planted in the sand. That was a picture she wouldn't soon forget. That, and that wonderful deep laugh of his.

But who knew what he was going to think of her? No respectable woman would be seen in wet clothes, let alone go into the sea with a man who was not her husband. How would she be able to face him?

Well, she couldn't worry about that now. The captain had elected to remain a little longer on the beach. But she'd had to get back and see about dinner. Martha did her best, but she was slowing down, and she really needed help.

Amity got to her feet. "There, I've done the best I could. It's time to go help Martha." She looked down at Hector. As usual, he was looking at her as though he understood every word she said.

"I know," she said. "If you could talk, you'd tell me I'm being foolish." She felt the heat reach her cheeks again. They must be bright red by now. "I *know* I'm being foolish." She heaved a deep sigh. "I just don't know how to stop."

Hector took his usual place on her shoulder. He didn't know how to help her—and he wanted to. If only Mistress . . .

*Patience.*

# Chapter Five

Dinner that night was strained. Adam had come back to the house expecting to see the same laughing woman who'd cavorted with him on the beach. Instead he found a stiff, rigid woman with a cold, distant expression, a woman who never once throughout the entire meal looked him in the eye. If he didn't know better, he'd think he'd run into twins, and this Amity was keeping the other laughing one a prisoner.

But it was the same woman. In spite of her stiff manner, wisps of her hair insisted on coming out of the bun and curling around her face. Just as they had at the beach. And there was a certain something to the way she held herself, to the way she walked, that . . .

He tried to make conversation. "The weather today seemed unseasonably hot," he remarked, dishing up some cobbler.

"Yes," she admitted. "It did." She took the pan he passed her and helped herself. "But August is often very hot here."

And she fell silent again. It was as if this afternoon had never happened. Except that he knew it had. She was even more distant than she'd been when he first came here. Whatever was wrong with her?

He didn't understand women, had never found it necessary to even try. But whatever was wrong with her would pass. And if it didn't, it really wouldn't matter. He'd soon be gone, back to the sea that was his life.

But in the meantime this sitting around was nervewracking. He was a man of action. He had to *do* something. "I was thinking about the widow's walk," he said at last. "The railing up there has a definite list."

"I know," she said, still staring at the cobbler. "George hasn't had a chance to fix it."

"Perhaps, that is—" Now why should he be stumbling around like this? He was a man accustomed to doing things. And she was only a weak woman. He'd faced the fiercest ocean storms. He would not let a mere woman unman him. "The thing is, I need something to do. This inactivity is very trying. And so I thought *I* might fix the railing. That is, if you have no objection."

Her head came up then, and she stared at him with big brown eyes. Why had he never noticed how big her eyes could grow? Or that her face, when it wasn't so cold, could be almost pretty?

"Not that George couldn't do a good job," he hurried on. "But as you've said, he has a lot to do around here. And I'm not busy at all."

She swallowed. He saw the convulsion of her

throat, as though she could hardly speak. "That would be very kind of you," she murmured finally. "In return I could take some off your room and—"

"No!" He didn't mean the word to jump from him so explosively, but to give her credit, she didn't move a bit. She must have been yelled at before. And more than once. "That is," he went on, "you'd be doing me a favor." He managed a smile he hoped was rueful. "There's very little time for sitting around when a man's at sea, you know. And if I don't get to do *something* soon, I'm going to go crazy."

A timid smile lifted her lips. "Well, Captain, I wouldn't want to be responsible for that. If you really want to, you may go ahead and fix the widow's walk. George will tell you where the tools and materials are."

"Thank you," he said. And he really meant it. Now why should he feel warmed by that timid little smile, or the fact that at last she'd looked him in the eye? Being on land must really be getting to him. He was thinking about things he'd never thought about before. And he wasn't at all sure it was good for him.

The days passed. August turned into September. Adam fixed the railing on the window's walk, and, with George's permission, replaced the missing spindles on the front porch. He did whatever other tasks of repair he could find to do. But Amity still seemed distant and removed. Oh, she looked him in the eye, from time to time, at least, but that easy friendliness they'd known that day on the beach was gone.

He hadn't imagined it—the fine time they'd had in the water. He was telling himself that one day when he came in from a walk along the dunes. He walked every day, morning and evening, but he had never seen Amity on the beach again. He had the distinct suspicion that she'd been avoiding him. And for the life of him, he couldn't figure out why. He hadn't done a thing to the woman. He'd been friendly and polite, even helpful. But still she was distant, as if he was some stranger she'd only just met—and didn't like very well.

He moved along the hall in his stocking feet. In deference to Martha's efforts to keep a clean house he'd taken off his boots to shake out the sand and decided not to put them back on right away. As he neared the half-closed door to the breakfast room, he heard the murmur of a voice.

He stopped to listen. Had Amity succeeded in finding another boarder? For some reason the thought didn't sit well with him. He'd better make sure about this new fellow. A person couldn't be too careful about the kind of people she took into her house.

"I just don't know what to do," Amity was saying. "I know it's foolishness for a woman my age to want a husband."

This couldn't be a boarder. Surely she wouldn't say something that personal to a boarder. Maybe she was talking to Martha, about woman-type things. He would move on. Amity had a right to her privacy.

"But he . . ."

He stopped again. What *he?*

"I know the captain wonders why I'm so stand-offish," she went on. "But I really do want to be married, in spite of all the reasons against it. And I'm afraid he'll think I've set my cap for him."

For him! His heart rose up in his throat. Didn't the woman know—

"And I know he's not interested in getting married. I know he loves the sea more than he could love any woman." She heaved a big sigh. "But I get so lonely sometimes. I wish we could just be friends. Like we were that day on the beach. Only I don't know how to go about it."

He listened hard. Surely someone would answer her, would say that she was still young enough to marry, though not him. Of course not him.

But there was no answer.

Finally curiosity got the better of him. He peered around the door. She was the only person in the room. It was the cat she was talking to. He could see Hector's tail swishing back and forth.

Adam backed away and tiptoed on past. Imagine that! He'd never have dreamed that *that* was the reason she was behaving so strangely. Still, now that he knew her reasons, her behavior made perfect sense.

Hector peered up at Amity from his place on her lap.

He knew the captain had been outside the door. He could smell him, smell his curiosity, and then his surprise. But Hector didn't move, didn't let Amity know someone was listening. It wouldn't hurt the captain to discover these things, to find out how Amity was hurting. She was hurting a lot, and Hector didn't know how to fix it.

He'd never thought he'd care that much about a human, but he found he did. He wanted Amity to be happy. He wanted it more than he'd ever wanted anything, even the trip to Mistress's secret tower room.

He rubbed his head against Amity's cheek. Poor girl needed all the comfort she could get.

Maybe now the captain would make an overture, at least be her friend.

He guessed he'd changed his mind about the captain. If Amity wanted to be friends with him . . . well, that was all right. Of course, what she really wanted, what she was afraid to say even to her own cat, was that she wanted to marry the captain.

He could understand that. A person, even an independent being like a cat, needed contact. Fur against fur, skin against skin. He hadn't forgotten the warmth of his mother's belly or the feel of her tongue against his body as she cleaned him. And he really enjoyed the stroking Amity gave him. It was natural to want such connections, such feelings.

Amity's hand moved on his back and he purred to let her know how much he appreciated her. She had provided him with a loving home. If only he could do that for her.

*Excellent.*

Now what did Mistress mean by that? What more could a cat do to make a woman feel loved? She needed the captain for that.

Hector swished his tail. He just didn't see any possibility of the captain considering marriage. Not the captain.

Unless . . . Unless something could be done to bring them together. But there was no one to do that but him. And he hadn't the least idea how to go about it.

That evening at dinner Adam decided to take matters into his own hands. He was tired of all this standoffishness, tired of eating meals with a distant stranger. "You know," he commented, helping himself to another slice of Martha's fresh-baked bread, "I really enjoyed that time last month that we spent on the beach."

Amity's face turned a trifle pink, but she said, "I did, too."

"Then why didn't we do it again?"

"I—I—" She looked around wildly, as though waiting for rescue. But it didn't come and she faced him bravely. "I didn't think it was proper. Oh, it was fun. But I want my boardinghouse to be a success, and if anyone had found out . . . Well, you must understand."

"I understand," he said. And he did. He understood that she wasn't going to tell him the truth, and for the very reason that she'd mentioned to the cat. "But surely propriety wouldn't be offended by a daily stroll along the beach. I think we'd both benefit from it. The sea air and all. And there's no harm in being friends. Is there?"

She stared at him. Had he come too close to what she'd told the cat? Did she suspect he'd overheard her?

But finally she let out a big sigh and smiled. "No, Captain, there's no harm in being friends."

"Good. Then let's start this evening. After we finish eating."

"I—Martha—"

"Martha can do the dishes," he said, perhaps more forcefully than he should have. "And George can help her."

Amity burst into laughter, a sound he'd been waiting to hear, it seemed, forever. "I'm afraid George doesn't believe in a man doing such chores."

Adam shrugged. "Then tell her to let them wait and *I'll* help her."

Her eyebrows went up. "You!"

"Yes. You forget, at sea there are no women to do things for men. They have to take care of themselves. So, is it a deal?" He looked down casually, as though the matter was of little importance to him. But actually his heart was pounding.

Foolish. He was being really foolish. Either the woman went with him or he went alone. Either way he'd get his exercise. So what did it matter?

But he wasn't fooling himself. It mattered. He wanted her to walk with him. He wanted it a lot.

# *Chapter Six*

They walked every evening after that, Amity and the captain. Sometimes Hector went with them, but he didn't care much for water, nasty stuff, and sand wasn't much better. It took such a lot of licking to get it out from between his toes. So he took to curling up on the porch when they left and waiting there for them to return.

He always waited hopefully, wishing that the captain would do something to make that special light come back on in Amity's eyes. But though she always seemed happy when she got back, it wasn't with the kind of happiness he was looking for. She and the captain were friends, all right, but Amity wanted more than that. And she wasn't getting it.

September drew to an end and still nothing had changed. One rainy afternoon Hector curled up in the chair in Amity's sitting room and tried to talk to Mistress. She hadn't been saying anything to him lately but that terribly irritating *patience*, but maybe if he could make her understand how important this was, how much Amity needed help . . .

He thought as hard as he could, but Mistress wasn't answering. She still hadn't told him what the task was he was supposed to do, but he wasn't worrying about that right now. It was more important to help Amity. If only he knew how.

The manual in its red leather cover lay on the table beside Amity's chair. *The Care and Feeding of the Modern Feline*, Mistress had called it. If only the captain had a manual to show him how to take care of Amity. Talk to her every hour. Stroke her. Share his bed with her.

Hector sat up straight, his whiskers quivering. Wait a minute! When she first read it, Amity had said that the manual made her think of loving a man. Why couldn't it make the captain think of loving a woman? Of loving Amity?

But how was he going to get the captain to read it?

He licked a paw. It didn't look like a very heavy book. He looked toward the window seat. It was raining out, so the captain was probably in his room. . . . Hector slipped from the chair and went to find out.

Ten minutes later, the manual held carefully between his teeth, Hector stood outside the captain's door. The captain had been leaving it slightly ajar when he was in there, an invitation to come in and be stroked. At least, that's the way Hector had been taking it. And he'd gotten a lot of stroking, so he was probably right.

He pushed through the opening. The captain sat in his chair, staring morosely at the rain falling on the sea. He looked down when Hector rubbed against his leg. "Hallo, what's this?"

Hector dropped the manual on the captain's shiny boot. The captain picked it up. "You certainly are a smart cat," he said with a chuckle. "Now you're even bringing me reading material. And a good thing, too, since I'm stuck inside on this miserable day."

He looked at the cover. *"The Care and Feeding of the Modern Feline.* What's the matter, boy, haven't I been treating you right? Is there something in here I need to know?"

Hector held his breath. If only the captain opened the manual. If only he read it. This idea had to work. Amity needed this man.

The captain leaned over and lifted Hector onto his lap. "Might as well be comfortable," he said, settling him there. "You won't want to go out in this rain either."

And he opened the book.

"I thought I would find you here!"

Hector looked up. Amity stood in the doorway, a smile on her face. That was good. She'd been smiling more since she and the captain had taken to walking on the beach. But the year was wearing on. And that's all they did, walk. When would they get to doing something else, something that would make Amity really happy?

"Hello," the captain said, closing the manual and gesturing to the other chair. "Come in, please, and have a seat."

Amity looked a little discomposed. Maybe a woman wasn't supposed to come into a man's room. Humans had such a lot of silly rules.

"Oh, come on," the captain said. "George and

Martha won't think anything of it. They know your good character. And you've no other boarders yet, to see what you do."

"Well . . ." Amity opened the door wider and stepped in. "I wouldn't have bothered you," she said, "but I was looking for Hector. It's time to . . ."

Her words came to a halt as she saw the red leather manual in the captain's hand. Her eyes grew bigger. "How did you get that?"

The captain waved a hand at the other chair. "Sit down and I'll tell you."

Amity sat, spreading her skirts down around her and smoothing her fresh white apron. "I'm sure I left the manual on the table in my sitting room."

"I wouldn't know," the captain said. "I was sitting here, staring at the rain and the sea, wishing I was out on the *Lady*, and Hector came strolling in, carrying this book. Since it was such a gloomy day and I had nothing else to do, I took to reading it. I trust you don't mind."

Amity made a dismissive gesture. "No, Captain, I don't mind. I was just surprised to see it in here."

She clasped her hands in her lap. She was nervous, Hector knew. Maybe he ought to go over there and give her some comfort. He jumped down and went to climb up in her lap. Right away her hands settled on his back. He could feel their slight trembling. Yes, she was afraid. She wanted to be here, talking to the captain, but she was afraid.

"It's quite an interesting book," the captain said. "But I'm surprised at such explicit instructions. I mean, for the care and feeding of a cat."

"When Hector came to live with me," Amity explained, "that manual came with him. I promised his former mistress that I would follow its instructions faithfully. And I have done just as I promised her."

The captain nodded. "But don't you find it a little excessive? I mean, you're supposed to talk to him lovingly every hour. And stroke him every hour."

Amity shook her head. "No, Captain, I don't. When you love someone—" She smiled. "—and Hector is a someone to me, you *want* to do those things."

The captain raised an eyebrow. "It also says you're supposed to let him share your bed."

Red flooded Amity's face and she got really busy scratching the special place behind his ears. "I have to admit that I hesitated a little about that. I've always slept—" She gulped. "That is, I'm not used to sharing my bed. But it has worked out very well. Hector is an excellent companion. I couldn't ask for better."

"Yes," the captain said. "I can see that he is. And this part about letting him come and go as he pleases, that makes sense. Cats and people both need freedom. But this book . . ." He looked down at the manual that he still held. "Does anything about it strike you as strange?"

She sighed. "Well, I suppose that people are not used to treating animals with such care."

"That's true," the captain said. "But that isn't what I had in mind."

Hector twitched his tail in irritation. Why didn't Amity come right out and say what she'd said when she had first read the manual? Or why didn't the captain say what *he* was thinking?

"What—what *did* you mean, then?" Amity asked.

*That's it*, Hector thought. *Keep talking to him*.

The captain cleared his throat. Goodness, both of them were afraid. Hector could smell it. "Well, it seems a little overdone," the captain said, "I mean, for an animal."

Amity pulled in a deep breath. Was she going to do it? Was she going to tell him?

"When I first read it I thought that it seemed— that it made more sense—that it ought to—"

"Apply to a person," the captain finished, looking a little red in the face himself.

Amity's breath left her body in a big whoosh. "Yes, Captain. That's what I thought."

"Well . . ." The captain looked thoughtful. "I haven't much experience with loving. I'm a man of the sea, and there's no place for women there."

"I know," Amity whispered, a world of disappointment in the two words.

But the captain didn't seem to hear it.

"But I have to admit that any person would probably relish such treatment."

"I've thought so, too," Amity said. "But I have no experience with loving either."

The captain smiled. "Except for Hector."

And Amity smiled, too. "Yes, except for Hector."

Well, at least they'd talked about it. That was something. But people were certainly slow. Cats would have handled this thing long ago. To both of their satisfaction.

Amity shifted him to her shoulder and started to get up. "Wait," the captain said. "I'm curious about these blank pages in the back. What are they for?"

Amity settled down again for a moment. "I don't know. Hector's previous owner said not to concern myself with them. And so I haven't. Anyway, I've been busy with the boardinghouse."

She started to get up again. The captain cleared his throat. "Ah, if you're not too busy now, please stay and tell me about this person." He smiled ruefully. "It's dreadfully dreary outside and I'd really appreciate your conversation." He put the manual on the table beside his chair. "I think Hector's had his share of talk for this hour. Maybe you could spare a little for me."

Yes! Hector thought. That's it! And he scrambled down into Amity's lap.

She settled back in the chair. She was going to stay!

When Amity left his room, the manual in her hand and Hector on her shoulder, Adam pulled out his albert, the short chain connecting his watch to a buttonhole. He looked at the watch. Then he looked again. They'd been talking for more than two hours. And it had only seemed like a few minutes.

He stared reflectively at the sea. He'd never really talked to a woman before, no more than a few words, at any rate. Usually to negotiate her price.

Women like Amity were pretty much unknown to him. And so was how to talk to them. During their walks by the ocean, they had talked some, but mostly about the sea or the weather, innocuous subjects. And even then he was sometimes hard put to know what to say.

But today he hadn't had to worry. Today she'd given him a glimpse of what it was like to be a woman. She'd talked to him about her feelings. About how lost and alone she'd been before she'd read that strange ad posted at the newspaper office and went to inquire about it. Yes, she'd told him a lot about her feelings, about her father losing his ships and drinking himself to death, and her mother dying of a broken heart. Neither of them seemed to have any regard for their child, though she hadn't said so. She'd even told him about losing her young man. That was too bad. She would make a man a good wife, a land-faring man, of course.

But to answer an ad in the paper! He shook his head. He probably wouldn't have responded to such a weird advertisement. In his experience, anyone who gave away money wanted something in return, and not just a home for a cat. But Amity had been in dire straits, more dire, he supposed, than she'd even admitted to. And so she'd ventured and she'd gained, not just the money but Hector, a valued companion.

Adam settled back in his chair and stretched his legs. It was odd how she'd been able to talk about personal things today. She'd always been close-mouthed about herself. And she'd never told him anything about her feelings. But probably it was the telling of the story that led her to speak more freely. She seemed to want him to understand why and how she'd gotten Hector. And her feelings were necessary to that.

He closed his eyes, trying to picture the odd woman she'd told him about, the exotic older woman with the rich red-gold hair and the slight accent. Why would any woman give away ten thousand dollars? Even a woman who lived on a huge estate and obviously had plenty of assets. The story about getting a good home for the cat didn't ring true. Anyone could have come in and *promised* a good home.

Of course, this woman *had* chosen Amity. So maybe she *was* a good judge of character. Amity seemed to be just the right person to be Hector's companion. She certainly did everything the manual said, even to sharing her bed with the cat.

He smiled. How she'd flushed when they discussed that part of the instructions. She was a modest woman, Amity was. Except when she was soaking wet from the sea.

If only they could repeat that day in the water. The weather was too cold now, though. And next summer he'd be gone. Boston—and Amity— would be nothing but a pleasant memory. He'd come back here, to the boardinghouse, whenever he was in port. But she'd have other boarders then. And it wouldn't be the same. Too bad women couldn't sail. . . .

He leapt to his feet. Now that was the stupidest thing he'd ever thought! He needed a walk. Rain or no rain, he had to get out of here.

Back in her room, Amity put Hector on the window seat and picked up her shawl. The rain made the air damp and chill. She pulled the shawl around her shoulders and settled into her rocker close to the hearth. George always kept a fire going in the grate this time of year. Now that they had plenty of money. Those days of cold and want seemed far away now, only half remembered. She was grateful for that, very grateful.

And now she had other things to think about.

"I can't believe it," she murmured as Hector jumped up into her lap and curled into a ball. "I can't believe I talked to the captain for so long. Or that I told him all those things about myself. About how I got you and everything. Even about Stephen going down with Papa's ship."

She sighed. Stephen was just a memory now. Even hazier than those days of want and misery. She could hardly even remember what he'd looked like. And even more distressing, whenever she tried to call up his face, she got the captain's face instead. And after that, usually, an image of the captain without his shirt and boots, standing in the sea.

"You know, Hector, I think I've made a mistake. I think I've fallen in love with the captain." Hector switched his tail and stood up to rub against her cheek. "Yes, I think that's what I've done." She sighed. "And it's really foolish of me."

She stared into the fire. "I suppose I should call a halt to our walks by the sea. And I suppose I should stop having conversations with him." Her breath caught in her throat. "But what good would that do? I already love him. And I already know it's useless."

She picked up Hector and stared into his deep green eyes. "What would you do?" Hector purred and rubbed against her arm.

She scratched behind his ears. "Well, I guess the damage has already been done. I'm not going to wake up and find that I don't love him. So I might as well enjoy what little time is left. You know, I've actually been praying that they won't finish repairing the *Lady* before winter sets in. That way he'll have to stay longer. Not that it would do any good."

She reached across Hector for the poker and stirred the fire. The flames reached higher, brightening the room. There was no sense lamenting her predicament. She was not like Mama—she wasn't going to curl up and die of a broken heart because she couldn't have what she wanted. She wasn't going to drown herself in a bottle either, like Papa.

"Come on," she said, putting Hector on the floor. "Let's go make an apple pie for supper. I think we have some apples left."

# *Chapter Seven*

The days passed. Hector watched the humans, watched and waited, but nothing happened. They seemed drawn to each other, seemed to want to be more than friends. But they still did nothing.

They took their walks on the beach, they talked to each other, even laughed together. But still there was that look of sorrow in Amity's eyes. No matter how she laughed and smiled, she couldn't quite hide it. At least not from him.

September turned to October. They had to bundle up for their walks along the sea, but unless it was raining they still went. And still nothing happened to erase the sorrow in Amity's eyes.

Then it was the day of All Hallows Eve. Late in the afternoon Mistress finally spoke to him. *Get Amity to take you for a walk by the sea. Just the two of you.*

Hector washed his whiskers. *It's cold out there. And wet.*

*The sun is shining. Do as I say.* Even in his head he could hear her impatience.

*But—*

*Do not question me. Do as I say.*

Well, there was no help for it. When Mistress said do something, a cat had better do it. He was going to have to go out in the wet and the cold. He went looking for Amity.

In the kitchen Amity looked up from the table where she was kneading bread. "Hector, stop scratching at the door. I'll let you out in a minute. Just let me finish this."

A bright ray of sunshine slanted across the room, hitting the bread dough with a shaft of light. "My, it looks nice out today," she said. "I hope the weather holds till the captain gets back from town and the shipyard. It'd be a good day for a walk."

Martha looked up from the rocker, where she was peeling potatoes. "Whyn't you go fer a walk anyway? You been stuck in the house the whole of this week, what with the rain and all. You need to get out. Get some of the stink blowed off."

Amity sighed. "A walk *would* be nice."

"Then go." Martha smiled. "I kin watch the bread. Ain't nothing much more to do for dinner. You go have yourself a nice walk."

"The captain . . ." Amity began.

"If the captain comes home afore you get back, I kin send him out to meet you," Martha said, reaching up to push back a strand of graying hair. "Now you just skeedaddle."

Martha was right. She'd been in the house too

long. Maybe out there on the seashore she could rid herself of some of these sad feelings. It would be nice to let them blow away with the sea breeze.

"I'll just put the bread in the pans, Hector. Then we'll go for a walk."

Hector quit scratching at the door and sat down beside it, waiting expectantly.

She laughed a little. "You know, Martha, I'd swear that cat understands every word I say."

Martha nodded wisely. "Sure and I don't see why he can't. Sometimes animals is smarter than people."

Ten minutes later, Amity had the bread in the pans and bundled herself into her heavy clothes, pulling her heavy cloak around her. She opened the door and Hector pranced out. He didn't run off as he often did, but seemed content to pace alongside her.

She went down the walk and paused to look back at the house. Well, she had done what she'd said she would. She had a boardinghouse. True, the captain's room payments didn't cover all the expenses, but there'd be time after he had gone back to sea for her to advertise for more boarders. Right now, she didn't want anyone else in the house. She still had money left from the ten thousand dollars. She could get by. Till spring and the captain—*Don't think about that.*

The house looked much better than it had when she had bought it back. The widow's walk didn't list anymore. The front porch railing was in perfect shape. The house could use a coat of paint, but there'd be time for that later, after the captain was gone.

Gone. Gone. The word kept coming back, echoing in her head like a funeral dirge. But she couldn't be thinking about that. "Come on, Hector. Let's take a walk. Get some of the stink blowed off, as Martha said."

She turned away from town. She'd like to walk in that direction. Maybe the captain would be coming back and she'd run into him. But he and she never walked that way. And it would look strange. Besides, Martha had said that if he came in, she'd send him after her.

"Well, Hector," Amity said, "I think you were right. It is a good day for a walk." The sun was bright—and the sky was a beautiful blue, with only a few fluffy white clouds.

"The world is a beautiful place," she said. "And I'm lucky to be alive."

Why didn't she *feel* lucky? She had everything she'd hoped to get when she answered the ad. She swallowed a big sigh. But when she'd answered the ad she hadn't known she'd meet the captain. She hadn't known that she'd fall in love with him.

Well, there was nothing to be gained by mooning about it. He was who he was. And he wasn't going to think about marrying. After all, he had the sea.

She'd be willing to share him with the sea. Oh, it would be hard. To stand up there on the widow's walk and see him sailing away when she wanted him to stay safely with her. But she could do it. It would be better than losing him for good.

"The trouble is," she said to Hector, "it doesn't matter what I'd be willing to do. The captain doesn't love me. And I have to accept that."

She lengthened her stride, moving toward the rocks that she thought of as their special place. In that place she had lost her feelings of shyness for a while and swam with the captain in the sea. That wonderful day would live in her memory forever.

"And even if it's all I ever have, it was worth it."

They'd started out defiantly, but her words ended in a half sob. She slumped down on a rock and pulled Hector into her lap. "I wish you could talk to me," she told him. "You're so wise. Maybe you could tell me what to do. How to make him love me. That's what I want, you know. I want him to love me."

Hector purred and rubbed Amity's cheek with his own. He wished he could talk, too. She was sadly in need of comfort, poor girl. But even if he could talk, what could he tell her? *He* loved her. But that wasn't enough.

She pulled her hooded cloak tighter around her and stared out into the sea. "That's my rival," she said. "That ocean out there. It's so beautiful. And so dangerous. I'm just a woman, and a plain one at that. I can't compete with a force of nature."

You're not plain, he wanted to say. You're beautiful inside, where it counts. But all he could do was rub her cheek with his. Why didn't Mistress tell him how to help? She'd sent him here to live, made him Amity's cat, the least she could do . . .

*Get down from her lap,* Mistress said.

*But she needs me, poor girl. She's in a bad way over the captain and . . .*

*Get down from her lap,* Mistress repeated, the sound more urgent. *You must run off.*

Hector froze. What on earth was Mistress talking about? Run off? Him? Why? He'd never run off. And Amity needed him now. She needed him a lot.

*You must do as I say,* Mistress said. *Remember the tower room.*

Hector trembled. He didn't care about the tower

room. He just wanted to help Amity. *I can't leave her. She needs me.*

*You must run off,* Mistress repeated sternly. Then the voice in his head softened. *This will help her more than staying. Trust my wishes.*

Hector hesitated. He had always trusted Mistress. She always seemed to know best. But it hurt him to desert Amity when she was feeling so sad.

*This is not desertion,* Mistress said. *This is what must be done. To make things right.*

*But how?* Hector asked. *How will my running off make things right?*

There was no answer.

Should he obey? How could he not? He'd always obeyed Mistress. Sometimes he hadn't understood why she told him to do as she did, but it always worked out for the best. So, much as he hated to leave Amity like this . . .

He stretched delicately and leaped down. Amity didn't seem to notice. She sat hunched in her cloak, staring dismally at the sea.

Hector stretched again. Run off to where? It would help if Mistress would have given him better instructions. But she hadn't.

He looked around. There were some rocks over there, and beyond them some tall sea grass. He didn't want to run too far. Amity might need him.

The wind swirled around her, tugging at Amity's hood and sneaking up under her cloak. A cloud covered the sun. She shivered and reached to draw Hector closer.

"Hector?" He wasn't in her lap. He had been, she was sure of that. But then she'd started staring at the sea, losing herself in dreams of what might have been—and would never be. And now Hector wasn't on her lap anymore.

She got to her feet and clutched the cloak tighter around her. "Hector? Hector, where are you?"

But there was no answer. This wasn't like him at all. Goodness, they'd walked on the beach many, many times and he'd never disappeared this way.

"Hector? Come on, it's time to go home. You must be getting cold."

But still he didn't come. She looked all around, squinting against the wind. But there was nothing to see but sand and sea.

"If you don't come, I'll have to go home without you," she called. "It's time to start dinner and I'm making a special dish for supper, a Halloween—"

Oh, no! Her blood ran cold. It was Halloween, and Hector wasn't to be left alone after dark. The manual said terrible things could happen if he was.

"Hector! Hector, please! Come back!"

But still there was no cat.

Snug in a little cave in the rocks, Hector twitched restlessly. *She's calling me*, he said. *She needs me.*

*You must not go. You must stay here. Out of sight. Trust my wishes. All will be well.*

He wished he could cover his ears with his paws. Amity's voice was breaking his heart.

Amity ran up the back walk and burst into the kitchen, one hand clutching the stitch in her side. "Martha, Martha! Have you—seen Hector?"

Martha looked up from the pan she was stirring. "Not since the two of you left. What's wrong, child? You look awful."

"It's Hector. He's run off."

"Now, now. That's nothing. Cats're running off all the time. That's the kind of creatures they are."

Amity fought to get her breath. "But it's—Halloween. And he's not—supposed to—be left alone."

The front door slammed. "Hello," the captain called cheerily. "Anyone around?"

"In the kitchen, sir," Martha answered. "Could you come out, sir? I think we'll be needing your help."

The captain appeared in the kitchen doorway. He took one look at Amity and hurried across the floor. "What on earth? Have you been hurt? Tell me what's wrong."

# *Chapter Eight*

Adam stared at her. Her hood had fallen carelessly
onto her shoulders, and her hair had come out of
its bun and clung wildly about her flushed face. It
was obvious she'd been out in the weather. But
that didn't account for her bedraggled appearance, or the way her bosom heaved as she tried to
catch her breath. Her entire gown seemed spattered with mud, especially the hem. Had she
fallen? Had she hurt herself? Something had happened to put her in such a condition. Something
bad.

"It's Hector." She struggled to get the words out.
"He's run off."

Adam swallowed a laugh. She was this dis-
traught because the cat had decided to take a
walk? "He's a cat," he said. "A male cat. He'll be
back."

"No, no!" Amity looked like hell warmed over.

"Don't you remember? It's Halloween."

He stared at her. Surely she didn't believe in Halloween and witches and all that folderol. "What has that to do with—"

"Don't you remember?" she repeated, glaring at him. "The manual says he's not to be left alone after dark on Halloween." She looked around wildly. "I've got to find him! I've got to."

He crossed the room to her side. "Easy now," he said, wanting to take her in his arms and comfort her. And not daring.

What could he do to help her? What?

Something was jiggling at his memory. Something in that manual. Come on. What was it?

Ahhh! A special call.

"Listen," he said, "isn't there something in the manual about a special call? Something guaranteed to bring him back?"

She looked up at him with tear-filled eyes. "Yes! Yes, there is. I forgot. I never had to use it. I'll get it and—"

"I'll get it," he said. "And we'll go back to the beach together."

Gratitude lit her eyes. She blinked and swiped at her tears, leaving smudges on her cheeks. "Thank you, Captain. Oh, thank you."

"Don't worry now," he said. "We'll get him back. We'll find him. In plenty of time. I promise."

He took the stairs two at a time. Why on earth had the cat decided to run off now? The little fellow had everything he could possibly want—a good home, a mistress who loved him. And beside that, the freedom to come and go as he pleased. A freedom he'd never used. Till now.

Stop this, Adam told himself. Nothing's going to happen to the cat. Even if it is Halloween.

But somehow he didn't believe himself. Amity's fears had taken hold in his heart and wouldn't be dislodged. He hurried into her sitting room and grabbed up the manual from its resting place on the table. It was in there somewhere—a call guaranteed to make any cat come. But where? What page?

The pages stuck to his hurrying fingers and he cursed impatiently. Where *was* it? Somewhere toward—There! At last. He repeated the page number to himself and started back down the stairs.

In the kitchen Amity paced the worn wooden floor. Though she'd wiped at her face more than once, the tears kept falling. She just couldn't seem to stop them. At least her side didn't ache any more. She shouldn't have run so hard to get back to the house, but she hadn't been able to think clearly. Hector was gone and she had to find the captain. That was all she could think of. And so she ran.

"Here now." Martha pressed a clean handkerchief into her hand. "Wipe your face. Just look at you," she clucked. "You're a real mess, you are."

"I know." Amity wiped at her wet face. "It's just—I'm so worried. I never should have taken him out today. I just wasn't thinking and—"

"Here, now." Martha tried to look stern, but she didn't have the face for it. "It ain't your fault the cat went and run off. He never done such a thing afore. How was you supposed to know he'd do it now?"

Amity wanted to take comfort from Martha's words, but she couldn't. "I promised! You know I gave my word to abide by the rules of the manual. And now my word will be broken. Hector is out there alone. On Halloween night. And it'll soon be dark."

Martha patted her shoulder. "Sure now, the captain'll help you find him. He's just a wee cat gone for some mischief. He don't know no better."

"Martha's right." The captain hurried into the kitchen, buttoning his heavy pea coat as he came.

"The manual—"

"In my pocket. I found the page. The call is in there."

He put his cap on and pulled it low over his ears. He eyed her spattered gown. "Are you sure you're warm enough? Maybe you should go up and change your—"

"There isn't time. We have to go now. It'll be dark soon." She turned toward the door. Hector was out there. They had to find him.

"Wait!" the captain called. "We'd better take a lantern. Just in case."

"Oh, all right!" Why couldn't he hurry? Something awful was going to happen to Hector. She just knew it. And it would be her fault.

The captain lifted a lantern off the shelf and headed for the door. "It'll be all right," he said to Martha, whose apple-cheeked face was creased with worry. "I'll take good care of her. I'll bring them both back safe."

Martha managed a little smile. "I know you will, sir. I've not a doubt of it."

Finally they were outside. Amity lifted her spattered skirts and hurried down the path toward the shore.

"Hold on," the captain called from behind her. "Save some strength for when we get there."

He was right, of course. She slowed her steps. But she was just so worried. Hector wasn't even full grown yet. She looked up. The sky didn't look threatening, but it was still cold, and a brisk breeze was blowing in off the sea. Hector didn't like cold. He liked to snuggle up against her back and—Tears filled her eyes again.

The captain fell into place beside her. "Where were you when he ran off?" he asked. "Did you see him go? See which way he went?"

"No. I—" How embarrassing. "The sun came out and it looked so nice. I wasn't sure you'd be back in time for our walk. And Hector was scratching at the door, like he wanted to get out." She pulled her cloak tighter against the rising wind. "Funny, he's never done that before, scratched like he wanted to get out. Anyway, I was kneading bread and he was scratching at the door. So I told him we'd go for a walk as soon as I finished. And he stopped scratching."

She stepped over a piece of driftwood. "We walked along the shore like you and I usually do. And I stopped by some rocks to—"

"What rocks? Do you remember where?"

She'd have to tell him. Hector was too important to let embarrassment stand in her way. "Yes, I remember. It was near the rocks where you found me swimming. Where the driftwood is piled up on the sand." She hurried on, hoping he wouldn't notice her flushed cheeks, or, if he did, that he'd think they were flushed from exertion. "Anyway, I sat on some rocks. Hector climbed up in my lap."

She circled a puddle of sea water.

"And then?"

"Well, I sat there for quite a while—staring at the sea." She looked toward it, toward the swell of waves. "You know how it can be. Sort of calm and soothing." Thank God she didn't have to tell him what she'd been thinking *about*: A life with him. A life that could never be.

"And then the sun went behind a cloud and the wind came up. I got chilly. So I decided to go home. But Hector wasn't on my lap any more. I don't know when he got down. Or which way he went." She wanted to sink down in the sand and wail. Instead she kept walking. "I just don't know!"

"It's all right." The captain's voice was deep, soothing. "We'll find him."

A little cry escaped her. "We've got to. I don't know what I'd do without him. I really—"

"It'll be all right." He raised the hand that held the lantern. "See? There are the rocks. We'll have him in no time—safe and sound."

She gazed up at the darkening sky and shivered. "We've got to. It'll be dark soon."

They reached the rocks and the captain set the lantern on a flat place. He reached in his pocket for the manual and opened it to the right page. "Here it is. The call is guaranteed to make a cat come to you."

He gave her a worried look. "Are you sure you're all right? You look half frozen."

"You—you try it," she begged, her teeth chattering. It must be nerves. She wasn't that cold.

"If that's what you want."

He glanced down at the manual, his lips forming the unfamiliar syllables. And then he voiced the call.

In some rocks, back from the shore, tucked away out of the wind, Hector raised his head. That was Mistress's special call, the one a cat *had* to answer. But that wasn't Mistress calling it. Or Amity. What was the captain doing out here? And why was he calling?

Well, it didn't matter. Amity must be with him. He could go home now, have a nice dish of warm milk and curl—

*No.*

He twitched his tail in irritation. *But that's the special call. I have to—*

*No. Do not answer.*

*But Amity's all upset. I know it. And I should go and—*

*When Amity calls, then you may go. But not until it gets dark.*

Dark? What did dark have to do with anything?

*Patience. All will be clear in time.*

Time. Patience. He was really tired of all this patience stuff. Why couldn't he just go home now and—

*Patience!*

# Chapter Nine

Adam voiced the call. He looked in all directions, squinting against the dusk till he thought his eyeballs would fall out, but nothing happened. No young tabby came bounding across the sand to leap into Amity's arms. He voiced the call again.

Then he listened with all his might, hoping for even the faintest meow. There were lots of rocks out here. If the animal was trapped somewhere—

He glanced at Amity. Her face had turned white, her brown eyes huge and tear-filled. "He isn't coming," she cried. "Oh, where can he have gotten to?"

Adam took a step toward her, ready to take her into his arms. But he stopped himself. What was he thinking? He couldn't do such a thing. However much she needed comfort, he was not the one to give it to her. Such an act could have long-reaching consequences. She might even think that he lov—He pushed the thought out of his mind.

"It's getting dark," she said, her voice choked with tears. "He won't be able to see us." A shiver shook her from head to toe.

This would never do. He could keep her warm, at least. He stretched out a hand to her. "Come on, we'll go over to the pile of driftwood. There's plenty there to build a fire. It'll keep you warm and—"

She shook her head. "I'm not cold! I just want to find Hector!"

She wasn't thinking of herself at all. How to—

"*I'm* cold," he said, trying to sound plaintive. "Besides, if we light a fire, Hector can see it. And us."

"Of course." She tried to smile, a poor effort. "I'm sorry. Yes, let's light a fire."

She put her hand in his and let him lead her—around the rocks, across the sand and up the beach to the jumble of driftwood and rock.

Strange how right it felt, having her hand in his. Right and good. Her fingers were like ice, though. He hoped the rest of her wasn't that cold. He'd build her a good big fire. Warm her up right. He could do that much. And maybe the cat would see it. And come to them.

He stopped by a flat rock. "You can sit here. I'll build the fire."

She sat, huddled in her cloak, a forlorn figure in the deepening dusk.

He lit the lantern first. The sky was darkening rapidly now, the sun sinking behind the dunes. He carried driftwood by lantern light, reaching deep into the jumbled pile for the driest material. Soon he had a nice blaze going. He dragged a log across from her and sat down.

"Warm your hands," he suggested, stretching out his own.

Her hands were pale. They trembled as she leaned forward to warm them.

He wracked his mind for something to talk about, anything to take her thoughts off the cat. "Did you do anything special on Halloween when you were a child?" A foolish question, but all he could think of.

She shook her head. "Papa didn't approve of heathen holidays. He said that's what it was—heathen. I didn't go out with the other children."

"Too bad. That was fun." He'd bet a pretty penny her father didn't approve of much of anything, the old buzzard.

"My mother used to tell me stories about Halloween in Scotland," he went on. "She said the people lit huge bonfires." He smiled. "Much bigger than ours. And they played games on that night, games to tell them who they were meant to marry."

Her expression didn't change at the mention of marriage. She just said, "Papa said the celebration came from some heathen ceremony. Samhain, I think he called it, when people built a big bonfire and danced around it. It had something to do with getting through the winter, keeping ghosts and goblins and witches away from their flocks."

She looked around again. "Where can Hector be?

Her gaze sought Adam's over the fire. So much pain burned in her eyes—not just the pain of losing the cat, but the pain of all the losses in her life—father, mother, young man. She had lost so much—and yet she carried on.

"Please, Captain," she begged. "Please call Hector again."

"I will." He consulted the manual once more,

holding it toward the light of the fire. For some reason he couldn't get the strange syllables to lodge in his memory. He got to his feet and voiced the call—again and yet again.

She looked up and down the now dark beach, turning in all directions, but the cat didn't come.

Adam sank down on the log and stared into the fire. This was all foolishness. A young tom was perfectly capable of getting along on his own through a night—several nights, in fact. Hector wasn't a black cat, so he had nothing to fear from the superstitious. He was probably just out having a good time.

A muffled sound came from across the fire. Adam looked up. Good God, she was sobbing, her head bowed in her hands. Now what was he going to do?

He got to his feet, feeling as frightened as a deckhand brought to the mast to answer charges of false conduct. But he had to do something. He couldn't just let her cry on, as though he didn't see. Or didn't care. Not knowing what else to do, he knelt beside her and touched her shoulder. "Come on, now. It's not that bad."

She raised her head. Her hood fell back, revealing the hair curling about her tear-drenched face. In the firelight that hair had auburn shadows.

"How can—you *say* that?" she sobbed. "You know—what the manual—says. He's not supposed—to be alone—on Halloween—night. He's not!"

He couldn't help himself. He gathered her to his chest and let her sob against him, his chin resting in her soft hair, hair that smelled of lavender. He disciplined himself not to notice it, not to notice the soft roundness of her body in his arms, or the heat he could feel through both their clothes. But his discipline didn't work very well.

Finally her sobs ceased. "Listen," he said. "Why don't *you* try the call? Maybe it only works for the cat's owner."

She raised her head again, hope in her eyes. "Yes, yes! That must be it."

He lifted the hood over her hair. No sense in her taking a chill. She drew back, away from his chest, and he felt an inexplicable sense of loss.

"Where is it?" she cried. "Where's the manual?"

He got to his feet. "Here, in my pocket." He pulled it out. "Just let me get the lantern so we can see to read it."

Hector stirred restlessly. This business of waiting was trying. Not that he was afraid to be out in the dark alone. He wasn't afraid at all. No self-respecting cat would be. Any other time he'd be enjoying himself. But tonight he was worried about Amity. She'd sounded terribly upset when she had called him earlier—and then when he didn't come, she'd gone hurrying off toward the house so fast he was afraid she'd fall and hurt herself.

If only he could understand why Mistress had told him to run off this way. It didn't seem right. Amity had been really good to him. He'd feel a lot better if he just knew—

*Patience. Soon all will be made clear.*

He certainly hoped so. He was getting so tired— Wait! This time that was Amity calling him. He'd know her voice anywhere.

He got to his feet and stretched. Nothing happened. No voice in his head. Mistress didn't tell him not to go. She didn't tell him anything. He took one step. Then another. Still no voice in his head. He set off across the sand at a run.

When Amity sank down in despair, Adam kept staring into the darkness. Why didn't the damn cat come? Amity couldn't take much more of this. She was about exhaust—

"Hector!" Amity leapt to her feet, the manual slipping off her lap into the sand. And out of the darkness the cat came bounding, jumping right into her outstretched arms. "Oh, Hector! You worried me so. How could you do such a terrible thing?"

The cat purred and rubbed against her cheek. Adam sighed in relief and put another piece of driftwood on the fire. Thank God the call had worked this time.

He looked around. It was rather pleasant out here, now that the wind had died down and Amity's fear was gone. The stars were bright overhead. No clouds, except near the moon. They might as well stay here till the clouds moved. It'd be a lot easier to get back to the house if they had plenty of moonlight. And that would give Amity time to get good and warm first.

He picked the manual up out of the sand. She might have disregarded it in her joy at seeing the cat, but she'd want it later. He dusted if off and put it back in his pocket, taking a seat on his log again.

Across the fire Amity and the cat were making joyful noises at each other. Adam stared into the flames. Amity really loved that cat. And the cat seemed to love her. So why had he run off?

If he, Adam, had someone who loved him that much, he'd never want to cause her pain. He'd never—A warning bell sounded in his head. He *was* going to cause Amity pain. He knew she would miss him when he set out on the *Lady* again. Just as he would miss her. But she didn't *love* him. They were friends, that's all, good friends. And those strange feelings of tenderness he'd felt when he held her in his arms, those were just the feelings of a friend. Nothing more.

After all, when he went to sea again, he'd be coming back. He'd stay at her boardinghouse. But it was still too bad women couldn't . . .

Enough! He put more wood on the fire and reached into his pocket for the manual. He'd just read for a while—while the two of them made up.

Amity sank back on the flat rock, holding Hector tightly to her breast. *Thank you, God, thank you*, she breathed silently. "Oh, Hector, I was so worried. I was sure something awful had happened to you. Don't you *ever* do that to me again."

Hector purred and rubbed his cheek against hers. As if he was saying he was sorry. But why hadn't he come? Had he been caught somewhere? Hurt? She looked him over. As far as she could tell by firelight, he looked fine, not hurt at all. She was so grateful that the—Oh, dear! She hadn't even thanked the captain.

She looked up. The captain sat across from her, reading the manual. He must think her an awful ninny, to be making such a fuss over a cat. The flames cast a ruddy glow on his face. Such a good-looking face. Even now, with the side-whiskers and beard he'd let grow since the weather started to turn cold. He looked handsomer clean-shaven, as he'd been that first day when she opened the door and saw him on her porch—and her heart almost stopped beating.

But it wasn't his good looks that endeared him to her now, not even when she thought about how he'd looked without his shirt that day at the beach—which she often did. Too often for her peace of mind.

No, the captain's exterior was a fine one—shipshape, as a sailor would say—but it was what was *inside* the man that made her love him. The way he talked to her—as if she was worthy of his respect—not yelling and blustering as Papa had. And, even more, the way he listened to her. Papa had never bothered to listen, even when she tried to speak. And Stephen had been much like Papa. Papa's choice for her husband, not hers.

Well, it was time she thanked the captain. She would never have been able to remember to look for that call herself. Well, maybe she would have, once she'd calmed down. But then she'd have had to go back to the beach alone. And would she have thought to build this nice fire, now giving off its warmth? She didn't know. But she did know that she was glad to have the captain for a friend, even if— Better not to think about that.

She pulled in a deep breath. "Captain?"

# Chapter Ten

The captain looked up from the manual, firelight dancing in his eyes. "Yes?"

"Thank you for helping me tonight. It was very kind of you."

"I'm glad I *could* help," he said. "That's what friends are for."

"Still, I must have looked silly, carrying on over a cat like that."

A shadow crossed his face. "Not to me. I know what it is to love something. And to fear its loss."

For a second her heart jumped up into her throat. But wait—he said some*thing*. He wasn't talking about her.

"You mean the *Lady*—your ship." She hoped she'd kept the disappointment out of her voice.

"Yes," he said, looking into the flames. "The *Lady*."

He fell silent then, and she didn't know what

else to say. She didn't want to talk about his ship. Or the sea. They were going to take him away from her. And she'd never—

She had to stop thinking about that. She looked up. "The stars are bright tonight, aren't they?"

The captain stuck a finger in the manual and looked up, too. "Yes, it's a crisp night. Beautiful. Only a few clouds. We should have some good moonlight soon. When those clouds over the moon's face move."

"Yes. I like to see moonlight reflected on the waves."

This was ridiculous. She was saying stupid things. And she couldn't just sit there staring at him. He might get the wrong idea. She felt the heat rise to her face. Or the right one. "I suppose we ought to go home."

"I thought we'd wait for more moonlight," he said. "It'll be easier to see." He frowned. "Unless you're cold."

"No, no. I'm quite warm enough." She had to find something else to talk about. "Are you looking for something special in the manual?"

He shook his head. "No, I just thought I'd reread it. These blank pages, though—I still don't understand why they're there. You know," his gaze met hers, dark and mysterious, "maybe it's the season or something, but sometimes I think I can almost see writing here. Strange syllables—like those in the cat call."

She laughed. That must be what he expected. He had to be joking. "Those pages are blank, Captain. We both know that. It must be the bonfire. And talking about ghosts and goblins."

"Perhaps," he said, "but let me show you."

He brought the book to her, bending so the

flames would cast their light on the blank pages. They *were* blank, but still—She stared, fascinated. "It must be the shadows from the flames. I know these pages are—"

The moon came from behind the clouds, sending bright rays directly onto the page. "Writing," she whispered, the breath sticking in her throat. "There's writing on these pages! But why couldn't we—"

"It must be a spell," the captain said, laughter in his voice, laughter and something else. "A spell to get what you want, I guess. See here? It says to stand by a bonfire in the light of the full moon. Take hands. Recite these syllables. Then say, 'Here and now. Now and here. Give me what my heart holds dear.'"

He looked directly into her eyes. "Shall we try it?"

"T-try?" she stammered, her heart pounding. He couldn't mean . . . "But—"

"You once told me Hector's mistress was strange." His eyes danced in the firelight.

"Yes, but—"

"The pages were blank before. They're not blank now."

"Yes, but—"

His gaze held hers. "There's nothing here about selling your soul to the devil or anything."

How could he joke about such a thing? She shivered and clutched Hector closer. "I wouldn't do that. Ever."

"I wouldn't ask you to, of course." The captain stared down at the manual. "It says here that the spell only works on Halloween. And only once."

She wanted to do it! Just once she wanted to do something wild and wonderful. But, of course, nothing was going to happen. They'd repeat the words and nothing would happen.

Then what was she afraid of?

"Don't you want to get what you hold dear?" he asked.

A spell wasn't going to get her that. Get her *him*. But she couldn't tell him that.

Disappointment shadowed his face. "Well, if you won't do it, I can't either. It takes two people to hold hands." He started to shut the book.

She put a hand on his arm. "Wait. I'll do it."

From his place on Amity's lap, Hector had been listening. A spell in the manual? A spell that only worked on Halloween?

*Yes*, Mistress said. *It is mine.*

*But I don't understand why you—*

*Patience. Soon all will be clear.*

Amity lifted him from her lap and looked into his eyes. "We're going to try this spell, Hector. The captain and I. It won't work, of course." Her voice quavered, and he knew she wished it would, wished it a lot. "But anyway, you stay here. By the fire. In the warm sand. No running away, now. Understand?"

He purred and rubbed against her cheek. He wasn't going to run away. All he wanted was a warm saucer of milk and their soft bed.

She put him down on the sand and stood up. The sand wasn't too bad. Not as good as her lap, but it was warm from the fire. He settled down to watch. If that spell had been put in the manual by Mistress—and she said it had—then it was definitely going to work. Maybe he'd be able to see how. At any rate, he'd just wait. As Amity had told him to.

She brushed the sand from her skirt and turned to the captain. "I'm ready if you are."

He handed her the manual. "First let me put some wood on the fire." He chuckled. "To do this properly we need a big fire."

He built up the fire till it blazed high against the night sky. "To keep away the ghosts and goblins," he added.

Amity laughed, but Hector could tell she was nervous. Excited, but nervous. She wasn't at all sure about this thing she was going to do.

The captain held the manual before them. "Can you see?" he asked.

"Yes." Her voice was just a whisper.

"Now we have to take hands."

Hesitantly, Amity extended her right hand. The captain took it in his left one. "All right," he said. "Here we go. First the syllables. Then the verse."

She nodded.

Hector listened hard, but the syllables ran together in a strange mumbo jumbo of sound. He couldn't make head nor tail of them. *Not for you,* Mistress said. *Only for them.*

*Only for them? But why? Why did you tell me to run—*

*Patience.*

"Here and now. Now and here." Amity's voice started out faint but grew stronger, till it matched the captain's. "Give me what my heart holds dear."

There was a flash of brilliant light. Hector blinked. Amity and the captain had disappeared. In their place stood two strange cats.

Hector took a step toward them. *No,* Mistress commanded. *Patience.*

And the two cats took off down the beach, running for all they were worth.

# Chapter Eleven

Hector sighed and moved a little closer to the dying bonfire. Amity—or the cat she'd turned into—had been gone a long time. He wasn't worried about her. The captain would take care of her. Cat or man, the captain would take care of her.

But Hector was hungry. He was tired, too, and getting cold. But most of all he was—hungry. It had been a long time since his breakfast saucer of milk. And his stomach felt empty and hollow.

At least things were starting to make a little sense. The spell would only work on Halloween, under the light of a full moon. Mistress had put the spell there in the manual—to be used by Amity and the captain, he guessed. Only them, she'd said. Hector preened a little. He had gotten them out there, under the moon. Of course, he hadn't known what he was doing—or why. But he *had* obeyed.

*You did well*, Mistress said. *Now you must wait*.

Patience again. He wished Amity and the captain would just settle this thing between them. And what good would it do changing them into cats? Surely *that* wasn't what their hearts held dear. On the other hand, *he* wouldn't want to be a person. People wasted so much time hemming and hawing around. And half the time they didn't even know what they wanted, even when everybody else could see.

Well, Amity had told him to wait. And that's what he was going to do, even if it took all night. He crept closer to the fire and found the warmest spot he could.

He slept finally, a little catnap, though his ears were still attuned to any human sound. And then, long past midnight, something woke him, some different sound. He sat up and looked around. The moon was high in the sky, the sand bright with its light.

In the distance, he could just make out two figures. Laughter came floating to him through the sound of the surf. He squinted harder, trying to see. There were two humans, all right. But that woman couldn't be Amity. He couldn't make out her face, but that woman's hair was all down, hanging free. And he could see the whiteness of her bare legs as she lifted her skirts with one hand. Her other arm was wrapped around the man—and his around her.

No, that couldn't be Amity. She'd never act like that. He settled down in the sand again. Wherever she was, he wished she'd get back here. He was getting tired—

"Hector!"

He leaped to his feet again. It *was* Amity. She and the captain drew closer.

Amity was a mess. Her hair was a wild tangle, her cloak and the front of her gown spattered with sand. So were her shoes. And the captain was in no better shape. He looked like he'd been rolling in the sand.

But it was Amity's face that caught Hector's attention. Her face was glowing with a special light. And her eyes—her eyes blazed out of her face. Eyes full of love and joy. No sorrow in there. Not a trace of it left.

She scooped him up and hugged him, rubbing her face against his. "It worked! Hector, the spell worked! Oh, it was wonderful. We were so free— wild and free. And yet together. We ran all night and—"

"Not *all* night, my dear," the captain said, his voice full of love. "There was about an hour or so—before we came back to our human shapes— and about an hour after—when we lay in the sand and—"

Instead of blushing, Amity threw herself into the captain's arms, nearly crushing Hector between them. He squealed indignantly.

She laughed and loosened her hold. "Sorry, Hector. But just listen." She reached up to kiss the captain full on the lips. "We're going to get married. And the captain—Adam, that is—" She kissed him again. "—is going to take me on the *Lady*, in the spring when she's ready, for our honeymoon."

No! Hector mewed as piteously as he could. They couldn't leave him behind. It wasn't fair. Not after all he'd done.

This time it was the captain who spoke, reaching out to scratch behind Hector's ears. "Of course you'll be coming along, old fellow. Plenty of mice on shipboard. We can use your help."

That was better. Hector rubbed against the captain's hand. As long as he could be with Amity he'd be happy. But wait! There was that task—whatever it was—that he hadn't even begun yet. The task Mistress wanted him to do. Maybe she wouldn't let him go.

*Your task is complete.*

What was she talking about? He hadn't even figured out what the task was yet.

*Your task is complete,* she repeated. *You have brought these two to love. You have done well.*

*This was my task? But I didn't even know. I just wanted Amity to be happy.*

*It matters not what you know. You have done well. You may come back to the tower room and choose your heart's desire.*

Choose? He hadn't thought about his heart's desire for weeks now. He'd been too busy thinking about Amity, trying to help her. Well, let's see. He could have anything he wanted. Mistress had said so. He wanted . . . He wanted . . .

Well, that was funny. He already *had* what he wanted. Love and happiness for Amity, and a good home for himself. And he really didn't care what was in the tower room. Not anymore. He snuggled closer to Amity.

*Thank you, Mistress,* he said, *but I already have my heart's desire.*

And he wriggled in between Amity and the captain, who were busy kissing again.

## HOLIDAY ROMANCE ANTHOLOGIES

*Trick or Treat* by Lark Eden, Lori Handeland, Stobie Piel, and Lynda Trent. From four of romance's most provocative authors come the stories of four couples as they experience the true magic of Halloween, and the ecstasy of everlasting love.

___52220-9                           $5.99 US/$6.99 CAN

*Midsummer Night's Magic* by Emma Craig, Tess Mallory, Amy Elizabeth Saunders, and Pam McCutcheon. In the balmy heat of the summer season, four couples venture into the realm of the wee folk and spirits, and in doing so, learn the true meaning of passion.

___52209-8                           $5.50 US/$6.50 CAN

**Dorchester Publishing Co., Inc.**
**P.O. Box 6640**
**Wayne, PA 19087-8640**

Please add $1.75 for shipping and handling for the first book and $.50 for each book thereafter. NY, NYC, and PA residents, please add appropriate sales tax. No cash, stamps, or C.O.D.s. All orders shipped within 6 weeks via postal service book rate. Canadian orders require $2.00 extra postage and must be paid in U.S. dollars through a U.S. banking facility.

Name_____

Address_____

City_____State_____Zip_____

I have enclosed $_____ in payment for the checked book(s).

Payment <u>must</u> accompany all orders. ❑ Please send a free catalog.

# A FAERIE TALE ROMANCE

## VICTORIA ALEXANDER

Ophelia Kendrake has barely finished conning the coat off a cardsharp's back when she stumbles into Dead End, Wyoming. Mistaken for the Countess of Bridgewater, Ophelia sees no reason to reveal herself until she has stripped the hamlet of its fortunes and escaped into the sunset. But the free-spirited beauty almost swallows her script when she meets Tyler, the town's virile young mayor. When Tyler Matthews returns from an Ivy League college, he simply wants to settle down and enjoy the simplicity of ranching. But his aunt and uncle are set on making a silk purse out of Dead End, and Tyler is going to be the new mayor. It's a job he takes with little relish—until he catches a glimpse of the village's newest visitor.

__52159-8                                    $5.50 US/$6.50 CAN

**Dorchester Publishing Co., Inc.**
**P.O. Box 6640**
**Wayne, PA 19087-8640**

Please add $1.75 for shipping and handling for the first book and $.50 for each book thereafter. NY, NYC, and PA residents, please add appropriate sales tax. No cash, stamps, or C.O.D.s. All orders shipped within 6 weeks via postal service book rate. Canadian orders require $2.00 extra postage and must be paid in U.S. dollars through a U.S. banking facility.

Name_____
Address_____
City_____ State_____ Zip_____
I have enclosed $_____ in payment for the checked book(s).
Payment __must__ accompany all orders. ☐ Please send a free catalog.

# BELIEVE
## Victoria Alexander

Tessa thinks as little of love as she does of the Arthurian legend—it is just a myth. But when an enchanted tome falls into the lovely teacher's hands, she learns that the legend is nothing like she remembers. Galahad the Chaste is everything but—the powerful knight is an expert lover—and not only wizards can weave powerful spells. Still, even in Galahad's muscled embrace, she feels unsure of this man who seemed a myth. But soon the beautiful skeptic is on a quest as real as her heart, and the grail—and Galahad's love—is within reach. All she has to do is believe.

___52267-5                                    $5.99 US/$6.99 CAN

**Dorchester Publishing Co., Inc.**
**P.O. Box 6640**
**Wayne, PA 19087-8640**

Please add $1.75 for shipping and handling for the first book and $.50 for each book thereafter. NY, NYC, and PA residents, please add appropriate sales tax. No cash, stamps, or C.O.D.s. All orders shipped within 6 weeks via postal service book rate. Canadian orders require $2.00 extra postage and must be paid in U.S. dollars through a U.S. banking facility.

Name_____
Address_____
City_____State_____Zip_____
I have enclosed $_____ in payment for the checked book(s).
Payment <u>must</u> accompany all orders. ☐ Please send a free catalog.
   CHECK OUT OUR WEBSITE! www.dorchesterpub.com

# A Stolen Rose

## CORAL SMITH SAXE

**Bestselling Author Of *Enchantment***

Feared by all Englishmen and known only as the Blackbird, the infamous highwayman is really the stunning Morgana Bracewell. And though she is an aristocrat who has lost her name and family, nothing has prepared the well-bred thief for her most charming victim. Even as she robs Lord Phillip Greyfriars blind, she knows his roving eye has seen through her rogue's disguise—and into her heart. Now, the wickedly handsome peer will stop at nothing to possess her, and it will take all Morgana's cunning not to surrender to a man who will accept no ransom for her love.

__3843-9                                    $5.50 US/$7.50 CAN

**Dorchester Publishing Co., Inc.**
**P.O. Box 6640**
**Wayne, PA 19087-8640**

Please add $1.75 for shipping and handling for the first book and $.50 for each book thereafter. NY, NYC, and PA residents, please add appropriate sales tax. No cash, stamps, or C.O.D.s. All orders shipped within 6 weeks via postal service book rate. Canadian orders require $2.00 extra postage and must be paid in U.S. dollars through a U.S. banking facility.

Name_____
Address_____
City_____State_____Zip_____
I have enclosed $_____ in payment for the checked book(s).
Payment <u>must</u> accompany all orders. ☐ Please send a free catalog.

## Bestselling Author of *The Mirror & The Magic*

Elinor DeCortenay hails from a world of castles and conquests, sorcerers and spells. So she has no trouble accepting the notion that a magic charm can send her to another time and place, where leather-skinned demons ride noisy beasts. What she can't believe is that the devilishly handsome man she mistakes for Satan's minion is really a knight of the present.

Since the death of his wife, Drew has become a virtual recluse, showing interest in little besides his passion for motorcycles. Then, while riding his souped-up Harley through the California countryside, he chances upon a striking beauty dressed like a resident of Camelot, and despite his misgivings, she wakens his lonely heart to a desire for the future. A medieval maiden and modern motorhead, Elinor and Drew are both trying to escape painful pasts—pasts that will haunt them forever unless they can share a love timeless, tempestuous, and true.

___4273-8                                    $5.50 US/$6.50 CAN

**Dorchester Publishing Co., Inc.**
**P.O. Box 6640**
**Wayne, PA 19087-8640**

**Bestselling Author Of *A Stolen Rose***

Sensible Julia Addison doesn't believe in fairy tales. Nor does she think she'll ever stumble from the modern world into an enchanted wood. Yet now she is in a Highland forest, held captive by seven lairds and their quick-tempered chief. Hardened by years of war with rival clans, Darach MacStruan acts more like Grumpy than Prince Charming. Still, Julia is convinced that behind the dark-eyed Scotsman's gruff demeanor beats the heart of a kind and gentle lover. But in a land full of cunning clansmen, furious feuds, and poisonous potions, she can only wonder if her kiss has magic enough to waken Darach to sweet ecstasy.

\_52086-9                                    $5.99 US/$7.99 CAN

## A Faerie Tale Romance

## Prince of Kisses

## COLLEEN SHANNON

Daughter of wealth and privilege, lovely Charlaine Kimball is known to Victorian society as the Ice Princess. But when a brash intruder dares to take a king's ransom in jewels from her private safe, indignation burns away her usual cool reserve. And when the handsome rogue presumes to steal a kiss from her untouched lips, forbidden longing sets her soul ablaze.

Illegitimate son of a penniless Frenchwoman, Devlin Rhodes is nothing but a lowly bounder to the British aristocrats who snub him. But his leapfrogging ambition engages him in a dangerous game. Now he will have to win Charlaine's hand in marriage–and have her begging for the kiss that will awaken his heart and transform him into the man he was always meant to be.

——52200-4 $5.99 US/$6.99 CAN

## GIVE YOUR HEART TO THE GENTLE BEAST AND FOREVER SHARE LOVE'S SWEET FEAST

Raised amid a milieu of bountiful wealth and enlightened ideas, Callista Raleigh is more than a match for the radicals, rakes, and reprobates who rail against England's King George III. Then a sudden reversal of fortune brings into her life a veritable brute who craves revenge against her family almost as much as he hungers for her kiss. And even though her passionate foe conceals his face behind a hideous mask, Callista believes that he is merely a man, with a man's strengths and appetites. But when the love-starved stranger sweeps her away to his secret lair, Callista realizes that wits and reason aren't enough to conquer him—she'll need a desire both satisfying and true if beauty is to tame the beast.

__52143-1                           $5.99 US/$6.99 CAN